Rose at the End
The Rose Garden Book 5

Casia Schreyer

This is a work of fiction. All characters are the creation of the author and any semblance to people, living or dead, is coincidental.

ROSE AT THE END – THE ROSE GARDEN 5
Copyright ©2019 by Casia Schreyer

Cover © 2019 by Sara Gratton

All rights reserved.
No part of this book may be reproduced, scanned, or distributed in any printed or electronic form without permission. Please do not participate in or encourage the piracy of copyrighted materials.

ISBN 978-1-988853-36-9
E-ISBN 978-1-988853-35-2

This series is dedicated to the
Rooswinkle Family

This book is dedicated to
Sheri Parent
Who demanded the series be completed
Sorry it too so long

1st of Starrise, 24th Year of the 11th Rebirth
The End of the World, The Isle of Light

A priest, seven royal guards, a tracker, a twice-named smith, and half a dozen servants sat together in the center of a small island off the northern coast of the Isle of Light. The island was perhaps a day's ride from south to north and slightly less from east to west. The clearing they were camped in was dominated by a stone arch, three men wide and two men high. The stones themselves were flat, anywhere from one to three inches thick, and cut in rough squares. Whomever had stacked them hadn't paid much heed to lining them up neatly. Moss grew over them, as it did over the flagstones of the small courtyard area surrounding the arch. In places the courtyard was framed by low, crumbling stone walls, overgrown with weeds.

The party had finished breakfast and were prepared for another day of waiting and standing watch in front of the gateway that connected the Isle of Light to the Wide World, the world they had left behind eleven generations earlier. According to the priests, this stone arch, this gateway, was the tether between the worlds.

And in the last twenty-four years that tether had weakened considerably.

"We didn't want to make this voyage at all, but High Priest Gold-Spark demanded it," the priest was saying. Most of the waiting group was paying him little mind but the smith, Kaelen Iron-Heart, and the tracker, Devin Sun-Stag sat in rapt attention. "The last time we tried, the priests who ventured over barely made it home."

"Why?" Devin said. "What dangers did they face?"

"Without five princesses, the gateway has become unstable, weakened. See how it flickers and threatens to close? It was worse the last time. And out here, at the edge of the world, we are too far from Airon and his temple, too far from the princesses we have found. We are vulnerable."

"Vulnerable to what? We have guards," Kaelen snapped.

"Dark Spirits," Devin said. "We're closer to their territory now, aren't we?"

"If they have a territory then yes, we are closer to it," the priest said. "They cling to the edges and this is the final edge for us."

Devin glanced northwards. Tall, scraggly trees obscured his view of the northern shore of the island a half-day's ride away, but he knew what it looked like. The island fell away and the sea beat upon the ragged cliffs with such vengeance that the spray topped those high rock walls to mist anyone who stood upon the stony edge. Though it had been full light when Devin had stood upon the cliffs, the stormy sea beyond was quickly lost in shadow. The cloudy sky along the horizon crackled with lightning.

The wind was strong, strong enough that it had threatened to drag him over the precipice more than once. More concerning had been the whispers in the wind, a voice so soft and low that Devin had not been able to make out anything resembling words. But the intent was not lost. Whatever that voice had said, the malice and danger carried through loud and clear.

Kaelen snickered and shook his head.

"You've seen the men and women affected by these Dark Spirits with your own eyes," the priest said.

"Aye," Kaelen said. "A real threat, I know that. But a here and now threat, not some dark, mystical force out to destroy our island."

Devin said nothing. He was the only person here from the Carainhithe, a people generally looked down upon by most of the provinces, especially the Metalkin, and though he was twice-named he'd not had contact with his family in years. Kaelen was an elder son, not the family heir, but high enough up the hierarchy of a powerful enough family to earn himself a place on this errand, even though he had no real purpose here. If Kaelen decided to make his life miserable it would be an easy task, and it would not end with the end of this voyage, not with both of them living and working in the capital.

Still, he had stood and faced the darkness, and something in the darkness had threatened him. *And I would bet any amount asked that the darkness was threatening more than just me. The darkness beyond the sea means to swallow us all whole.*

The swirling, flickering lights of the gateway seemed to shudder for a moment and then the edges became solid, firm for the first time since they'd arrived here. The clouds parted, and the clearing was bathed in golden sunlight.

A young woman stepped through the gateway. "Bloody hell!"

Everyone in the camp shot to their feet at the sharp sound of her words, spoken with passion in a heavy, rolling accent. Behind her four priests stepped through the gate, their faces lit up in excitement. They were all speaking at once.

The young woman stared at everything with wide green eyes. Her thick, red, shoulder-length hair framed her face accentuating the rosy blush of her cheeks. She wore men's clothes, cut in an odd fashion and dyed vibrant colours. Aside from that first exclamation of surprise, she said nothing. In fact, aside from the priests, no one said anything.

They found her, Devin thought. *The fifth princess, they actually found her.*

She took an unsteady step forward. Her gaze shifted from everything else to her own feet. She frowned. She tried another step, but her knees were noticeably trembling. Her mouth transformed into a silent 'o' of concern and she stopped trying to walk. Her face came up again and she looked at each person around her in turn.

The colour drained from her face, making the freckles stand out like pinpoints. Her gaze met Devin's and lingered. "Bloody hell," she said, softer this time.

And then her eyes flickered shut, her knees buckled, and she dropped to the mossy stones.

There was a moment of absolute silence, and then pandemonium.

"She's opening her eyes."
"Give her a little space."
Bodiless voices penetrated her consciousness. She groaned and rubbed her head. "What happened?"

"You're in shock," said the young man at her side. "You fainted. Aside from a bump on your head you're just fine. I have some water here if you're thirsty."

"Please. My mouth feels like cotton."

He helped her sit and held her elbow as she drank from the odd leather sack.

She wiped her mouth on the back of her hand and looked around. She was sitting on moss-covered cobblestones in the middle of a forest clearing. Everyone around her looked like actors at some sort of Shakespeare play. Finally, she said, "I guess they weren't lying. And I guess it wasn't a bad trip. Unless I'm still tripping?"

"You didn't trip on anything," the man said. "Not that I saw. You're likely in shock. Can you stand? I can help you."

"I will help her," said a deeper voice. "She is my princess, not yours."

She turned. She hadn't noticed the large man with a black beard kneeling just behind her until now. "Who are you?"

"Kaelen Iron-Heart," he said, bowing as best he could when he was already on his knees. "Princess Ashlyn, it is an honour to meet you at long last."

"Ashlyn?" She looked back to the first man. He was smaller, leaner, and had lighter hair. Both were dressed in archaic fashion but there was a vast difference in the quality of their clothes. "I don't …"

"You're up! Excellent!" One of the priests, the eldest, bustled over.

The woman's eyes flared. "You!" She struggled to her feet and both men scrambled to assist her. The priest took an uncertain step back. "Where am I? What is this place? What did you do to me?"

"We told you when we found you in the Wide World. You are the lost princess, one of five rulers of the Isle of Light. You were able to see us, you were able to see the gateway, and you were able to pass through the gateway."

"The swirling portal thing on Beech Hill Road?"

"I don't know how you name your landmarks and towns," the priest said. "But yes, it was a swirling circle of light. You saw it, you agreed to walk through it."

"I didn't think anything would happen! This is impossible. Take me back, now."

"I can't, it's …"

"TAKE ME BACK!!"

"Miss," the lean man said, drawing her attention away from the quivering priest. "What is your name?"

"Her name is Ashlyn," the large man grumped.

She pulled her arm free of the large man's grasp and said, "My name is not Ashlyn, that's not even my middle name. My name is Mallory Catherine Brock." She focused on the lean man in the odd leggings as he seemed to be the most rational one in the group. "I want to go home."

"He's right, the priest. He can't take you back now."

"Why not?"

"After you and the priests of Airon returned through the gateway, it closed. We don't know how to open it."

"It ... what do you mean it closed?"

"See for yourself." He turned her so that she was facing the giant stone arch. It looked like a ruin, like the walls on either side had crumbled and whatever wooden door might have been there had rotted away leaving nothing but the arched doorframe.

For a long moment she stared through the arch at the trees beyond. "Where is the portal?"

"The light went out. There is no gate. There is no way to travel between the Isle of Light and the Wide World without that gate."

"So? Open it again."

"We can't."

"You opened it before. You opened it and you came through and you tricked me into coming here. Now open it back up and let me go."

The priest stepped forward again, trembling. "My apologies, Princess. We did not open the gate. Airon does that."

"Well, where is this Aaron? Tell him to open the gate."

"Airon is a god," the lean man said. "The sun god. Chief among the spirit guides of the island. It is his power, and his magic, that created the gate and it only opens when he wills it."

"Say a prayer. Burn some damn incense! Get him to open the gate."

"He won't, Princess," the priest said. "He wants you here. We *need* you here."

She pulled her other hand free and scrubbed both hands over her face. "Okay, fine, I can't get home that way. Any other options?"

"None," the priest said.

"Fine, fine. When the acid or whatever this is wears off, I'll wake up in a puddle of my own drool and the girls and I will laugh about this over a pint this weekend. Until then, can I get something to eat? And can someone tell me what's going on?"

"We have food right over here," Kaelen said, reaching for her arm again.

"Hold on," the other man said. "Let me finish checking her for injuries."

"You're not a healer," Kaelen said.

"I know more than you, more than anyone else here," he insisted.

Mallory watched the exchange. "Let him do his job," she snapped.

Kaelen bowed. "Of course, Princess."

She scowled and turned away from him. "What do you need to do?"

"There's a bench here," he said, "Probably more comfortable than the ground. Most likely you just need food and rest but I need to be sure."

She nodded and followed him. It was quieter here, away from the group. "I don't know your name," she said.

"Devin Sun-Stag. Does anything hurt?"

She shook her head. "What's the story with that Kaelen fellow?" She was being careful not to be overheard.

"He's wealthy," Devin said. "And a Metalkin noble."

"I have no idea what a Metalkin is," she said, "But I understand rich and noble. That explains a lot. Are you a noble too?"

"My family is, but my father was fairly far down the line of inheritance and worked at a guild hall. You can move your legs all right? No pain when you move your head?"

"Everything feels fine," she said.

"Just shock then. I'm sure Kaelen is eager to get you fed."

"Why him? Why not you?"

Devin smiled sadly. "You're the Metalkin Princess, Metalkin is a group of people, a province. You're Metalkin, and so is Kaelen. I am not. It is an honour to have met you, and I will continue to serve you any way I can."

"Thank you, Devin Sun-Stag, for your care and for being the only sane one here."

Against Devin's better judgement they camped in front of the gate that night. Waiting for Mallory to wake up from her faint had taken up the better part of their afternoon and it would take several hours to get the small boats back to the North Shore.

"It will be safer on shore," Devin insisted. He'd been patrolling through the trees on and off all evening. "There's something not right here, something is coming, I can feel it."

"We might be safer on shore," the eldest priest, Honourable Bernard, conceded, "But we'd be vulnerable in the open water. You're one of the Animal People. You know how many fishermen are lost to the Dark Spirits each season. We'll be safe here in the clearing. This is a sacred space, a space built by Airon himself at the time of The Pact."

"Maybe," Devin said. "But I don't think Airon is here right now. I think his presence left when that gate closed."

Still, Devin knew the risks of being on the open water at night. They'd have no room to maneuver in a fight in those little boats, and the channel was too shallow here for one of the larger trade ships. With the sun settling lower on the western horizon they had no choice but to wait for morning.

Mallory was seated by the fire right next to Kaelen. Devin didn't care for the Metalkin man and it went beyond provincial bickering. He'd lived and worked in Golden Hall all of his adult years and found the majority of people there to be decent folk. This Kaelen on the other hand was turning out to be pushy at the very least.

It's only for a few more days. When you return to Golden Hall your chances of seeing him again are slim. For now, there are more important things to think about than hot-headed nobles.

Quietly Devin made the rounds to all of the guards. Half of them were from Metalkin, half were from the Sun Temple, all were armed with the special blades, blessed by Airon to kill the Dark Spirits.

"Be wary tonight," he told each of them. "We'll double the guard and sleep lightly." He could tell by the way they nodded and the tension in their jaws and shoulders that they all felt it too. They were no longer welcome here.

Mallory sat on a log stool by the fire with a wool blanket over her shoulders. Kaelen handed her a wooden bowl filled with a thick stew. At least she thought it was stew. It was very greasy, and the meat was cut in rough chunks.

"I'm sorry, we had to travel light."

She gave him a puzzled look.

"The bowl. You're the Metalkin Princess, you deserve better than a common wooden bowl."

"Right now, I'm just grateful for food and warmth," she said. "If I wake up here in the morning and I really am stuck here, I'll try to figure the rest out then." She took a bite of the food and found it more flavourful than she expected. It didn't compare to curry, but it was still good.

Honourable Bernard came over and sat on the other side of her. "We've decided to stay here tonight and sail back to the Metalkin coast in the morning."

"It's not that dark yet," Mallory said. "How far is it to the coast?"

"Not far," the priest said. "A few hours from here to the boats, and a few hours on the water."

"We can't make it tonight?" Mallory said. "I don't know if I want to stay here." She glanced around and pulled the blanket tighter with her free hand. The hair on the back of her neck kept standing at attention and she couldn't stop shivering.

"We never travel this close to dark," the priest said somberly. "Too much risk?"

"Bears? Wolves?"

"Dark Spirits."

A short burst of a laugh escaped her, but she stifled it when she noted the absolute seriousness of the man's face. Whatever these dark spirits were, this man believed in them completely, and believed them to be a very real threat. *Apparently, superstition goes hand-in-hand with swords and strange religions. What did you expect, Mallory? Come on.*

"We'll do what you think is best," Kaelen said.

"I'll have them set up the extra tent for Princess Jewel-Rose."

"Thank you," Kaelen said.

Mallory just groaned. She'd been camping once, at nineteen, with a bunch of friends, and it was one of the worst experiences of her life. *And they probably don't have insulated sleeping bags here either. At least there are no mosquitos or anything, not that I've seen yet.*

"If we're staying here tonight then I guess I'll turn in as soon as I'm done eating. Uh ... where can I use the washroom?"

"What do you need washed?"

10

He sounds like a bad joke. She sighed. "Bathroom? You know, when I need to pee?"

"Ah. Well …" He actually blushed. Most men when they reddened looked adorable, or vulnerable, but Kaelen just looked silly, his rosy cheeks peeking out from behind the thick black beard. "Hunter!" he hollered.

The lean man looked over, scowled, and approached them. "You know full well that's not my name."

"Princess Ashlyn requires a latrine."

"Come with me, I'll show you the way." When Kaelen stood too he said, "I think one strange male while she's taking care of something so private is more than enough, don't you?"

The Metalkin noble glowered. "You think I'm leaving her alone with you?"

"I'm not sure what you think I would do." Devin said.

"I'm capable of peeing without supervision," Mallory said. "And can we please stop it with the whole 'Ashlyn' thing. I have no clue who Ashlyn is."

"If you wanted to escort her, you wouldn't have called for me," he said.

Kaelen huffed and sat back down. "Fine." He crossed his arms. "I'll wait here."

"Why thank you, that's so considerate." He lightly touched Mallory's elbow. "This way."

"You're a hunter, and a tracker, so I can see you being useful on a journey of any kind, but what does Kaelen do?" Mallory asked softly.

"He teaches apprentices at the Blacksmith's Guild, I believe," Devin said. "I've had little contact with him before this trip."

"What is a blacksmith instructor doing here?"

"I don't know. It wasn't my place to ask. Here. It isn't much but you're the only woman here so we didn't actually think of this."

'Isn't much' was being generous. It was a shallow hole in the ground with a log suspended over it like a skinny little bench. From the smell, she wasn't the first to use it.

"I'll wait here. With my back turned," he said. "Just, don't take too long. I don't like being in the trees, even a little bit, this close to dark."

"Right," Mallory muttered. "Dark spirits or boogey men or whatever." She took a deep breath and approached the makeshift bathroom. *This is even worse than the last time I was camping.*

She returned to the fire where Devin left her with Kaelen. When her bowl was empty Kaelen led her to a tent that was little more than a thin panel of leather draped over a pole and tacked firmly to the ground. Inside was a leather sleeping roll, lined with something soft and surprisingly warm. She bundled the wool blanket up to make a meager pillow and closed her eyes. Her last thought before sleep took her was, *On second thought I'm never telling anyone about this bad trip.*

2nd of Starrise, 24th Year of the 11th Rebirth
Edge of the World, Isle of Light

Out in the clearing the shadows between the trees were moving even though the evening was still and none of the trees swayed. When one detached itself from the dark and moved silently across the clearing the guard on duty raised the alarm.

Devin was sleeping by the fire and roused instantly, his hand going to his sword. He saw a second Dark Spirit coming from the other side and shouted, "Up! Up! Everybody!" The other sleeping guards staggered to their feet, unsteady and groggy.

Devin leapt over a log and swung at the Dark Spirit. Though it carried no blade it raised an arm in defense and Devin's sword connected with the appendage with a resounding clang. Soon similar sounds of fighting filled every part of the clearing as the Dark Spirits poured in from the trees.

"Protect the Princess. Surround her tent! Don't let them reach her!"

Inside the tent Mallory huddled in her blankets, shaking. The fire outside was casting shadows on the side of the tent, larger than life figures dashing about, swinging weapons. *If this wasn't a nightmare before, it is now.* She shivered.

A shout had woken her, followed by others, and then the sound of metal on metal.

Mallory's life had not been free of violence, she'd witnessed bombings and shootings on the television and read about them in the papers. She'd heard the shots in New Delhi from her bedroom window. Her mother had been scared to send her to school in Ireland because of the IRA. None of it had ever occurred as close to her as this fight.

Someone burst into the tent and she screamed.

"Princess, are you hurt? Are you all right?"

"Kaelen, you scared me." Mallory took a few gulping breaths. "I'm fine. Nothing came in until you. What's happening?"

"We're under attack, but I will remain here with you and defend you, even to the death if I have to."

The sounds of the fight surrounded them and they were getting louder. Mallory shut her eyes and covered her ears, willing it to be over.

She felt a hand on her wrist and looked up. Kaelen was sitting on the bedroll, concern creasing the skin around his eyes. "My Princess do not fear, I swear it, nothing will hurt you tonight."

"Why aren't you out there fighting?"

"I'm not a guard, Princess. I have some training, but my place is here by your side. I will protect you, not only from harm but from fear."

"Why?" Her heart was pounding too fast, the fighting, the yelling it was all too much. And now these vague sentiments from a man she hardly knew, it was enough to shift her emotions from fear to anger. Anger she could deal with, anger she could control.

"Because of the way I feel about you."

"If you start waxing poetic about my beauty …"

"It is not your beauty," he said. "I will not deny that you are as attractive as any beautiful woman I have seen, but that is not why I am here."

"Great," she muttered. "They believe in true love at first sight."

"No," he said. "Love does not work that way, not for most people. But you are a Princess of Airon, your prince was chosen for you at the moment of your birth."

"Pre-destined love?" She cringed as the scuffle drew closer for a moment. When the sounds of fighting faded a little, she went on. "I don't believe in that."

"Neither did I. But Airon's priests teach that each princess has a soul mate, a single man who will complete their soul and strengthen The Pact that keeps the island safe."

"Great, so not only am I stuck here, with swords and superstitions and strange religions and probably no electricity, but I'm expected to marry someone just because *God* demands it? Great, just great."

"Don't worry, Princess. Finding your prince will not be difficult."

"That's not what worries me," she muttered. Something bounced off the taut tent wall and she cringed. "When will this end?"

"They will drive the attackers off," Kaelen said. "The guards are the very best fighters in all of Metalkin."

"I wish they'd be quicker about it."

"As do I. But at the same time, I cannot help but be happy. I knew when I first saw you, but I couldn't believe it. How could it be possible. But speaking with you last night, sitting with you now, as dawn approaches, I know what I feel."

She groaned. *Don't say it. Don't say it.*

"Princess Ashlyn Jewel-Rose, I love you with all that I am and I believe that I am the prince Airon destined you to wed."

Devin was certain it was no single act on the part of any of the men that drove the Dark Spirits back, not the fighting of the guards, not the prayers of the priests. No, the only thing that saved them from the tireless onslaught was the coming of the dawn.

As the sky paled and rays of light peaked through the eastern trees the Dark Spirits silently melted back into the trees, leaving a picture of chaos in their wake. One tent had been ripped, another knocked over. There were burning embers strewn across the ground. Packs, dishes, and supplies were scattered, some of the food smashed and no longer edible.

For a long moment the men stood, weapons at the ready, waiting, watching the trees in case the Dark Spirits returned. Gradually they relaxed and lowered their weapons, looking from the trees to each other.

"They're gone," one of the guards said. "I don't think they'll come back now."

"Not today," one of the priests said. "But we'd best be leaving. I think it best we were as far from here as possible before night falls again."

"Where is Princess Ashlyn?" Honourable Bernard said. "Has anyone seen her?"

"She's here," Kaelen said, rising from the tent opening.

Mallory crawled out behind him. She glanced around, nervous. "It's over?"

"Yes," the priest said. "Come. We'll eat what we can and then we'll leave. If we have to leave the tents behind to make better time, so be it."

"You're afraid they'll follow us."

"It's quite likely," Bernard said.

Mallory took Kaelen's hand and allowed him to help her out to her feet. She paused and looked at the mess the fighting had caused.

The devastation didn't match what she'd seen on television but then there were no buildings to bomb and no dead bodies.

At the far end of the clearing two guards helped Devin to his feet. His eyes were clenched shut and his mouth was a thin line. He was holding his ribs on one side.

"He's been hurt," said one of the guards.

"I's not bad," Devin said, the words slurring slightly. "Hurts but no blood."

"Let me see," Mallory said.

"Leave him," Kaelen said, not letting go of her hand. "He's likely infected."

That last word drew her up short. She had travelled to Ireland to attend veterinary college, and she knew enough about medical sciences to know that infectious diseases were no laughing matter. "Infected with what?"

"I'm fine," Devin said. "Took a knock to the ribs, lost my breath. I can't even feel anything broken. We need to leave. We need to get back to the boats. Pack what we're taking along. We have to move fast."

"They wouldn't come back in daylight," Kaelen said.

"It's not full light yet, and we have an unwed Princess with us. That's always been our biggest fear, losing a princess before her wedding. Let's not have it happen now." He took a deep breath that made him wince and shouted, "Pack up!"

"We should eat," one of the priests said.

"Grab bread or cheese and eat while you walk. I have jerky in my pack as well. We can take turns eating in the boats, trade off with the rowers. Let's go."

Mallory sat alone by the fire while everyone else packed up the tents and supplies. Every now and then a shiver would pass through her and she'd rub her arms. *This isn't a bad drug trip, and this isn't a dream. This is really happening. I'm really on a magical island and they really think I'm a princess. I guess it's time to start figuring this stuff out then.* Her stomach rolled. *What if I never get home again?*

When everyone was packed, Kaelen helped her up and they started walking for the southern edge of the island.

They piled into the small boats and the men took turns rowing towards shore. From the edge of the island Mallory could clearly see the shoreline of the mainland and the dock that awaited them, but as they pulled away into the water the island seemed to recede behind them at a faster rate than the shore approached. By the time they beached the boats the island was nearly out of sight.

She stood on the damp sand, staring towards the northern horizon, as the men emptied the boats.

"I don't understand," she said when Honourable Bernard stepped up beside her. "Where is the island? It wasn't that far away before."

"That is Airon's island, a sacred space. It has no tether in this world and drifts near only when it is time for us to cross the channel to its shores."

"No, that makes no sense. An island doesn't just float. An island is a rocky outcropping that is taller than sea level is high. That's all. You can't swim under them."

"Airon is mysterious and powerful. It is our place to give thanks and live our lives in accordance with his teachings, not question his abilities."

His blind faith irked her. *I don't think they're ready for science, or atheists,* she thought.

"The horses are ready," someone called.

Bernard touched her elbow. "We want to get away from the shore, if possible, before we have to camp again. There are a few estates nearby where we would be safer for the night."

Mallory nodded, the sight of the still-receding island made her cold. *Will I never see home again?*

There was an argument in process when Mallory and Bernard joined the others at the road. "The Rose-Gold estate is just southwest of here," Devin was saying. "It's closer."

"But it's further from Golden Hall," Kaelen said. "It will make the next few days' journeys even more stressful. The Iron-Smith estate is just east of here. We can make it this evening without straining the horses. And it's closer to Golden Hall."

"I think it's too far to risk," Devin insisted. "It's shorter as the hawk flies, but the road east is winding. We'll lose time and end up pushing the horses …"

Kaelen's face was getting redder and his voice was getting louder. "A little push today will save us hours in the days to come."

"The Iron-Smith estate is too close to the coast. We'd be putting Mallory at risk." Devin turned to Bernard, his expression pleading for help.

"We're wasting precious time," Bernard said. "Golden Hall is southeast so those are the directions we must travel."

"Mount up," Kaelen shouted. He gave Devin a smug smile. "We ride east."

Mallory expected Devin to fight back but he lowered his head in a shallow bow. "As you see fit," he said. He swung into the saddle and rode ahead to join the guards.

She watched him go, confused not only by his lack of reaction, but by her disappointment as well.

Kaelen approached Mallory, his smug smile turning to a look of adoration and respect. "Can you ride, my Princess?"

"Yes," Mallory said. "I've had lessons."

"We have a gentle beast for you. She'll follow the others without too much trouble. I apologise that we didn't bring a carriage for the return trip, but there was no time."

"I guess you're forgiven? It's fine, really. I like riding." He showed her the mare, the smallest of the group, and helped her up. Around her all the men were mounting up as well. They guided the horses to the road and pointed them east.

Riding lessons and a few trail rides over the years had not prepared Mallory for over five hours in the saddle. By the time they arrived at the walled estate that evening her legs, back, and butt hurt worse than they ever had in her life.

She gratefully let Kaelen help her as she slipped from the saddle. He caught her as her knees tried to buckle.

"You're hurt."

"No, just sore and tired. I'll get used to it. Give me a minute before I have to walk anywhere."

"Take all the time you need, we're safe now," he said.

Around them there was a flurry of activity teenage boys, and boys as young as nine or ten, came out of the low building to collect the horses. Several people were also coming out of the doors of the main building, which Mallory assumed to be the manor or estate.

"Master Iron-Heart," one man said, striding towards them. "This is unexpected. What brings you ..?" He stopped short when he saw Mallory on Kaelen's arm. "They found her."

"This is Princess Ashlyn Jewel-Rose, the lost princess."

"My name is Mallory," Mallory said, but already the newcomer was bowing deeply.

"Princess Jewel-Rose, my house is honoured beyond measure. You and your entire escort are welcome here, of course. I am Lord Iron-Smith, the head of this family and lord of this estate. Whatever you require, we will provide."

"I'd love a hot shower," she said. When he gave her a puzzled look she said, "So I can wash up."

"Of course. I'll have a room prepared and a bath prepared."

Mallory took a deep breath and said, "A bath would be fine, thank you."

"Kaelen, old friend, I'd like to speak with you about some other matters while you're here. Word reached me from my nephew about a promising development."

"I'll come see you in a moment. I'd like to escort the princess to her rooms."

"Of course." He bowed to Mallory. "Whatever you need, just ask one of the servants and they will provide it. We already have the cooks working on dinner." He left them, making his way over to the priests they were travelling with.

A young woman, a few years younger than Mallory, appeared before them and curtsied. "I will show you to way to your rooms, Your Highness."

They went inside. Like the old buildings Mallory had grown up in, this one was entirely made of stone. Unlike Mallory's home, which had been hot and oppressively humid, this one was cool and a little damp. The lines were simpler, straighter, the trim mostly black metal and bulky.

"This one is for you," she said, opening a door and indicating Kaelen. She opened the one across the hall. "And this one is for you, M'Lady."

Kaelen kissed the back of Mallory's hand. "I'll leave you in good hands to wash up and I will see you down at dinner." When Mallory had disappeared into her room he turned and went back the way they had come.

Lord Iron-Smith's study was dominated by a large wooden desk but unlike most wooden furniture where the joints were connected as unobtrusively as possible, this one had bold iron fastenings holding the legs in place. The bookshelves against the back wall were similarly constructed. There was a black iron ring hanging from an iron chain above the desk with twelve candles arranged around it and the candle holders on the wall were also iron.

Kaelen glanced around, nodding in approval. "What's this news?" he said.

Lord Iron-Smith leaned back in his chair. "My nephew holds a high position in the Iron Guild in Stones Shore and has taken over the contract of an iron mine in the mountains. There have been gem stone finds in the area in the past."

"You think we'll get lucky this time."

"I'm sure of it."

"And your nephew, he knows what to do?"

Lord Iron-Smith nodded. "Yes, yes, he's trustworthy. He's a Loyalist with no fondness for the Stone Clan peasants he's forced to endure. If he finds something, he'll find an excuse to remove the Stone Clan mine supervisor and then the gems will be shipped north."

"That's excellent. The mines between here and the Animal Province have all come up empty thus far. It would be nice to have something to show for all this work."

"Our work is at the mercy of the damn ground," Lord Iron-Smith said. "Your work, however …"

"You don't think I'm trying?"

"We pulled a lot of strings to have you sent on this expedition."

"I didn't ask to be chosen for this."

"Did we make the wrong choice?"

"No, I didn't say that. I'll do what I have to do."

"I don't want to doubt the colour of your heart, Kaelen."

"There's nothing to doubt. My heart is iron, just like yours."

"Good. The rewards we reap will be worth all of this, I promise."

Kaelen stood. "So you all keep saying. Let's hope this isn't in vain. I'll see you at dinner. If you don't mind, I'd like a little time to myself before I have to perform for her again."

"Of course. Our hospitality extends to you as well. Whatever you need, just ask."

Kaelen nodded and retreated. He was still angry at his father for volunteering him for this instead of his brother, but he understood why he'd been chosen. Knowing why didn't make it any easier.

No, it makes it worse. Would it have been so bad? Would it really have stained the family name? So, she wasn't wealthy. Her father was a Loyalist. No. There's nothing to be done now except see this through to the bitter end.

The room looked like something out of a fairy tale movie, complete with canopy bed and stone fireplace. Unfortunately, the bath was also like something from a fairy tale movie, but without the talking animals. She stripped and stepped into the giant wooden bucket of surprisingly hot water. She sat and found that the water barely came up to the bottom of her ribs and she could not straighten her legs, which meant her knees stuck up like twin islands. She scrubbed as best she could with the rough cloth and the bar of plain, soap that had been left for her. When that was done, she sat for a moment trying to figure out how to wash her hair without drowning herself. She settled for kneeling in the tub with her head down and using the pitcher someone had left behind to pour water on the base of her neck so that it ran over her hair.

She wound up with a face full of water, but she was wet. She used the same soap to wash her hair and then rinsed it, shutting her eyes tight against the harsh suds. By the time she was done, she was shivering.

There was a stool by the fireplace with a stack of what looked like towels, but they weren't fluffy. She unfolded the top one to find that the fire had warmed it nicely and started drying off. She wrapped a second around her hair and pulled her clothes back on. They were dusty and sweaty and smelled of horse, but they were all she had.

She was halfway dressed when the door opened and the girl returned, another pile of fabric in her hands. "Oh! You're done. I was just coming to help with your hair."

"Oh, I'm not used to having someone help me bathe. I managed."

"You can't wear those clothes to dinner. It wouldn't be proper."

"I have nothing else to wear. I'm fairly certain naked would be worse."

"Lord Iron-Smith thought that might be the case and sent me with these. They belong to his daughter who is about your age."

"It would be nice not to smell like a horse at dinner."

"I'll help you dress and then I'll see that you have clean clothes for tomorrow morning."

"Thank you."

The borrowed clothes turned out to be a simple wool dress with long sleeves, a full skirt, and a modest neckline. It had been dyed a deep red and trimmed with cream lace. She ran her hands over her hips, smoothing the skirt.

"Wow. This is lovely, heavy, but lovely."

The girl ran a brush through Mallory's hair. "They're waiting downstairs for you already or I'd do something more with your hair. A pity it's so short. I'll show you the way."

Mallory stepped out after the serving girl. "What's your name?"

"Kendra, M'Lady."

"Kendra, I'm very new here and very confused. I don't know how to address people, I don't know anyone's names …"

"I call everyone 'sir' or 'ma'am' but I'm a servant and you're the princess. Oh, 'honourable' is the correct form of address for a priest."

"That helps," Mallory said. She took a deep breath. "Well, everyone knows I'm new so maybe they'll be forgiving."

"You're the princess," Kendra said again. "I'm sure no one will yell at you."

"Do they yell at you?" she said.

"Sometimes. I'm sorry. I should not speak so of my employer. This is the dining room." Kendra curtsied and hurried away, leaving Mallory alone in front of a heavy wooden door.

She took a deep breath and pushed open the door.

There was a long table down the middle of the room. At the head sat Lord Iron-Smith. At one hand sat an older woman and next to her several adults of varying ages with enough similarities that Mallory assumed them to be Lady Iron-Smith and her children and assorted relations.

On the other side of the table was an open seat, then Kaelen and the priests. Since there was only one empty place Mallory went straight to it, trying to ignore the fact that everyone was staring at her.

Kaelen stood and drew back her chair for her, tucking it in as she sat. As he resumed his spot servants appeared with food and wine.

"Where are the others?" Mallory said.

"The others?" Lord Iron-Smith said, obviously puzzled.

"There were several other men riding with us," Mallory explained.

"Ah. The guards are eating in the barracks with our estate guards," he explained.

"That makes sense," Mallory said. *The staff at the embassy didn't eat with the politicians and diplomats. It only makes sense that they'd have a similar rule here.* "What about Devin?"

"I'm not sure who you mean," Lord Iron-Smith said.

Honourable Bernard leaned forward. "We had a guide with us, a hunter and tracker from the Animal People, Devin Sun-Stag."

"I assume he's eating with the guards, then," Lord Iron-Smith said.

There was an awkward pause and then Lady Iron-Smith leaned forward and said, "The dress looks lovely on you. I'm glad it fit."

"Yes, thank you for your generosity."

"Nonsense, we're honoured. I know you're the princess and above such things, but there are a few other dresses that might suit you. You could take them with you, for your travels. There will be clothes for you in Golden Hall, of course."

"Perhaps," Mallory said. "I mean, it's very nice of you to offer, and I don't mind hand-me-down clothes, but this is a lot to get used to."

"I understand," she said.

For the most part, the dinner conversation made little sense to Mallory. They spoke of lords and ladies she'd never met, politics she didn't understand, and gods she had never heard of. Then again, her answers to their questions left them equally confused.

She ate her fill and drank a few glasses of wine. The food was bland compared to what she was used to, but the wine was amazing. When she stood at the end of the meal the room wavered a little.

She put a hand on the table and the other to her lips, trying to hold back the giggle. "I'm sorry," she said. "I think I've had one too many glasses of that delightful wine."

"I'm glad you enjoyed it," Lord Iron-Smith said.

"I'll walk you to your room," Kaelen said. To his friend he said, "Send someone up to help the princess to bed."

"Of course."

Arm-in-arm Mallory and Kaelen made their way through candle-lit halls. "I'm glad you're enjoying yourself," Kaelen said. "It's nice to see you relax. Lord and Lady Iron-Smith are very important and influential people at court. I'm glad you're becoming friends with them."

"They seem nice," Mallory said.

"You look beautiful in that dress."

"I feel silly, like I'm playing dress-up, or going out for Halloween. I've never worn a dress like this in my life."

"That's too bad, it suits you. The colour brings out your freckles and your hair. You need an emerald necklace to highlight your eyes."

Mallory laughed. "I don't own any emeralds."

"You do now. You're the princess. The crown owns many fine things and they'll all be at your disposal."

"Imagine that. I'm a fairy princess. If only my friends back home could see me now."

Kaelen opened the door and led her into the room. "Princess, what I said this morning in your tent, I meant every word of it."

"I hardly know you. I don't feel anything for anyone, just a lot of confusion." He was standing too close to her. The dress and the alcohol were making her feel too warm. She wanted to step back but he was holding her hand to his chest.

"You're overwhelmed. Your feelings are lost in all that confusion, and that's okay. I know what I feel, I know the truth. Just trust in me. Soon, when you've grown accustomed to this place, you'll see what I say is truth." He bent over her and kissed her, pulling her body close to his. When he stepped back someone cleared their throat.

Kendra was in the doorway. "It's time for the princess to get some rest," she said.

"Of course. Good-night my princess. I'll see you in the morning."

"Yes, good-night," Mallory murmured. She was feeling a little dazed. Kendra led her further into the room and helped her undress for bed.

Kaelen went out and shut the door. Lord Iron-Smith was hovering a short ways down the hall and hurried over.

"Well?" Lord Iron-Smith demanded.

Kaelen wiped his mouth with the back of his hand and nodded. "It's done. She saw. She'll tell the priests, I'm sure of it, and then it's done. I should be wed to Mallory by the end of the month."

"The sooner the better."

"Yes, yes, I know. I was told what was expected, should she actually be found."

Lord Iron-Smith put a hand on his shoulder. "You've done well. This won't be forgotten."

4th of Starrise, 24th Year of the 11th Rebirth
Iron-Smith Estate, Metalkin Province

"Where are my clothes?" Mallory asked.

"In the wardrobe," Kendra said from across the room.

Mallory, stood, one hand on the open door, her face set in a frown. "I'm looking in the wardrobe. They're not there."

Kendra appeared at her shoulder. "Yes, Princess. All these dresses are yours. Lady Iron-Smith said you could have them. You've been wearing them since you arrived."

"That was very nice of her, but I want *my* clothes. I want my jeans and my shirt."

"I've never seen pants that colour before," Kendra said. "And the shirt was so soft."

"Yes, I know. It's my favourite. I'd like it back. It was very nice of Lady Iron-Smith to lend me these dresses while I was a guest here but if I'm going to be travelling again, I want to be comfortable."

"You'll want one of these day dresses then," Kendra said, reaching past her.

"I can't ride in a dress."

"You won't be riding. Lord Iron-Smith has provided you with a carriage. Do you want the grey dress or the brown one?"

"I don't want either of them! I want *my* clothes!!"

"I'm sorry Princess. Honourable Bernard instructed us that you would no longer be needing them. They were disposed of."

"Honourable Bernard said? Disposed of? They weren't his clothes!"

"I'm sorry. I'm just a servant. I was given instructions and …"

"I'm the princess of this country, yes?"

"Uh, you're the Metalkin Princess, yes."

"So, I outrank everyone else in this house?"

"I suppose so."

"If I told you to throw things away or burn them or rip up books, would you?"

"I would have to check with Lord Iron-Smith. This is his home."

"And those were my clothes!!!"

"I'm sorry Princess. I wrongly assumed the instructions had come from you, to him, and then to me. I'm sure Lord Iron-Smith would reimburse you for …"

"I don't want his money. I can't take that money and replace my clothes. No one here wears clothes even similar!"

"There's nothing I can do now, Princess. Unless you wish to go in your underclothes, you'll have to wear one of the dresses."

Mallory felt like screaming. She cast about, her gaze settling on a clay vase. She seized it without thinking and threw it as hard as she could against the far wall. The vase shattered.

"Princess!"

"I'll take that vase in exchange for my clothes," she said. "Pick me a dress I can travel in. And be quick about it. They'll be waiting for me."

She marched down to the front door, her face set in a scowl. Kaelen smiled at her. He had been her near constant companion during their visit with the Iron-Smiths, flattering her and holding her hand, and he was at it again today. "You look lovely again this morning."

"I don't want to hear it," she snapped, walking past him to the group of priests. She pointed a finger at Bernard. "My clothes were destroyed on your orders."

"You no longer needed them."

"They were mine. You had no right! If you ever do something like that again I'll … I'll … I don't know what I'm allowed to do to you, but I'll find something, and it won't be pleasant."

She stopped talking to realize that everyone was staring at her, wide-eyed.

She took a deep breath. "What? I'm ready to go. Let's get this over with."

Everyone busied themselves grabbing the last of the bags and they went out into the courtyard, hurrying through the rain to be on their way before they were soaked to the bone.

7th of Starrise, 24th Year of the 11th Rebirth
North Road, Metalkin Province

Mallory hadn't spoken to Bernard in three days, outside of 'pass the bread', not even to say 'thank you', and she planned to continue giving him the silent treatment for as long as possible, especially since it so obviously made him uncomfortable. That left her with few people to talk to. She was politer to the other priests but didn't feel like listening to their zealous rants about the glory of Airon. The guards answered when she asked them questions but kept their answers short and did not respond with questions of their own, making conversation difficult.

That left Kaelen, who often rode in the carriage with her and sat with her when they stopped for meals, and Devin who always rode when they travelled and stuck with the guards when they stopped. Sometimes, while Kaelen rambled on about her loveliness, or the grandeur of the home she was moving into, she would find herself staring at Devin with great curiosity.

He was thinner than the other men, except for the priests, and fairer, not blonde but not so dark either, and with finer features. His clothes were simpler, sturdy, well-worn but well-cared for. He moved with an easy grace, but she noticed the way he looked at everything, all the time, like a deer in a field, waiting for something to jump out. She wanted to speak with him, ask him questions, since he'd been the easiest to talk to when she'd first come through the gate, but Kaelen made that impossible.

Kaelen presented a different mystery. How could she believe that this man had fallen madly in love with her just by laying eyes on her? He'd spent much of the last three days attempting to explain soul mates to her, but it scared her.

Today was no different. They were sitting around the fire in the common room of an inn, enjoying a hot meal. The stone fireplace took up most of one wall and the innkeeper's counter took up most of the opposite wall. There were eight tables of varying sizes spread around the remaining space. The guards had taken up a couple of tables near the door and were playing some sort of game that involved dice, drinking, silver coins, and loud laughter. The priests had retired to their rooms. Devin sat alone with his back against the far wall where he could see everything in the room.

"Did you want another bowl of stew?" Kaelen said.

Mallory's attention was drawn back to him. "No, thank you. I'm stuffed." She sighed and sunk a little lower in her chair. "Some more wine would be nice."

He nodded and took the dishes back to the counter. He returned with two cups of wine and a bowl of stew for himself. "It will be nice to get back to Golden Hall," he said. "The food there is much better than at these little inns, better even than at the Iron-Smith estate."

"It will be nice to eat something other than stew," Mallory agreed.

"We would have arrived in the capital sooner, but the priests insist on stopping at every village to speak at length with the village priest. And we're not pushing the horses at all. I'm sorry, I didn't mean to complain. What I meant to say was, soon we'll be arriving in Golden Hall and I hope you won't send me away."

"Where would I send you?"

"Back to my family's home in the city. I hope you will welcome me into the castle. I hope you've come to see me the way that I see you."

She sighed again, this time out of frustration rather than contentment. "Kaelen, I don't understand any of this. We don't have soul mates where I'm from. We don't believe in love at first sight. I don't know you, I don't really feel anything for you, good or bad. I just – more than anything I feel confused and lost and frustrated."

"Then please, trust me. I grew up here. Everything that is new and confusing to you is normal to me. I know what's happening between us." He took her hand. "I don't know you either, I don't know anything about you or the world you grew up in, and that scares me too."

Mallory looked away. "Don't."

"Princess, please, don't turn me away. Our union will bring peace and stability to the island, it will stop attacks like the one that happened at the gate."

She turned back to him, slowly, deliberately, her eyes wide. "You're saying that if I don't marry you, horrible things will happen?"

"Horrible things are already happening because it took them so long to find you. It falls to us to put aside our fear and confusion and set things right."

"I don't know. I'm tired. I'm going to my room. Alone." She stood, leaving her wine untouched and walked away without offering him a good-night.

Devin should have been paying attention to the door and the innkeeper – the two unknown factors that he might have to guard against. Instead he was watching Mallory and Kaelen. He saw Kaelen hover too long at the counter, fumbling with the pouch at his belt while he fussed with the food and drink. They'd been talking all evening, alone in a booth near the wall. Kaelen oozed charm but Mallory appeared to shy away from him. Finally, Mallory walked away and he watched Kaelen throw the contents of her untouched cup in the fire.

Something is not right. A deep anger welled up inside of him. His fist clenched, the other tightening around his cup. He'd left his knife in his room, trusting the guards to have their weapons, trusting that in a Metalkin inn this close to the capital they would have no trouble. *That's not it at all. You didn't trust what you might do with the knife.*

The whisper had started at full dark each night since they'd left Airon's Gate and it made it hard to think. The only thing that was easy to pay attention to was Mallory.

Kaelen turned, saw Devin staring, and glowered. He marched over. "Is there a problem?"

Devin shook his head. "Just enjoying my wine and the dance of the fire."

"Just watch yourself, *hunter*."

"Always, sir." He lifted his wine to his lips and turned his gaze back to the fire.

Kaelen harrumphed but went up the stairs, his great heavy steps betraying his anger and frustration.

9th of Starrise, 24th Year of the 11th Rebirth
Golden Hall, Metalkin Province

Golden Hall was a large, walled city filled with tightly packed buildings and tightly packed people. Their procession through the streets drew quite the crowd. Mallory didn't want to be the center of all this attention, but she stared out the carriage window anyway, not caring who stared back. There was too much to see.

They came in the gate at the north end of town and turned east. Near the gate, the buildings were small, simple, and built so close together only a child could pass through the spaces between them. They looked old, their roofs falling apart, their stone walls weather-beaten. They passed a small market where men and women shouted about goats and pigs and chickens and bread. On the other side of the market, the houses began improving in quality and size. Here the roofs were slate, and the houses had small front yards surrounded by black-iron fences.

Some of the buildings had signs over the doors declaring them shops or guild halls. Her window was so small that even at their easy pace it was hard to take it all in.

Kaelen had fallen silent a few miles before they'd reached the gates and he hadn't shared anything about the buildings they passed as they moved through the city. He wasn't looking out the window either, his gaze locked on some spot on the carriage wall.

They came to a second gate which opened before them and entered the courtyard of the castle. When the carriage halted, Kaelen got out and offered his hand to Mallory. "Welcome home," he said.

Puzzled by the lack of enthusiasm in his words, she stared at him for a moment before turning to face the castle. It wasn't the Taj Mahal but it was glorious in its own right. The courtyard was grey cobblestone and contained several low wooden buildings. She could hear the ring of metal on metal and shouting from nearby but since no one else appeared to panic at the sounds she assumed they were from training, not an attack. The stone walls were grey and clean-cut, perfectly straight and stretching three stories tall. The double doors were a dark-stained wood with heavy ornate iron fittings.

There were people everywhere: working with the horses, unloading the carriages, talking to the guards, all hurrying to finish before the rain began again. Two men in white robes and green sashes stood waiting by the door. They had to be waiting for something because they were the only two people in the courtyard not doing anything.

They're probably waiting for me. Mallory glanced at Kaelen but he stood stiffly at her side letting the business flow around him.

Honourable Bernard stepped up on her other side. "Welcome to Golden Hall, the castle for which this city was named, and the ancestral seat of the Metalkin royal family. This has always been the home of the Jewel-Rose princess and we're honoured to have you with us once more."

"Only half of that made sense," Mallory muttered. "Who are the men waiting there?"

"Your stewards. I will formally introduce you, and Master Kaelen, to them, and them to you."

"Why Kaelen?"

"He is your soul mate."

"Right. That." She took a deep breath. "All right. Lead on." She took a step before she noticed that Kaelen had put his arm out to her. Blushing she stopped and put her hand on his arm. "Sorry," she whispered.

They went together, a step behind Bernard, to the front doors.

The two men were like night and day. The one of the left was older, his hair mostly grey, his narrow features heavy with the fine lines of age, but his eyes were bright and the barest hint of a smile played at the corner of his mouth.

The man on the right was younger, if he was ten years older than Mallory she would have been surprised. He was dark, like Kaelen, but clean-shaven and not quite as large. He had dark eyes that seemed too small for his face and thin lips.

"May I introduce Princess Ashlynn Jewel-Rose, the eleventh rebirth of Airon's chosen protector, ruler of the Metalkin, and her prince, Master Kaelen Iron-Heart of the city of Golden Hall."

The two men exchanged a startled look.

"Princess, may I introduce to you Master Jaspar Black-Kettle, and Master Emilio Spirit-Light."

Mallory assumed the elder, fair-haired man was Master Spirit-Light and the younger, dark-haired man was Master Black-Kettle. She smiled, unsure of what to do next.

The men bowed and Master Spirit-Light said, "Welcome. I had hoped to see your return. Please, come inside with us, this morning's rain has stopped, for now, but it looks like it could start again at any time. We have much to talk about."

Mallory just nodded and followed them inside.

Devin took his horse to the stables and personally removed the tack, brushed the animal down, and saw to its food and water. He liked the horses, more than the hawks or the hounds, liked the smell of the leather tack and even the dry sweet smell of the hay. The dim dustiness of the stable relaxed him. It was warm here, and dry. He breathed deeply. *You can't put this off.* Squaring his shoulders, he walked back out into the rain and hurried up the wide stairs into the castle.

He took the time to change out of his riding clothes, not that his other clothes were any fancier, but they were clean and not covered in several days' worth of road dust, wash his face and hands, and comb his hair. He nodded to servants and guards as he passed them in the hallway, pausing to exchange a few words with several of them – just little things like asking after their children or checking how things had been since he'd left the castle.

Finally, he made his way to the round, dome-ceilinged temple. It was quiet, nearly empty save for a few acolytes who were sweeping and dusting and peeling up puddles of melted wax from floors and shelves. A few candles still burned on the altars around the room and the smell of burnt wicks and old incense lingered in the air.

He was halfway across the room when an acolyte stopped him. "Can I help you?"

"I need to speak with Honourable Bernard."

"Honourable Bernard has only just returned from a …"

"I know. I was with him on the journey. It's important. Tell him it's Devin Sun-Stag and it's about what happened our last night at the gate."

The acolyte nodded but didn't look impressed or convinced.

Devin took up a seat near the doors to the priests' quarters and waited, his gaze wandering around the temple. He wasn't a frequent visitor of this place, he preferred to worship the old spirits of his people out in the open spaces where the animals preferred to be, but he admired the beauty and craftsmanship in the pillars and mosaics.

He heard two sets of feet on the stone floor and stood to greet Honourable Bernard. The acolyte seemed flustered and gave Devin an odd look before returning to his duties and leaving the two men to talk.

"Thank you for seeing me. I know you must be tired for the journey and you likely have much to do."

"Yes, but this sounded important."

"It is. Is there somewhere we can speak where no one will hear us."

Bernard frowned but said, "Follow me." He led Devin to his personal room. "Let's hear it then."

Devin took a deep breath. "You remember the attack at the gate?"

"Of course. We were lucky to escape unharmed."

"We weren't that lucky. Not all of us."

Bernard took a step back.

Devin nodded.

"I'm sorry. I'll have to take you to the healers, they'll know what to do."

"They'll sedate me and restrain me. Please, I can't exist like that. I'll go mad before the Dark Spirit has a chance to destroy me."

"The rules …"

"I'm fine still. I made it back here without any of you guessing. Please. All I'm asking is for a few weeks, even a few days, just let me live my life until I can't hide it and then I will go with you to the healers and I'll submit. I know there is no surviving this, no coming back. I know what my end will be. I'm tempted to end it myself before it comes to that."

"You wouldn't be the first." Bernard sank into his chair and sighed. "This is a highly unusual and potentially dangerous request."

"I understand that."

"I want to call someone else, get their opinion. He's trustworthy, I promise, a very learned man. If he agrees with what I have in mind, then we will proceed. If not, then I have no choice but to send you to the healers."

"All right."

Bernard summoned an acolyte. "Go and fetch Master Spirit-Light at once. I know he's busy and he'll try to turn you away but he must come. Tell him this is a matter of utmost importance, it cannot wait."

"Yes sir."

"And have someone bring tea for three. The rain has left me chilled."

"Yes sir."

"Good." He turned back to Devin. "Now, while we wait, I have some questions for you."

"Of course, Honoured One. I'll do my best to answer."

"How do you know you're possessed?"

"While we were awaiting your return through the portal I was exploring Airon's island, I looked North and I saw the storms on the horizon. I heard on the wind a dark voice, and though I understood no words I felt in my soul that something out there meant the whole island harm. I hear that voice within me, whispering, urging me to embrace my anger, my rage, my darkest desires."

"That is why you walked away from every fight Kaelen laid at your feet on the journey home."

"Yes. If I had given in, if I had fought back, I would have fed a little piece of my soul to the darkness and I would never have gotten it back."

"No one has ever been able to describe these things before. I wonder …"

There was a knock at the door.

"Yes, enter," Bernard said.

A girl came in with a tea tray and set it on the only clear spot on the desk, which was only clear because there was usually a tea tray there. She curtsied and disappeared again.

"I was saying. I wonder why your case is so different."

"Perhaps it was being around the princess."

"We've always assumed that would …"

There was another knock.

"Oh, really now," Bernard said, then louder, "Come in."

This time it was Emilio Spirit-Light who came through the door. He was a slender man with fine features that bordered on being delicate. He wore a linen robe, similar to Bernard's but his sash was green and gold, as opposed to Bernard's whose was yellow and silver.

"Honourable Bernard, I hope we can make this a short emergency. I've only just finished the official meeting with the new princess and I've much to do this evening."

"I know, I know," Bernard said. "I would not have bothered you today of all days if it weren't important. Devin, tell him your story."

Keeping to the important details, Devin retold the story of the attack and his possession.

"Absolutely remarkable," Emilio said.

Bernard nodded. "Just as I said. This presents an interesting opportunity. You seem remarkably composed for a man who has been possessed for a week now. I have seen men become monsters in less time and never have I seen one show no outward signs after seven days."

Devin shrugged. "I don't understand it myself."

"No one would. Now, here's what I suggest we do. You will come to either me or Master Spirit-Light every few days so we can observe your condition closely. We know so very little about these spirits, perhaps this is our chance to learn something of value. We will also monitor your possession for signs of danger and will report you to the healers if I feel you're progressing too far. If this is all right with Master Spirit-Light."

Emilio held his chin in his hand, his long fingers curling about his mouth. "Yes," he said. "I think you're right. It will be dangerous, but with two of us watching him, we should be able to avert any trouble. But you mustn't miss a meeting or we'll have to send you straight to the healers."

"I understand." Devin bowed to the priest. "I cannot thank you enough. Both of you."

"You may not thank me when this is over. Stop at the altar on your way out and ask Airon for strength. I suspect that you will need it."

"Of course, Honoured One, Master Spirit-Light. Thank you." Devin left Bernard and Emilo musing together and returned to the temple proper.

There were five altars in the temple, with the altar to Airon and the altar to the Metalkin spirits being the largest and fanciest. They were bedecked with candles and offerings and there was always an acolyte at each, dusting, sorting, and keeping the candles fresh and the incense lit.

The other three altars were smaller, plainer, barely tended, and rarely used. It would have been an insult except that the people of stone, plant, and animal only came to the temple here to worship Airon. They worshipped their own spirits in their homes, or in their work.

Devin stopped at Airon's altar. He hadn't brought anything with him that he could offer so he just stood there for a moment, trying not to shuffle from foot to foot. He supposed he should say something, even silently, some request or offering of thanks, but the words wouldn't form. He brushed his fingers over the edge of the altar and walked out.

The rain had stopped but the day remained damp and chilly. He went back to the stables, the stable hands paying him no mind as he entered, picked up a brush, and started on a dusty looking horse. The repetitive motion soothed him and as he relaxed the words he needed came to his mind.

I don't know why I haven't yet succumbed to the monster inside of me, but I pray that the spirits of horse and deer, of hound and hawk, will protect me long enough to be of service. And when the end comes, may it come mercifully.

16th of Starrise, 24th Year of the 11th Rebirth
Golden Hall, Metalkin Province

Mallory paced her bedchamber, wringing her hands. The last few days had been filled with dress fittings and shoe fittings and meeting staff and arguing with everyone about her name. And of course, dining twice a day with Kaelen who seemed to alternate between adoring and cold without reason. It left her feeling unsettled and confused.

Today she was nervous for another reason. She was in no way ready for the meeting that was about to happen.

In the last week she hadn't seen much of the castle, just the few rooms she regularly used and the hallways connecting them, and even less of the city outside the walls. To be honest, she'd been too busy to go exploring, and it looked like the foreseeable future would be just as busy.

They'd told her she was a princess, but she didn't know what that meant or what permissions that gave her. Kaelen and Jaspar had assured her that once the hectic rush of preparations for the wedding, and the wedding itself were over they would help her learn everything she needed to know. "But until then, just trust us to handle everything," her steward had said.

She was grateful for their support.

The knock on the door startled her enough that she jumped. "Who is it?"

"Your guests are ready for you." The voice was soft and feminine.

Probably one of the girls that's been helping me. "All right. I'm ready." She hiked up the front hem of her skirt so that she wouldn't step on it and marched to the door.

She followed the girl down busy hallways. She was used to the servants' presence now, even if she wasn't used to the extent that they waited on her. Growing up in an embassy, the daughter of an ambassador, she hadn't done her own laundry or cooked her own meals until she'd moved out for school. But she had dressed herself every morning and brushed her own hair and drawn her own bath. Not that she wanted to draw her own bath here. The thought of carrying all that water up from she didn't even know where made her cringe.

Today the halls were crowded with finely dressed guests who were probably as surprised to see her out and about as she was to see them at all. She tried to keep her chin up and her back straight as she passed them, but they all stopped and stared at her, some of them bowing or curtsying. By the time she reached the day room where she was meeting her special guests, she had her head down and her shoulders up and she was sure her cheeks were as red as her hair.

The girl opened the door and went in ahead of her, curtsying deeply. "May I present Princess Ashlyn Jewel-Rose."

Everyone in the room stood and faced her. Taking a deep breath, she stepped fully into the room, raised her face, and said in the firmest voice she could muster, "My name is Mallory Brock and I would appreciate it if people would stop calling me Ashlyn."

Four women roughly her age and an older man just stared at her. Then one of the women started laughing. She had a round face and wore a dark green dress. "Oh, I like her already!"

The man glared. "Princess Betha, control yourself." He cleared his throat and turned his attention, and a softer stare, back to Mallory. "Welcome. I am High Priest Balder Gold-Spark."

All her fear and confusion sharpened into white hot rage that bubbled up with bitter words. "You're the one that sent them to kidnap me."

"I was informed you made the choice to step through the portal of your own free will."

"I didn't believe it would work," she muttered. Then she huffed. "Fine. I'm here. Now what?"

"I'm pleased you already found your prince," he went on. "That is the first duty and greatest honour of any princess and will ensure peace and prosperity for your province. After the wedding tomorrow there's the matter of your education, and then you take over governing this province."

"Great." She was muttering again. "I never wanted to go into politics."

"Allow me to introduce the other princesses of the Isle of Light. They rule the other provinces." He gestured to the round-faced woman who was still grinning broadly. "This is Princess Betha Rose of Roses of the Evergrowth."

"They call me the Thorn Princess," she said proudly.

The wispy girl beside her rolled her eyes and said, "I don't think they mean it as a compliment."

"This is Princess Taeya Living Rose of the Animal People."

Mallory saw Taeya cringe slightly and her smile became tight. "Welcome to the island," she said.

"This is Princess Rheeya Stone Rose of the Stone Clan."

"I live about as far from you as I can get on this island," Rheeya said, "But if you ever need anything, just write."

"Yes, I suppose calling you on the telephone is out of the question," Mallory murmured. Her cheeks flushed when she saw everyone staring at her. "No, nothing. Just, never mind." She cleared her throat. "Thank you for the offer."

"And this," Balder went on, his voice taking on an even grander tone, "Is Princess Vonica Bright Rose of the Sun Temple."

Vonica had been looking down at her hands since Betha's initial outburst. She glanced up just enough to make the barest eye-contact with Mallory and then looked down again. In the softest voice, she said, "Hello."

Mallory frowned. From the priest's introduction, she'd been expecting more.

"I'm sure you have lots of questions," Balder continued.

"Oh yeah," Mallory said. "Like what the heck is this place? What's with the portal? Why does everyone keep calling me Ashlyn? And when can I go home?" She took a deep breath. "And that's just for starters."

"I was going to say, that after the wedding your steward of religious matters will be able to answer most of them. Why don't we all have a seat? There are a few pressing questions I can answer for you now so that you'll feel more comfortable here." Once everyone was seated, he said, "To answer your last question first, you are home. For you to leave now would be devastating to the stability of the island."

"I don't really care about your politics," Mallory said. "Find someone else to rule."

"I meant the physical stability of the island," Balder said. "Your soul is a key piece in keeping our island physically safe from utter destruction. Even if it were safe for you to leave, there is no possible way. The gate will not open now until it is time for us to locate your rebirths."

"You look Irish, but you talk like a Hindu," she said, ignoring the puzzled looks her words created. "Kaelen mentioned reincarnation on the trip here. He said something about me being this Princess Ashlyn everyone is going on about."

Balder cleared his throat. "Essentially, yes. You are the reincarnation of the Metalkin Princess, Ashlyn Jewel-Rose. If you had been found at the usual time you would have grown up here and that would have been your name."

"It's not my name," Mallory said. "I'm not changing my name."

"I'm sure we can work out a compromise," Balder said. "I understand it would be difficult for you, after twenty-four years, to change the name everyone addressed you by on a day-to-day basis. But the name and title carry much symbolic significance."

"I'm already letting you call me Princess."

"I mean 'Jewel-Rose'. This was the name given to the first Ashlyn by Airon himself as a symbol of the pact between him and the five provinces."

"Airon is the sun god," Betha put in.

Mallory had gotten that much from the priests she'd travelled with, but she was thankful someone was being considerate enough to offer explanations. "Sounds like he's a big deal around here," Mallory said. "I'm guessing that's why all of your last names sound the same? It's all part of this pact?"

"Basically," Betha confirmed.

Mallory nodded and after a moment's consideration, she said, "I don't want to be called Ashlyn, not day-to-day, not by the priests, not at ceremonies or rituals or whatever you people do, not in official documents, nothing. It's not my name. I will not answer. *But you can tack Jewel-Rose onto my name. That's a compromise I can make.*"

"Then we will inform everyone that your name is Mallory Jewel-Rose and …"

"Mallory Brock," she said, interrupting him. "Mallory Brock Jewel-Rose."

Balder frowned but said, "Mallory Brock Jewel-Rose. We will address you as such at the wedding tomorrow and all future official documents will bear that name."

"Thank you." Her stomach rolled again. She'd been so busy arguing the looming wedding had slipped her mind. She swallowed the lump that was rising in her throat. "There's one other thing; it can't wait until after the wedding."

"Whatever you need." Balder said the words but the tone of his voice was impatient.

"I don't understand how I'm supposed to marry someone I just met two weeks ago. I don't know him at all." She cast her gaze about the room, hoping for some sign of support or understanding from the other princesses.

"Your soul knows him," Balder said. "Because your souls are parts of the same whole. Your marriage tomorrow is mainly about making that soul bond official as part of the sacred pact that keeps this island safe. You'll get to know him in time."

It was becoming apparent that no one, not the servants who dressed her, not her stewards, not the other princesses, and most certainly not this high priest, was going to listen to her concerns and cancel the wedding. "Then I'm not sleeping with him," she said, a last, desperate act of defiance. "I don't sleep with dudes I've only just met. I like to get to know them a bit first."

"You wouldn't be the first princess to request separate accommodations from her prince," Balder said. "Kaelen has a suite of rooms here, I assume?"

Relieve flooded her. "Yes, he's been living here since I got here."

"Then that will suffice. You can inform him that he is not allowed in your rooms without your permission and inform your stewards that Kaelen will not be vacating those rooms after the wedding. If any of them give you trouble about the matter you can send them to me. I'm sure that in time, as the two of you get to know each other, you'll change your mind."

"If I do, I'll let you know," Mallory said. *But I don't think I ever will.*

"Master Emilio Spirit-Light is your steward of religious matters. You've met him already?"

Mallory nodded. "Yes. I like him, I think. He seems nice enough."

"He will answer any questions you have about our history and religion. He's a very learned man. It is his job to guide you in all religious matters, and any political matters that involve the other provinces. Master Jaspar Black-Kettle will assist you with court and dealing with the guilds within your own province. He's younger as the steward who was trained to work with you passed away shortly before you were born, and quite suddenly, it was very unexpected. But he has been doing an exemplary job of running the province in your prolonged absence."

"Can I wear pants?"

"Of course not," Balder said, looking taken aback by the very suggestion. "A certain level of respectability is expected from you. You're the princess, the leader of this province. You have a full wardrobe and seamstresses to make necessary alterations. Your day dresses are simple, and I'm told comfortable. Do they allow you to wear pants in the Wide World?"

"Of course."

"Hmm. That isn't what the historical records of the Wide World say."

"When was the last time you were a part of the world?"

"You are the eleventh rebirth."

"So, ten generations, give or take, depending on how closely the length of days and years lines up and the difference in life expectancy. Yeah, a lot has changed in ten generations. Women wear pants if they choose and cut their hair and work outside of the home. It's not totally equal yet, but we even get to vote."

"Vote? Vote for what?"

"Government. I live in a country with a democratic government. We vote for our leaders. I mean, we still have a queen and all that, but she's just a celebrity really. She has like no political power anymore."

"You will have to speak with Master Spirit-Light at length about these things," Balder said. "He will make a record of them for the library. The priests who go over once each generation to locate the princesses don't have the chance to explore or learn much about the changes in your world."

"This could take a while. I don't even know where to begin. Democracy, electricity, women's liberation, civil rights. Basic geography?"

"I'm sure you two will figure it out. Now, I'm sure Princess Mallory has a great many things to do to prepare for tomorrow and I *know* the four of you have meetings this afternoon, and I have things to prepare for the wedding as well. So, we will part ways now and get done whatever duties we have to do."

"But you barely let us talk," Betha said. "I have so many questions!"

"Then I will provide you with a copy of whatever book Master Spirit-Light writes based on Mallory's information," Balder snapped. "Princess Mallory found her prince within the first week of her being on the Isle of Light. The four of you have been looking for five years and nothing! All of the reports I receive from your stewards point to all of you being difficult and stubborn. So, you

52

will go and see to any official business that is required of you while you are here and you won't complain to me about it. Understood?"

"Yes sir," Vonica said.

Balder nodded sharply and stood. When no one else moved he said, "Girls?"

The four other princesses stood, curtsied to Mallory, and filed out after the high priest. A moment later one of the serving girls appeared in the open door. "Princess Ashlyn? If you're ready, the seamstress is here for the final dress fitting for tomorrow."

"It's Princess Mallory," she said. "Tell the others. I don't ever want to be called Ashlyn again."

"My apologies. It's habit. We were taught …"

"I was taught magical islands don't exist. We all have to learn new things. Let's get this dress fitting over with."

It wasn't often a member of the Carainhithe court was invited to Golden Hall, and even rarer that it was someone Devin knew. Martin Black-Kite had grown up one town over from the Sun-Stags and had courted one of Devin's sisters for a short time before both had turned their romantic attentions to others. The romance hadn't lasted, but Devin and Martin's friendship had.

The two men wasted no time in getting caught up over wine in Martin's room.

"How did you manage an invitation to this wedding?" Devin said.

"Luck," Martin said. "I got hired on to help the aging Hawk Master in the castle. I was sent along to oversee the transport of a young Sun Hawk."

Devin whistled. "Now that is something. And for that you're rewarded with a seat at a royal wedding."

Martin laughed. "I'm not attending the wedding. I don't rank that highly. What about you?"

"I might stand in the back of the temple with the other servants, but I won't be welcome at the dinner either." He was going to the ceremony, wouldn't miss it for anything, even if the thought of watching Mallory wed that pompous oaf made his stomach churn.

"Well then, we'll have dinner together that night."

"We probably won't get fed if we stay here," Devin said. "Every cook and servant will be busy with the wedding feast."

"Then we'll ride into town. Someone will feed us."

The shortest route between the Guest Wing and the Servant's Wing was through the Royal Wing. Servants, including Devin, were only allowed in the Royal Wing if they had work to do, but Devin didn't feel like going all the way around. *If I get stopped, I'll make up some errand,* he thought, trying to walk casually.

He heard voices behind him and looked over his shoulder, worried a guard might be making a regular patrol down the hallway. He ended up walking right into someone.

"I'm sorry," he said. "I'm sorry, that was my fault entirely, forgive me," he said, bowing deeply. The chances of it being a servant or a noble were split almost even. *Better to be on the safe side.*

"Devin?"

He looked up. "Princess Jewel-Rose."

Her expression darkened. "If you don't call me Mallory, I'm going to scream."

"I'm sorry, Princess, it wouldn't be proper. I just work here." He bowed again.

She growled in frustration. "Will you at least call me Princess Mallory then?"

"Yes, I can do that."

She nodded sharply. "Good."

He should just walk on, maybe apologize again, but he hesitated. "Were you going somewhere?"

"I'm tired of being in that room!" She pointed over her shoulder. "I'm going exploring."

"Are you looking for something in particular?"

"I don't know," she said. "I just need to get away from all the fuss and bother."

"Why don't I show you around a little," he said.

Her gaze turned wary. "Why?"

"Because it's a polite thing to offer?"

"You're not going to keep me out of places?"

"Well," he said. "I might suggest not walking into an occupied guest room, but otherwise, it's your home, isn't it?"

"That's what Kaelen said when I got here, but no one will show me around and everyone keeps telling me I don't need to know yet."

"That's silly. This is you home. You should be getting used to it. What sorts of spaces do you like?"

"Open ones," she said. "Brightly lit ones. Something with fresh air."

"I know just the place," he said. He led the way up several flights of stairs and opened a seemingly random wooden door to reveal a sitting room with a large balcony. "Go ahead," he said. "The view is amazing."

She took tentative steps across the room, her gaze sweeping back and forth, pausing on the paintings and tapestries. She stepped out, closing her eyes a moment and letting the sunlight warm her. After a few slow, deep breaths she opened her eyes. Directly below the balcony was a garden, and beyond that the wall that separated the castle grounds from the city.

She was expecting something small and quaint but Golden Hall stretched out before her, a patchwork of rooftops and towers and trees. The edge of the city was much closer to the castle wall on one side then the other and beyond the buildings she could see the roll of pasture lands and the dark green of trees. She could hear the ringing metal and swell of voices of the men training down in the yard, and somewhere nearby, the more consistent pounding of a blacksmith at work in his forge. A hawk's cry pierced the air and she spotted the quick form just before it disappeared into the cityscape.

"Thank you," she said as Devin joined her. "It's lovely."

"I don't get to come up here often," he said. "I spend a lot of time away from the castle."

"How far do you travel?"

"Just into the forest there," he said, pointing. "I hunt, or I do routine checks of the hunting and lumber camps there for your stewards."

"Oh. You don't go north?"

"No, I don't go to the coast."

"So, you can't help me get back to the gate?"

"No, and even if I could, I couldn't open the gate to send you home again."

"It's just not fair!" she said, suddenly angry again. "I'm supposed to be a princess on a fairy tale island, but no one listens to me! This wedding is happening too fast. I don't know where anything is. I'm not allowed to do anything for myself. I want my clothes back!!"

"Hold on," he said. He disappeared inside and returned with a chair for her. A second trip yielded a chair for himself.

"Are you allowed to bring these outside?" she said, stopping her rant to eye the chairs.

"Do you want them outside? They belong to you now."

She laughed a little and sat. "I guess they do."

"You seem upset, and rightly so," he said, trying to approach the subject as gently as possible. "If you want to talk, I'll listen."

"You'd be the only one," she said. "I'm surprised they're letting me keep my name. That *man*, that *high priest*, he brushed off every one of my concerns. There's no way for me to delay the wedding, I'm just lucky they aren't making me share a room with him!"

"With Prince Kaelen?"

She nodded. "Who else do I need to share a room with?"

"No one," he said.

"Good. I just … I don't know what I expected. No one else could see the portal. They all just walked through like it wasn't there. I thought the same thing would happen to me and it didn't. Then I was here and everyone insisted there was no way home. I just want to go home. I keep trying to do the right thing, be the princess everyone wants me to be, do a duty I didn't even know I had, but I just want to go home."

"I understand," he said, nodding.

She blinked at him. "You do? You're not going to yell at me? Or scold me?"

He shook his head. "No, I understand completely. I …"

The door opened and a young woman stuck her head in. "No, it's empty, there's no one … hold on, I've found her. She's here." The woman, a servant by the way she was dressed, came into the room. "Princess A-Mallory, we've been looking for you. Honourable Bernard is waiting for you to review the wedding ceremony."

"No one told me I had another meeting today," Mallory said.

"We didn't know you had other plans," the girl replied. "We thought …"

"That I'd just sit in my room waiting to be herded from one place to the next?"

She dropped her gaze. "I'm sorry, Princess."

Mallory looked over at Devin. She'd rather stay here and talk to him. He'd been about to say something before they were interrupted, but this wedding was happening tomorrow, there was no stopping it, and she had no idea what to expect.

The last time I walked into a situation without knowing what to expect, I wound up here. Maybe I should go and learn something before this ceremony. At least then I can ask questions beforehand.

It was rational, responsible, and she still wanted to stay here and talk to Devin instead. "Wait in the hallway," she said to the servant. "I'll be out in a moment." When the woman had gone Mallory turned back to Devin. "You work here, right?"

"Yes."

Her eyes burned into his. "So, that means you work for me?"

"My jobs generally come from the stewards, but yes, I'm employed by the crown, and that means you." *Airon help me, whatever you ask of me I'll do.*

"How do I contact you?"

His heart leapt. "You send a servant in search of me." He hoped he sounded calm.

"That won't work," she said. She tapped her fingers on the chair. "I really need a phone right now," she muttered. "If I send you a note, would the servant delivering it read it?"

"No," Devin said.

The certainty in his voice was enough for her. "When I need your services, I'll send a servant with a note," she said.

"I'm not sure what services I can provide, other than what your stewards already assign me."

She laughed a little. "It's an excuse to get you here the next time I need someone to talk to."

"Oh." He smiled. "I'm honoured, Princess Mallory."

"And I'm grateful." She huffed. "I have to go. If you don't see *Honourable* Bernard at the ceremony tomorrow expect a summons to help me hide the body." She stood, squared her shoulders, and marched out leaving Devin to hope that she was joking.

17th of Starrise, 24th Year of the 11th Rebirth
Golden Hall, Metalkin Province
The Wedding of Mallory Jewel-Rose

Though the wedding wasn't until noon preparations began mid-morning, at least for Mallory. Someone came and helped her into her old-fashioned undergarments, including a corset, and then a simple wrap dress to protect her modesty.

Two girls worked on her hair, combing it smooth and then twisting it into elaborate braids. Fresh roses were pinned into her hair in a cascade pattern. She protested that, but the girls did it anyway. Afterwards, looking in the mirror, she had to admit the effect was stunning.

Finally, they started on the dress, which had over fifty little white buttons which all needed to be slipped into their loops and she couldn't help with any of them since they went down her back where she could neither see nor reach. So, she stood helpless, arms outstretched, on a low stool, while the girls buttoned and pinned and adjusted. The roses on the dress, at least, were cloth, and not as bright as Mallory was expecting, but against the cream of her dress, they looked amazing.

She was led through deserted hallways to the main temple with two girls helping her carry her skirt and another carrying her train. They stopped in the foyer where a set of large ornate doors loomed between them and the temple proper. She stood before the doors while the girls fussed over her dress again and then Master Jaspar Black-Kettle came over and shooed them away.

"You look every bit a princess," he said. "Everyone is awaiting your arrival."

"I didn't need to know that," Mallory muttered as butterflies descended on her stomach. "I guess eloping is out of the question."

Jaspar gave her a puzzled look. "If you're ready I will invite Prince Kaelen in to escort you."

"No, I'm not ready."

"What do you need?"

"I need to go home. I need to wake up now. I need to not be here."

"I'm sorry, I don't think ..."

She took a deep breath. "No, it's okay." Another deep breath. "I'm ready. Let's just do this."

He nodded, looking relieved, and disappeared.

The next person to approach her was Kaelen. When she'd met him, he'd been dressed for travelling and had been on the road, away from whatever conveniences this place could boast for several days. She'd had dinner with him nearly every night since arriving back at the castle and he'd cleaned up well. Today, however, was a step above. His jacket was black and cut in what Mallory would describe as a military style. *Like those old paintings of Napoleon.* The trim was all gold. His dark hair was combed back, and his beard neatly trimmed. He cut an impressive, almost imposing figure. There was something eager in his eyes, an impatience that echoed in his rigid posture and somber face.

He held out his arm. "My Princess."

She smiled weakly and placed her hand around his arm.

The doors opened with a creak, revealing a large round room. The nobles and guests were arranged around the circle, the central portion left open. She took a deep breath and when Kaelen stepped forward she did too.

They made their way to the compass rose inlaid on the floor, centered under the building's domed roof. Mallory had met Bernard here yesterday and had spent more time studying the copper and gold inlay on the floor than she had listening to what she was supposed to say and do. Again, today, even with the crowd of nobles around her, the mosaic was by far the most interesting thing in the room.

Her attention was quickly pulled from the polished gleam of the floor to High Priest Balder when he started speaking.

Mallory had to be prompted each time it was her turn to speak. *This is a lot more complicated than repeating back vows a few lines at a time and saying 'I do' at the end. All these 'blessed be's and 'by his light's and 'may his light ever shine upon us's – I don't know which to say when!*

For his part, Kaelen stood stiffly by her side, intoning responses and oaths in a flat, emotionless baritone.

When the rituals were over, Balder raised his arms high and said, "Princess Mallory Brock Jewel-Rose and Prince Kaelen of house Iron-Heart. May their union return unity to the island, may their happiness bring peace, may their long lives bring prosperity."

There was a great cheer from the crowd and Mallory was relieved that she wasn't expected to kiss Kaelen in front of everyone.

The wedding ceremony, which had doubled as a coronation ritual, had lasted most of the afternoon. Mallory had barely half an hour of quiet to recover and rest her feet before being led into the great hall for dinner.

The room was full of people and the sound of voices and laughter filled the room. Mallory could only stare blankly at the crowd of strangers. *This is it. It's done. I'm the princess now. There's no going home, no going back.* She looked over at Kaelen and was surprised to find he was standing rigid at her side, his face cold. *I thought he, at least, would have been happy today.*

The meal was elaborate and delicious, soups and salads and roasts and potatoes and hot bread cut thick with butter. Servants came around constantly with fresh platters of food and pitchers of wine. Mallory ate, surprised to find she was actually hungry in the face of all the nerve-wracking activity.

Nearby the four other princesses sat together at a small table. Mallory studied them, trying to remember their names. The round-faced one was Betha, she knew that. She liked Betha's boldness. The slender one staring at her hands was probably Vonica. The other two she wasn't sure about. She was still staring at them when a large man suddenly stepped up in front of the table, blocking her view.

At his appearance Kaelen scrambled to his feet and hastily straightened his clothes.

Mallory blinked and gave her head a rapid shake, more surprised at Kaelen's reaction than the stranger's appearance. She quickly realized the two men shared many of the same features, the heavy brow, dark hair, and dark eyes, the large frame, the thick hands.

"I didn't … I'm glad …" Kaelen stuttered. He took a deep breath. "Welcome. Please, allow me to introduce the two of you." He reached out and took Mallory's hand, tugging her to her feet. "Mallory, this is Lord Shane Iron-Heart, the head of my family seat, and my father. Father, this is Princess Mallory Brock Jewel-Rose."

Shane bowed. "It is a pleasure to finally meet you. In the excitement of your arrival and the haste to see you two wed, there wasn't time for a visit." When he straightened he held out his hand.

Mallory placed her hand in his and he kissed the back. "It's nice to meet you too. Kaelen mentioned you on our trip here. Maybe in the next few weeks we can come to visit you? Or you and your wife can come and visit us here."

"Oh, no," Kaelen said. "My mother passed away many years ago."

Mallory looked from father to son and back. "I'm so sorry. He never mentioned it. I hope I didn't …"

Shane chuckled. "It's been many years, as Kaelen said. There are times I miss her, to be sure, but the pain is greatly lessened. You haven't offered offense."

Mallory couldn't help but sigh with relief. "The offer still stands. You are welcome to visit."

"My thanks. I'm sure that Kaelen and I will be able to find something that works for all of us, and soon. I look forward to getting to know the love of my son's life." He smiled broadly at them. "I will return to my table now. I'm sure there are others who will come to introduce themselves to you this evening. Airon bless you both." He bowed a little as he stepped back.

Mallory turned to Kaelen. "That was a nice surprise," she said, only to realize that Kaelen was standing as stiff as a poker. She touched his hand and he jerked it back away from her. "Kaelen?"

He looked down at her with cold, hard eyes, the corner of his mouth curling up, twisting his face into something ugly. For a heart-pounding moment they stared at each other.

Finally, Kaelen's who body relaxed, his face returning to neutral and then to sorrowful. "I'm sorry," he said. "I shouldn't have done that. He caught me off guard."

His words sounded empty and insincere but there was a huge room full of people and most of them kept looking in their direction, so Mallory smiled. "Let's sit and finish the meal."

Kaelen nodded.

"Maybe someday you can tell me more about your family," she said. *And why you reacted so strongly to your father today.*

"Perhaps," he said. "If there is time. The next few weeks will be very busy."

"So I've been told. I guess we should enjoy the evening." *Or at least try.*

18th of Starrise, 24th Year of the 11th Rebirth
Golden Hall, Metalkin Province

Master Emilio Spirit-Light rose early in spite of the late night the night before. He met with the other princesses, ensuring they had everything they needed for their journeys home, and then saw them off. The other guests would be gone by the end of the day, returning to nearby estates or making the trek to other provinces.

Nina Copper, the head of housekeeping, would have her hands full, coordinating the airing and cleaning of all the guest rooms, but Emilio knew she was quite capable. He also knew he'd get a heavily worded request for additional hands if the work proved too much for her regular group of girls.

What he wasn't expecting that morning was the timid girl who knocked on his door to report that Mallory was not opening her door and had refused breakfast.

"It was a late night," Emilio said kindly. "Give her time."

"Of course, sir, I wouldn't worry, except that I could hear her crying in there."

"I see. Thank you for informing me. Have you told anyone else?"

"No, sir. I came to you first. I can inform Master Black-Kettle or Prince Kaelen if you see fit."

"No. Don't bother them with this. I'll speak with her myself."

"Yes, sir."

Emilio had spent a lot of time these last twenty-four years in the Princess's rooms, examining the artwork and wondering what their missing princess would be like, if she were ever found. Now, here she was, and he wasn't sure what to think of her yet. She had amazing strength, he could see that, but she was obviously scared, confused, and angry. *And rightly so. But at some point, she must move on from that or her presence here will do us little good. Master Black-Kettle has been in charge long enough, I think.*

He knocked on the door. "Princess?"

There was no answer.

"Princess, may I come in and speak with you?"

"No." The word was muffled, and not just by the heavy door.

"Are you dressed?"

Again, no answer.

Keeping his eyes on the floor, just in case, he let himself into her room.

Mallory was sprawled on the bed in a robe, face in her arms, the sound of her sobs now unmistakable. He closed the door softly behind him.

"Princess, why don't you come and sit with me by the fire?"

"Go away."

With a sigh, he went to the chairs and turned one around so that it was facing the bed then settled into it. "Mallory, I'm sorry this happened to you, I truly am. I cannot imagine what you are going through right now. I left the Sun Temple for the first time when I was twenty-one and came here. That was difficult enough. The Metalkin live very differently and value different things. But this is still the Isle of Light, and whatever differences I faced are nothing compared to what you must be facing."

"I want to go home," she said in a hushed voice.

"I know."

She sat up and adjusted her robe so that she was covered, swinging her legs over the side of the bed. Her eyes were red and puffy from crying. She was expecting brisk lectures about getting over it and moving on, not compassion or consideration.

"Most Honourable Gold-Spark informed me that your world has changed immensely since we last had the opportunity to see any of it. We will have to discuss those changes some time, over a glass or two of wine, when you feel up to it."

"I thought this was a dream. I kept hoping I'd wake up. And every time I woke up, I was still here. I … I don't know what to do. Before, I was on my way to school, I was going to study, become a veterinarian, and now that's all gone. I never wanted to get into politics."

"Then let's take this one step at a time. Prince Kaelen and Master Black-Kettle are … capable of the day-to-day tasks involved in running the province while you learn more about us and our way of life."

Mallory nodded.

Emilio felt his heart soften towards the young woman and he smiled gently. "You have questions and I'm betting neither Kaelen nor the High Priest answered them to your liking."

"Balder … the High Priest told me to ask you after the wedding."

"Well, it's after the wedding and here I am. Ask me anything."

"I understand about the reincarnation. Will I ever remember anything about my past lives?"

"We've never had a princess remember her past lives, no."

Mallory nodded. "Okay. At least I don't have to deal with someone else's weird memories on top of everything else. But if I don't remember being me, how do you know you have the right person?"

"Airon guided his priests to you, you were able to see them when no one else could, and you were able to see and use the portal."

"There's no chance of mistake?"

"Not if you're here. Maybe you could have seen our priests but to use the portal? No. Airon chose you."

"Everyone talks about Airon but people keep mentioning spirit guides too."

"Each province worshipped their own spirits, and those spirits guided them towards certain trades and skills. Generations before The Pact Airon's prophet united the island under his guidance. The other provinces, including the Metalkin, still worship their spirit guides, of course, but Airon is the chief among them."

"Airon is your spirit guide?"

"Yes. I hail from the Sun Temple Province just south of here."

"What do I do? I mean, day-to-day. If I'm going to be princess here, what are my jobs?"

"You'll hold court each day to hear the petitions and concerns of the people. Sometimes there will be a serious case that requires your judgement. There will be letters from various guilds and nobles and the other princesses to answer. And there is a certain amount of entertaining that is expected of you, hosting members of the guilds for lunch or noble families for dinner. There are several religious ceremonies throughout the year which you are required to attend and participate in."

"If I have to deal with all those people, I need to know what to call them. Sir? Lord?"

"Lord is reserved for the patriarch of each family. He governs the family estate and surrounding lands. 'Lady' is the proper address for a lord's wife."

"What about earls and dukes?"

"I've never heard those terms before."

"That will make it easier at least. And Honourable is a priest."

"Yes. You can also use 'Honoured One'. Most Honourable and Most Honoured One are reserved for the High Priest. Master is used for anyone who holds an elevated position. These are the men and women who have achieved the highest form of training or education in their guilds or hold a position of authority in the guild. They are business managers, stewards, or scholars as well."

"What about calling someone 'sir'?"

"Members of the Royal Guard. Otherwise, you outrank everyone so you don't need to 'yes sir' or 'yes ma'am' anyone."

"There's so much to remember." She sighed. "I'm kind of hungry."

"I'll have food sent up to you. You can eat and wash up and dress and then we can continue our discussion."

"All right. And Master Spirit-Light?"

"Yes, Princess?"

"Thank you for your understanding."

He nodded and exited. *We've a long way to go before she's ready to sit at court but with a little patience we should get through this just fine.*

Mallory had changed from her robe to a simple dress by the time the girl came with her breakfast tray. *Though I suppose, given the time of day, it's probably brunch. I wonder if they know that word here.*

The girl had raven black hair in a thick braid down her back. She looked to be about sixteen. Mallory had seen her almost every day over the last ten days and still didn't know her name, didn't know the names of any of the servants who helped with her hair and clothes.

She smiled. "Thank you."

The girl nodded. "Of course, M'Lady."

"What's your name?"

"My name?"

"I shouldn't really call all of you 'girl' or 'hey you'."

"I'm Cecilia," she said with a deep curtsey.

"Hello Cecilia. How long have you worked here?"

"Nearly a year."

"Do you like it?"

"Princess, working in the castle is one of the most coveted jobs for a young woman with no ties to a guild or trade. I am grateful to work here."

"You're desperate for this job and you're afraid if you speak out against someone here, you'll lose it, is that it?"

"M'Lady, I didn't say …"

"I come from a very different world, Cecilia. You work for me now, not for the other nobles living here, not my stewards, not the priests. Me. So tell me, if you could safely ask for something here to change, would you?"

Cecilia looked at the floor at her feet. "Princess, no job is perfect. Excuse me, I'm supposed to be helping with the guest rooms. I'll come back for the tray later."

"Thank you."

Mallory sat at her desk with her breakfast. It meant facing the wall, but she didn't like eating in the arm chair, it was too plush, and the table was in an awkward spot. *Maybe I can have a small table brought in. The room is large enough.*

She had more important things to think about than tables and chairs right now.

It was obvious now that this was all real, that she wasn't dreaming or tripping out on some designer drug, no matter how long and hard she had hoped otherwise, and it was equally obvious that she wasn't going home anytime soon, if ever. The people here seemed to think she was important, not just a political figure head, but tied to the safety of their island by magic.

Part of her didn't care. Part of her wanted to return home, even if it meant the whole island would collapse. But that part was shrinking each day.

It wasn't fair, she knew that. It wasn't fair that she'd been forced to give up her dreams for some impossible fantasy, a fantasy that wasn't even hers. But here she was.

So, I will make the most of it. And that means learning as much as I can, so I can be the best princess possible for these people. Because it was obvious to her that things in Golden Hall were not as great as the priests and stewards made it out to be. *I saw enough of the IRA's anger back home to know what happens when the government ignores the people's needs and desires.*

She finished eating and then went to explore the book shelf in the corner. She found one titled 'History of Airon's Pact' written by a Master Scholar Julianus Winter-Sun and pulled it off the shelf.

Master Spirit-Light found her in her chair engrossed in the book a short time later when he returned to check on her.

"Do you feel better now that you've eaten?"

She nodded. "Who is in charge of hiring staff here?"

"The stable master, head of housekeeping, and captain of the guard all work with Master Black-Kettle to ensure there are enough people in the correct places to make life here in the castle run smoothly."

"Who fires someone when they do something wrong?"

"Complaints are brought to the person's superior and they bring the serious ones to Master Black-Kettle."

"I want to deal with those complaints from now on. You said I had to sit in court every day, right? That's one of the things that will be brought to me. If the stable master, or whoever feels that the matter is beyond their ability to discipline properly, or that the only appropriate course of action is to dismiss them, then it has to come before me."

"Are you sure, Princess? There will be many things that you have to deal with. I'm sure something small like this could continue to be handled by Master Black-Kettle."

"It could be, but I don't want it to be."

"All right. I'll inform Master Black-Kettle. I see you've found something to read."

"I needed to start learning about your history. I'm going to need a lot of help, but I hope one day I can rule this province with the same confidence and ability as the other princesses rule their provinces." She wanted to mean the words, but they were hollow, just something she was supposed to say. What she really hoped for was the chance to go home.

"I hope so too. And whatever I can do to help, I will do."

A brief smile passed between them and then Mallory said, "You'd best sit down then. I have some questions about this book."

19th of Starrise, 24th Year of the 11th Rebirth
Golden Hall, Metalkin Province

"Princess Mallory, your first tutor is here to see you."

"Thank you, Cecilia, you can show him in." Mallory put the book she was reading on the side table and stood. She had done a lot of reading already and was eager to talk to someone about it.

Cecilia opened the door, allowing the older man to enter. "I'll run these down to the laundry," she said, lifting a large basket to her hip.

"Thank you. I'll ring down for lunch later."

Cecilia nodded and went out.

The older man bowed. "I am Master Iron-Blood. Master Black-Kettle hired me to be your tutor."

"It's nice to meet you," she said, holding out her hand.

He crinkled his nose. "It appears we have quite a bit of work to do. We'll start with greetings, but I want to get a look at you first. Stand still."

"Excuse me?" she said but he was already walking slow circles around her.

"Hmm, yes, we'll want to work on posture and bearing as well, hopefully you sit better than you stand."

"I'm not a dog," Mallory said. "What sort of tutor are you exactly?"

"Princess, the Metalkin are a proud and prosperous people with strong traditions and high expectations. You are their princess, you must set an example with your behaviour and actions."

"I don't see how my posture has anything to do with being a successful ruler."

"You did not grow up here. You are an outsider. They will obey you out of obligation, but only after fighting you on every decision. If you are a proper princess, you will set them at ease and they will follow you more willingly."

"So, you're here to teach me how to act like I grew up here?"

"Yes."

"I'm sure I can just learn those things over time. Aren't there more important things for me to learn? Like how your taxation system works? Or …"

"As I understand it, those things are being dealt with for you. Now, let's begin, we have much to do. Greetings."

"What's wrong with 'it's nice to meet you'?"

"You're the princess, this is a formal meeting, you need to sound formal. 'It's a pleasure to meet you' would be more appropriate, or a simply 'thank you for coming'. You are the princess, so you only offer deferential greetings to the High Priest, or to the other princesses *if* you are visiting their provinces. If they are visiting here, they defer to you."

"The High Priest is 'Most Honourable'."

"That's right. I'm pleased to see you're a quick study. You will curtsey only to High Priest Gold-Spark, or when you present yourself to the princess you are visiting. Once the formal greeting with the other princesses is complete, you may take a more casual and equitable approach."

"Can I sit down while we discuss this? I'm not used to these slippers yet."

Master Iron-Blood frowned. "Yes, yes, you may sit. At least I'll be able to see your posture."

"I'm not sitting all prim and proper for you just to listen to you talk about how to greet people," Mallory said, settling into her chair.

"Then I will deal with that later. Now, the nobles."

"I already know about Lord, Lady, and Master," Mallory said.

"Mistress or Madam is the equivalent of Master," Master Iron-Blood added. "When you greet a lord, lady, or guild representative they will bow or curtsey to you. You nod in response, but the nod should involve some movement of your shoulders."

"But not a bow."

"No."

Mallory sighed. "Anything else?"

"For anyone else of noble birth, a simple nod accompanies the greeting. For commoners, maintain a serious and formal appearance at all times, and do not nod when greeting them."

"You're not going to make me practice this, are you?"

"Possibly. Now, sit up straight. When you hold court, everyone will be watching you. Poor posture is a sign of laziness and sloppiness."

Master Iron-Blood had her practice how to sit at court, how to sit at meals, how to sit at meetings, how to stand when greeting guests, how to walk in a suitably regal manner, how to curtsey, and just how far to bow her shoulders when addressing nobles. He had rules for whose hand she could hold, and when it was more appropriate to link arms or simply place a hand on their arm. He had rules for eating and drinking. He had rules for processions. He had rules for religious celebrations.

Finally, her head spinning with details and her toes pinching in her slippers, Mallory said, "Enough. That's all I can take. I'm going to ring Cecilia for an early lunch and do some more studying."

Master Iron-Blood nodded. "Of course, Princess. I will return tomorrow to see how much of our lesson you remember. Hopefully, within a week, you will be proficient enough to attend court to observe how Master Black-Kettle and Prince Iron-Heart deal with petitions."

"A week? No, never mind, I don't feel like arguing about it now." She waved her hand in dismissal of the conversation.

"Enjoy the rest of your day, Princess," he said, bowing deeply and with much flourish before leaving.

26th of Starrise, 24th Year of the 11th Rebirth
Golden Hall, Metalkin Province

It turned out that not only were there plain day dresses and semi-fancy dresses and ball gowns, there were also private day dresses for quiet times in her room and public day dresses for court and informal occasions. Mallory just sighed and allowed Cecilia to select the proper dress and shoes. Her hair was still too short to do much with so they clipped her back from her face and added a hair comb. While Cecilia fussed Mallory studied her face in the mirror. She still looked the same, dress aside, but she didn't feel the same.

"You're ready," Cecilia said.

"Thank you," Mallory said.

"You know, you're the only Metalkin in the castle who thanks a servant for anything."

"No one else says thank you?"

"Oh, the nobles thank each other, and anyone they deem worthy of respect, and the other provinces, their people are a little more considerate, but working for you is proving to be a delight."

"I like you too," Mallory said, smiling.

"You'd best go, you don't want to keep them waiting on your first day."

"No, I guess I don't."

"Do you remember the way?"

"Maybe?"

Cecilia laughed. "I'll walk with you, at least part of the way. Come."

The two women walked nearly side-by-side in silence. Their quickly growing friendship was something they both knew had to remain behind closed doors, at least for the time being.

Master Black-Kettle was waiting for them in the back room behind the main hall. He bowed hastily. "It's all arranged," he said. "Prince Kaelen and I will deal with the petitions on your behalf today. All you need to do is listen and learn. After each decision is made, I will ask you to approve it, just say yes and we can move along to the next petition."

"What happens if I don't approve? Or if I have questions?"

"Save your questions for afterwards," he said. "Prince Kaelen is waiting for us." He ushered Mallory through the door into the main hall.

For most of the morning, Mallory sat and listened to guild representatives argue back and forth about taxation rates and trade rates. She wasn't sure what normal was here, so she didn't know who was arguing for special privilege and who was arguing for fairness. Several times over the morning she found herself wishing for a pen and paper.

I'm not going to remember all the questions I have about this. I wish they would slow down and explain some of this to me! Oh, what is this one saying now?

When Master Black-Kettle said, "I'll hear the final petition now," Mallory breathed a sigh of relief.

The man who stepped forward was finely dressed with the dark hair and eyes Mallory was learning to associate with the Metalkin, but he was poker thin and as tall as Kaelen, if not a little taller. He bowed to Master Black-Kettle and Prince Kaelen, ignoring Mallory completely.

"Thank you. I have been an honoured guest here at the castle for several weeks while assisting with various tasks that required cooperation between the castle staff and local guild workers. I've been fortunate that my wife and daughter have been able to stay with me and I thank you for the hospitality."

"You are most welcome," Kaelen said.

"I am, however, gravely concerned about the safety of my daughter. On more than one occasion a member of the palace staff has been overly familiar with her."

"Is she hurt?" Jaspar said amid gasps and shocked mutters from the nobles sitting on the sidelines.

"No, sir. No physical contact has occurred between them, thankfully. However, his speech has been full of romantic hints and suggestions."

"I see. If you have the name of the servant …"

"Jeffery Irons, sir."

"Thank you." Kaelen turned to one of the guards posted in the room. "Fetch Jeffery Irons to court immediately."

"Yes, My Lord."

After a brief wait the guard returned with a simply-dressed man in his early twenties. He approached the front of the court, stopping a step behind the nobleman accusing him, and bowed deeply. "How may I be of service to the court?"

"I have some questions," Kaelen said. "Are you familiar with this man?" he gestured to the nobleman.

"Yes, M'Lord. This is Master Iron-Hearth, a master of the Iron Guild who has been staying in the guest wing of the castle with his family."

"Do you work in the guest wing?"

"On occasion, M'Lord. I assist some of the girls with the heavy lifting when they ask, and I was helping fetch and carry for the guild workers who were doing repairs in one of the suites down the hall from the Iron-Hearth suite."

"Are you familiar with Master Iron-Hearth's daughter?"

"I know who she is, yes M'Lord, though I wouldn't claim to be familiar with her. I've run the odd errand for her, and her mother."

"So, you don't deny having spoken to her?"

"No, M'Lord, I don't. I'm sorry, M'Lord but I'm not sure what this is about."

"What was the extent of your conversations with Master Iron-Hearth's daughter?" Kaelen went on, not bothering to explain anything to the commoner.

"Conversations, M'Lord? You're mistaken. I've spoken with her regarding the errands I've been sent on, but I've not conversed with her."

His words were met with quiet heckling from the nobles in the gallery.

"Are you calling Master Iron-Hearth a liar?" Kaelen said.

"No sir. I'm afraid I don't know what Master Iron-Hearth said before I arrived, though, so I don't know if I might be implying that or not."

"You were flirting with my daughter!" Master Iron-Hearth bellowed.

Jeffery cringed and took a step back then looked desperately at Kaelen and Master Black-Kettle. "No, M'Lord, I swear I did no such thing. I was polite, and nothing more. I laughed at a funny thing she said. I didn't realize such a thing would be too familiar. I didn't want to offend her. Please. You must believe me."

"My daughter wouldn't be casually joking with a servant," Master Iron-Hearth said. "So, either he is lying and was flirting with her, or he was eavesdropping on a private conversation, or he was laughing at her."

"I wasn't doing any of those things," Jeffery said. "I was just being polite. I swear it."

"I have no way to prove that you weren't out of line," Master Black-Kettle said. "And I have a responsibility to protect the guests of this residence. Effective immediately you are no longer employed at the castle."

"No."

Everyone turned to look at Mallory.

"No?" Master Black-Kettle said.

"I gave Master Spirit-Light a direct order. I am the only person in this castle who can dismiss an employee of the crown from service. He was supposed to inform you of this."

"I'm sorry, Princess. I was just acting in your name and …"

"No, you were not. Do not dismiss this man."

"He is in the wrong."

"You have no evidence of that. If you must discipline him, find a punishment that doesn't involve him losing his job … or you will lose yours."

She'd expected an uproar in response to her words but was met with only silence. Finally, Jaspar cleared his throat and said, "Of course, Princess." He turned back to Jeffery. "You are forbidden from working in the guest wing in any capacity, effective immediately and you will assist the stable lads in cleaning the stables for the next month."

"Yes sir. Of course, sir," Jeffery said, bowing deeply. He turned and bowed to Mallory. "Thank you M'Lady, you are most kind and understanding."

He turned and rushed out, without waiting for permission.

Master Iron-Hearth cleared his throat and said, "Thank you for taking steps to protect my family." He bowed, barely, and walked stiffly out of the room.

"Court is dismissed for the day," Jaspar said. He and Kaelen rose and herded Mallory out the private door behind the throne.

Jaspar said, "I have other duties to attend to."

Kaelen nodded. "I can handle this."

As Jaspar hurried off, Mallory said, "Handle what?"

"Your behaviour in there."

"He was going to dismiss a servant without proof of wrongdoing."

"You're claiming Master Iron-Hearth is a liar."

"You're claiming there is no way Master Iron-Hearth could be mistaken."

There was no way for Kaelen to argue that, and since he didn't care for the other man, he didn't feel like defending him too strongly. "The validity of Master Iron-Hearth's claim aside, you should not have interfered that way. You should have taken the decision up with Master Black-Kettle after court."

"After the damage was done, you mean."

"Mallory, you humiliated Jaspar in front of the nobles and the guilds. All he's ever done is serve you, even before you arrived. He's kept this province running for you. You should be thanking him, not threatening him. He is your closest ally, aside from me. He can't effectively deal with the nobles if they're second guessing him or if they feel they have permission to undermine him."

Mallory felt her anger evaporate like mist in the sun. "I didn't think of that."

"No, you didn't."

"He disobeyed an order."

"An order you gave to Master Spirit-Light. Did you stop to think that maybe that order hadn't reached Jaspar yet? That maybe he forgot out of habit?"

"He argued with me."

"You asked him to temper his decision, but you didn't lead by example."

"I'm sorry. I let my temper get in the way."

"You're strong, Mallory, and that's a good thing, I promise. We need a strong princess. But we also need a princess who understands our culture and traditions, a princess who knows when to ask for help, and a princess who does not lose her temper in court. We need you to study and learn, not interfere in matters you don't yet understand."

"I know. I'm just frustrated by how slowly things are moving."

"Nothing big or important is happening right now. You don't need to rush. Focus on your studies so that if an emergency arises, you'll be ready to help. Can you do that?"

"I'll try. Should I apologize to Master Black-Kettle?"

"I will pass it on to him the next time I see him. Why don't I walk you to your room? I'm sure this whole thing has upset you." He turned her and started walking with her down the hall. "I promise, things will be easier for all of us if you just trust us to help you."

Mallory tried reading but there was something restless stirring inside of her making it difficult to focus. She set the book aside and muttered, "I was only trying to help, Jaspar just wouldn't listen." She went to her desk and scratched out a quick note before ringing for a servant.

"Deliver this to Master Sun-Stag immediately," she said. She made her way upstairs to the sitting room he had shown her before the wedding. Just stepping into that room, with its wide, open balcony, made her feel better. She went to the rail and leaned over, letting her eyes follow the garden paths below.

When she felt more relaxed, she went back into the room and fetched the chairs, arranging them on the balcony. All that was left was to sit and wait.

Devin swung down from the horse and walked the animal from the gates to the stable. A nervous looking young woman was hovering near the paddocks and she rushed forward when she spotted him. "Master Sun-Stag. A message for you, from the Princess."

Devin felt a surge of heat through his body as he reached for the letter. "Thank you." He opened it, quickly read the words, and then whistled sharply, his excitement edging towards panic.

A lad appeared at the stable door at his whistle and Devin handed the horse off to him. "Apologize to Master White-Hart for me, I'm needed elsewhere, immediately."

"Of course, I'll look after her for you."

With a brisk nod, Devin took off across the yard. He considered going to change first but he didn't know how long the girl had been waiting for him, hadn't thought to ask. *I hope she didn't get tired of waiting and leave.*

When he entered the sitting room he spotted the chairs out on the balcony and smiled. Her face appeared around the side of one chair and lit up in a smile. "Devin, you got my message."

"Only just," he said. "I wasn't in the city, I just returned. Have I kept you waiting long?"

"I don't mind, the view is lovely. I needed a break, and someone to talk to."

He settled into the second chair. "I haven't seen you since before the wedding. How are you holding up?"

"Were you there? At the wedding? There were so many people …" Her cheeks darkened.

"I was in the temple, way at the back. I barely saw you either, and it was your wedding. I wasn't invited to the dinner."

"Oh. I didn't even see the guest list."

"Don't worry about me. What have you been doing since the wedding?"

"Reading. Learning to walk and talk like a princess. I feel like I'm being erased. It's bad enough that no one understands the slang I'm used to."

He gave her a sheepish look. "I don't know what slang is."

She rolled her eyes. "There's formal language, and informal language, right? Well, slang is part of the informal, they're just odd words and sayings that people use. Like 'cool' means interesting or popular, so does 'tubular' and 'rad'. 'Cat's meow' means something or someone that's the best or your favourite. So does 'the bees knees'."

"Do bees have knees?"

"Well, they have articulated legs, so I guess they do, but that's the point, it's not literal, it's just a saying."

"I like it," he said, smiling.

"No one else does, they look at me like I'm crazy. I'm so tired of it. I feel like I'm losing myself. And what's so important about standing straight and sitting straight and how I hold my hands, anyway?" she said as her bottled-up anger bubbled over again. "I want to learn important things like taxation rates and guild trade rates."

"I agree with you," he said, "But I can't help you."

"At least you're not arguing with me," she said. "I got to observe at court today. Jaspar tried to fire a servant for laughing at some nobles' daughters' joke."

"He did what?"

"A visiting noble complained that a servant was flirting with his daughter. The servant claims he'd barely spoken to her, but had, on one occasion, politely laughed at something she said to him."

"That's a fireable offense?"

Mallory shrugged. "The noble claimed he was afraid for her safety. Are servants here in the habit of taking advantage of noble girls?"

"No, I can't say that they are. I've never heard of it happening. Was Master Black-Kettle really going to dismiss him just on that?"

"Yes. I wouldn't let him." She looked down at her lap and tugged at her fingers. "I *may have* lost my temper a *tiny* bit in the process though. I sort of threatened Jaspar's job."

Devin started chuckling. "I wish I could have seen his face."

She looked up again, confused. "Everyone was angry at me for it, and you're laughing?"

"I'm not from this province, and I firmly believe that most of the nobles here need to be reminded that they're not gods."

"Tell me about your home, before you came here."

"The small villages on the island are all very much the same. There's a central market area built around the inn and the chapel. Depending on the size of the village you might have one or a few permanent shops and space for travelling merchants. There are some homes around the square, teachers, healers, a blacksmith, the guild offices, anyone who doesn't live or work on a farm. The rest of the village spreads out around that, wheat farms, vegetable farms, goats, sheep, chickens, whatever is needed to sustain the village."

"But what was *your* village like?"

"We were near the edge of a wooded area so there were hunters and woodsmen. That meant a lot of women on their own while the men were off in the camp in the trees. They looked after each other, watching each other's children and helping each other with heavy chores. Growing up it was like have two dozen aunts, and none of them were afraid to holler at you."

"I grew up very alone," Mallory said. "We lived half a world away from my parents' families. There weren't a lot of children who spoke English where I lived. I went to a special school but I didn't really have friends until I was a little older. I was looking forward to university in Ireland, to finally making friends."

"You can make friends here," Devin said.

"I guess so. I don't know what to talk about."

"You're doing fine now."

"*You* actually want to hear about my home. Emilio does too, but only so he can record it for research. No one else that I have the chance to speak with seems to care."

"Then they are missing out," Devin said. "Tell me about things that we don't have here that you have in the Wide World."

"You won't understand half of it," she said.

"I'll try. Back at Airon's Gate you kept talking about tripping over something that I couldn't see."

She laughed. "Oh, because that's a *great* place to start!"

Emilio had gone to the palace healer for a tea to help with his persistent headache. On his way back to his rooms he heard rich laughter drifting down the halls. He took a left instead of a right and peered around the next corner, curious to see who the joyous voice belonged to.

There were two figures in the hall ahead, the nearest, with his back to Emilio, was a slender male in working clothes. Beyond him was a woman in a fine dress, her face blocked by her companion.

"Next time you will have to explain this telo-vision," he said.

She laughed again. "You'll think it's magic," she said.

"Can you blame me? Metal birds that fly without flapping their wings and are big enough to carry hundreds of people? It must be magic, or the people of the Wide World worship very powerful gods."

"Yes," she said. "We call one god Science and the other Technology, and I will teach you all about them."

Metal birds? Telling-vision? Science? Technology? Is that Mallory? Emilio thought. The young man turned, and Emilio ducked back behind the corner. He hurried to the nearest room and slipped inside, leaving the door open just enough that he could peer through. The young man was whistling as he walked. *What is Devin doing up here? There's no work for him at this end of the castle,* Emilio thought, recognizing Devin as soon as he walked past the door.

When it was clear, Emilio hurried to the place where he'd seen Devin with his pretty companion, but the girl was gone. *She wouldn't be in a rush. Perhaps I can catch up with her.*

He passed a young lad in a cap and stopped him. "Did you see a woman go by just now?"

"You mean the Princess? Sure, you're not far behind her."

"You're sure it was her?"

"I haven't seen anyone else with hair like that," he said.

"Of course. Thank you." *Well, that is very troubling in deed.*

27th of Starrise, 24th Year of the 11th Rebirth
Golden Hall, Metalkin Province

Devin felt like a goat at a farmers' auction the way Honourable Bernard and Master Spirit-Light were circling around him, studying and poking at him. When they finally stepped back, Honourable Bernard said, "I just don't believe it. It's not possible."

"I received word from a holding steward at the southern-most end of the island," Master Spirit-Light said. "They've had several sightings of Dark Spirits there and one possession. The man was dead within a week."

"I've never heard of one dying so quickly," Bernard said, "Except for a few cases where the possessed individual recognized their affliction and ended their own suffering before it progressed too far."

"I got the impression this was a death caused by the natural progression of the possession," Emilio said.

"Odd that we see the quickest and slowest cases of possession at the same time."

Emilio turned to Devin. "How are you feeling?"

"It's not bad during that day," Devin said. "I work with the animals and keep busy and that helps. It's worse at night. I can hear that whisper inside of me. I've taken to sleeping in the stables."

"Why would you sleep in the stables?" Emilio said.

"His spirits guides, of course," Bernard put in. "He's Animal People. He draws strength from being close to the animals. But we've never seen that sort of protection or immunity before."

"Perhaps we should send him to Caranhall. Being among his own people, closer to his own spirit guides …"

"No."

Both priest and steward looked at Devin.

"I won't go back there."

"Even if it meant saving your life?" Emilio said.

"Even then."

"May I ask why?"

"My family and I had a falling out. I'd receive no help or support in Caranhall. I've been shunned."

"I see," Bernard said. "Well, considering how well you're coping with the possession while living here I see no real reason to move you. Besides, the journey would likely prove too dangerous."

"Then we'll continue to keep an eye on you," Emilio said to Devin. "And you will inform us at once if you feel any change in your situation."

Devin nodded and pulled his shirt back on. "Of course." He hesitated a moment. "Have you told anyone else about this?"

"No," Honourable Bernard said. "Though I suppose I am obligated to notify the High Priest, I haven't."

"I haven't written to the scholars either," Emilio said. "I haven't even informed the palace healer yet. Is there someone you want us to inform?"

"No. I'd rather no one else knew."

"I thought you might feel that way," Emilio said.

Someone knocked at the door and the three men looked at each other. "I'll get it," Devin said. "Since I do work for you."

There was a maid at the door. She held out a note. "This is for Devin Sun-Stag," she said. "I was told he was here."

"Thank-you," Devin said. "You've found him."

She curtsied and went on her way.

Devin smiled at the note. He hadn't expected her to summon him again so soon.

"From the Princess?" said a soft voice over his shoulder.

Devin looked up to see Emilio standing over him. "How did you …"

"I saw the two of you leaving the sun room yesterday."

"Nothing improper happened. She's craving companionship, someone she can be Mallory around instead of always having to be Princess Jewel-Rose."

"I trust your intentions," Emilio said. "But do you really thing it's wise, given your condition, for you to be alone with the princess?"

Devin could feel his pulse, a dull aching thud in his chest.

"Whose best interests are you looking out for? Is this what's best for her? Or something you crave? And is it really you, or the beast inside of you?"

"You're telling me not to go, not to answer her."

"I'm asking you to do what needs to be done to keep her safe."

Safe, happy, that's all he could want for her. *He's right. I'm a danger to her. If something happened to her, if I did something … no, the price is too high.* "I understand. I won't put her in any further danger."

Emilio put a reassuring hand on the younger man's shoulder. "I knew you could be counted on. We'll see you in a few days."

When Devin had left and one of the acolytes had brought in a tea tray the two men settled in to discuss the darker side of Devin's possession, things they didn't want to say in front of the younger man.

"What we're doing here is increasingly stupid and dangerous," Emilio said. "He's a danger to us all, and especially to the princess."

"We both understand that but the potential knowledge we could learn from him? How can we simply lock him away to rot?"

32nd of Starrise, 24th Year of the 11th Rebirth
Golden Hall, Metalkin Province

Mallory had quickly learned the most direct path from her rooms to the main hall but Cecilia had still accompanied her almost daily, just so they could enjoy each others' company. Today, however, Mallory made the walk alone.

She caught Master Black-Kettle off-guard and he hurried to bow to her as she strode up. "Princess, you're early this morning. I'm glad to see you've come to observe again today."

"I won't be observing today."

"Oh. I'm sorry to hear that, but you didn't have to come to tell me in person. You could have sent a servant to inform me."

"I'll be making the decisions today."

He stared at her. "I'm not sure if you're ready to …"

"Everyone keeps telling me I need to act like a princess. Shouldn't I be doing this?"

"Well, of course. We just want you to settle in first, get your bearings and all that."

"I'm bored. I need something to do. You can sit right beside me and walk me through everything, but I need to start being involved. Please."

"I suppose there's no harm in seeing how it goes for today. If you're not ready you can always return to observing tomorrow."

"Thank you. Can we begin?"

"I was waiting for Prince Kaelen. His knowledge and experience will be of great value."

"All right, we'll wait for him."

After several minutes of awkward silence, Kaelen sauntered up. "I'm ready to begin," he said.

"Then I will announce you to the court," Master Black-Kettle said, heading for the door.

"Good morning," Mallory said.

He nodded to her. "Yes. Good morning."

"I haven't seen much of you this last week."

"We've both been busy. I thought you were busy with a tutor this morning."

"I cancelled the lesson."

He frowned. "I don't think …"

Master Black-Kettle was waving to them from the door.

"We'll talk about this later." He strode purposefully forward only to have Master Black-Kettle stop him at the door. "Yes?"

"The Princess first," he said.

Kaelen scowled but took a step back.

Mallory took a deep breath, straightened her posture, and walked through the door. She took her place on the throne, an elaborate chair with iron legs adorned with vines. The back was topped with curling vines and silver roses. Fortunately, there was a cushion on both seat and back, done in gold and silver cloth, woven into the pattern of roses. Mallory arranged her full skirts and sat as Kaelen took the seat to one side and Master Black-Kettle on her other.

As they were settling into their seats there was a flood of whispers from the gallery which quieted when Jaspar called for the first petition.

It took Mallory three of four times as long to work through each petition as it took Kaelen and Jaspar when they were working without her. One of the men had to offer explanations to every statement addressed to her and they were both full of suggestions on how she should handle each situation.

She slowed the process down further by insisting on asking questions instead of simply accepting their suggestions out of hand. Only when she was comfortable that she had a basic understanding of the petition did she accept a solution for it, sometimes offering her own suggestions in response to information she was given.

After several hours of this Jaspar said, "That will be enough for today. I thank you all for your patience. Court is dismissed."

"Was that the last petition?" Mallory asked Kaelen softly as he escorted her out.

"It must have been," he said.

"There weren't as many as I thought," she said. The door closed behind them.

"I'll be down to see you shortly," Kaelen said, his hand too tight on Mallory's arm. "I have some people I promised to speak with."

"Of course," Mallory said, cringing. "I'll have tea brought up for us."

He released her and stalked away. Mallory turned and fled in the other direction, tears springing to her eyes. It was difficult to see clearly and somewhere between the main hall and her room she took a wrong turn, winding up in a part of the castle she wasn't yet familiar with.

She slowed her pace, looking around at the hallway lined with pictures she'd never seen before and doors she didn't dare open. *There's always someone working somewhere in this castle,* she thought. *I'll run into a servant sooner or later and get back to my room, hopefully before Kaelen does.*

The study closest to the main hall had been set aside exclusively for Kaelen's use and he wasn't surprised to find several noble men, Loyalists all, waiting for him there after court concluded for the day. And none of them looked happy.

"What exactly was Princess Mallory doing in court today?" said Lord South-Mine. "You were given this position to stop her from interfering in this province's governance."

"I understand my job," Kaelen said, bristling. "Did you take into account the fact that she wouldn't be satisfied with just watching? She has the priest and that damned Sun Temple fool, Emilio, filling her head with ideas of what she *should* be doing. Jaspar and I are trying to keep her busy but she just showed up this morning, insisting that she was ready to do this job."

"She won't stop now," Master Silver-Mine said. "I assume you and Jaspar will continue to sit with her and advice her accordingly?"

"Of course."

Master Silver-Mine nodded and went on. "Even that may not be enough. We're moving into the final stages of our plans and any interference now could lead us all to ruin."

"It won't come to that," Kaelen said.

"We'll have to make sure of that." Lord South-Mine thought for a minute then went on. "Kaelen, I'll have my wife send you an invitation to visit our estate. You'll encourage Mallory to accept. Tell her it would be a good idea for her to meet the ruling families in this province. I'll see to it that you receive similar invitations from other families, and the guilds, on a regular basis. She can't hold court if she's not in the castle."

The other men nodded. "Simple, effective, I like it," one said.

"And then Jaspar is free to make the needed rulings that will allow our agents to travel and collect what we need from the other provinces," Lord South-Mine added.

"Then I look forward to your invitations," Kaelen said. "Now, I am meeting my wife to discuss her rash behaviour today. I don't know if she'll listen. She comes from a different world, a world where she was never expected to follow a man's lead. She may be difficult to convince."

"Then these visits will serve two purposes," Lord South-Mine said. "She'll be able to see firsthand how a good Metalkin wife acts. I must write my wife. Don't let us down, Kaelen."

"I won't," Kaelen stood stiffly by the door as the men filed out of the room. When they'd gone he took a deep, trembling breath and leaned heavily against the doorframe for a long moment.

A passing servant paused. "Do you require anything, Prince Jewel-Rose?"

"No, I don't," Kaelen snapped. "If I needed something, I would tell you."

"My apologies." The servant bowed and went on his way.

Kaelen pulled away from the wall and straightened his clothes. He had another meeting to attend to, one that had to be handled with great care.

Just as the panic was starting to settle over her a door up ahead opened and she felt relief flood her body. Mallory hurried forward.

"Hold on," she called. "Please wait."

He turned, and their eyes met. She stopped short, suddenly breathless. *Devin.*

"Princess? What are you doing at this end of the castle?"

"I – uh – took a wrong turn," she said. "I'm lost."

"Yes, you are. These are the servant's quarters."

"Oh. But you're twice named!" She put her hand over her mouth. "I'm sorry."

"Don't be," he said. "When you're the younger son of a younger son for a few generations there's nothing to being twice named except the name. I have to work just like the commoners and that doesn't make me popular with other nobles. I think they're afraid that the same fate might befall them. I remind them that their position and wealth is vulnerable."

"I can see that. The nobles here are very concerned with wealth and status, aren't they?"

"More so than any other province, yes." He turned and led the way back down the hallway, still talking. "It's always been like that."

"I wasn't sure I'd ever see you again, even though you live here, and work here," she said. "I spend most of my time in my room still. Cecilia has been taking me on regular tours of the castle though, so I am starting to learn my way about."

"That's good. This is your home. You should feel comfortable here."

"I know I should," she said, looking down at her feet. "I'm trying, I really am, but I'm letting everyone down."

"This way," he said, directing her around the corner when she tried to go straight at the next intersection.

"I don't remember turning here," she said.

"I'm taking a short cut." He smiled at her. "I wasn't reprimanding you, by the way."

"What?"

"When I said that you should feel comfortable here. I wasn't scolding you for not feeling that way yet. Golden Hall should be more welcoming to you, that's what I meant."

"A place is just buildings, they aren't … anything."

"Then I'm blaming all the people and situations that are making it difficult for you to settle. You are their princess, they've waited for you for twenty-four years, they should be bending over backwards to make this feel like your home, to make you want to be here."

"Thanks for saying that. I feel like everyone has such high expectations of me, but they won't tell me exactly what those expectations are or give me the tools to meet them."

"What about your husband?"

"I hardly see him. We haven't dined together since the wedding. He's been busy with meetings and stuff – doing the things I'm supposed to do, I suppose."

"You should put your foot down and just jump in and start ruling."

"I tried. Every time I try to assert myself, they have another reason for shutting me down. I feel like I'm going about this all the wrong way."

"Is Master Black-Kettle helping at all?"

"No. I barely see him either. He sends tutors though. I might shoot my etiquette instructor though. The man is insufferable."

"Etiquette? Are they teaching you history or politics or anything like that?"

"A little now that I've been observing at court. I tried holding court myself today. I'm tired of feeling useless."

"That's a good first step. I'll …"

They came around the corner and Devin nearly collided with Kaelen.

Kaelen glared at the smaller man and took a deep breath, obviously ready to yell.

Mallory smiled. "Ah, there you are. And if you're here then I must be back in the right place. Thank you, Master Sun-Stag for your assistance. I'm sure my husband can see me the rest of the way."

Devin bowed low. "Good day," he said. He bowed to Kaelen as well and then left.

Kaelen stiffly offered Mallory his arm and she meekly slipped a hand into the crook of his elbow. "Where were you?" he said. "What were you doing with that man?"

"I got lost," she replied. "Master Sun-Stag was showing me the way back."

"Any servant could have done that. That's not *his* job."

"He was the first servant to cross my path. And he's a servant, his job is to serve, isn't it? That was the service I required." The words made her feel slightly queasy but appeasing Kaelen's anger was, at this moment, more important than her own comfort.

"You didn't send for tea, did you?"

"I didn't see anyone I could ask. I'll ring for … the girl as soon as we're back at my room," she said, almost calling Cecilia by name.

"Good. I could use the refreshment."

Mallory opened the door to her room and realized this was the first time Kaelen was setting foot in the space. If this had been her room back home she'd be worried about underwear on the floor and dirty dishes in the sink, but Cecilia kept the room spotless and she didn't have a kitchen of her own. Still, she felt nervous allowing him to enter.

He paused just far enough inside that she could close the door behind him and looked around. It was very similar to his rooms down the hall with a few books on the shelf, paintings on the walls, and pretty vases tucked on side tables and shelves. None of the vases held flowers but the Metalkin were more interested in the decorative metalwork than what the vases could hold.

Mallory hurried to the bell pull and then back to the door. It didn't take long for one of the girls to answer her summons. "Tea," she said softly. "For two, please, and some food, something nice but easy."

"Yes, Princess," she said and disappeared again.

She turned to find Kaelen had made himself comfortable in one of the chairs by the fireplace. There were also two chairs by the big windows, but it was raining at the moment, so the view was dreary. Mallory settled in the other chair. "What was it you wanted to speak about?" The formality of the Metalkin culture still felt odd in her mouth and she sounded awkward in her own ears.

"The tea is on its way?"

"Yes."

"Then we'll speak on it after the tea arrives. I don't want to be interrupted by some gossiping servant."

Mallory sighed. "Okay then. How was your meeting?"

"Fine. Everything is being taken care of."

"What was it about?"

"I was speaking with a coalition of nobles who have been working to maintain Metalkin culture and the prosperity of this province in your long absence."

"Oh. That's nice of them. I didn't know such a group existed. I should like to meet some of them." She smiled brightly.

"I'm sure they'd like to meet you as well." He didn't sound nearly as excited as she did.

There was a knock at the door and Cecilia came in with the tray. She set it on the table between Mallory and Kaelen and curtsied. "Do you require anything else?"

"No, thank you," Mallory said. Kaelen was already reaching for the nut rolls on the tray.

"Ring when you'd like me to fetch the tray," Cecilia said.

When they were alone again, Kaelen said, "You embarrassed me today."

She stiffened. "What are you talking about? How? By doing my job?"

"By not warning me about what you planned to do today. I am your prince. I deserve to be involved in any important decision you make. How else am I supposed to do my job to guide and support you?"

"I'm sorry. I haven't seen you outside of court all week and you're always too busy before and after to talk."

"You could have called for me."

"Would you have answered? Or would you have been too busy again?"

"Running this province is a lot of work, of course I'm busy."

"I'm trying to help."

"You help by watching and asking questions, by studying with your tutors, not by taking on tasks you cannot handle."

"I'm trying to be a good princess."

His voice softened. "I know that. We all see that. You have to trust us. I know it seems odd to you, the importance we put on etiquette and appearance …"

"If I have to continue those lessons can you at least assign a different tutor?"

"I'm told Master Iron-Blood is the best at what he does."

"Are the two of you related?"

"Pardon?"

"Your families, Iron-Blood and Iron-Heart, are they related somehow?"

"Not to my knowledge. There are a lot of twice-named Metalkin families with 'Iron' in their names. Iron is an important metal on this island, not as flashy as silver or gold, but far more useful."

"Is your family involved in iron mining or iron smithing?"

"You're changing the subject," he said.

"I'm sorry. I didn't realize there was more you wished to speak about."

"Do you understand that Master Black-Kettle and I are just trying to look out for you? And this province?"

"Of course, I understand that. But I'm trying too."

"And I'm so proud of the progress you're making. I just don't want to see you make a mistake."

"That's sweet of you but I'm going to make mistakes. No one is perfect."

"But I'm here to help you avoid the worst of the mistakes that you'll inevitably make. Let me help you."

"I relied on your council at court today."

"And I thank you for that."

"Did I do a horrible job?"

"No, but they were simple petitions today. I worry that when something politically charged comes up you won't understand how we need you to deal with it. Your life in that other world was so different, you learned such different things."

"Not all of that is bad. There's so much I could teach you, and everyone else, about …"

"I know. It's important to you, and I do want to know about your life from before."

"When? You never have time. We're supposed to be getting to know each other but you won't talk about your family and you won't let me talk about mine."

"I've been busy."

"Yeah, you said that already." She sighed. She didn't really want to push him on that particular point as she didn't mind not seeing much of him. It was a horrible thing to think about her husband but more and more it was becoming the truth.

"Why don't we share the midday meal tomorrow? I really shouldn't let work get in the way of us strengthening our soul bond." He smiled at her.

This change in his attitude confused her. "Okay," she said. "I don't have any other plans so it should be fine. Is there a dining room or something?"

"Yes. Your maid can show you the way."

"It will be nice to talk to you again," she said. She wasn't sure she meant it, but he was her husband and supposedly soul mate, so it made sense that she make an effort to get along with him.

"I have things to attend to before midday," he said, rising from his chair. "Promise me you'll consult with me before making any further decisions."

"I will ask for your council," she said.

He nodded. "Good. Have a good day. I will see you tomorrow for our meal together."

When he had gone she called for Cecilia to fetch the tray and then settled in to read some more until her tutor came.

As soon as Devin was sure he was out of sight of Kaelen he broke into a jog. Instead of heading back to the servants' quarters, or outside as he'd originally intended, he continued through the private wing of the castle where Mallory, Kaelen, and the two stewards, lived. He had to stop several passing servants before finding one who could direct him to Master Emilio.

He waited in the hallway outside the study while Emilio finished the meeting he was in, waiting so long that he wound up seated on the floor with his back against the wall and his eyes closed before the door opened. He listened to Emilio say good-bye to whomever he was meeting with and then said, "I hope you have a moment to spare for me."

Emilio startled at the unexpected sound of Devin's voice and had to glance about the hallway to find him. "Come in, quickly," Emilio said, this time glancing about to see if anyone else had noticed his caller. "Is there a problem? Are you feeling all right?"

"I'm fine, concerned, but fine. This isn't about me."

"I see," Emilio said, visibly relaxing. "What's on your mind?"

"I just spoke with Princess Jewel-Rose. She was lost and I assisted her back to her rooms."

"Kind of you, though we already discussed you breaking off contact with Princess Mallory."

"I know the risk. The beast was sleeping. She wasn't in any danger, at least not from me. I'm concerned that she's not getting the education she needs."

"I offered to help with that, but Master Black-Kettle assures me that he has the best tutors working with her."

"Did Master Black-Kettle mention that one of these tutors was a master in etiquette?"

Emilio frowned.

"It's not my place, I'm just a guide and a hunter. She isn't even my princess, and this isn't my province, but she's frustrated and scared and that should scare you, a lot. I'm taking a huge risk speaking to you candidly about this. Prince Kaelen or Master Black-Kettle could have my job over this if they found out."

"No, the princess insisted that she be the only person in the castle allowed to handle the termination of the staff here."

"That's not very reassuring when the two men who dislike me most in this castle are the same two men working to limit the princess's power and control what they can't limit."

"I think you're overreacting a little. I agree that it is concerning but you make it sound like a coup!"

Devin bowed quickly to hide the anger. *That's exactly what it looks like to me.* "My apologies, that was not my intent," he lied. His hands were bound at this point. He didn't possess enough influence to push the matter, no matter how much he wanted to protect Mallory. "I allowed my frustrations to get the better of me and lead me to speak out of turn. I understand that Kaelen and Master Black-Kettle are responsible for the political well-being of the province, and the political education of the princess, but I'm sure there is something you can do, something that would fall under religious guidance ..."

"Yes, of course. I can certainly do my job without overstepping my bounds and see if I need to speak with Jaspar about anything."

"That's all I can ask. I was not born here but this is my home now. I would hate to see The Pact fail now."

"As would I, but Mallory has been found, the island will begin to mend. All this doom and gloom is pointless."

"You're right, of course. Thank you for your time, today, Master Spirit-Light. I will, of course, visit you and Honourable Bernard in the next few days, as agreed."

Emilio watched Devin go, his mind spinning with possibilities. He gave his head a shake, trying to clear the thoughts away, dismissing them as unfounded. "Those Animal People are an excitable bunch, and not the most knowledgeable about political matters, but at the very least, I can check on Mallory's well-being. There's no harm in that."

33rd of Starrise, 24th Year of the 11th Rebirth
Golden Hall, Metalkin Province

Cecilia looked up in surprise when the princess's bedroom door burst open short minutes after she'd begun stripping the bed linens. "Princess! I didn't expect you back so soon. I thought you were holding court again today."

"So did I, but apparently, according to Master Black-Kettle, there are no petitions to hear today."

"That does happen," Cecilia said.

"Did I do something wrong? Did I make a bad decision yesterday? Is it so wrong of me to want to rule? Isn't that what I'm supposed to do?"

"Uh ... I'm sorry, Princess. I don't know how to answer those questions."

Mallory sighed and dropped into a chair. "You don't have to," she said. "I was just venting."

"I'm not sure what that means."

"It's a saying. It means I was just giving voice to my frustrations so that I'd feel less ... frustrated." Trying to explain idioms was harder than it looked.

"I see. If you'll excuse me, I should take this to the laundry."

Mallory waved a hand dismissively and slouched deeper into the chair. She didn't think anything of it when there was a knock on the door a few minutes later and said, "Yes, yes, come in," expecting Cecilia.

"Good-morning Princess."

The masculine voice surprised her, and she sat up straighter, her attention going to the door. "Oh, Master Spirit-Light. I thought you were Cecilia, come for the rest of the laundry."

"Yes, your maid came to fetch me this morning. She said you were 'feeling frustrated' with your situation."

"Tattle tale," Mallory muttered, slouching again.

"She's not the only one concerned about you," Emilio said. He gathered his robes and settled into the other chair. "You're probably still feeling a little lost. That's understandable. How are your lessons coming?"

"I can walk across the room without dropping the damn book," she replied. "I don't trip on my skirts, and I know how to smile and curtsey to my tutor's approval."

"I meant your history lessons."

"I don't get a lot of those yet. I understand there are five provinces, each with its own set of talents and spirit guides and that I'm the princess of the Metalkin, people gifted to work with metal. We're jewellers, silversmiths, iron workers, and black smiths. We mint money, we make weapons, we make horseshoes and iron fittings. We are the wealthiest of the provinces and there is a strong sense of provincial pride among the people here."

"Yes, Metalkin pride can border on arrogance at times," Emilio said. "And other provinces see them as egotistical and elitist."

"That's not good."

"No, but these last two dozen years have strongly reinforced that idea. The Metalkin are aggressive in trade and in all negotiations. You'll find a lot of your petitions will be dealing with conflicts between Metalkin guilds and guilds from other provinces that must work closely with them."

"If I'll ever be allowed to hear petitions."

"You will. The other princesses didn't hear petitions on their own for years after moving to their own provinces. Be patient."

"I'm trying. And I'm trying to do a good job at this whole princess thing but I keep messing it up."

"Mistakes are expected. You'll figure it out in time." He reached over and patted her hand. "Why don't you make a list of everything you have questions about and everything you're having troubles with and give it to me tomorrow. I'll see what I can help with and what I can bring to the attention of your tutors."

She nodded. "Okay. I can do that."

"Good. I'll leave you to it. You may also consider writing to the other princesses. I'm sure they'd be more than willing to write back."

"Maybe."

He nodded and rose from his chair. "I'll see you tomorrow then. Good day, Princess."

"Yeah, I'll see you tomorrow."

Lunch rolled around quickly, and Cecilia walked Mallory down to the dining room where Kaelen was supposed to meet her. The room was small enough that two people wouldn't feel lost or out of place there, but still big enough to comfortably seat about a dozen people. Though the artwork displayed around the room was very different, it still reminded her of the dining room in the embassy where she and her parents had eaten breakfast each day, just the three of them. Her father would read the paper while he sipped his coffee and listen to her mother rattle off upcoming social engagements. Someone would ask her about her schooling and tell her to eat her eggs and then they'd all be off in their own directions for the day.

The memory actually made her smile.

Kaelen came in behind her, grinning broadly. He leaned over her shoulder and kissed her cheek, startling her.

"You're in a good mood," she said, unsure how to feel about the kiss.

"I have a letter here I can't wait to share with you. Come sit, we'll have the food brought in and you can read it."

"All right."

He pulled a chair out for her, nudging it under her as she sat. He handed her the letter and then went to signal the servants before joining her at the table.

She quickly skimmed the contents of the letter. It was from a Lord South-Mine. Mallory hadn't been introduced to him yet, but the last name suggested that he was Metalkin or Stone Clan. He appeared to be inviting them to his estate for a visit.

"Where is this estate?" she said.

"It's near the southern end of the province, nearest the Sun Temple province. I hear he has some marvelous gardeners working for him and the estate is simply beautiful this time of year."

"You're really thinking of going?"

"Of course. Aren't you excited?"

"I'm sorry," Mallory said as servants loaded the table with food. "Should I be? I mean no disrespect, but I don't know these people and I'm not sure about the social etiquette of the situation."

"Don't worry. That's why this is so exciting. We'll have a few days with no pressures or jobs, just the two of us and our hosts. You'll have a chance to interact with Metalkin nobles and learn a bit about our culture and traditions without the pressures of court or stuffy tutors. I know Lady South-Mine would be honoured to meet you in person." He started serving himself.

"I suppose if I had grown up here, I would have met a lot of these people already." Mallory too filled her plate as she talked, and they started eating.

"Yes, I suppose you would have."

"And it would probably offend people if I declined without good reason, correct?"

"Oh, most likely."

"Do I have a good reason to turn down this invitation?"

"There are no emergencies at this time that need your undivided attention. And you can call this all a part of your education."

"Will you take care of the reply? I'm not sure I can handle writing an official letter with all the titles and such just yet. I have been practicing."

"Yes, I can send the letter."

Mallory took a deep breath and added, "You'll remember to tell them about our sleeping arrangements?"

"I will make all the arrangements, don't worry about a thing. Just let your girl know when you return to your room and she'll have a trunk packed for you."

"When would we be leaving?"

"Tomorrow morning, if I can clear it with the captain of the guard. It's not far from here. We can spend a few days visiting. I hear Lady South-Mine is quite good at Stones and Crows."

"What is 'Stones and Crows'?"

"It's a game that nobles enjoy in the evenings. She will have to teach you. I'll send the reply after we finish eating. And I'll let the kitchens know to have a hearty breakfast sent to your room in the morning so you'll be ready for the trip south."

His excitement about the journey was contagious and Mallory found herself smiling. "All right. It sounds like fun."

Kaelen sat at the desk in his office, his heart heavy and his mind dark. In front of him was the finished letter to Lord South-Mine telling him that Mallory had bought the ruse and that they'd be arriving for dinner the following evening. He set the letter aside and pulled out a fresh piece of paper.

Dearest Emilia,

I miss you terribly. I'm sorry that I've been so busy lately. Find it in your heart to forgive me? I will find the time to visit you soon.

Unfortunately, this letter does not contain the news you wish to hear. I will not be able to dine with you for your birthday this week. Duty has called me away to one of the southern estates. I leave in the morning.

I promise you, Dearest, that I will make the time to visit you as soon as I return. You have my highest word of honour on that. I miss you and I crave your presence like the unshaped iron craves the heat of a forge. You are the fire that melts my heart, the spark that lights my life.

Always yours,
Kaelen

For a moment he was tempted to throw the second letter in the fire. It's what his father would expect, and it might be less painful in the long run. In the end he couldn't bring himself to do it. He rolled up both letters, sealed them, and took them to the aviary to oversee the sending of them personally.

He had a bottle of wine sent to his room. He planned to have a glass and wound up drinking the whole bottle and even that did nothing to numb the ache in his heart.

34th of Starrise, 24th Year of the 11th Rebirth
Golden Hall, Metalkin Province

Strange. Yesterday Kaelen looked and sounded excited to be going on this trip. This morning he's surly and red-eyed. I wonder what kept him up late last night? Or if he was merely restless. With nothing to do to assist with the preparations Mallory had stationed herself off to the side of the steps, out of the way of the servants and guards, where she could watch everyone.

The way Kaelen now snapped and snarled at everyone concerned her. *Do I really want to be stuck in the carriage with him all day? I hope he's riding with the guards.*

The rush of servants back and forth had slowed and then stopped and even the guards appeared ready to leave but Kaelen was caught up in a heated discussion with the Captain of the Guard on the far side of the courtyard.

Mallory approached the carriage and flagged down one of the stable boys. "Introduce me to the horses," she said.

"Princess?" the boy stammered, staring at her with large eyes.

"I'd like to meet the horses," she repeated.

"Oh. Uh. Sure. Just be careful. These are the Sun Mares and they've got a lot of spirit."

The horses were a creamy golden-brown colour with blonde manes and tails. They were stomping and snorting, obviously impatient to be off.

"They get like this as soon as we put the tack on them," the boy explained. "This here's Starlight. She's my favourite. She's the oldest of the Sun Mares here in Golden Hall so she's a little quieter." He stroked the horse's nose then added softly, "Sometimes the other Sun Mares scare me a bit."

"They are fantastic creatures," Mallory said, reaching out to stroke Starlight's face. "You say Sun Mare like they're a special breed."

"They are. They're descended from the mares blessed by Airon himself at The Pact. They're stronger and faster than other horses, but harder to breed and harder to train. That's why only the Princesses get to use them. You can push them a bit faster if you need to make it somewhere before dark. They'll keep you safe from Dark Spirits."

"You're very smart."

The boy beamed.

"Let's go," Kaelen said, his voice sharp.

"Thank you," Mallory whispered to the boy before making her way to the carriage.

"Was he bothering you?" Kaelen said. He was holding the carriage door open for her.

"No."

"Why were you fussing around with the horses?"

"I was bored just waiting."

"Horses and stable boys are beneath you."

She sighed. "Because I'm the Metalkin Princess, I know." *Never mind that I like horses.* She climbed the step and arranged her skirts as she sat. "Are you riding with me?"

"No. I'll ride with the guards. I'll see you at midday when we stop to water the horses."

"All right," she said, hoping she didn't sound too relieved.

He closed the door and a moment later the carriage started forward. Outside she could hear hooves on cobblestone and the clatter of the wheels.

3rd of Cloudrise, 24th Year of the 11th Rebirth
Golden Hall, Metalkin Province

"At least you get to wear one of the nicer dresses today," Cecilia said, fussing in the wardrobe. "Green? Or red?"

"I don't care," Mallory said, pacing the room in her dressing gown. "Whatever you think is best. I'm too nervous about this. I can't believe they're actually letting me go out into the city to meet with the Guild Masters in the guild halls."

"It's important," Cecilia said. "You should see what your people do, what gifts and talents they have."

"Do you really think they'll give me a tour of the hall? Or will I be stuck in an office having tea with the officials?"

"I don't know. You should request a tour as soon as you walk in. You said the Jeweller's Guild today? Green I think." She pulled out a dress and carried it over. "Take the robe off so I can help you with this."

"I don't know what I'd do without you."

"Someone else would help you," Cecilia said. "Want a little advice?"

"Anything! Please!" Mallory laughed. She'd only been back in the capital since the first and she was still fretting that she'd made a fool of herself during her first estate visit.

"If you walk into that guild hall and tell them how excited you are and how talented they are and how you would so love to see the work they do in your best over-excited, in-awe voice you'll be more likely to get that tour than if you walked in and made a demand."

"Do you think that would work to get my way with Jaspar and Kaelen?"

"Not likely. They're too used to the real you now to know what you're up to. But you can try other things. Or rather the same thing in another way. These Metalkin nobles, they are prideful and arrogant. If you challenge them head-on, they bristle. If you compliment them and thank them and ask for favours, or ask for their help, they feel flattered."

"So, say 'thank you' more often?"

"And 'what would I do without you?' and 'I hate to bother you but you're the only one who can help me with this and it's so important'."

"How do you know all this?"

"My family has served for generations, either here at the castle, or at noble homes in the capital. We see how the nobles interact with each other, we see the best ways for lower class people to get what they need from the nobles."

Mallory gave her head a shake. "Your world is so very different from the one I grew up in. I'm glad you're here to teach me these things. Why wasn't my etiquette teacher explaining this to me?"

"Because then he'd have to admit that those behaviours work to manipulate nobles, particularly noble men, though noble women are particularly susceptible to flattery. Honestly, I'm not even sure that the nobles are aware of it."

"Hopefully, in time, they'll respect me enough that I don't have to fall back on grovelling and flattery," Mallory said. "Until then, I'll use whatever works!"

She took an open-top carriage through the city, pulled by one of the regular horses, a gelding with a speckled grey coat and iron-black mane. She wore a shawl to protect her from the chill of the moving air, and to protect her dress from the road dust.

It was nice to be able to see more of the city as she passed through it. The houses were stone but the iron fittings on the doors and windows were bold and obvious. The fences were all wrought iron, some plain and straight, others with curls and accents along the tops. The houses were large here, all of them two-stories and spacious. It made sense that the district closest to the castle was filled with wealthy homes.

They stopped in front of a modest two-story building with an ornate silver crest on the door. Kaelen climbed down from the carriage and offered her a hand. Normally she was fiercely independent and would have scoffed at such a gesture, but she'd come to realize that navigating in skirts was harder than it looked, especially when climbing down a set of narrow steps above a muddy road.

She accepted his arm and he led her up the well-tended walk to the oak and iron door. The crest she'd seen from the road was even more impressive up close. The image was framed with a chain that crossed at the top to hang down in a loop. From the loop was suspended the image of a pendant and below that were two interlocking rings.

Kaelen lifted the iron knocker that hung beneath the crest and rapped it twice against the wood. The answer came swiftly and a middle-aged balding man in a linen robe ushered them inside with a deep bow.

"Welcome, welcome. The Jeweller's Guild is honoured by your visit."

"To be honest," Mallory said. "I couldn't wait to visit. The work you do here, that your jewellers do, it's so detailed, so beautiful. I hope you will honour me with a peek at least."

"My dear, I'm sure tea can wait. If the two of you would like to follow me, I would gladly show you the workrooms where we train our apprentices."

Mallory stretched the tour out as long as she could, asking questions and gushing over everything from the finely wrought silver chains to the details of the pieces being pulled from the silver molds.

"You're all so talented, and patient. Oh, just look at the detailing on this gold pendant."

When there was nothing else to see they were led upstairs to a study. Fresh tea was ordered up and the senior members of the guild joined them.

"It's quite concerning," said the Guild Master. "Never in all my years have I seen the Stone Clan raise their prices to such an extent. It's almost criminal. How can we turn a profit on the pieces we make if we have to pay that much for the gems?"

"Does the Gem Cutters' Guild have anyone else to sell their gem stones too?" Mallory asked.

The men all looked at each other for a moment. "No, not really," the Guild Master said. "I'm sure some nobles have purchased unset stones for collections, but otherwise, it is only the Jeweller's Guild that would have need of them."

"None of the other artists on the island would have use for them?"

"Perhaps a sculptor," one man said. "But I've never heard of it being done. Why?"

"Well, it seems to me, that if you have only one market for your product, you would not do something to endanger your relationship with that market without good cause. Obviously, pieces with gems are worth more, but you could still make jewelry with just silver, gold, and other metals, yes?"

"Of course," the Guild Master said. "Some of our finest pieces have been made that way."

"So, they need you to buy stones, but you don't need stones to make your product. Raising prices without good reason hurts them far more than it hurts you. For the time being, I recommend reducing the number of gems you buy until the reason behind these price increases becomes known."

"That is a good short-term strategy," the Guild Master said. "But in the long-term …"

"We can plan for the long term when we have more information," Kaelen said. "I'm sure other options will become available soon."

"Yes, of course," the Guild Master said. "We look forward to working with you on this problem."

The conversation shifted to lighter matters and Mallory asked about each man's family and how long they'd been in the guild. When the tea and snacks were gone Kaelen offered her his hand.

"We should be going. We need to return to the castle. I have letters to write this evening."

"Yes. I should write Princess Stone Rose. Perhaps she has some answers."

"We are in good hands," the Guild Master said.

The men bowed, and farewells were exchanged. The ride back wasn't as interesting as they took the same roads, but Mallory didn't mind. It felt like a day well spent.

Upon their return, Kaelen disappeared into the castle, headed for his private study and whatever letters he had to write.

Mallory decided not to return directly to her room, asking one of the passing servants to find Cecilia for her and then waiting in the shade along the edge of the courtyard.

"You're back," Cecilia said, curtseying.

"Yes. Your advice paid off."

"I'm glad I could be of service. What did you need?"

"I need to speak with Master Spirit-Light. I had a thought today and he seems like the best person to talk to about it. I don't know where to find him ..."

"Hmm. I can show you to his study. If he's not there, perhaps we can find someone who does know."

"And you're experiencing no dizziness? No weakness?" Bernard said. He was poking Devin's back.

Devin shook his head. "No, nothing like that. And you can ask the stable master and the guards, I haven't had a single outburst, haven't called anyone rude names, not even a snarl."

"You're still helping in the stables then?" Emilio said. He was seated in one of the chairs, taking notes in a small leather-bound book.

"Yes sir, when the guards don't need a guide and the cook doesn't need fresh venison."

"The horses aren't acting strange around you?"

"More affectionate than usual, if anything," Devin said. "I haven't been bitten or attacked or anything though."

Emilio nodded and jotted the information down.

"I really don't understand it," Bernard said. "This is not a normal possession. Perhaps you are not really possessed?"

"If you could hear the voice in my head, hear the things it suggests to me, you wouldn't ask that."

"Perhaps ..." The priests words were cut off by a knocking at the door. "Put your shirt on," he said.

Devin nodded, shrugging into his shirt as Emilio went to the door. He saw the steward open the door just wide enough to peer out.

"Yes? I see. Just a moment." He turned into the room. "It's the princess," he said softly.

Devin felt his pulse begin to race.

"I think we're done here," Bernard said. "We will take our leave and let you return to your duties as steward."

"I'll see you both in a few days." He peered into the hallway again. "Yes, I can see her right away."

Mallory felt odd, waiting a few steps down the hallway as Cecilia spoke to Master Spirit-Light on her behalf. Finally, the girl waved her over. "He's here. He'll see you."

As Mallory reached the door it opened fully, and Devin Sun-Stag stepped out, the two of them nearly colliding with each other.

"I'm sorry," she said, stepping back.

"I should have been watching where I was going. He said you were here to see him. I should have known."

"I didn't realize he was with someone, I shouldn't have interrupted."

"We were already done. You're not interrupting."

In the doorway, Honourable Bernard cleared his throat.

Devin bowed. "Airon's light bless you," he said and then he hurried off down the hallway.

"You're not interrupting a thing," Bernard said. "I've hardly seen you since the wedding. How are you feeling?"

"Just fine," Mallory said. The shift in her voice, posture, and mood was so fast it startled even her but that didn't stop her from remaining cool towards the priest. "If you'll excuse me, I must speak with Master Spirit-Light. Alone."

"Yes, of course. If you ever need guidance …"

"That's what I have stewards for."

"Of course, of course." He bowed and hurried off down the hallway.

Next to her, Cecilia curtseyed. "Will you be okay to find your way back?"

"I'll manage, thank you," Mallory said, relaxing again. She went into the study and closed the door behind her.

"You've returned from your visits," Emilio said. "Come sit. Tell me what's bothering you, and then tell me all about your trips."

"I realized something today that had me thinking," she said as she arranged her skirts into a chair. "Why am I named Jewel-Rose? The Stone Clan is in charge of mining, cutting, and polishing gem stones. The Metalkin only set them."

"Ah, yes, that," Emilio said, taking the chair opposite her. "You're not the first princess to point that out. Sometimes the Metalkin princess catches it, sometimes the Stone Clan princess. It was an error made at the time of The Pact, and of course, after the ritual was complete it could not be undone."

"You would think that, if The Pact were so important, time would be taken to do it right."

"Yes, well, you must understand," Emilio said, shifting in his seat as he spoke. "It was a politically difficult time and a delicate and contested matter. As the story goes, the girls volunteered against the wishes of their fathers. I'm sure there was a bit of pressure to complete the ritual before someone changed their mind or interfered."

"You have guards."

"It's a small thing and …"

"Not really. I'm named for something that isn't even covered by my spirit guides or my provinces talents or anything."

"I mean, it was a small error, a slip of the tongue. It was supposed to be *Jewelled* Rose. Because of the jewellers, not because of the stones themselves. Somehow the '-ed' was dropped, perhaps it wasn't said, perhaps it wasn't heard. Whatever the case, Jewel-Rose became the official title and it was weeks, maybe even months, before someone realized what had happened. By then it was too late to change."

"Why not just change it to the way it should have been? If that's what Airon intended …"

"It's not about intent. You understand contracts?"

"Of course."

"You can have a contract between two people, or between two guilds. In the first case, if one person dies the surviving person would have to negotiate a new contract with their estate or heir."

"Of course."

"In the second case, the contract would stand even if the guild representatives who signed it died because they were signing on behalf of the guild."

"I know all this. What does this have to do with The Pact?"

"The Pact is the biggest, most important contract our people have ever signed. And we signed it with an immortal god. And it was signed by Princess Stone Rose of the Stone Clan, Princess Living Rose of the Animal People, Princess Rose of Roses of the Evergrowth, Princess Bright Rose of the Sun Temple, and."

"And Princess Jewel-Rose of the Metalkin," Mallory cut in. "So, if I became Princess Jewelled Rose instead then I wouldn't be held to the pact."

"We would have to redo the rituals, at the very least, if that would even work at this point. The Pact has become so delicate with your prolonged absence and the difficulties the other girls have faced finding their princes. Any further actions that *might* weaken The Pact would be disastrous."

"Well, that explains things at least. I still think it should have been caught sooner."

"You're right, of course, but sometimes the person in charge of these things is overwhelmed by other details and things are missed. Even important things like the official name of the Princess of Metalkin."

"Wait. Why did High Priest Gold-Spark allow me to keep my first name?"

"At the time of The Pact the tradition of keeping the girls' first names hadn't yet been established, so their first names were left out of the contract, as it were. The contract allows for a change in given name, but not title."

"Well, that was lucky. I don't think I could ever get used to being Ashlyn."

"You've had two political visits now, correct?" When she nodded, he went on. "Tell me about them. What did you think of the **LN** family? What did you think of the guild?"

"The visit today went well. I went to see the Jewellers, which is how I came to this question of names, we were discussing the rising cost of gem stones. They actually gave me a tour of the hall. And we talked about more than just business. I actually felt like a proper part of things for once."

"That's good. The guilds here can be ... snobbish and secretive."

"All of the guilds are out for themselves, aren't they? I mean, not just the Metalkin guilds, but all of them, in all the provinces?"

"The purpose of the guilds is twofold. First, they recruit and train artisans and workers within a specific craft and maintain the professional standards of that craft. You know that all guild-backed healers are properly trained to deal with your broken arm or fever. You know that all guild-backed stone masons will be able to build you a house that doesn't fall on your head."

"That's a good thing," Mallory said.

"It is. The second purpose of the guilds is to protect the guild's interest in the market and protect its members. That means ensuring that everyone from the men who dig the mines to the stone cutters to the jewellers are all working in appropriate conditions and are paid accordingly. There are some guilds that work more closely with each other because they have needs or supplies that overlap. Other times that overlap generates tension. Sometimes guilds contain people from more than one province."

"Oh. I thought ... which guilds?"

"The weavers, for example. Linen comes from flax. Wool comes from sheep. The dyes are almost all plant-based. There are Evergrowth and Animal People both in the weaver's guild and they generally work well together."

"That makes sense," Mallory said, nodding.

"Things here are not black and white. There are many complications, all delicately intertwined with each other."

"I'm beginning to see that." She sighed. "Every time I think I'm beginning to understand this place, something like this comes up and I realize just how much I still have to learn."

"The other princesses have been studying for twenty years now. You're making amazing progress."

"Thank you."

"Are you going to tell me about your trip to the South-Mine estate?"

"The journey was uneventful. We had no troubles on the road. They have a lovely home and an amazing garden. We were there two full days, plus dinner the day we arrived and breakfast the day we left."

"I know all that," Emilio said. "Princess, I'm not Metalkin so your opinion of one of their noble families will not insult me. And I am sworn to serve you. Gossiping about your opinions to someone who might let word slip to the people we're discussing would not be serving you. I want to know what actually happened during your visit."

"Lady South-Mine was nice, but very snobby. She showed me around, showed off her art collection, and the garden she hired someone to tend for her. She introduced me to her daughter, and cousins, and nieces. I lost track of all of their names and how they were related to her, or her husband. Tea time and meal time was filled with gossip. Did I know so-and-so yet? Wasn't this one a slob and that one acting above her station? It was very petty. I saw very little of Lord South-Mine or Kaelen the entire time I was there."

"Did you enjoy yourself?"

"Not really. I was bored and I was tired of pretending to smile."

"We're still getting used to what type of princess you'll be, and you're still getting used to the people you're ruling so I'm not surprised that it was an awkward visit. They say the people, and the court, take their temperament from their ruler. As the people get used to you, they'll want to mimic you. But, you're back now, and you're safe. Hopefully you did learn something about the Metalkin culture."

"I guess so."

"Good."

"Master Spirit-Light, were you surprised to learn Kaelen was my prince?"

"Yes, I was. And not just because he happened to be along on that voyage. There were a few suitors I had mentally placed near the top of the list, Joseph Rose-Gold was one of them, Clarence Silver-Wrought was another, because they showed a certain affinity for the castle, and the temple. I would not have bet money on Kaelen Iron-Heart. I guess that goes to show how difficult these things are to predict."

"I'd like to meet a few of these other suitors, if you can find a reason that won't make people suspicious or Kaelen jealous."

"Do you have a reason for wanting to do this?"

"I'd like to meet people Kaelen isn't interested in introducing me to."

"I'll see what I can arrange. Is there anything else you need?"

"No. Just a good night's sleep."

"All right. I'm glad you're back."

"Me too."

5th of Cloudrise, 24th Year of the 11th Rebirth
Golden Hall, Metalkin Province

Yesterday had been filled with meetings with various scholars and historians, all of whom had dry, dusty voices. Today, Mallory was going to visit the Gold Guild, and that meant the cloth of gold dress.

Aside from her cream-coloured, rose-adorned wedding dress, this was the finest dress Mallory had ever worn in her life, and she'd owned a few ball gowns and a collection of silk saris made by some of the finest artisans in India. None of that compared to the decadence of this dress.

The fabric was heavy and stiff, but it shimmered in even the smallest sliver of light. The bodice was snug with a low neckline. The sleeves were snug too, from shoulder to elbow, and then flowed to her wrists, the extra fabric making her arms feel heavy. The skirt was full, held up by a petticoat that, for all its layers, was lighter than the skirt.

"Are you going to make me wear the cloth of silver dress to meet the Silver Guild?" Mallory asked while Cecilia fussed with the skirts.

"Most likely, yes," she replied.

"Isn't this a little too obvious? A little clichéd?"

"You look beautiful. Trust me. The Gold Guild especially is obsessed with wealth. You'll discover that all those men are wearing cloth of gold sashes or have gold trim on their vests. And chains of gold around their necks. We have to choose a necklace for you, something eye catching but the right length for that neckline."

"Are you common born or noble born?" Mallory asked.

"Common," Cecilia said. "But as I said, my family has served for generations and my mother taught me everything she learned working in a Metalkin noble household."

"You could have fooled me."

"I've never owned anything worth even a tenth of what that dress cost to make," Cecilia said. "But I have an eye for beauty and the chance to dress you in the finest things. Don't expect me to pass that up."

"Okay," Mallory said, laughing. "I'm just glad I don't have to think about this stuff every day. Before I came here my biggest concern was if the clothes were clean enough to wear."

"You did your own washing?"

"Well, not when I was growing up. We had house staff when I lived at the embassy in India. But I was a university student for a few years before the priests found me. I lived on my own, and yeah, I had to do my own washing."

Cecilia came over and took both of Mallory's hands, turning them over, examining each finger. "You did not."

Mallory laughed again. "We had electric machines that did the actual washing. I had to go down to the dorm's laundry mat and put everything in the machine once a week or so."

"What a strange world. And yet, it would be nice not to scrub the clothes by hand." She released Mallory's hands and turned to the dressing table. "Here. You won't want to wear something with a stone, they may take it as a slight. This etched gold pendant is just right." She hung it around Mallory's neck and adjusted it so it hung straight. "There. You look beautiful."

"Are you all done then?" Mallory asked with a cheeky grin. "You don't want to paint my face or play with my hair some more?"

"You need to grow your hair out more," Cecilia replied, smiling back. "Go, or you'll be late."

Mallory caught Cecilia's hands before the girl could turn away. "Thank you. I really don't know what I'd do without you."

They shared a smile and then Cecilia pulled her hands free. "Someone is coming up to dust and tidy today while you're gone. I'll see you this evening."

"All right."

The Gold Guild was located south of the castle instead of west so even though it was closer to the castle Mallory got to see a new part of the city.

Everything here was fancier and more elaborate than it had been at the Jewellers' Guild and it rivalled even the formal rooms at the castle. The Guild Representative who met them at the door was less susceptible to flattery than his counterpart in the Jewellers' Guild and he offered Mallory a thin smile in response to her excited greeting.

"If there is time after the meeting we'll see about a tour. The senior guild officials are already waiting for you upstairs with hot tea and cakes."

"Of course," Mallory said. "I don't want to keep them waiting. Please, lead the way."

He nodded, obviously satisfied with her answer, and led them up a wide staircase.

18th of Cloudrise, 24th Year of the 11th Rebirth
Golden Hall, Metalkin Province

It had been a busy two weeks, full of meetings and visits. After her meeting with the Jewelry Guild on the third and the Gold Guild on the fifth she'd gone to the Silver Guild on the seventh in a cloth of silver dress and the Iron Guild on the ninth. Several members of a prominent Metalkin family arrived from the Stone Clan province so she'd had a long dinner meeting with Kaelen and her stewards on the seventh to prepare her and she'd spent the eighth visiting and entertaining her unexpected guests. An invitation arrived on the eleventh, so she'd left with Kaelen for her second estate visit on the thirteenth to return yesterday.

Today there was a service in the temple to mark mid-month which she attended, though it was optional, so she could gain more understanding of the religion and culture of her new home. Now she was enjoying afternoon tea, alone, on the little stone patio outside her room.

It bothered her how evenly spaced all of her activities had been, how quickly both Kaelen and Jaspar had switched from 'stay here, read, listen to your tutors' to 'go out, meet people, explore the city and the province'. Together it made her very suspicious indeed. In the last two weeks she'd managed to get to court only twice and on both occasions, there had been nothing pressing or important to deal with.

"Either this is the most boring province in the world or they're working very hard to keep me from doing anything useful," she said to the rose bush growing next to her. It was starting to bloom, the large red flowers a stark contrast to the dark green leaves. She didn't know much about plants at all, but she liked this bush. She liked the patio too, with it's cobblestone paving and neatly tended flower beds. She was just glad she didn't have to tend it herself.

"Princess?" came a voice from behind her, somewhere in her room.

"Yes, I'm out here."

The girl came over. "Cecilia said you were in here but then you didn't answer …"

"I'm sorry, I didn't hear you at the door."

"It's okay. I don't mean to disturb you, but a letter just arrived for you, from Princess Stone-Rose."

"How nice. Thank you."

When the girl was gone, she opened the letter.

To Mallory Jewel-Rose, Eleventh Princess of the Metalkin,

May this letter find you well. I hope your first month on the Isle of Light has been, well, liveable I suppose. If you ever have need of anything, please write me.

I really hate to burden you with this when I know you're still trying to find your feet, but the situation is important. Though I'm certain my steward would say it's a problem of my own making.

I had a petition today and it was discovered that the Iron Guild had breached the terms of a contract and were underpaying Stone Clan workers. I am hoping this incident will prove to be isolated to one guild hall and one contract, but I thought I should warn you.

I will be writing to Princess Bright Rose as well. We had a similar complaint against the Merchant's Bank. I am praying those two incidents are not connected, and honestly, I have no reason to suspect they are. And yet ... No, I need not burden you further with imagined scenarios.

If you do choose to look into the matter, please write me if you happen across anything. Or if you don't. It would be good to know that it was, in fact, isolated.

May Airon's light ever shine upon you,

Princess Rheeya Stone Rose, Eleventh Princess of the Stone Clan

Mallory rang for a servant and met the girl at the door. "I need you to fetch both of my stewards, and Prince Kaelen, immediately."

"Yes, Princess, of course."

The men arrived one shortly after the next. When they were all seated in her room, she held out the letter. "Princess Stone Rose just wrote me. The Iron Guild was found to be in breach of contract and she's concerned about overreach and possibly corruption on the part of the guild outside of Stone Clan territories."

"This is highly unusual," Jaspar said. He cleared his throat. "I will write to the head of the Iron Guild and make sure he is aware."

"Please have him send me a report when he is finished looking into this matter," Mallory said. "I would like to know what he finds, and what he decides to do about it."

"Of course," Jaspar said.

"This Princess Stone-Rose sounds a bit distracted," Kaelen said, pointing to the letter. "Here, where she mentions 'imagined scenarios', can we even be sure there is a problem?"

"I'm not dragging people to trial," Mallory said. "I'm just asking the guild to look into it. And besides, Master Black-Kettle is the one who actually suggested that the guild investigate."

"Fine," Kaelen huffed. "While they're seeing to this investigation, you and I can visit the …"

"Is it outside the city?" she interrupted.

"What? Yes. It's an estate, the …"

"We're not going."

He sat staring at her. "We're not? You haven't even looked at the invitation. They'll be offended."

"Write then with my apologies. Until this matter with the Iron Guild is cleared up I want to be here in Golden Hall to receive any further letters from Princess Stone-Rose."

Kaelen stood. "Of course, I will write them at once. Hopefully, they will be understanding and will issue another invitation later."

2nd of Thornrise, 24th Year of the 11th Rebirth
Golden Hall, Metalkin Province

36th of Cloudrise

To Mallory Jewel-Rose, Eleventh of Her Name, Princess of the Metalkin

Further to my earlier letter regarding the Iron Guild and the contract issues at the Black Mountain Iron Mine, I wish to inform you that there have been further collapses at the mine.

The Iron Guild representative in charge here is Jared Iron-Smith. He was here when I arrived at the mine this morning but this evening he has gone down to the village on an errand and is not available to answer questions I have about the mine. I am concerned that while Master Iron-Smith was in control of this mine (a direct violation of his contract) he made decisions which negatively impacted the mine's productivity and put lives in danger.

Until I speak with him further or receive confirmation from other sources this is merely educated speculation.

I hope to have more information for you in the coming days but any information you can provide me regarding the Iron Guild's operations would be beneficial.

Princess Rheeya Stone Rose of the Stone Clan

Mallory frowned at the letter. *Getting information on the Iron Guild could be tricky. They hardly let me hold court, and when I do, they basically tell me what to say.*

She pulled out pen, paper, and ink and started writing, one letter to the Iron Guild requesting information, and one to Princess Rheeya, promising her cooperation.

She had the letters written and sealed and had summoned a servant to take them to the aviary before she realized she hadn't shown Kaelen the letter, and hadn't asked his guidance in the matter.

Well, I haven't actually done anything other than ask for more information. I'm sure there's nothing wrong with that.

3rd of Thornrise, 24th Year of the 11th Rebirth
Golden Hall, Metalkin Province

There were two letters from Rheeya today:

Princess Mallory Jewel-Rose,
This letter is to inform you that Jared Iron-Smith has been stripped of his access to the mine. The Iron Guild has been stripped of all rights to the Black Mountain Mine, as well. I have informed the Iron Guild here in the Stone Clan that we will not longer deal with Jared Iron-Smith and that it is in their best interest to remove him from a position of authority within the guild hall. I have no authority over whether he remains employed by the guild in another province.
Princess Rheeya Stone Rose

Princess Mallory Jewel-Rose,
This is an official request for reimbursement. Please find below a summary of costs incurred by the Iron Guild and their mismanagement of the Black Mountain Mine. It is up to you whether you wish to pay this amount from the royal account or have the Iron Guild pay some or all of it.
I suggest that you allow your stewards, and mine, to handle the actual transfer of money. Dealing with the bank can be complicated.

Jared Iron-Smith has fled the Black Mountain region. While he may turn up at the Guild Hall in Stones Shore, it is equally, if not more likely that he will return to Golden Hall or his family's estate. Though his employment in Stone Clan territory is at an end, his presence is still required. I have formal charges to lay against him.

Should you have knowledge of his whereabouts, or discover where he has gone, I request that he be returned to Stones Shore to face trial.

Princess Rheeya Stone Rose

Mallory summoned Emilio first. "How bad of an offense would a person need to commit for me to summon them back from another province?"

"You mean, what crimes would a Metalkin need to commit in another province in order for you to summon them back here?"

Mallory shook her head. "No, I mean someone from another province. If they were to commit a crime here and flee, how bad would it have to be for me to be allowed to demand they be returned for trial?"

"Generally, each princess takes care of what happens in their own province, no matter who has committed the crime. If a commoner were to steal something small in Golden Hall and flee to the Animal People's province, you would write a letter to Taeya and she would arrest the criminal, try them for theft, and punish them, at your request, sending back any compensations to injured parties."

"I have a letter here from Princess Rheeya. She says a man named Jared Iron-Smith has committed a crime, she doesn't say what, and she's politely demanding he be returned to Stones Shore for trial."

"Oh dear. That he's noble born, and she's still demanding his return? This is severe."

"More severe than breaking a contract or mismanaging an iron mine?"

"Quite a bit more severe, yes."

"Then I am morally and legally obligated to fulfill her request. Thank you. That will help me deal with Master Black-Kettle, and my husband."

"You think they would argue against sending him back?"

"I know they are friends with the Iron-Smith family, and I know that they know more about your legal system than I do. Any information I have can only be helpful."

"Do you want to summon them now? I can stay."

"No. It's late. I want to think on this tonight. I will call a meeting after court tomorrow."

Emilio nodded. "Perhaps that is for the best. Given the dates on these letters, I'd say you have a little time before Jared arrives in our province anyway."

"I was hoping that would be the case. Thank you for your assistance."

"It is my duty to serve," he said with a bow. "Is there anything else?"

"Not tonight, but I hope you will attend the meeting tomorrow morning."

"Of course. Good night, Princess."

4th of Thornrise, 24th Year of the 11th Rebirth
Golden Hall, Metalkin Province

Mallory was starting to feel more comfortable with daily court, though they still weren't letting her deal with anything important. She wasn't sure if there was nothing bigger than property line squabbles to deal with, or if they were postponing the important stuff, of if they were holding a second court session each day without her knowledge. Whatever the case, court was soon out of the way, and that meant meeting with her stewards, and Prince Kaelen, to discuss the letters from Rheeya.

She took a deep breath and squared her shoulders before entering the sitting room where the men waited. "Thank you for coming this morning," she said. "I'll make this quick. Princess Rheeya is dealing with a crisis at the Black Mountain Iron Mine and requires assistance. She has identified several costs that were incurred because of the Iron Guild directly, or one of its members. We need to review that list and decide what will be paid by the crown and what will be paid by the Iron Guild."

"You're going to pay without even questioning it?" Kaelen said.

"Of course not," Mallory fibbed. "Why do you think you're here? We're reviewing the account right now."

She'd copied the account onto a fresh sheet of paper before coming, allowing her to keep the rest of Rheeya's correspondence quiet for now. She'd also taken the liberty to reword the description of some of the items on the list to make it more difficult for anyone to deny the need to pay them.

In the end, they agreed that every item on the list was, in fact, a Metalkin responsibility, and divided the list with most of the payments being delegated to the Iron Guild.

When that was done and the appropriate letters signed and sealed, Mallory turned to Kaelen. "You are friends with the Iron-Smith family, correct?"

She saw him stiffen but he said, "Yes, you know that. We visited their estate when you first arrived on the island."

She did know, she had remembered, but she smiled and nodded. "That's right. I knew the name was familiar."

"Are they somehow tied up in this?"

"No, I don't think so, at least, not the entire family. Rheeya is looking for information on a Jared Iron-Smith. I was wondering if you knew him."

"I've heard the name," Kaelen said. "The Iron-Smith family is quite large, and they have members in all five provinces working at both the Iron Guild and the various smithing guilds."

"Hmm. That might make it difficult to locate him then."

"Locate him?"

"Yes. Princess Rheeya has some questions for him and he's gone missing."

"What sort of questions?"

"She didn't elaborate. I assume it has to do with the mine he was overseeing. I'm travelling to the Iron-Smith estate to speak with Lord Iron-Smith about this, I'm sure he would be cooperative in this matter. Kaelen, you'll accompany me?"

"Of course," Kaelen said.

"Then I will see to writing a reply to Rheeya to keep her up to date. Is there anything else we need to discuss?"

"When exactly do you plan to leave?" Jaspar asked. "We need to make travel arrangements. You need an escort. Wouldn't it be better to send the Captain of the Guard and some men instead?"

"I was certainly planning to bring guards along. I can't travel without them," Mallory said.

"Why don't I just write them?" Kaelen said. "It would save you the journey."

"I want to ask them in person."

"Summon them here."

"When I last visited them, they said I was welcome any time."

Jaspar looked from Kaelen to Mallory. He knew the other stewards used the excuse 'it's too dangerous for you to travel' with the other princesses, but with the amount of travel they'd foisted upon Mallory in recent weeks that excuse would ring hollow. "This is very short notice."

"I understand that, but this is a pressing matter. I want to handle it personally. Please. You won't let me handle serious petitions. You all get angry with me for trying to make decisions on my own. I didn't ask to come here, I didn't ask to be your princess, you all wanted this. Please. You wanted a princess, let me be a princess."

"I, for one, am impressed with your willingness to take on these difficult tasks," Emilio said.

Jaspar sighed. "I will see to your escort and the other necessary arrangements."

"Fine," Kaelen said. "But I think you're overreacting, and I think a simple letter would be better."

"I know you do. Please, try to understand, I need to do this."

Kaelen shook his head. "You're looking for trouble where this is none, and you're dangerously close to betraying your people."

"Kaelen, if Jared Iron-Smith can help Princess Rheeya in any way, I need to convince him to do so."

"She's right," Emilio said. "Balance and support are crucial in these trying times."

"When do you want to leave?" Kaelen said.

"After lunch," Mallory said.

"After lunch?" Jaspar said. "I thought you'd leave tomorrow."

"After lunch," Mallory said again. "I already have my girl packing my things. I will be in the courtyard as soon as I finish eating."

"I ... I guess I have a lot to get done. Excuse me," Jaspar said, bowing. He hurried from the room.

"I'll go pack," Kaelen growled.

When they were alone, Mallory said, "Thank you. I think the fight would have been worse if not for you."

"I don't understand the two of them. They are clearly trying to hobble you, but I don't know why."

"Will you keep an eye on Master Black-Kettle while I'm away?"

"Yes, of course."

"Thank you. I feel like you and Cecilia are the only ones around here that I can trust." *What about Devin?* She thought she could trust Devin but he'd stopped answering her letters, hadn't joined her in the sun room in weeks. *Better not to mention Devin.*

5th of Thornrise, 24th Year of the 11th Rebirth
Iron-Smith Estate, Metalkin Province

Devin rode into the Iron-Smith estate's courtyard just behind Mallory's wagon. They'd made good time, but it was starting to get too close to sunset for his liking. He dismounted and set about helping the stable lads employed at the estate with the horses. The chaos around him was more than the usual for the arrival of a guest. He glanced over at Kaelen who had been more irritable and hostile than was normal, even for him, since they'd left Golden Hall.

Mallory climbed down from the carriage and straightened her skirts. She spotted him and hurried over, paying little mind to the horse he was leading. "Master Sun-Stag, I'm glad you joined us. Please stay close to me for the next little while, I'll have a job for you very soon."

He bowed. "Of course, Princess. Anything you request."

The front doors opened and Lord Iron-Smith hurried out, his steward close on his heels. "Princess Jewel-Rose, this is a surprise. I wasn't expecting you. I will have rooms prepared and a meal cooked. What brings you here?"

"Jared Iron-Smith."

"What about him?"

"I need to see him at once."

Lord Iron-Smith glanced at Kaelen but the prince only shrugged. "I'm sorry, Princess. I haven't seen him in years. He lives in the Stone Clan Province. He wrote about a month ago, something about a mine he was overseeing, but that was it."

"You've not seen or heard from him in the last week or so?"

"No, Princess."

"I wish I could take your word for it but Princess Stone Rose is prepared to lay serious charges against him and I must be sure." She turned to her guards. "Search the estate."

Kaelen and Lord Iron-Smith were both protesting loudly as the guards fanned out across the courtyard and headed into the house. Mallory ignored them.

"Master Sun-Stag, come with me," she said, walking back towards the carriage. "Go speak with the stable hands and the stable master. Maybe you'll be able to tell if there is a horse missing from the stable, maybe he'll be willing to tell you something."

Devin nodded and jogged in the direction of the stables.

It didn't take long for guards to start reporting back, all of them saying they'd found nothing. Mallory was starting to think she'd set herself up to look like a fool when Devin returned.

"Stable master says he was woken in the middle of the night. A rider had arrived. He was tasked with saddling a fresh horse and then tending the one the rider had come in on. Said the poor thing was in a sorry state from being ridden so hard. He doesn't know who the rider was or where they were headed. Must have been an emergency though, to be out at night like that."

Mallory nodded and went back to Lord Iron-Smith. "Someone arrived here last night, who was it?"

Outright denial wouldn't work since it was obvious the princess already knew about the rider, and since he'd given the man a horse it would be hard to convince her that he didn't know the rider's identity. "Local patrol," he lied. "He works for the estates in the area. We generally don't see him at night, no one travels at night, but he was carrying important news west and needed a fresh horse."

"You're willing to swear an oath that it was not Jared Iron-Smith?"

"I've already told you, I haven't seen Jared in years."

"Excuse me, Princess," Devin said as he approached. "I found this in the stables." He handed the scroll to Mallory.

Lord Iron-Smith went pale.

Mallory unrolled the letter and read aloud. "To Jared Iron-Smith, this letter is to confirm that the latest shipment of iron has been safely received. Compensation has been made to the Black Mine account. Signed Master Forge of the Iron Guild. I wonder how this found its way to your stables?"

"I didn't know," Lord Iron-Smith said. "I didn't know Princess Stone Rose planned to lay charges against him! He wrote, said there was an emergency transfer at the guild, said he would be stopping here for a fresh horse. He didn't tell me he was in trouble. I would have held him here, I swear it."

"Where did he go?" Kaelen said.

"I don't know. I swear it. It was dark and he didn't say. He just rode out of the courtyard. Maybe one of the guards saw which way he went."

Mallory turned to her guards. "Find out." She turned back to Lord Iron-Smith. "I understand family loyalty," she said. "And I believe only the man guilty of a crime should be charged for it. But understand this: your first loyalty is to me."

"Yes," Lord Iron-Smith said. "Of course."

"We need to impose on your hospitality tonight," Mallory said. "And we will be leaving first thing in the morning."

"You don't have to leave first thing in the morning on my account," Lord Iron-Smith said. "Now that you're here, we'd be honoured to host you for a day or two."

"I'll consider it," Mallory said. "I was only planning to be away overnight."

A guard ran over, panting. "Princess, the guard at the wall last night says he went south from the gate but there's a crossroads that way so there's three or four villages he could have gone to."

"Come with me," she said. "Lord Iron-Smith, I need a map."

"Yes, of course, this way," he said, bowing.

They went inside and Lord Iron-Smith led the way to his study. He unrolled a map on the desk. "We're here," Kaelen said, pointing. "Here's the crossroads."

Mallory traced the roads and pointed to the three nearest towns. "Send men to each of these towns. I want him found."

The guard nodded. "Yes, Princess."

Lord Iron-Smith rolled up the map. "Shall we sit somewhere more comfortable and discuss more interesting and entertaining things until dinner? I know I'm feeling a little flustered by all this."

Mallory smiled. "Yes, that would be lovely. I haven't seen you or your wife since I first arrived on the island. It would be nice to visit."

"I'll call my wife, and we'll meet you in the sitting room."

"I know the way," Kaelen said.

9th of Thornrise, 24th Year of the 11th Rebirth
Golden Hall, Metalkin Province

"Are there any other petitions this morning?"

"No," Jaspar said. "But the Captain of the Guard is here to see you. I can have him meet you after we finish here."

"No need. Just have him come in now."

Jaspar nodded and relayed the order to the guard by the door. A moment later a tall man in a stunning deep-red uniform marched in. Mallory smiled. "Captain Shield-Forge, it is good to see you again."

"And you, Princess Jewel-Rose. I suppose it's a good sign that we don't need to meet too often."

"A very good sign. What can I do for you today?"

"I'm merely here to report. Jared Iron-Smith has been found and is on his way to Stones Shore, under guard."

Amid the gasps and whispers from the gallery Mallory said, "Where did your men find him?"

"A smaller village along the northern coast. He had booked passage on a ship bound for the southern end of Evergrowth. He had some interesting papers on him, papers that would have introduced him to the Iron Guild in Evergrowth as a Master Silver-Hearth."

"I see. That would have made it twice as difficult to find him, at least. I'm glad your search was successful. There were no complications?"

"None at all, and it appears he was travelling alone."

"Please make sure his wife and children are safe. I don't want anything to happen to them. They are not at fault here."

Captain Shield-Forge bowed. "It will be done."

Mallory wrote a letter to Princess Rheeya while she had her tea that morning, informing the other princess that Jared had been found. After tea she had a meeting with Master Spirit-Light and one of the young men he'd been watching as a potential suitor.

As she came into the sitting room both men rose and bowed. "Princess, this is Master Joseph Rose-Gold. He's been working here at the castle for several years. Joseph, this is Princess Mallory Brock Jewel-Rose."

"A pleasure to meet you. I was pleased to hear of your return to us." Joseph wasn't a tall man but he had the striking black hair of the Metalkin and a kind, round face.

"I'm getting accustomed to being here," she replied. "Sit, please. You work here at the castle, doing what?"

"Oh, a little bit of everything I suppose. I work as an assistant to Masters Black-Kettle and Spirit-Light."

"Officially," Emilio said. "Unofficially he's done some work as an investigator and spy."

"I wasn't sure I could tell her that."

Mallory smiled, as much at his words as at the twinkle in his eye. "Well, this is certainly good timing then. I need an investigator."

"I live to serve," Joseph said.

"Princess Stone Rose has voiced concern over the conduct of our guilds in her province. I'd like to hire you to travel there and do an accounting of their records. Actually, I'd like you to do all the provinces."

They stared at her for a long moment. "Say that again," Emilio said.

"I need to do a full accounting and review of all of the Metalkin Guilds on the island," Mallory said, matter-of-factly.

"I – That's a very big job," Joseph said. "I could do it, but it would take months at least."

"I understand that."

"You may not want me working for you that long," Joseph said.

"And there are things we must consider," Emilio said. "He'll need a letter from you that gives him permission to access guild records, he'll need a letter of introduction that will get him into noble households, and into the other castles. He'll need …"

"Clothes, food, a horse, an escort, money for inns …" Joseph cut in.

"Okay," Mallory laughed. "He doesn't need to leave today! Both of you make a list of what is needed and we'll sort out how to get it all. In the meanwhile, why doesn't Joseph review the Iron Guild here in the city for me. Tell me what needs to go into one of these letters and I'll write it right now. We'll have a chance to see if I can handle having you work for me or not."

"That sounds like a plan," Emilio said, handing her paper, ink, and a quill.

Mallory was surprised to see a second plate set out next to hers at lunch, and even more surprised to see Kaelen seated there. He had hardly spoken a word to her since they'd left the Iron-Smith estate on the fifth. Swallowing her surprise, she joined him at the table.

"I didn't see you at court this morning," she said. "You missed Captain Shield-Forge's report."

"I heard the news," Kaelen said. "You really handed one of your own noblemen over to another province?"

"Kaelen, I may be new here, but everywhere I go I hear everyone talking about balance, unity, and interdependence. You live on a single island. Whatever is here, that's what you have. There is no one else to trade with or ally with. A war here would ruin everyone, even the victor."

"You don't know that."

"Don't I? What's the most violent thing you ever witnessed? A fist fight? A duel? You've never seen war. You've never seen children crawling bloody from the wreckage of their homes. You've never seen armies fighting in the streets and the piles of dead bodies along the roads. You have no photo, no video, no record of these things in your past except for writing and writing is dull."

He scoffed. "And you have seen these things?"

"Yes. In the Wide World war is common. Acts of terrorism are common. I've seen buildings destroyed with people still inside of them. A few years before I was born they dropped bombs so powerful they …"

"What's a bomb?"

"A big metal tube full of stuff that goes boom and destroys things. One of these bombs levelled an entire city. Imagine the entire city of Golden Hall gone, levelled to its foundations, in the blink of an eye."

"That's not possible."

"Not here, thank-god, whatever name you give him. It was horrible. And the ones who survived? Their injuries were horrifying."

"What does all of this have to do with Jared Iron-Smith?"

"Jared Iron-Smith was accused of a crime, or multiple crimes, and at least one of these was severe enough that Rheeya wouldn't tell me what they were. I talked to Emilio. If this was about breach of contract, then I could have dealt with him here. This is something severe enough that Rheeya is insisting on dealing with it herself. What was I supposed to do? Shelter a criminal?"

"You don't know that he's done anything wrong. There hasn't been a trial."

"And now there will be. Innocent or guilty he needs to face this. And whatever happened at that mine, or whatever happens at the trial, the Stone Clan are our allies. We're supposed to cooperate with them."

"We're not supposed to allow them to trample on our people!" Kaelen bellowed.

"Am I supposed to allow my people to trample all over Rheeya's? Is that balance?"

"You have no idea what's going on here. None. You've been here three months."

"Eighty-one days. It has been eighty-one days since I walked through that portal. Eighty-one days since I was last able to call and speak to my parents or any of my friends, eighty-one days since I saw my pet goldfish, eighty-one days without coffee or television or a proper bra! I know exactly how long I've been here. I know what I gave up, and I know full well that eighty-one days is not nearly long enough to figure out the politics at work here. But I'm trying. And I'm trying to do what's right."

"How could you possibly know what is right?"

"Because right and wrong aren't exclusive to your precious island. I may not know the political power structures of your guilds or any of your history, but I know right from wrong. My father was a politician. I know what nationalism is. I know what greed and imperialism are. I know what is morally right, even if I don't know all of your laws."

"You're right, you don't understand our laws. You are supposed to be our protector! And you just threw Jared to the enemy!"

"Enemy!? Rheeya is not the enemy! That's what I don't understand. How can you see a peaceful neighbour and economic partner as an enemy? You have no idea what a real enemy is!"

"The Sun Temple raises the girls in seclusion, makes them all best friends, so they think exactly like that. I thought you'd be different since you grew up without them."

"I am very different," Mallory said. "But I grew up through a period of political turmoil. The hippies have the right of it."

"Hippies?"

"People who believe in peace, in loving everyone, in equality."

Kaelen heaved a sigh. "You don't understand. We have no war here, so words like enemy don't mean the same to us as they do to you. You're reacting like I've called her the worst curse word imaginable. I'm not going to wage war on her, and I don't think she'll wage war on me, but she is not Metalkin, and that makes her other, it makes her …"

"Different? What would you do without her? Without her people?"

"The Metalkin are more self-sufficient than you realize. I hope, in time, you'll come to see the importance of what we're doing, and that our ties to the other provinces are less important than the priests tell you."

"What about balance and unity and mutual prosperity?"

"Maybe it's not necessary. Didn't you say that you grew up in a world where people could choose their own paths? That the place of your birth, or your last name, had less control over what you could do with your life? I'm a master in the Blacksmith Guild because that's what my father is, but maybe that's not what I wanted from my life. I've seen children and youth from every province experiment with things they aren't allowed to do or be. I've seen Metalkin girls trying to grow flowers on their windows until they're deemed too old for such things and they're taken away. I've seen Stone Clan lads keeping rabbits for pets until their fathers find out and toss the animals in the stew pot. You're the Metalkin Princess, you will never have the chance to work with animals."

All of Mallory's initial doubts and confusion about the Isle of Light and its people came back to her. Hadn't she wondered all the same things? Hadn't she mourned the loss of her dream to be a veterinarian?

"None of this changes the fact that Jared Iron-Smith broke the law. I had to hand him over to Rheeya. He must stand trial. But, I will review Rheeya's sentencing and if there's anything in there I don't agree with I will ask her to overturn it. And, if he is innocent, I will ensure he receives a formal apology from Rheeya, and the Mining Guild, and that reparations are made for his time and trouble."

Kaelen nodded. "That's something at least. I will reassure Lord Iron-Smith that you are taking the trial of his kin seriously and will look out for Jared's best interests."

"You really are lucky, you know," Mallory said. "You escaped a world of pain and war. Those strangers who came to your island all those years ago, they wouldn't have respected your ways and there would have been war."

"You don't know that for fact," Kaelen said.

"That's their pattern of history," Mallory said. "You had resources and they wanted them."

"We could have arranged a trade deal with them."

"Maybe," Mallory said. "I wonder how different world history would have been if you had stayed in the Wide World."

32nd of Thornrise, 24th Year of the 11th Rebirth
Golden Hall, Metalkin Province

Mallory rolled the letter up and looked at her stewards. "It is done."

"And?" Jaspar pressed.

"And, Rheeya is sending Jared back to Golden Hall. She has revoked the Iron Guild's rights to the largest iron mine in her province. They will have to renegotiate a new contract in order to access that mine again."

"She's put her own miners out of work too," Jaspar said.

"Apparently not. They will be strengthening the mine tunnels that were weakened by Metalkin neglect and they found a deposit of gemstones."

Kaelen's face grew serious. "I hope negotiations are quick."

"That will depend on the Iron Guild. I don't think Rheeya is in the mood to be charitable right now."

"What else happened at the trial?" Jaspar said.

"Jared has been forced to personally pay reparations for every injury and death at the mine, and all of the materials required for the rescue and for repairs. I have already paid Rheeya some of that so, Master Black-Kettle, you will provide Jared's family with a total of that sum. He will need to repay me as well."

"That could bankrupt him, and the entire Iron-Smith family."

"Rheeya was aware of that and has given Jared the option of going to prison until the full debt is paid."

"That's not much of an option," Kaelen growled.

"Men died," Mallory said. "And, on top of all of that, Jared attempted to have the Stone Clan prince assassinated."

Emilio had been nodding along with all of the political and economic talk but sat up straighter at this news. "He did what?"

"Exactly as I said. The man with the knife turned himself in rather than even attempt the act. Rheeya's prince is safe and well. But Jared was charged with treason. He, and every member of the Iron-Smith family has been banished from Stone Clan territory until her next rebirth can rule on the matter. And they owe a yearly tribute to the Stone Rose family for the remainder of this rebirth."

"She's ruined them," Kaelen said. "She's bankrupted the entire family."

"I believe that Rheeya's words on the matter were, 'your family can work, or you will live out your days in a debtor's prison', and I agree with her. Jared is returning under guard. When he arrives put him in a simple room, not in the guest wing, but I don't think he needs to be put in a cell at this point. I want to meet with him. I need to ensure that his family pays and that he doesn't try to run again."

"That is reasonable of you," Jaspar said.

"You're not going to fight this decision?" Kaelen said. "She's embarrassed and ruined one of the prominent families in your province."

"No, the Iron-Smith family embarrassed and ruined themselves. I won't fight it, and I won't let you fight it either."

"You mentioned that Princess Stone Rose had found her prince?" Emilio said.

"I hardly think that's ..."

Mallory cut Kaelen off. "Yes, she did. And the date of the wedding has been set for the eighteenth of Daggerrise. Master Black-Kettle, you'll make arrangements for the trip to …"

"Stones Shore," Emilio said.

"Thank you, yes. I've been so busy learning family names and the names of the local officials that 'Stones Shore' slipped my memory for a moment."

"Perhaps you should focus on your lessons until we leave for Stones Shore," Kaelen said. "You've neglected them throughout this investigation."

"I didn't neglect them, I put them aside. And yes, I will resume them, as soon as I've spoken with Jared Iron-Smith. Is there anything else?"

"I don't think so," Emilio said. "I would like to speak to your tutors to ensure you're getting pertinent lessons on our Stone Clan neighbours before your trip."

"I will speak with the captain of the guard about your escorts and such," Jaspar said.

"I have a meeting to attend," Kaelen said.

"Oh, I'm sorry. I haven't made you late, have I? You should have said something sooner."

"No, this was important. I will see you later." He left with Jaspar close behind him.

Emilio hesitated. "This was a trying time for all of us," he said. "No one expected a reputable guild representative to do something like this."

"Yes, I suppose that's it. I can't really expect Kaelen to be happy with the results of this matter. He's good friends with the Iron-Smith family. We stopped at their estate on the way south from Airon's Gate."

"My job is to guide you in matters of religion, and matters involving the other provinces, but I have lived here for just over thirty years now and I have noticed that most of the powerful nobles families in this province are good friends with one another. I hope you aren't faced with their combined displeasure in this matter."

Kaelen knew they would be waiting in his study and hurried his steps through the castle. He did not want to attend this meeting but he could not reschedule it and if he missed it the repercussions would be worse than anything he would face today.

He paused outside the study door, took a deep breath, and entered with as much confidence as he could muster. They were waiting for him, and he expected, and there was no where left for Kaelen to sit. He glanced about once but no one offered him their spot. He closed the door.

"You're late," Lord South-Mine said. Kaelen may have been 'prince' now, but *he* was the leader of the Loyalists.

"Mallory requested my presence and since she'd received a letter from Princess Rheeya, I thought it best to go there first."

"We've all received letters from family in Stones Shore," Lord South-Mine said. "Jared's trial was public."

"A spectacle," Lord Iron-Smith said. "They made a fool out of him and ruined our family. I can't afford to pay what she's asking. She's left me no choice but to disown Jared, strip him of his second name, and strike him and his sons from our family records."

"You'd really strip his nobility?" Kaelen said.

"What other choice do I have? The man was foolish enough to get caught. I'm glad he's only a second cousin and not one of my own sons. Jared's father and brothers will be upset, of course, but to protect myself and my sons I have no other choice."

"The fault is Rheeya's, of course," Lord South-Mine said. "She was out of control. The reports we've gotten have been full of inconsistencies, but the general consensus is that the Stone Clan Princess has acted inappropriately in this matter."

"Mallory would not agree with you," Kaelen said. "I don't know what reports you've received but I can at least clear the air there and provide you with the truth of the charges and punishments." He proceeded to recount everything he'd learned in his meeting with Mallory.

Lord Iron-Smith shook his head. "He was a fool. And arrogant too. To order the assassination of someone you have a business disagreement with? Even in an attempt to cover your tracks? For that alone I would disown him. Bad for business, and stupid too."

"And you say Mallory supports Rheeya in this?" Lord South-Mine said.

Kaelen nodded. "She refuses to dispute the rulings and has forbidden me from pursuing it in any way."

Lord South-Mine shook his head. "We were trying to avoid this. Why didn't you go to Gold-Heart estate as planned?"

"Mallory refused to go. I tried to talk her into it. Right when the invitation arrived she received a letter from Rheeya. She wanted to stay here, learn as much about the guilds as possible, just in case. There was nothing I could do to dissuade her."

"Kaelen, you were put in this position to control her! Jared discovered a pocket of gems in that mine and was trying to get them out without the Stone Clan being the wiser for it. Now we have to renegotiate with the Stone Clan just to regain access to the iron there!"

"I can't control Princess Rheeya!" Kaelen shouted. "And I can't control Jared Iron-Smith!"

"Iron," Lord Iron-Smith said.

"Whatever," Kaelen snapped. "You're asking me to control matters that are beyond my reach. As for visits, we are leaving in two weeks for Stones Shore to celebrate Princess Rheeya's wedding."

"Encourage her to relax when you return from this trip," Lord South-Mine said. "Perhaps if she sees you trying to care for her she'll be more open to resuming these estate visits and guild visits."

"Maybe hold off on the guild visits until she's forgotten about investigating for more corruption," Kaelen said. "We need to find something to distract her, something she enjoys or someone she enjoys spending time with."

"That was supposed to be you," Lord Iron-Smith said. "I hear you two still sleep in separate rooms."

"She doesn't believe in love at first sight," Kaelen said. "I will not force myself upon her."

"We're not asking you to do something reprehensible," Lord South-Mine said. "But you need to do something to create some sort of bond between the two of you. Find out what she likes to talk about, find out what she did for fun before coming to the island. We're all counting on you."

"I understand."

"If she discovers what we've been doing, if she discovers what we did two-dozen years ago, it could mean all our heads."

Kaelen felt his lunch crawling back up his throat and swallowed hard, resisting the urge to bring his hand to his neck. "It won't come to that," he said. "I'll get control of the situation."

"Good. Be certain you do. And quickly."

**10th of Daggerrise, 24th Year of the 11th Rebirth
Golden Hall, Metalkin Province**

Mallory came outside and was surprised to see two carriages. She stood blinking at them as servants loaded trunks and prepared the horses. Kaelen appeared at her elbow. "Are you ready to see more of the island?" he said.

"Yes, but why do we need two carriages?"

"We're going a lot further this time …"

"Is one going to break down?"

They stared at each other a moment and then he said, "No, we need to bring some servants with us. I believe that girl who's been working with you regularly is coming."

"Cecilia? Oh, that's good. But …"

"One for us, one for the servants," he explained.

"Ah, I see. Wait, you usually ride."

"I have some paperwork to do and that's near impossible on horseback. Besides, we haven't had much time to talk. What good is it to go on a vacation together if we don't have time together?"

"I guess I shouldn't have packed so many books."

"I'm sure you'll still be glad to have a selection. I'm going to check on the preparations."

17th of Daggerrise, 24th Year of the 11th Rebirth
Stones Shore, Stone Clan Province

They were the last to arrive but Mallory was relieved to find out that Vonica had beaten them only by a few hours. "We've waited dinner," Rheeya said as she led Mallory inside.

"You didn't need to do that."

"Of course we did. We were all looking forward to spending the time with you. You can freshen up here and change if you want. Ring when you're ready and someone will show you down to the dining room."

"All right, thank you."

Mallory glanced around the room. The windows were smaller and the décor simpler but otherwise there wasn't much difference between here and Golden Hall. Someone had already brought her trunk up, so she pulled out a dress while she waited for Cecilia to find her.

The door opened, and she turned, ready to greet her maid, but came face to face with her husband. "Can I help you?" she said.

"Uh, this is my room," he said. "They just directed me here."

"Rheeya just escorted me here personally. She said this was … oh no."

"You're thinking that Master Black-Kettle forgot …"

"Or chose not to mention it. I'll ring for someone. They can fix this, I'm sure. It's a big castle."

"It's two nights," Kaelen said. "The bed is huge. You stay on one side, I'll stay on the other. I'll be a perfect gentleman. I'll even wait in the hallway while you dress."

"I don't know. I'd be more comfortable in my own room."

"Can it wait until after dinner, at least? We're both tired and hungry. I don't need to change, so I can give you privacy."

"All right."

Kaelen passed Cecilia in the doorway. The maid looked over her shoulder at the prince then at her princess. "You two have spent a lot of time together already this trip."

Mallory groaned inwardly. The conversation on the journey from Golden Hall to Stones Shore had left much to be desired. Kaelen didn't seem inclined to talk about history or culture or religion, in fact, certain questions made him very defensive. He wasn't interested in asking about her life before coming here, wasn't interested in music or art, and didn't like talking about his family. "You're not going to start playing matchmaker, are you?" she said.

Cecilia just smiled. "You've picked a dress, I see. Let me help you change so you can go eat."

"What about you?"

"They have rooms for us in the servants' wing and we'll be fed in the kitchens while you're eating. Don't worry. Princess Stone-Rose takes good care of her guests, even the near-invisible ones."

"I don't think you're invisible."

"It's the nature of our job to be discreet and subtle. We clean rooms while no one is in them, we serve meals quietly, without drawing attention to ourselves."

"True. It was like that at home too. How's my hair?"

"I'll run a quick brush through it. Luckily you weren't riding or it would be a real mess."

Mallory sat and let Cecilia fuss over her for a moment. "As soon as you're done, can you ring for one of Rheeya's servants? She said she'd have someone show me the way."

"Good, because I've never been here before. You're ready. Try to relax."

"I will. Thank you."

Dinner was a small, simple affair, with just the five princesses, plus Prince Kaelen and Prince Tomas in attendance. Everyone wanted to hear all about the trial and the assassination attempts and Rheeya's time at the mine.

Mallory had been worried about joining them, since they'd known each other all their lives and she was so new but they welcomed her into the conversation, explaining things in light voices and asking her friendly questions.

Just after the soup course Rheeya said, "I know you're hovering just outside the door. You're just getting under foot. You might as well come in here."

A boy of eight appeared in the doorway. "I was trying to stay out of the way." His voice was innocent, almost pleading, but his eyes darted everywhere with obvious excitement.

"I could hear them scolding you. Never mind, you're here now. Fetch the stool from against the wall and set it next to Tomas."

He went quickly before she could change his mind.

"Who's this now?" Kaelen huffed.

"This young man is James Quarry. He is a distant relation of Tomas' and he lives with us here. After the festivities he'll begin his schooling," Rheeya said.

"Why here?" Kaelen pressed. "Why isn't he with his parents?"

Mallory was staring down at her lap. Rheeya's face had gone hard. The boy, James, just smiled. "Oh, I don't have parents anymore." He glanced at Tomas then added, "Sir." He looked around the table. "They don't look anything like you, do they?"

Taeya and Vonica blushed. Mallory looked up again, suddenly curious. Betha grinned.

"We're not twins," Rheeya said.

"Common rabble," Kaelen muttered.

Vonica, who was on the other side of Kaelen, glanced his way, shocked. Luckily no one else seemed to hear. In fact Mallory was smiling.

"Tell me James," Mallory said. "What will you be studying?"

"Dunno yet. To read I guess. Rheeya thinks I could be a steward, or the Captain of the Palace Guard. I hope they teach me to swing a sword."

"Excuse me," Kaelen said. He pushed away from the table.

"Where are you going?" Mallory said.

"To our quarters." He flashed a quick, forced smile in Rheeya's direction and left.

He returned to the room he was sharing with Mallory and dug through the desk there for paper and ink. He sat and wrote an angry letter to Lord South-Mine.

~The situation in Stones Shore is worse than we anticipated. Rheeya's prince is indeed a commoner, single-name and all. She has dressed him up in fine clothes but there is nothing else polished about him. Worse still, she has taken in a common orphan! She plans to teach the boy to read with the aims of making him a steward someday.

She's dismissed Evan Fire-Stone from her service. He was as much a fool as Jared Iron but at least he understood how things are supposed to work. Now, we will be negotiating with Tomas Mason, Prince of the Stone Clan. This does not bode well for us.

None of the others seem to have a problem with this either. We need to alert the other Loyalists in the other provinces and warn them. We may all face serious trials in reaching our goals if this trend continues. ~

He included a short recap of his journey and his attempts to win Mallory over, knowing in the back of his mind that his storming out of the dining room like this wouldn't help matters. He sealed the letter and rang for a servant.

"Take this letter to the aviary and have your Hawk Master send it to Lord South-Mine in the Metalkin Province. And have someone bring me a bottle of wine."

"Yes sir," the servant said with a deep bow.

Kaelen stayed in the room with his wine, staring into the fire, until Mallory finally returned from dinner. Not wanting to discuss dinner, his behaviour, or their accommodations, with her, he closed his eyes and let his head slump against his shoulder.

"Kaelen, did you …" Mallory stopped. She'd spotted Kaelen as soon as she'd entered but now noticed that he hadn't moved. She peered around the chair and pursed her lips. In a softer voice she said, "Are you awake?"

He didn't stir.

Still frowning Mallory quickly changed into her nightgown and crawled under the covers. Dimmed the bedside lantern and snuggled down, intent on getting some sleep before the big ceremony the next day.

**18th of Daggerrise, 24th Year of the 11th Rebirth
Stones Shore, Stone Clan Province
The Wedding of Rheeya Stone Rose**

Mallory woke alone to an empty room. She rang and Cecilia quickly appeared with another servant in tow. "He'll take your breakfast order and bring you a tray," Cecilia explained. "While I get you dressed." She helped Mallory into a robe as she talked.

"Oh. Uh, an egg, maybe some bread and sausage?"

"Of course, Princess," he said with a bow.

"Do you know where Prince Kaelen is?"

"I haven't seen him this morning but I'll ask the other servants."

When he'd gone Cecilia set to work on Mallory's hair. The dress would have to wait until after Mallory ate.

"How did you sleep?"

"Well enough. I feel like I've only just gotten used to the bed in Golden Hall and now I have to sleep somewhere new. It was nicer than the inns. Is your room okay?"

"Yes." She couldn't help but smile. "You are an odd one."

"I grew up in a completely different world."

Mallory paid close attention to the wedding service. Her own had passed in a blur and now she wanted to hear the prayers and oaths that were being said.

The temple here was similar in construction to the one in Golden Hall, a round room with a compass rose inlaid in the floor and small altars around the walls. It was more modestly decorated, with carved stone pillars rather than silver trinkets and cloth of gold table runners. It was also the first room she'd seen in the castle with decent windows.

Rheeya was a radiant bride and she and Tomas couldn't stop smiling at each other through the entire service, even when everyone else was yawning and their attention was faltering. Mallory glanced over at Kaelen who sat stiffly with a bored expression on his face.

Even during those first days he didn't smile at me like that. Oh, he looked all adoring, but he didn't smile like that. I have never seen him smile like that for anyone. Perhaps it's just a difference in each provinces, but I wish he wasn't so stiff and serious all the time.

Mallory's wedding dinner had been huge, filling the great hall at Golden Hall to bursting with nobles and guild representatives and visitors. She hadn't fought it because it was tradition, but she'd felt completely overwhelmed by the whole thing, and other than her run-in with Kaelen's father, she remembered very little of it. She was surprised when they were led back to the modest dining room after the service.

All the princesses, and Prince Kaelen were there, along with James and a middle-aged man with a minor limp who was introduced as Tyson Mason and could only be Tomas's father. Two other couples were seated at the table and were introduced as Lord and Lady Black-Mountain, and their son Dwayne with his new wife.

The atmosphere at dinner was light-hearted and casual. The laughter was loud and frequent. The only one who refused to relax was Kaelen but Mallory found it easy to ignore him with James sitting on her other side.

With a conspiratorial glance around the table James nudged Mallory and said, "Did you want to hear the frog story now?"

Mallory smiled. "Tell me."

"Rheeya and the other princesses grew up in the Sun Temple. There's these special rooms there just for them when they're little. They had lots of classes and stuff but they got to play too. One day they were outside and they were catching frogs even though they weren't really supposed to. They snuck all the frogs back into the palace with them. But then they had all these noisy squirmy frogs and no real place to keep them. That's when they got the idea."

"Who got the idea?"

"Oh, Rheeya says she doesn't remember. I think she does but she doesn't want to point fingers at just one of the girls. Besides, they all wanted to do it and they all helped. Even though Rheeya insists she had 'very little to do with the whole thing'."

"Oh, I'm sure she likes to say that," Mallory said, grinning. "Where did they put the frogs?"

"There was this one priest …"

"No."

James was nodding, grinning. "Honourable Mathias. He was a priest and a scholar but he was in charge of the kitchen staff that worked directly with the princesses."

"In his shoes?"

"No. They stuffed them all in cooking pots in the kitchen cupboards. They thought the kitchen staff would find them first but Honourable Mathias was doing an inspection or something."

"Oh!" Mallory let out a laugh so loud she drew smiles from Vonica and Betha and a scowl from Kaelen.

James kept grinning and nodding. "Rheeya says there was a lot of shouting. The girls were in some history lecture with one of the scholars and they could hear him from like a huge distance away. They were all trying not to laugh, or smile, or anything. Can you imagine all those frogs hopping around the kitchen and the Honourable Mathias going red in the face and chasing them with a frying pan?"

"He didn't?"

"I don't know. That's just how Rheeya tells the story."

"Oh, that's fantastic. That beats anything I did as a child."

"You have to tell me some of your stories now!"

"Okay, okay, just let me think."

She and James talked and laughed through the entire meal, sometimes just the two of them, sometimes being drawn into larger conversations around the table. Betha and Lord Black-Mountain were enjoying a similar loudly joyous conversation at the other end of the table.

At some point Kaelen left, though Mallory wasn't exactly sure when. Vonica too turned in early, but she took the time to say goodnight to everyone before leaving. When Mallory finally retired for the evening her cheeks hurt from smiling and her ribs hurt from laughing so much.

26th of Daggerrise, 24th Year of the 11th Rebirth
Golden Hall, Metalkin Province

"It's good to be home," Kaelen said as he stepped down from the carriage. Whatever good mood he'd been in before the trip had evaporated while they were in Stones Shore and the return trip had been tense and quiet.

"Yes, it's good to be back," Mallory agreed, if only because it was nice to be out of that carriage and off the road. She wasn't quite ready to think of this as 'home' just yet.

They'd made it just in time it seemed. The sun was disappearing behind the western skyline of the city. The stable lads were out in full force, trying to get the horses stabled as quickly as possible. There had been a stable near the embassy in India where she and other wealthy or privileged children had gone for lessons. She knew she wasn't supposed to go into the stable here, especially while they were so busy, but she missed the smell and the sounds, so she hovered along the edge of the courtyard, just watching and enjoying what she could.

"Hey! Watch it!"

The sudden raised voice and resulting confusion drew her attention to the other corner of the courtyard. A man in a dark travelling cloak had collided with one of the stable lads, sending a saddle tumbling to the ground. The lad was stammering and trying to pick the saddle up again.

"That saddle is worth more than you are," the man said. "Watch where you're going next time."

"Yes sir. I'm sorry sir."

The man pushed by and stalked across the courtyard, his face set in a scowl.

Mallory watched him with a mixture of displeasure and intense curiosity. She hurried to the stable and caught the lad on his way out again. "Are you all right?" she said.

The lad stared at her for a long moment and then bowed so low she thought his nose might brush his knees. "Princess Jewel-Rose."

She smiled. "It's okay, you can stop bowing. Were you hurt just now?"

"No. And the saddle is fine too," he said, still bowing.

"I'm not worried about the saddle."

"You're not?" Now he looked at her, surprised.

"Who was that man?"

"Oh. I don't know his name. He showed up here maybe a day after you and the prince left for the wedding in Stones Shore. Don't know what he does. He sort of drifts through each evening."

"Is he always like that?"

"I don't know. That was the first time I talked to him."

"Thank you. Is the Stable Master about?"

"Yes Princess, but he's busy. I can fetch him though."

"No. I should go in and eat. Tell him I'll come and speak with him after my dinner."

"Yes Princess."

It was much quieter when she returned to the stables that evening. The stable master was waiting just inside for her, though he was puttering with some tack while he waited. She smiled at that. *There are just some people who can't stand to be idle.*

"Horse Master," she said, announcing her presence.

"Princess," he responded, setting the job aside and turning to her. "You left quite the impression on the lad."

"I do hope he wasn't hurt."

"No, no harm done. What can I help you with?"

"That man, the boy said he arrived shortly after I left. Do you know his name?"

"You mean the scowl-faced gentleman in the dark cloak?"

"Yes."

"He goes by 'Hunter', don't know if that's his given name or his family name, it's the only name he's ever given. He spends a lot of time with the guards in the evenings, throwing dice and drinking. He's got a mean look about him."

"You've no idea where he came from or why he's here?"

"No, Princess. I will say that with a name like that, he's almost certainly from among the Car … the Animal People. And in my opinion, he's trouble waiting to happen."

"Thank you for that. I'll see if I can find out why he's here, without speaking to him directly." As she left the stables she paused. She knew the stable master was right, and that she should heed his advice and stick to her own as well. And yet that nagging curiosity from earlier had returned. *There will be guards about. He won't try anything.*

Instead of crossing the courtyard and going straight inside she turned and walked towards the side doors closer to the temple, taking the path that would lead her past the barracks.

She could hear men's laughter ahead and someone was playing a stringed instrument. There were a few men lounging outside the barracks and by the sounds of it, more inside. She walked along, only occasionally glancing their way, as if her reason for being there was only to get somewhere else.

At first, she didn't see him. With his hood up, he blended into the shadows. He had his feet up on a log and there was smoke drifting up from the shadows around his face. One of the guards nudged him and he accepted a tankard of whatever the other men were drinking. He didn't seem to notice her at all, none of them did, even though she'd paused there on the path to watch.

The smoke was coming from a pipe that he pulled from his lips before taking a long drink from the tankard. He said something to the guards that Mallory couldn't hear, and the other men laughed.

Mallory shook herself out of her reverie and continued down the path. She wasn't sure why she was so interested in this stranger and the intensity of her curiosity scared her. *He's trouble. Stay away from him from now on.*

From under his deep hood Hunter watched the princess retreat along the path and smiled. *So, she's back, is she? Well, that make things much more interesting.*

27th of Daggerrise, 24th Year of the 11th Rebirth
Golden Hall, Metalkin Province

Emilio Spirit-Light was on his way back to his sitting room for a quick midday meal. He'd had a productive morning and was looking forward to chatting with the princess later. He hummed a little as he walked, his mind running through things he had to do and questions he wanted to ask people.

"Master Spirit-Light," called a voice from behind him.

He paused and turned. There were several servants and castle staff walking in either direction, but none were really looking at him. He saw a hand raised and stepped to the side to see around a maid with a basket of laundry just as Devin Sun-Stag stepped around the slower moving servant.

"Master Spirit-Light, I was looking for you." He stopped next to the steward.

"I'm just on my way to eat. Can this wait?"

"No. But don't let me keep you from your meal."

Emilio stifled his sigh. "I can ring up for a second place setting."

"No, no need. I'm not very hungry. In fact, I'm not feeling very well at all and I'm deeply concerned about it."

His annoyance became concern and he started walking again. "Join me then. I'd best hear this now."

"Thank you."

"Have you been to see Bernard yet?"

"No. If I couldn't find you, I'd have gone to him. I'd rather talk to you about his. You're far more reasonable, and rational, then he is."

Emilio didn't know if the words were empty praise meant to flatter him or a genuine observation, but he was inclined to agree with them either way. "You were right to seek me out." He opened the door and ushered Devin inside. "There will be servants coming any moment with my food. We'll wait until they've left to discuss this."

"Of course."

An awkward silence settled over them. Thankfully it was short-lived as three servants entered with food, wine, and dishes. One stopped and stared at Devin. "I didn't know you were entertaining. I'll go fetch …"

"No need," Emilio said. "He's already eaten. I'm just sneaking in an extra meeting while I eat."

"Of course. We'll wait for your summons before coming to tidy up then." He bowed, and they left the steward to his food and his guest.

"Sit. Tell me what is troubling you."

Devin did as he was bid. "It started about two weeks ago I guess, I'm not even sure. I noticed I was tired in the mornings, like I'd had a restless night. I turned in early a few nights, trying to catch up on my sleep but it didn't seem to help. I didn't pay it much mind until this morning. I woke up with this." He rolled up one pant leg to reveal a bruise.

"How did you get that?"

"I don't know. From the size of the bruise, I'd say I'd certainly remember running into something."

"Could it have happened while you slept?"

"There's nothing in my bed that could have done this, and I'd have remembered rolling out of bed. Unless I was sleep walking, I don't see how that's possible."

Emilio frowned. "I'm not sure what this has to do with me, or the Dark Spirit you claim is possessing you. Do you think the Dark Spirit did this? Perhaps it's trying to get out."

"I'm not sure why it would try to exit through my leg," Devin said. "The thing is, last night is the first time in days, maybe weeks, that I remembered anything I dreamt."

"What did you dream?" Emilio had little interest, but he wanted the man gone and the quickest route to that goal seemed to be humouring him.

"I dreamt about Princess Mallory. In my dream it was late. She was walking though the castle grounds, and I was watching her. The Dark Spirit was watching her, I could feel it looking through my eyes. It was very interested in her. It's just a dream, I know, but …"

As Devin spoke Emilio's interest and concern grew. "But for you to have this dream, and remember it, the same night that Mallory returns home?"

"She's back?" Something leapt inside Devin's chest.

Emilio was studying him. "You didn't know?"

"I didn't go to the stables yesterday, or today. No one has any real reason to tell me her comings and goings."

"This is strange indeed. If I had to guess, I'd say your restlessness is due to the Dark Spirit wrestling with whatever it is in you that is keeping it in check. It's been months, and you've shown no outward sign. I would recommend you continue to turn in early. Dark Spirits are strongest at night. Maybe you'll keep it at bay longer this way."

"Or maybe it sees me as weaker when I sleep. Maybe I should be sleeping during the day when it is weak also."

"Maybe. We have no information on this. You are the first person to our knowledge to ever last so long with a Dark Spirit possessing you. Continue doing what you're doing for a few days and we'll monitor if it gets better or worse. Then we'll make a decision about whether or not you should change what you're doing. And please come to see me or Honourable Bernard daily from now on." He turned his attention to his meal.

Devin hesitated a moment. "I know I have a room in the staff wing here, but I was thinking of moving out to the stable for a bit. Maybe if I'm closer to the horses it would help. And being away from people in case something does happen isn't a bad idea either."

"Yes, yes, if you think it will help, and if the Stable Master approves."

"Thank you for seeing me," Devin said as he left. He wasn't sure what he'd expected from Master Spirit-Light. This entire time both the steward and the priest had shown only a passive interest in his condition. *They probably don't even believe me. I wouldn't believe me. It's not possible. But I feel this thing inside of me, fighting harder every day.*

The only reason he continued to go to either Emilio or Bernard was because he knew they would take his failure to show as a sign the Dark Spirit was taking over, and they'd order him tied to a bed somewhere. The only reason he continued to trust in their advice was because he didn't know what to do either.

34th of Daggerrise, 24th Year of the 11th Rebirth
Golden Hall, Metalkin Province

The last time Mallory had attended a service in the Golden Hall Temple, Honourable Bernard had waxed poetic about Princess Vonica Bright Rose finding her prince and adding further stability to The Pact. It hadn't taken Vonica long at all after her return from Stones Shore to find her prince and now Mallory and Kaelen had to leave for another royal wedding.

Thankfully, this time Kaelen intended to ride with the guards. That meant only one carriage and Mallory could travel with Cecilia. Since the Sun Temple province neighboured the Metalkin province so they had a shorter trip ahead of them and it would help that they weren't stopping to visit any nobles this time. On the way home from Stones Shore Kaelen had insisted on stopping to visit his second cousin's family. The visit had lasted only a day, but Mallory had been bored out of her mind.

"The Sun Temple has the grandest library," Cecilia explained as the horses, guards, and carriage started on their way south. "And the largest temple to Airon. I hope I have time to visit the temple. There's an altar to the Metalkin Spirit Guides there and I want to leave an offering."

"I'll have meetings and such, and you're not responsible for my laundry while we're away, so I'm sure there will be time."

Cecilia went on. "My father sent a few things with me, things he wanted me to put on the altar there, if I had the chance."

"That's one thing I still have trouble with," Mallory said. "All this stuff about gods and spirits."

"You don't think they're real, do you?"

Mallory couldn't tell if Cecilia was amused by this or just curious. "I don't know. Where I come from there are close to a dozen religions and philosophical traditions and they all think they're right and they all think their gods are real, or that no gods are real. Some believe in saints, others in ghosts, others in demons or monsters or powerful spiritual beings."

The serving girl mulled this over for a moment. "How strange. Which group worshipped Airon?"

"None did. There were religions that worshiped sun gods, and there are some similarities between Airon and some of the deities back in the Wide World, but I hadn't heard his name until I came here."

"He's real. We've all seen the results of his power."

The absolute certainty in the girl's voice grated at Mallory. "But have you seen any sign of that power with your own eyes? Or have you just heard stories?"

"You mean like the miracles of the Prophet Abner? No one alive today has seen miracles like that. And it's been eleven generations since The Pact. No one alive today, except for you and the priests who fetched you have seen the Wide World or the people who live there."

Mallory pushed on. "How do you know the Pact happened? Or that it really was eleven generations ago? How do you know the miracles happened?"

Cecilia's reply was softer. "Well, I don't. But what about the miracle in South Bay? Or the one at the Sun Temple?"

"What? You mean the glowing lights around the princesses when they found their soul mates? Okay, I'll admit that's pretty neat and I don't know how it happened, but why didn't it happen when I met Kaelen?"

"That's something you should ask a priest," Cecilia said. "I'm not educated enough to answer that question for you."

"We're headed to the Sun Temple, so I just might do that."

36th of Daggerrise, 24th Year of the 11th Rebirth
Golden Hall, Metalkin Province

"Ah, Emilio, there you are."

Emilio stopped, turned, and quickly buried his impatience and irritation under a thin, professional smile. "Jaspar."

"I have some papers here, the Equine Guild, and thought you could help me with them. They seem to be going on about …"

"Jaspar, can this wait until tomorrow?"

"I'm meeting with them tomorrow. This proposed change in their contract is bothering me and I can't see a reason for it."

"Why are you meeting with them tomorrow? The princess just left yesterday for the Sun Temple. Shouldn't this wait until she returns?"

"These contracts must be dealt with. I think it's a good thing I'm dealing with it, personally. I think the Animal People are trying to take advantage of Mallory's inexperience. That's what this clause is. They want to know what they can get away with."

"Jaspar, I'm on my way to a meeting. I cannot help you with this now."

"Oh. I didn't realize. I thought, with the princess gone, you wouldn't have much to do, whereas my job is that much more important when she's gone. She relies on me to …"

"You don't rule here," Emilio said. "We're stewards. We were never meant to rule."

"Yes, yes. I'm sorry to have bothered you. I'll deal with this on my own." Muttering he wandered back up the hallway the way he'd come from.

Emilio gave his head a shake and hurried on his way.

He entered the study and turned to shut the door, talking as he went. "I'm sorry I'm late. I was held up by …"

"Well, it's about time."

Emilio stiffened and turned. "Excuse me?"

"It's rude to keep someone waiting."

Emilio just stared at the man who leaned against the wall near the window. He was dressed in simple, earth-tone clothes and had the same light-coloured hair as Devin Sun-Stag, but his posture was arrogant and his face, set in a sneer, was that of a stranger. "Who are you? What are you doing in here?"

The stranger laughed. "What am I doing here? You told me to come here."

Emilio frowned. "Devin?"

The stranger laughed. "In a way, yes, I suppose I am."

Emilio tried to study the man. Aside from the hair and the clothes he was about the right height to be Devin, though he held himself taller, and he had the same slender build. The eyes were the same colour but they lacked any warmth or compassion. The face though was different, enough so that a quick glance would have convinced Emilio they were two different people. Now, the longer he looked, the more he thought they could have been related.

"You're possessed," Emilio said. "It's starting to show."

The stranger, Hunter, laughed.

"Why now?"

The question was met with a wide, toothy grin. "Wouldn't you like to know," Hunter said in a sing-song voice. He laughed again and pushed away from the wall. He strode past the steward and out the door.

"Airon preserve us," Emilio muttered.

1st of Hoofrise, 24th Year of the 11th Rebirth
Sun Temple Complex, Sun Temple Province
Wedding of Vonica Bright Rose

Mallory could have been imagining things, but she was certain Balder Gold-Spark was making even more grandiose statements at this wedding than he had at either hers or Rheeya's. *Probably because Vonica is the Sun Temple Princess.*

She had to admit that everything about the Sun Temple Complex was impressive. The buildings sprawled out around a central courtyard, each wing opening into the wide, sun-lit space, and each wing connecting to the temple itself. She'd had a tour yesterday, but she was certain she'd get lost here for weeks if not for servants and scholars to point her in the right direction or take her where she needed to go.

After the ceremony there was a dinner and ball. Mallory and Kaelen were seated at a table with the other princesses and with Prince Tomas and the boy, James. James and Betha were deep in conversation all evening and often one or the other would burst into joyful laughter.

"I like this place," she said to Kaelen at one point in the evening.

"I suppose," Kaelen said. He was focused on his food.

When they were done eating Kaelen took her around and introduced her to nobles and guild masters while music played and people danced. A few times she looked at the dancers wistfully but there was always someone else to talk to until she thought she'd scream at the forced politeness of it all.

When Kaelen excused himself to go talk to a few nobles waiting to have a word with him, Mallory slipped unnoticed from the hall and returned to her room early.

2nd of Hoofrise, 24th Year of the 11th Rebirth
Sun Temple Complex, Sun Temple Province

Mallory woke up alone. She was more accustomed to that than to waking up next to Kaelen as she had the day before. This was far more pleasant. She'd told Cecilia to take the morning off since she wasn't sure when she'd be rising so she dressed herself in a simple day dress, wishing all the while for a pair of jeans and a proper bra. She pulled her hair back in a simple pony tail and went out in search. It didn't matter at this point if she found her husband, one of the other princesses, a servant, or some food.

In some ways the Sun Temple was so similar to Golden Hall it confused her. The hallways were the same grey stone, lined with woven tapestries and broken by heavy wooden doors with their black iron fittings. And yet, this hallway should turn left, not right, and the tapestry at the end was one she'd never seen before.

It's like those first few days in Golden Hall all over again, only now Cecilia can't help me.

"Mallory!"

She turned at the sound of her name and smiled, as much delighted as she was relieved. "Betha, Taeya, good morning."

"Have you eaten?" Betha said.

"No. I was just looking for someone to point me in the direction of breakfast."

"We ate in our rooms."

"I didn't think of that. I'm not used to servants and room service, even after three and a half months. I mean I eat in my own room at Golden Hall but I wasn't sure that would be okay here."

"It's okay," Taeya said. "For us this is normal, but for you …"

"For me this is still very strange," Mallory laughed.

"Where's your husband?" Betha said. "Didn't he call for breakfast?"

"I don't know where he is," Mallory admitted.

Taeya looped an arm through Mallory's. "Let's get you breakfast. There's nothing formal going on until midday."

They wound up in a small, informal dining room with tea for all three of them and breakfast for Mallory. "How are you settling?" Taeya asked.

Mallory sighed. "You live very different lives here, like something out of one of our history text books. The clothes, the food, the books, it's all … ancient. And the people …"

"You really didn't have servants?" Betha said.

"Oh, well, my father was an ambassador. He, uh, didn't live in the country where he was born. He worked with a foreign government on behalf of his government. There were some maids at the embassy, and we had a cook for formal events, but I dressed myself and bathed myself and generally made my own meals or went to a restaurant."

"Restaurant?"

"A dining establishment, like an inn but just for food, no bedrooms."

Betha nodded in understanding.

"It's not the servants, really, it's the fighting. Does everyone in your court fight you every step of the way?"

"Not really," Taeya said.

"Sometimes," Betha admitted. "I'm sure your stewards just feel you have a lot to learn. They're overbearing most of the time, but they are there to help."

"It's not just my stewards. The guilds refuse to deal with me, they refuse the reviews and even my husband tells me I shouldn't be investigating, that I'll offend people. Somehow I just know that this investigation Rheeya started is onto something but no one in my province will support me."

"No one?"

"Well, there are a few people who are helping me, but I feel like every step forward is hindered by two or three steps backwards."

"Stand your ground," Betha said. "Don't be afraid to shout orders and give ultimatums, at least sometimes. I don't know how the governments worked where you came from, but here, you're the princess. Everyone answers to you."

Mallory sighed. "I hope it's that easy." *Because so far, it hasn't been.*

A few years ago, a friend of her mother's had gotten her the job in the palace. The work was hard, carrying linens, scrubbing floors, dealing with entitled nobles, but Cecilia had been grateful for it. She was only common born, and only a servant, but among servants, working in the personal wing of the palace carried its own mark of prestige. She'd worked hard, proving her worth to the head of housekeeping time and again, and her reward had been an assignment to the personal rooms of Princess Jewel-Rose herself.

She'd expected to remain anonymous, just one of the many girls who tended to the princess's needs. Instead she'd become Mallory's personal maid and primary companion, travelling with her to Stones Shore, and now to the Sun Temple itself.

Hard to believe a common born maid from the poorest district in Golden Hall is placing an offering on the altar in the Sun Temple.

This Temple was the same as the one in Golden Hall, same round room, same domed roof, same sun mosaic on the floor, only this one was much larger. There were five alcoves around the edge of the main chamber, each corresponding with a capital city's location on the compass rose, each dedicated to a different spirit guide. The Metalkin altar was in the northeast alcove, a chest-high iron table surrounded by and adorned with offerings and candles. There was a low stool, also iron, but someone had placed a thin cushion on it. Here, Cecilia sat, meditating on the gifts of her people, her body and mind open to the voices of her spirit guides.

The voices she heard first belonged to people. Men. She assumed priests or acolytes until she heard one say, "You're sure we're alone?" There was something familiar about that cold voice.

"Yes, we're alone. The priests and acolytes had a vigil yesterday while the rest of us were at dinner. They're all in bed still or eating. The temple is closed to the public today."

"We'd better not be interrupted by any acolytes."

"I've got this under control."

Cecilia kept herself tucked in the shadows of the alcove, moving with practiced silence until she could see out across the temple with little risk of being seen. There were two men, seated in the benches near the palace wing doors where Cecilia had entered only minutes earlier. One she'd never seen before, but from his hair and clothes she guessed he was Metalkin and wealthy, though she couldn't see his face. The other was Prince Kaelen.

"Do you?" Kaelen was saying. "Because I thought the whole point of shipping the gems through this province was to keep the operation secret!"

"How was I supposed to know the blacksmith would see them? And how was I supposed to know he was a Rosie?"

"You should have known his loyalties, that's part of having all of this under control! You should have known he was untrustworthy and planned the transport route accordingly."

The other man looked away. "What's done is done. We've covered our tracks."

"A fire? Having a man killed?"

He looked back at the prince, pinning him with a hard stare. "You're not getting squeamish, are you?"

Kaelen bristled. "Of course not. But these are not subtle means. We're trying to stay out of sight."

"No, *we're* trying to stay out of sight. *You're* supposed to be trying to get control of that princess! Is she going to back us against the other provinces or not? And if she's not, how are we going to keep her out of our business?"

"I'm working on it," Kaelen growled. "So far she hasn't been a problem. We've managed to stall her investigation at every turn. There's nothing for her to discover."

"Oh, there's a whole lot for her to discover. And if she finds out, she's going to wipe out half the nobles in Metalkin Province."

"Wipe out? Do you really think she'd start beheading people?"

"Yes. Some of us are destined for the block if this fails. Some will be stripped of their second name, their titles, their lands, their wealth. If we fail it will reshape Metalkin society. If we succeed, we'll …"

The clang of metal against stone cut his words off abruptly. Cecilia sucked in a breath and looked down at her feet. She'd been trying to get a better view and her toe had caught a shield leaning against the altar, sending it crashing to the ground. Both men stood.

"What was that?" Kaelen said. "You said we were alone!"

A door opened and both men turned the other way as a priest and three acolytes entered.

"...must be scraped off the stone and fresh candles set in all the holders along... Prince Kaelen, I didn't know you were in here."

Kaelen glared at the now bowing priest and his flock of acolytes. "Yes. We were just taking a few quiet minutes of reflection before I have to return home."

"Of course, of course. We will go about our work as quietly as possible."

As they spread out across the temple Kaelen elbowed his companion. "Come. Let us visit the Metalkin altar once." They walked slowly together, looking in all of the alcoves as though they were admiring the art and offerings there.

They paused at the Metalkin Shrine and Kaelen's companion bent and picked up the shield. "It was likely just this we heard," he said. He leaned it against the altar again. "It slid, all on its own, until it hit the floor."

"Are you sure? If someone heard us..."

"Who? The temple was closed. The priest was expecting the temple to be empty when he came in. We both know what has to be done. We'll go our separate ways, now that our moment of quiet reflection is over. Hopefully the next time I see you we will be celebrating the success of all our plans."

They continued around the room until they got back to the door that led to the palace wing. The door was ajar. Kaelen paused, staring at it for a moment. *The priests came in the other door, from their own wing, and I'm sure I closed this one when we came in. Was there someone here? Who? And what did they hear?*

Cecilia ran through the halls, out of breath. She knew full well it was only the timely appearance of the priest that had saved her. She'd slipped from the alcove, staying low and out of sight while Kaelen made his search of the room. While he studied her hiding place she'd eased open the door to the palace wing and slipped through, leaving it unlatched behind her so as not to make a sound.

What do I do? What do I do? Who do I tell? Mallory. I need to tell Mallory!!

She ran back to the princess's rooms but they were empty. Completely out of breath, and with no idea where to look, she dropped into one of the chairs to await Mallory's return.

After the council meeting Mallory spent some time exploring the library and then met with Kaelen, the princesses, Prince Tomas, and Prince Johann for dinner. She was delighted to discover James was attending as well but James was occupied with Betha all evening.

The meal was quiet and simple and they all stuck to light-hearted topics, avoiding talking about the council meeting or politics in general.

After the meal Kaelen stood. "We'd like to leave early tomorrow so we should turn in."

"Oh," Mallory said. "I suppose so."

"It was good to see you again," Vonica said.

"Keep in mind what I said," Betha said.

"Hopefully we will see you again soon," Taeya added.

They walked back to their room together. "We really must remember to request separate rooms next time," Mallory said.

"It's tradition," Kaelen said.

"Most Honourable Balder said I wasn't the first princess to request separate rooms from her prince."

"It has happened before, of course, but this isn't tradition, it isn't normal. The staff at Golden Hall are willing to accommodate us because that is our home. When we're visiting, things are different, and we have to compromise."

"If you say so. These places are so big, I can't believe it would be a bother."

"It's one of the things you'll get used to."

They entered the room to find Cecilia setting out Mallory's night gown, robe, and slippers. She curtsied. "Princess, Prince, do you need any further assistance this evening?"

"No, thank you," Mallory said.

"Are you ... uh ... both turning in?"

"Yes," Kaelen said.

"Is something wrong?" Mallory said.

"No, of course not. There was some small matter I wished to speak with you about, that's all."

"Can it wait until later?" Kaelen said. "We have an early start and we're both tired."

"Of course," Cecilia said. "It's not an emergency. I'll speak with you later, Princess. And I'll arrange for an early breakfast for you both. Good-night."

"Good-night, Cecilia," Mallory said.

Kaelen watched the servant leave, suspicion setting his mental wheels moving. "You know," he said. "I've missed you today. Perhaps I'll ride in the carriage with you tomorrow."

"Oh. But we didn't bring a second carriage for Cecilia."

"It will be a little tight, but we'll manage. I could use the break from riding, and it would be nice to spend some time with you."

"Well, it's as much your carriage as it is mine so if you want to ride with us there's no problem at all."

5th of Hoofrise, 24th Year of the 11th Rebirth
Golden Hall, Metalkin Province

As soon as the carriage clattered into the castle's courtyard in Golden Hall, Kaelen said, "Mallory, I need to borrow your maid for a moment."

"Oh? Why?"

"I have some things that need taking care of and I don't want to waste time hunting down another servant."

"Oh, well, I suppose so," Mallory said.

Cecilia's heart was beating too fast. "If you tell me where," she said. "I can send someone along to help you. I'm supposed to see to …"

"No, it'll be easier if you just come with me." That carriage rocked to a halt. "Come. I don't want to waste time."

Trembling a little, Cecilia followed Kaelen out of the carriage and into the castle. As they walked, he said, "Where are you from, Celia?"

She grimaced at the error but didn't correct him. "From here in the city."

"You have family here?"

"Some. Mother and father. My sister works at an estate just over the Animal People border. I haven't seen her in a while. Why?"

"Follow me." He took her to Jaspar Black-Kettle's study and ushered her inside.

"Ah, you're back," Jaspar said. "Who is this?"

"This young lady is the maid who has been taking such good care of the princess."

"Oh?" Jaspar said, raising an eyebrow. This was the first he'd heard of the girl and wasn't sure why Kaelen was bringing her to his attention.

"I've been impressed with her service these past months and I thought a reward was in order. She's just informed me that she has a sister working west of here, at an estate in the Animal People province. I'd like you to fund a trip for her to visit her sister, provide her with transportation or pay a caravan to take her, and bring her back in a few weeks. I'll write a letter to her sister's employer, requesting a spare bed and some time for the two of them to spend together."

"That's very generous of you," Jaspar said.

"Yes," Cecilia said, still trembling a little. "Very generous. But Princess Jewel-Rose …"

"While the other girls don't know her the way you do, I'm sure she'll still be well looked after," Kaelen said. "Please, it would warm my heart to be able to do this small thing for you."

It's that easy for him to send me away on a vacation, how easy would it be for him to send me away for good? Or arrange an accident? He suspects, and men like Kaelen don't need proof to act out of self-preservation. "All right. A thousand times, thank you. This really is too generous."

"Leave me the name of the family your sister works for and go pack," Kaelen said. "I need to speak with Mallory and then I will see you on your way."

Making sure I don't speak with her before I leave. Could I leave a note? Would it be safe? Or should I wait and try again when I return. If I return.

I'm not safe any longer, no matter where I go. "Of course. It won't take me long to pack."

When Cecilia had gone, Jaspar said, "Why her? Why such an extravagant gift? Another lover?"

Kaelen scowled. "No. I suspect she may have overheard something dangerous and I'm trying to keep her away from Mallory. Have her ride arranged within the hour if possible. I want her away from the castle today."

"I see. I'll get it done."

"Good." Kaelen went to Mallory's room to find she was just thanking the servants who had brought her trunks up from the courtyard. "Do you have plans this evening?" he said.

"I was hoping Cecilia would come and help me unpack," Mallory said. "Otherwise, no. I was just going to relax for the evening."

"Actually, Cecilia is going to visit her sister in the Animal People province for a few days, maybe a week or so."

"Oh? When did this happen?"

"Just now. You inspired me to do something nice for someone whom the nobles tend to overlook. Servants rarely get time away from their job, and when they do, it's the odd day to do their own laundry and attend church services." He reached out and took her hand, kissing the back like he'd done those first days after she'd come though the gate. "She's taken such good care of you, and I wanted to thank her properly."

"Oh. Oh wow. That's so nice of you. I'm sure she's excited. Well, another girl can come and help me while she's gone."

"I'll find someone. Did you want a bath this evening?"

"That sounds nice," she said. *Not as nice as a bath back home would have been. I wonder how much effort it would take to get them to make me a longer tub?* "And some dinner."

"Of course. May I dine with you this evening?"

"All right. I think I'd like that."

Kaelen kissed her hand again and then, with a smile, he was gone.

2nd of Starfall, 24th Year of the 11th Rebirth
Golden Hall, Metalkin Province

It had been nearly a month since Mallory and Kaelen had returned from the Sun Temple. Mallory had been making do with other maids as Cecilia was still off enjoying her visit with her sister. It didn't really matter who helped her dress or brushed her hair, but the truth was, she missed Cecilia. She'd come to rely on the girl for advice as much as for dressing.

And some advice would have been welcome. She'd been struggling these last few weeks.

After Rheeya's run-in with both the Merchant Bank and the Iron Guild, and Vonica's discovery of deep-rooted corruption, it was clear to all of the princesses that something needed to be done. Only they hadn't really settled on a plan during their conference since Most Honourable Gold-Spark had been focused on getting Princess Betha and Princess Taeya married off.

Still, Vonica had given her some good ideas on where and how to start and she'd come home ready to be useful and productive.

She quickly realized that neither Kaelen or Jaspar had forgiven her for Jared's trial, or her approval of Rheeya's sentencing. Whatever she suggested, they had a dozen reasons why it wouldn't work, or would have to wait, or would have to be done a different way, or would be too much work or alienate too many people. And when she asked them for suggestions, they asked her to be patient, told her it would take time to develop an appropriate plan.

She was so frustrated that she wanted to scream, and not just a wordless release of emotion, she wanted to yell at Kaelen and Jaspar, wanted to demand action and answers, to accuse them of sabotaging the investigation. But, it was that type of heated response to Jared's arrest that had caused this problem to begin with so she swallowed her frustrations for days until, in the middle of a meeting with Jaspar, she broke down sobbing.

"Princess, are you all right?"

She'd shaken her head, no, but the sobs came too fast and too hard for her to speak.

"I'll call for Prince Kaelen."

She shook her head even hard and managed to choke out a "no".

"You need something, someone," he said, rushing out. He'd come back with the palace healer, a grey-haired woman with an apron that had dozens of little pockets sewn on it.

After a quick examination, the healer, Madam Bella, had recommended rest and so Mallory had been shuttled off to her room for three whole days.

When she returned to court after her mandatory bed-rest, she found one of the petitions piqued her interest. The stable master, Jeremy White-Hart, reported that a horse had been taken without leave from the palace stables the night before.

"Oddest thing," he said. "Horse was saddled and everything with no one even noticing. One of the lads saw horse and rider leaving, well after dark. No one travels after dark like that, it's far too dangerous."

Mallory ignored the night-fear superstition and stuck to the facts. "Did anyone see the rider's face?"

"No, he wore a cloak with a deep hood. He rode right past the gate guard without heed."

"What does the horse look like? We should release a description, maybe someone in the city has seen it."

"That's the thing, Princess," Master White-Hart said, twisting his cap in both hands. "The horse was back in her stall when I got up this morning. She was brushed and fed."

"It seems no real crime was committed. Why are you here?"

"I have to report it, Princess. Those are your horses, and no one is supposed to ride them without your permission. If the mare had been injured, we'd find ourselves in a real bind."

"Keep an eye on the horses and keep an eye out for this mystery rider. When he's found I'll have him brought up on mischief charges. I'll find a suitable punishment for his inconvenient behaviour."

"Yes, Princess," Master White-Hart said, bowing.

It was a few days before the hooded figure appeared again, stalking through the courtyard in the deep shadows of late twilight. Mallory heard about it the next day in court as the two guards who'd approached him appeared to testify.

"We stopped him, as you asked," the first said. "He wasn't very polite or respectful."

"I've seen him around before. He sometimes drinks with the off-duty guards, throws dice with them. I've seen him with the stable lads from time to time as well."

"Hunter," Mallory said.

"Aye, that's what he said his name was," the first guard said. "We told him you wanted to speak to him about the horse he borrowed, and he broke my partner's nose before sprinting off. I've never seen a man move so fast before."

"I assume you went to see the healer?" Mallory said.

The second guard nodded. "She did what she could, but my nose will likely be crooked for the rest of my life."

"Hunter is now wanted for the assault of a guard," Mallory said.

"I'll see to the warrant," Jaspar said.

The next day Emilio presented a letter to her in court. She reviewed it quickly and then read it out loud.

"To Mallory Brock Jewel-Rose, Princess of the Metalkin, my deepest apologies. I fully admit to taking a horse from the palace stables without going through the proper channels. Master Spirit-Light had an assignment for me and it was imperative I leave without hold up. The horse was returned, no worse for wear, and well-tended.

"I fully admit to the assault of a guard the other night as well. Nothing excuses the behaviour, of course, no amount of alcohol or sense of urgency. My temper got the better of me. The customary reparation for this crime has always been ten gold and a short jail sentence. I have left the gold with Master Spirit-Light, plus an additional five gold for the crown. I hope that my continued service to Master Spirit-Light will serve for the rest of my sentence. I will be away from Golden Hall for several days." The signature at the bottom bore Hunter's name. Mallory looked up at Emilio. "You have the gold?"

"Yes, Princess."

"You gave a wanted man further work instead of bringing him before the court."

"In all fairness, Princess, I gave him the assignment before I knew he'd assaulted a guard. The letter and gold were found in my study."

"Where is Hunter now?"

"I can't say, precisely. He's been tracking Dark Spirits."

A murmur went through the court. Mallory just rolled her eyes. "I'm sure it's very important work." She turned to Jaspar. "Is this letter correct in the customary sentencing?"

"It is," Jaspar said.

"Then see that the gold is given where it is due. And Master Spirit-Light, I suggest you get your agent under control before he commits a more serious crime."

"Of course, Princess," Emilio said, bowing deeply. "There will be no further issues." He left court and ran into Devin Sun-Stag who was waiting in the hallway for him.

"How did it go?"

"The payment was accepted. All that remains is keeping Hunter out of sight for a week or so."

"All right. Are you sending me away or locking me up?"

"You're taking this well."

Inside the weight of what was happening was starting to crush his very soul. "It was only a matter of time," he said sadly.

"I think it's time we inform the palace healer of what's going on. We should keep you close for observation, at least for a few days. Now let's go, before someone sees us and figures out that I lied to the princess."

With the investigation stalled and Hunter gone on some errand, there was nothing for Mallory to do except sift through a pile of letters. Most of them were invitations to dinner parties in the city, or invitations from the heads of various families, inviting her to visit their estates. None were from the guilds offering up assistance in the investigation, and none contained information on Hunter's whereabouts or where he'd come from in the first place.

She was about ready to throw the whole pile in the fire when a servant arrived with yet another scroll, this one from High Priest

Balder Gold-Spark. She set the other correspondence aside and opened this new scroll.

It was another invitation, this time one she could not choose to ignore. She called for Kaelen and her stewards; a wedding invitation meant planning a trip and she'd need help from each of them.

"Princess Taeya is getting married," she said when they were all seated. "We are expected in Dinas Rhosyn for the ceremony and dinner on the eighteenth."

"You're mistaken," Kaelen said. "Taeya is the Animal People's princess. The service will be in Caranhall."

"That makes travel much simpler," Jaspar said.

"That's not what the invitation says," Mallory said. "Taeya went to Dinas Rhosyn with Betha after Vonica's wedding. I assume she met her prince while there and they're having the ceremony there so his family can attend."

"That's not how this works," Jaspar said. "Each princess must be wed in her own province. It has to do with vows and oaths and The Pact. Master Spirit-Light, tell her."

"The wedding is being held in Dinas Rhosyn," Emilio said. He held up a second scroll. "I received this letter from Master Star-Fire, one of the Evergrowth stewards. There's been some upheaval this last month or so."

"What sort of upheaval?" Jaspar said. "How much trouble could two girls get into?"

"Enough," Emilio replied. "And he assures me there is no error in Most Honourable Gold-Spark's letter. Taeya Rose of Roses is being wed at the temple in Dinas Rhosyn on the eighteenth of Starfall."

"Taeya Rose of Roses?" Kaelen said. "What are they talking about? Taeya's title is Living Rose."

"Not anymore," Emilio said. "I'm sure you and Mallory will hear the full story while you're in Dinas Rhosyn."

"You'll need to leave on the twelfth, no, thirteenth," Jaspar said.

"Twelfth," Kaelen said. "It would be better not to push the horses through the Great Wood."

Jaspar nodded. "I'll have everything ready."

"Ten days," Mallory said. "I don't suppose Cecilia will be back by then, will she?"

"I'm not sure," Kaelen said. "If she is, then of course, she will travel with us. Otherwise, I'm sure we can find suitable maids for you."

"Of course," Mallory said. "The other girls are doing a fine job."

"I'm glad to hear that," Kaelen said. "I have some letters to write. Master Black-Kettle, I know you have this well in hand."

When Jaspar and Kaelen had gone Mallory turned to Emilio. "What do you think happened?"

"How do you mean?"

"With Taeya and Betha? Why this change in names? Why is the wedding being held in the 'wrong' location?"

"A mistake happened, somewhere, at sometime in the past. Probably before the girls were twelve. I don't know what or how, and I'm sure Most Honourable Gold-Spark has his hands full trying to figure it out."

17th of Starfall, 24th Year of the 11th Rebirth
Dinas Rhosyn, Evergrowth Province
Wedding of Taeya Rose of Roses

They had arrived mid-afternoon, and Taeya's change of name was not the only surprise waiting for them. They were greeted by the Evergrowth stewards, Master Avner High-Oak and Master Nunzio Star-Fire, and a younger man wearing the robes and sash of the High Priest of Airon.

"Princess Jewel-Rose, may I introduce you to Most Honourable Baraq Silver-Cloud, the newly appointed High Priest of Airon," Master Star-Fire said.

Mallory curtsied as best she could, she still hadn't fully gotten the hang of it, while Kaelen and Baraq bowed. "I see a lot has happened in the last month," Mallory said.

"Yes. And it's as much a surprise to me as to you," Baraq replied. "I'm sure you're eager to see the other princesses, I know Betha is waiting to speak to you, but I was hoping to borrow you, and Prince Kaelen, for a moment."

"Of course," Mallory said.

"I'm sure the two of you have questions," he said as he led them through the castle's temple to a sitting room in the priests' quarters. "Let me get you caught up on what's happened here."

"The invitation was a surprise," Mallory said.

"We've concluded that somehow the girls were mixed up when they were very young. Taeya and Betha will be keeping their first names but will be switching official titles. Taeya will now reside here in Dinas Rhosyn with her prince. Betha will be moving to Caranhall. Hopefully this will sort everything out and will make it easier for Betha to find her prince."

"Where is High Priest Gold-Spark?" Kaelen said.

"I escorted him back to the Sun Temple myself," Baraq said. "He was struck blind by Airon during the ritual we performed to sort his mess out."

"That's unexpected," Mallory said. "Airon is certainly a hands-on god."

"He hasn't been before now," Baraq said. "It's got a lot of people on edge. I can honestly say the news of High Priest Gold-Spark's sudden ailment and my unorthodox and untraditional ordination did not go over well at all. Do either of you have any questions at this time?"

"No," Kaelen said quickly. "We'd like to get settled, it's been a long journey."

"Of course," Baraq said. "Mallory, there will be a council meeting the day after the ceremony. You're free to return home any time after that."

"We'll be leaving the next day," Kaelen said. "Excuse us."

"Couldn't we stay longer," Mallory said as they followed one of the servants to their rooms.

"No. I have things to do back home."

Mallory sighed but didn't argue. *At least the council meeting after the wedding means I get one extra day before returning home.*

18th of Starfall, 24th Year of the 11th Rebirth
Dinas Rhosyn, Evergrowth Province
Wedding of Taeya Rose of Roses

Mallory was becoming accustomed with the prayers that were said at regular services. Though she wasn't yet sure she believed in Airon or Spirit Guides, she understood that she was more than just a political leader to these people; it was her duty to be familiar with their religion, even if she didn't follow it in her heart. Weddings were a different matter altogether. She'd only been to five, including her own and this one, since her arrival on the island. She followed along with the responses as best she could and waited for it to be over.

Baraq Silver-Cloud was a pleasant change. His voice was rich and melodious, a far cry from Honourable Gold-Spark's dry drone, and he seemed to genuinely wish the couple happiness.

After the service they had a grand dinner. Mallory and Kaelen were seated at a table with Vonica, Johann, Rheeya, Tomas, James, and Betha. The food was delicious, heavy on the breads and the vegetables, but also heavily seasoned. The evening would have been a delight except that Betha was in a horrible mood and was snapping at everyone except James.

Mallory was about to make a comment to Betha about her attitude when conversations all around them stuttered to a halt.

Mallory turned to look at the head table. Taeya was standing, waiting patiently for silence.

"Twenty-four years ago, four infant girls were brought to the island instead of five. This was only the beginning of what is becoming the most unusual of rebirths. Perhaps the biggest upheaval came only weeks ago when we discovered that Princess Betha and I were given the wrong names at birth and sent to the wrong provinces twelve years ago. The next few months will be a time of change and adaptation as I learn how to be the Evergrowth Princess. But today is a joyous day, and there will be plenty of time in the coming weeks to discuss serious matters. Let's spend this evening celebrating a future of peace and prosperity."

Francis stood and escorted Taeya onto the dance floor as the music began. Conversations resumed, and other couples moved to dance. Johann stood and offered his hand to Vonica. "Shall we?"

She smiled and accepted both his hand and his invitation.

"Excuse me," Kaelen said. "There are people here I should speak with while we're here."

When he'd gone Mallory sighed, her gaze lingering on the dance floor. A new song was just starting when a young noble approached the table and bowed. "Princess Jewel-Rose, you look lovely this evening. Would you honour me with a dance?"

"I'm not really familiar with your ..."

"Yes, she will," Betha said. "Go, have fun."

Mallory smiled and took the young man's hand, following him to the dance floor. True to her word, she really wasn't familiar with any of the formal dances; Kaelen hadn't danced with her since their wedding, and even then, it had only been two dances. Still, the young man was patient with her, showing her the steps and laughing with her when she made mistakes, turning the dances from something stiff and solemn to something fun and casual.

Much later she excused herself and went to her room, smiling from ear-to-ear. Not even having to share a room with Kaelen for a few nights could ruin the evening for her.

19th of Starfall, 24th Year of the 11th Rebirth
Dinas Rhosyn, Evergrowth Province

Mallory liked Dinas Rhosyn, it reminded her of home. The embassy in India had a large garden too and she'd spent many hours walking those stone paths in the cool reprieve of the evenings. She met up with Taeya after breakfast and the two girls walked together through wide hallways to the council room.

Baraq was already there and Rheeya and Vonica joined them soon after. "We'll need Betha before we can start," Baraq said.

"I'll send someone to remind her," Taeya said.

"How are things with your family?" Mallory said to Rheeya. "We haven't had much time to catch up yet."

"Nothing prepared me for raising an over-active, inquisitive, eight-year-old boy. Nine. He just passed his birthday recently."

"From the stories I've heard of the four of you, that might just be karma," Mallory said.

"I've never heard that word before," Baraq said.

"Oh, it's the idea that what you do comes back to you. So, theoretically, people who do good deeds with good intentions will receive good things back and people who do bad things, or do things will selfish or bad intentions, will get what they deserve. But it's not instant, and it's a subtle thing. I don't know. It sounds so simple but it's really not."

"We were never this bad," Rheeya said.

"James did tell me about the frogs," Mallory said, smiling.

"You think the frogs were bad! We couldn't find him the other day, spent hours searching for him, calling him, nothing! We found him in the kitchen."

"Had he been there the whole time?" Vonica said. "Because that seems an obvious place to look."

"Oh, we did look there. Three times. We found him there the fourth time."

"Where was he?" Taeya said, returning to her seat.

"Up on the castle wall. He'd gone up to see the view and followed some stray cat. Now, the wall is wide and has a high ledge to protect the guards, but that ... that ... *monster* of a boy, was up on the ledge! Apparently he found some perch near the aviary tower with a good view and lost track of the time!" The other girls were laughing, and even Baraq was grinning. "It's not funny!"

"It really is," Taeya said.

"Come now," Vonica said. "You're loving every minute of this."

"I don't know about every minute," Rheeya said. She huffed and then she laughed too. "It's certainly been an adventure. He keeps me on my toes,"

"James?" Betha said as she entered.

Rheeya looked over. "Yes. I was just telling them about his latest adventures."

"I probably heard his side last night."

"I guessed as much," Taeya said.

Betha responded only with a cool smile and took her seat. Mallory looked from Betha to Taeya and back again. The last few times she'd come together with the girls, Betha and Taeya had been thick as thieves, always seated together, always laughing and chatting together. Mallory wasn't sure about Betha's reserved response today but guessed it had to do with the current upheaval.

"Let's begin," Baraq said.

They discussed the Black Mountain Mine, Vonica's progress with the guild records, and Betha's plans for meeting suitors before being interrupted by a servant looking for James.

"For his sake I hope she finds him before Tomas does," Rheeya said, making Mallory grin. "Is there anything else?"

"Travel plans," Taeya said.

"I'm leaving in the morning," Vonica said. "I've too many ledgers to read. Mallory, you're welcome to travel north with me as far as the temple."

"I'll inform my guard, and Kaelen, and we'll leave with you in the morning," Mallory said.

"I'll travel with you," Baraq said. "The priests here have everything well in hand. There's no need for me to linger."

Mallory's face brightened. "I have some questions about history and politics and such. Maybe I can pick your brain on the road."

Everyone stared at her, their expressions a mix of confusion and disgust.

"It means 'ask questions' or 'make use of your expertise'. No head splitting involved," Mallory said quickly.

"What a strange saying," Taeya said.

"I like it," Betha said.

"I'm leaving tomorrow too," Rheeya said. "We'll go north, check on the village that was destroyed in the landslide, and then take the central pass."

"Betha's staying a few days," Taeya said.

Betha glared. "I can answer for myself. I leave day after tomorrow. I'll come north and stay the night at the Temple."

"We'll have a room ready," Vonica said.

"I'd like to speak with Madam Olga while I'm there."

Vonica didn't seem surprised by Betha's request. "I'll send word to her as soon as I arrive home."

Betha turned to Baraq. "How did this happen? Aren't there rituals? Traditions? Something in place so this doesn't happen?"

"Yes. There are five sacred items and the spirit of your people would have guided you to the right one."

"So, how did Taeya and I both choose the wrong ones?"

"I don't know yet," Baraq said. "But I'll be looking into the matter when I return to the Sun Temple."

Rheeya pushed back from the table and stood. "If there's nothing else, I should help find James."

Baraq nodded.

Taeya rose as well. "I need to check in with my stewards and then maybe I'll come down to your room, Betha, and help with any names your friend provided."

Betha frowned and said, "It looks like I'm going to pack."

"I should do that too," Vonica said.

"Me three," Mallory added. "Kaelen will insist on breakfast before we leave tomorrow."

"I'll insist on breakfast before we leave," Vonica said with a laugh.

"Oh. I don't generally eat until ten … er … midmorning." Honestly, all the early breakfasts were starting to annoy her.

"We'll pack something for you," Vonica said.

Vonica and Mallory made their way to the guest wing together, chatting about the weather and how Mallory was adjusting to her new life. They paused outside Mallory's room and Mallory absently opened the door as they were talking. She peered inside, not wanting the conversation to end, but not wanting to keep Kaelen waiting, if he was waiting. She glanced into the room.

"Oh, Kaelen's not here."

"Hmm, well, I'm sure he's with Johann and Francis and Tomas."

"Wasn't Tomas off looking for James?"

"I wonder if they ever found him, and where. Why don't you come join me then? I was thinking of going out to the garden."

"In a little bit, maybe."

"Okay. Don't get lost."

"Because you've been here before and know your way around," Mallory said.

Vonica laughed. "True. I will try not to get lost either."

Mallory wandered the halls, enjoying the artwork and the wide windows. She wound up at the main doors so she went out. Across the courtyard she could see the stables and off to one side, one of the many low gates into the garden. She was headed in that direction, intending to find Vonica, when she heard a familiar voice behind her. Stepping behind one of the trees she carefully glanced back.

Kaelen had just come out of the stables. He was with another man, a noble from his cloth of gold vest.

"It hasn't been easy. We were told the girls wouldn't be a problem," the other man said.

"I understand," Kaelen said. "Your assistance in these trying times has been greatly appreciated." He produced a small pouch. "This should cover the shipping expenses and any further costs you accrue, trying to keep this whole matter quiet."

The man tossed the pouch lightly in his hand and nodded approvingly. "Yes, this will help some. Won't help Lucien Sun-Harvest though."

Kaelen sneered. "It's just Harvest now, isn't it?"

"Oh yes. His wife left him, did you hear? Returned to her family and their name."

"He shouldn't have been so careless," Kaelen said.

The man's face hardened. "Those men you sent here shouldn't have been so careless. What they did to that foal was unnecessary. You put me at risk."

Kaelen bristled by brushed the criticism aside. "Yes, yes, a horrible mistake. We won't make it again."

"Good. Best keep your collectors at home for a while. Suspicions here are too high."

Kaelen nodded his agreement. "In the mines too. But no matter, we'll weather this little storm and be back on track soon enough."

"I should hope so, for all our sakes."

Trembling, Mallory took off in the direction of the garden, hoping that neither man noticed her. She didn't bother searching for Vonica, instead she entered the first door back into the castle that she passed and asked a servant to show her to her room. She did not come down for dinner that evening, begging off sick, and was in bed, pretending to sleep, when Kaelen came in.

For all her pretending, sleep was a long time coming, and she lay there staring at the shifting shadows, her mind a turmoil of dangerous possibilities.

25th of Starfall, 24th Year of the 11th Rebirth
Golden Hall, Metalkin Province

Cecilia stood at the edge of the yard, fussing with her skirt. She'd been back in Golden Hall for nine days, returning only days after Mallory and Kaelen had left for Dinas Rhosyn. She'd come out here to wait the last few days, wanting to be ready the second Mallory returned. Several long, whispered conversations with her sister had convinced her that whatever Kaelen might do to her, she still had to tell Mallory the truth of what she'd seen and heard.

She was beginning to think the princess would be another day on the road when the gates opened and the processions of guards came through with the carriage behind them. As soon as it was safe she darted forward, heading for the carriage, eager to see Mallory again.

A hand clamped down on her shoulder, stopping her in her tracks. Trembling she looked up. Kaelen smiled down at her. "Back from your trip I see. I hope you had a pleasant time."

"I did. Thank you again for your generosity. It had been some time since I'd seen my sister."

"Why don't you come with me a moment?" he said, turning her towards the castle.

"I should tend to Mall … Princess Jewel-Rose. I've been away so long …"

"And she's been fine without you. This will only take a minute." As they went in a swarm of servants was coming out. Kaelen led her through the crowd and into an empty sitting room. He pushed her inside and shut the door behind them.

Cecilia stumbled forward but caught herself before she fell. She stood as tall as she dared, her chin lifted in defiance. "What do you need, my prince?"

"Just a moment of your time," Kaelen said. "I'm glad you had the chance to see your sister. That makes this easier. Whatever you think you saw in the temple, you're better off keeping it to yourself."

"I'm sure I don't know what you're talking about."

"See? You've already got the hang of it. Just keep saying that and you'll be fine. More importantly, your sister will be fine. Of course, if any ugly rumours were to start, or if anyone should try to tell lies or unfounded gossip to the princess, your sister might not be so well."

Cecilia's face went pale and she could feel her knees trembling under her skirts. "I don't know what you're talking about," she said again.

"Good. See to it that it stays that way. Or your sister won't be the only one that suffers. The princess is waiting for you." He opened the door for her and stood there, waiting for her to go out past him.

She kept her steps measured and even and her chin up, refusing to cower beneath his stare.

She found Mallory just coming in from the yard. The princess's face lit up in a smile. "Cecilia! You're back. Come, run me a bath and you can tell me all about your sister. I'm so happy to see you again."

Cecilia pushed the ugly meeting from her mind and tried to smile back. "I've missed you too," she said. *Forgive me Princess. I must keep my family safe.*

26th of Cloudfall, 24th Year of the 11th Rebirth
Golden Hall, Metalkin Province

For four weeks Cecilia had done her work and kept her head down while the secret of what she'd seen and heard burned inside of her. A few times, Mallory had asked her if something was bothering her but each time she'd lied, and the guilt of those lies was beginning to weigh heavily on her.

Nine days ago, she'd sent a letter to her sister, the only person she'd dared to share the events in the temple with and she'd carried the reply in her pocket since it arrived a few days ago. She didn't dare leave it with her things for fear Kaelen had someone spying on her.

She was making Mallory's bed when the door burst open and the Princess stormed in, slamming the door shut. "I can't get anything done with the two of them around!" she shouted in frustration. She cast about, searching for something, unsure of what she was looking for until Cecilia appeared at her elbow offering up a tea cup.

Mallory seized the cup and flung it against the far wall with a scream. The crash of clay on stone seemed to shock her out of her rage and she stood blinking at the mess she'd made. "I'm sorry," she said in a small voice.

"It was cracked anyway" Cecilia said. "I'll just tell the cook I dropped it." She moved to clean up the pieces.

"I don't want you to get in trouble."

"Then I'll tell them that you dropped it," Cecilia said. "I'm sure the cook will catch my meaning."

Mallory smiled despite herself. "I missed you while you were on your vacation. The other girls were nice enough, but I can't trust them the way I do you."

Cecilia shut her eyes a moment, glad her back was to the princess. The words of her sister's note glowed in her mind's eye. *Don't worry about me, I can look after myself. The princess needs to know the truth.'*

"Forgive me," Cecilia said. "I haven't been honest with you." There was no turning back now.

"What are you talking about?" Mallory said.

Cecilia left the pile of tea cup shards on the ground. "When I travelled with you to the Sun Temple, I saw something, heard something, I should have told you sooner but it wasn't safe."

"Kaelen," Mallory said.

Cecilia nodded.

"Come sit," Mallory said, pulling the chairs closer together. "Tell me everything."

The words came out in a rush. "I saw Prince Kaelen speaking with another man. They mentioned transporting gems and the blacksmith being a 'Rosie'. The other man said Kaelen's job was to control you. They want to know if you'll back them, whoever they are, against the other provinces. They're afraid you'll behead or demote all the nobles in Metalkin territory. That's all I heard. I stubbed my toe and knocked something over and they heard it hit the floor. I barely got out. Kaelen suspects it was me, I know it."

"So, the vacation was to keep you away from me."

"And he threatened my sister when I returned. I should have spoken up sooner."

"You were afraid, and I don't blame you. I've heard the Iron-Heart family is very powerful, and not very kind."

"What are you going to do?"

"I don't know. But you are going to fetch us some tea."

"Us?"

"Yes, us. Lie to the cook, tell her I have a guest. Get two cups and lots of cakes. We need it."

She nodded, still feeling shaken. By the time she returned from the kitchen with the tray she was feeling steadier, though it was still bewildering to be taking tea with the princess in her rooms. She frowned as she set the tray down. "You cleaned up."

"I threw the pieces in the fire place," Mallory said. "That tea smells lovely."

Cecilia smiled and set the cups out. They sat for a few minutes in silence, both lost in thought. Finally, Cecilia said, "What are you going to do?"

"I'm not sure what I can do. Kaelen and Jaspar are impossible to deal with. I thought what happened at Dinas Rhosyn was an anomaly, I honestly tried to think up excuses for the man, can you believe it? But if what you say is true, and I'm inclined to believe you, then Kaelen's actions are deliberate, and they form a disturbing pattern. I don't know. Every time I think I know what I need to do something else comes up. I don't even know where to begin now."

"Are you going to tell the other princesses about this?"

"Not yet. I have no proof. I don't know how much weight your word will carry. I only heard a part of a conversation. No, I'll write them, but best to keep these details between us for now. I need to do this alone."

"You need to do this here," Cecilia said. "And you need to find proof, but you don't need to do it alone."

Mallory smiled at her maid, her friend, and said, "Thank you."

**32nd of Cloudfall, 24th Year of the 11th Rebirth
Golden Hall, Metalkin Province**

Mallory hurried through the castle, cursing the seamstress for taking up so much of her time. She was breathing hard as she burst out the door into the courtyard. Servants and stable lads were busy with luggage and horses. The Living Rose crest adorned the side of the carriage, so Mallory knew it was Betha who had arrived.

"You didn't tell me it was a princess coming to visit," Kaelen said, stomping over to her.

"A guest is a guest," Mallory said. "Is everything all right? Where is she?"

"She's in there," Kaelen said, flinging an arm in the direction of the stables. "She's talking to the Stable Master, of course. This is the problem with Animal People, they have no sense of propriety. I've been stuck waiting here while she's in there chatting away. Who knows how long she intends to take. This shows a complete lack of courtesy on her part. What's she doing here anyways?"

"She's here to help me."

"With what? You have me, two stewards, and as many tutors and scholars as you want. How much more help do you need?"

"The tutors you hired didn't teach me what I needed to know and Master Black-Kettle spends more time finding reasons to put the investigation on hold than he does assisting with the investigation."

"Fine," Kaelen said, his voice softening. "I understand you're frustrated, but we talked about this. You're supposed to talk to me before you make any big decisions so I can help you and so I know what's going on."

"I really didn't think this was a huge deal. She's my friend. She's allowed to visit."

"We're busy. She's busy. She has her own province to take care of. And, I didn't know she was coming, I was caught off guard, unprepared. That's embarrassing for me."

"Well, she's here now and …"

"For how long?"

"I'm not sure, exactly. We didn't set a firm date."

"An open-ended visit? In the middle of a political investigation?"

"I don't see why you're so upset. You're not interested in the investigation anyways."

A sudden, heavy silence hung between them and Mallory could see hot anger playing over Kaelen's features.

"I'm sorry," she said. "I know you care, I know you're invested in this too, it's just the frustration talking."

"You're here now. I'll leave you to wait for your guest while I return to my own duties." He marched past her and she heard the door slam shut behind her.

She closed her eyes and took a few deep breaths. Her hands were shaking.

"Everything all right?"

Mallory turned to Betha, plastering a too-bright smile on her face. "Sure! Everything's fine. Let's get you settled in." She led the way towards the castle. "I received your letter and burned it as you instructed." She lowered her voice. "I really didn't intend for you to drop everything and ride down here."

"Your letter sounded desperate."

"Things have not been going well here, I'll be honest about that. But how will they view me if I go running for help at every turn?"

"I'm your friend and ally. And this is a common problem we share. And I already know the foals we are looking for passed through Golden Hall."

Mallory's steady steps faltered. "What? When? How did you learn that?"

Betha glanced around. "Maybe that's a story for another time. Once I'm settled, we can plan a course of action."

"Oh, by the way, this arrived for you a few hours ago. Apparently, it arrived in Caranhall a few hours after you left there." She produced a letter and handed it to Betha. "I'll go see about dinner, a private affair for just the two of us."

"Thank you." Betha took the paper and followed the servant into the guest room.

Mallory took another deep breath and turned on her heel. *I'm sure a private dinner will be easily arranged. I don't think Kaelen wants to speak to me right now. And I'm not as bothered by that as I should be.*

33rd of Cloudfall, 24th Year of the 11th Rebirth
Golden Hall, Metalkin Province

Kaelen's horse was saddled and waiting for him after dinner. "When will you be back?" the stable master asked.

"Late."

"Forgive me sir, its none of my business, of course, I only ask so we have someone here for the horse when you return."

"See that you do," Kaelen said. He pulled himself into the saddle and rode off at a brisk walk. The guard at the gate waved him through. The city was busy, even at this hour. Most people were on foot, moving aside to let his horse pass, but paying him little attention otherwise. If Mallory had been with him everyone would have stopped to stare but for now he was just another noble. *As it should have been.*

Emelia paced the front hall, her heart pounding. Her parents had gone to dinner and she'd sent the servants away for the evening, all except the stable hand who'd be needed to see to her guest's horse. He was running late and with each passing moment she became more convinced that the next knock on the door would be a messenger coming to give her his regrets.

She was so worked up that she jumped when someone did knock. She rushed forward, absently smoothing her immaculate skirts, and jerked the heavy front door open. "Kaelen," she said, the word coming out with a heavy exhale. "You made it. I was beginning to worry."

He stepped past her into the house. "I couldn't get away without arousing suspicion. Where is everyone?"

"Gone. We have a few hours." She closed the door and threw the lock.

"Good." He caught her by the shoulders and kissed her. When he stepped back again, he said, "I've missed you Emelia."

Her eyes were downcast, and she remained silent.

"What's wrong?"

"You used to visit all the time. We were in love. You said you'd propose to me. And then you married the princess."

"This wasn't my choice," he said, following her to the sitting room. He'd known it was only a matter of time before the hiding got to be too much, only a matter of time until they had to have this conversation. That didn't make it easier.

She laughed, a short, dry, bitter laugh. "Yes, fate and soulmates and Airon's will. Everyone else is fooled but my father is a Loyalist too. I've heard the talk. You weren't chosen by Airon."

"I was chosen by a dozen old men who didn't bother consulting me!"

"You could have refused. You could have asked me to marry you and then made a public announcement about our engagement."

"And then we both would have been disowned, me for disobeying, you for marrying a single-named failure."

"I wouldn't have cared. I loved you. You! Not your family's fortune, not your family name."

"Loved?"

She looked away.

"Emelia, please, don't do this. I love you."

"You did. Now you've become consumed by this Loyalist plot, just like our fathers."

"I want out," Kaelen said. "I'm tired. Mallory and I fight all the time. I cannot imagine thirty or forty years of that. I know she's beginning to suspect. Betha too. What happens if she meets her real prince? What happens if there's a sign, like in Dinas Rhosyn?" They could hang me for treason and our fathers would abandon me to my fate."

Emelia reached out and took both of his hands in hers. "What do we do?"

"I need to get out."

"Go to Mallory, tell her everything. If you help her shut this whole Loyalist plot down maybe she'll forgive you. I'll speak on your behalf."

"I'd be dead within twelve hours of opening my mouth. The steward, Black-Kettle, is one of theirs. How do you think he got his second name?"

"Then what?"

"I need your help."

"Do you really love me?"

"Yes, oh Emelia, yes. More than life itself. You don't know how much I regret everything."

She sighed. "Okay, I'll help. But you must act quickly. My mother wants me to marry soon. She's throwing suitors at me."

"You must stall her, please. I can't lose you." He pulled her close, staring deeply into her eyes. He could feel her body trembling slightly. "Emelia, I'm sorry. I've hurt you. You're right, I should have refused from the start. But I'll set it right. I'm not afraid. If you promise to stay with me, I won't be afraid of them anymore. I'll get out. We'll be together."

She nodded. "Okay."

He kissed her, savouring the feel of her. "Don't worry. I know what to do."

**6th of Thornfall, 24th Year of the 11th Rebirth
Golden Hall, Metalkin Province**

Mallory was expecting a fight; everything had been a fight with Kaelen lately, so when he responded to her recounting of the day with a 'that's nice' she sat back and stared at him, completely speechless for several minutes. When she did find her voice back she said, "You're not angry with me for offering to pay the Rose-Gold family's medical expenses?"

"I think it's a good idea to send Master Rose-Gold to Stones Shore," he said. *Now he can't make trouble here.* "And with his father so ill, this was the kindest and most efficient way to get him to go." *A small price to pay. Now to make the best use of his absence.*

"Okay," Mallory said. "I'm glad you're not upset."

"And when is Betha leaving?"

"In a week," Mallory said.

"You've had a nice visit?"

"Yes," Mallory said, wary now.

"That's good. If you'll excuse me, I have some business in town."

Mallory watched him go. Part of her was relieved that they hadn't fought, but part of her was suspicious; his attitude was too different, too fast. *What's he up to?*

She rang the bell cord and when the servant arrived she said, "I need to send a discreet letter here in the city. I need a lad to run it for me but I need someone absolutely trustworthy."

The woman nodded. "I'll fetch my younger brother."

While she waited she composed the letter which she handed to the young man when he arrived.

He glanced at the folded paper and said, "I know where the Rose-Gold house is."

"You're not going to the Rose-Gold house," she said. "You're going to follow Kaelen."

"But the letter …"

"Is a ruse. Wait a few minutes after he goes inside then knock and present the letter. They'll scold you for being at the wrong house. Apologize and return to me. I want to know where he's going and who he's meeting with, if possible. Hurry now, or you'll miss him."

Mallory waited until she was past sick of waiting, though she paused to consider it, she wouldn't have to wait at all if the messenger had missed Kaelen. *Waiting just means the plan is working.* The thought did little to appease her impatience.

When the young man returned, fake letter in hand, his face was serious.

"Did the plan fail?" Mallory said, rushing to offer him a seat.

"No, it worked. A young woman opened the door, said it was the Iron-Forge house."

"That's more than I knew before."

"There was a man inside, I didn't see him, wanted to know who was at the door. He addressed her as Emelia."

"Was she a servant?"

"She was dressed too fine and she told me I was useless."

"Another servant would have been more forgiving of the error."

He nodded. "Without a doubt."

"So, a young noble woman with no servant to open the door for her." Mallory pondered a moment. "Newly wed, perhaps? Just getting established, new home, no servants yet."

"It was one of the old-family homes, the sort that belongs to lower branches of big families. Given her age I'd have guessed she lived there with her parents, though it's possible she lives there with her in-laws."

"Give me a reason a nobleman would have his daughter open the front door rather than a servant."

"The family is in financial distress, but given who the home belonged to, I highly doubt it."

"I take it you hear a lot of gossip?"

"Sometimes. And I have a cousin in the Blacksmith's Guild, an apprentice. There's a Master Iron-Forge teaching there."

"Give me another reason then."

He paused to consider the question. "Private meeting. Prince Jewel-Rose is meeting someone in the house and they want no potential eavesdroppers, or no witnesses."

"Is he meeting this girl's father? Or her husband?" *Or is he meeting with her?* Something twisted in her gut, something cold and painful. *Am I jealous?*

"I don't know. I saw no one else."

"You've done well," Mallory said. "Keep this little errand out of the palace gossip, if you can."

"My lips are sealed," he said.

When he'd gone, Mallory went to her desk and wrote, "Emelia Iron-Forge" on a paper. "How do I learn more about you?" she murmured.

15th of Thornfall, 24th Year of the 11th Rebirth
Golden Hall, Metalkin Province

"Princess Betha is on her way home," Mallory said as she joined Emilio on the study's balcony. From here they could see the gardens and the city wall, but not the castle courtyard. The morning sun cast the garden in rich, golden light and the balcony was warm.

"The two of you had a good visit?"

"Yes. It felt nice to talk about home. Actually, I had a question about The Pact."

"Of course."

"The whole point of the pact was to protect the island from the people you refer to as 'the strangers'?"

"Yes. They threatened the balance of our way of life."

"I think those Strangers were the ancestors of the Irish people. From what I can piece together, the Isle of Light *is* Ireland, or was. I've seen the map, the shape is certainly eerily similar, it's just the topography that's different. I think somehow, Airon made it so your island phased out of synch with the world, like it's vibrating at the wrong frequency. It's still there, it's just invisible. That's why I was born there, and the other girls. For some reason, when we're reborn, our souls phase back to the normal frequency and you have to come fetch us. My soul resonates at the frequency of the 'Wide World' and my soulmate's soul resonates at the frequency of the island. Our union creates a harmony that keeps the island far enough out of synch that it's invisible, and intangible, but close enough that it's still tied to the fabric of reality. I'm betting, based on average lifespans here, that it's been seven hundred and fifty, maybe eight hundred years since The Pact for you, but it's been closer to two and a half thousand years on Earth."

The whole time Mallory had been rambling Emilio had been staring at her with fascination. "I didn't understand all of that, but it sounds like a fitting theory."

"Betha mentioned a second island, and then more land beyond that?"

"Yes. That's how it was before The Pact. We didn't explore very far beyond the shores of the other island, but we had stories from the Strangers before The Pact separated us."

"If I sketched out a map of Earth, of the Wide World, you'd see England off the cost of Europe, and Ireland off the coast of England. The geography makes the most sense."

"For someone who claimed to have questions you seem to have a lot of answers already."

"Oh, well, I have no proof, of course. Maybe if there were some old maps somewhere?"

"Not in Golden Hall but I'll see what the scholars back at the Sun Temple can find for you."

"It's all just theory, guess work really."

"I don't understand all this about resonating more or lest frequently, but I think it's as good a theory as anything our scholars have come up with."

"I didn't believe in magic, and I was having trouble adjusting to your religion, but if Airon really did this, I think I should start believing in his existence."

"Yes, it might be a little awkward if the chosen one doesn't believe in the god who chose her."

Mallory laughed. "Chosen one, right, I forgot about that part."

"What are your plans for today?"

"Writing letters, reviewing guild records, remembering to eat, boring stuff."

"I will write to the scholars and see about having some maps sent over. I'm interested now to see how much of your theory we can prove."

"It will certainly be more interesting than guild accounts. If you hear back from them, let me know."

"Of course, Princess. And if you need help with anything." He hesitated for a moment. "Even things that might not be my job, precisely, you will let me know?"

They studied each other for a moment and then Mallory nodded. "I will, yes. Thank you."

"No, thank you. I once told you that a princess has great influence over the attitudes of her people. I know it's been hard for you, but I think this province needed you, more than you know."

30th of Thornfall, 24th Year of the 11th Rebirth
Golden Hall and Surrounding Forests, Metalkin Province

"Princess, this is highly unusual," Master White-Hart said.

"I didn't grow up here, so I don't have the same reservations when it comes to horses. I love riding and I've been missing it terribly. I have an entire stable full of horses that are mine and I'm tired of not being allowed to ride them. Bring one out for me. I'll brush it and saddle it. I insist."

"Yes, Princess. Of course." He came back with a sweet looking mare and tied her to the fence. Behind him came a couple of the stable boys, one with a bucket of brushes, the other with the tack.

"Thank you," she said. She pulled a brush from the bucket and got to work. The smell of the horse and the feel of the warm body under her hand was already relaxing her.

The two stable boys hovered nearby, silently watching her. She did her best to ignore them. She needed this time to just be Mallory Brock and not Princess Jewel-Rose. She'd spent the last two weeks pretending to investigate the guilds and the nobles, so she could watch Kaelen and Jaspar and what she was learning was highly disturbing.

They were corresponding with the guilds behind her back, warning them if she planned to search an office or estate, buying them time with excuses so they could hide their records and alter their books.

She'd kept lists of who Kaelen and Jaspar were in contact with and had conscripted the help of the hawk master, the stable master, and several guards and servants. *The only people I can truly trust are Cecilia, Emilio Spirit-Light and Joseph Rose-Gold.*

"Good afternoon, Princess."

Mallory looked up. *And Devin Sun-Stag. He's been employed by the crown, and Master Spirit-Light since before I arrived here and I've never heard a negative word about him, except from Kaelen.* "Good afternoon."

"You seem very at ease with that mare."

"She's a beautiful animal," Mallory replied. "She seems to like the brushing." She lowered her voice. "But I think I'm making the stable hands uncomfortable."

"They aren't accustomed to this. Would you like help cleaning her hooves?"

"I know how," Mallory said. "But maybe you'd keep her calm?"

"Certainly." He stood stroking the mare's nose while Mallory fished a pick out of the bucket and started deftly cleaning manure, straw, and pebbles from the soft part of the mare's feet. "Her name is Lily," Devin said.

"An interesting name," Mallory said. "Who would name a horse after a plant?"

"She has a white mark here, on her nose. It's not so obvious now but when she was little, it looked like a lily."

"Did you hear that story from one of the hands? Or did you see it yourself?"

"You're asking how long I've been in Golden Hall?"

"I suppose I am."

"I saw her born, right here at the palace stables. I was working with the Royal Tracker at the time, barely older than the lads by the fence there."

"Is your family from the city here?"

"No. My parents live in the Animal People's territory."

"You've been away from home a long time."

He didn't answer.

"I'm sorry. I get the feeling you don't like talking about it."

"I don't," he said. And then, because this was the first time that he hadn't felt the sting of shame at the mention of his parents, he took a deep breath and said, "We had a fight. It was foolish, but my father and I yelled at each other a lot for a few weeks and ignored each other when we weren't yelling. It escalated until we weren't fighting over one thing, we were fighting over everything."

"Do you remember what the one thing was? The one that started it?"

He nodded. "The royal escort had come through our village when Taeya … Princess Living Rose … was twelve. I met her, briefly, but it was enough to know that she was a complete disappointment to me. When I was a little older my father wanted to send me to Caranhall and I refused."

"Yes, I get the feeling everyone takes this whole suitor-soulmate thing very seriously."

"She wasn't my princess," Devin said. "I mean, she wasn't my soulmate. I couldn't have known she'd turn out to be the Evergrowth princess."

"What about Betha?" Mallory said.

"I met her when she came for your wedding, and again when she came to visit you. The first time I wouldn't have known I was even a possible suitor for her, but I didn't feel anything special either time. No, she's not my princess either."

"Do you miss your family?"

"I miss my sister. A family friend wrote me and told me she'd gotten married. No one invited me. I wish I could have been there for her. I just know she was stunning. The rest? No, I don't miss my parents, or the farm."

"I miss my parents," Mallory said. "I never thought I'd miss my dad, but I do. It hasn't even been a year. I know they're still looking for me."

"I'm sorry, you know. I'm sorry we had to pull you through that portal. I'm sorry the priests didn't give you more time or warning."

"It's done," she said, forcing a smile. "And so are her feet. Help me with the saddle."

"You're going to ride around the paddock?"

"That was the plan. Now I think I'd like to go for a real ride. And you're going to be my escort."

His heart leapt. Here and now, talking to her, even about something as painful as his past, he felt at peace for the first time in nearly a year. She'd given him a command and his first instinct was to obey without hesitation. And more than that, he wanted to go with her, wanted to spend time with her without guards and stable hands and Prince Kaelen watching their every move, hanging on their every word. He'd felt this way before, back at Airon's Gate, and he never thought he'd feel it again.

But he knew it was a bad idea. He shook his head. "I'm honoured, Princess, but you need a proper escort. A guard, or two …"

"I'm tired of guards," she said. "You're a tracker and a hunter, right? And I can see you're armed."

"Yes," he said, drawing the word out. "But this isn't proper. It's not safe. It's already late in the afternoon. I don't …"

"Get a second horse," she said. "We're going. The other princesses keep telling me just to put my foot down and issue orders so that's what I'm doing. You and I are going for a ride, just a short one. We'll be back by dinner."

He sighed, forcing his face to remain serious. "I have to obey," he said. "But I'm still going to tell you that this is a bad idea."

"Your opinion has been noted. Now fetch the horse."

Emilio strode through the halls of Golden Hall, his eyes only half on where he was going, his attention divided by the letter he held in his hand. He stopped every second or third servant he passed and asked them if they knew where the princess was, but the answer was always a 'no'. Finally, a guard at the door was able to provide a more substantial answer.

"She went out to the stables," he said. "She looked dressed for the outdoors."

Emilio crossed the courtyard and entered the stables. The nearest lad bolted in the opposite direction and came back a moment later with the stable master.

"Master Spirit-Light, what can I do for you today?"

"I'm looking for Princess Jewel-Rose."

"You've just missed her. She insisted on going out for a ride."

"Out? Ride? Where? When will she be back?"

"She went out, with an escort, to see the forest on the edge of the city. As I said, she insisted. Her escort promised to have her back for dinner, though whether that will be a late meal or an early one I don't know. I trust him to have her back well before dark."

"How many men went with her?"

"Just the one, sir. I tried to tell her she needed more guards, but she refused. I'm sorry, but I'm just the stable master. These are her horses. I couldn't exactly stop her."

"You should have called for me, or Prince Kaelen, or the captain of the guard."

"She wouldn't let us. She insisted that she'd be fine, that she knew how to ride and that she needed the time and fresh air to clear her mind."

"This is most unusual and highly inappropriate."

The man just shrugged. "She's the princess, I have to obey."

"Fine. Fine, it's done. I can't bring her back without sending out guards to hunt her down and that won't impress her or solve the problem. I suppose I have no choice but to await her return." He turned to leave.

"Don't worry," the stable master called after him. "Devin Sun-Stag is the best tracker and most capable hunter I know. He will keep her safe."

Emilio rounded on the man. "What did you say?"

He took a step back, cringing, though he was physically larger than the steward. "I said that she went out with Devin Sun-Stag. He's trustworthy, I swear it. He's a good man and means her no harm. He'll protect her with his life."

"Airon protect us, you may have doomed us all."

Mallory was having the time of her life. She had missed riding so much. Her legs were aching from the effort, and from taking nearly a year off from the saddle, but she was happy, and she didn't care one bit that she wouldn't be walking much tomorrow. The company was a welcome change too.

Kaelen hated her, she was sure of that now, and Jaspar was a sycophant, saying what he could to please her while still working more for Kaelen than her. She could only really count Emilio and Cecilia as friends. And Betha but she was so far away. She'd never really had a chance to talk with Devin, not without Kaelen cutting the conversation short, even though she'd found Devin far more interesting, and attractive, that first day at Airon's Gate.

Once they were out of the city they cantered to the trees, their speed and the pounding of horses' hooves making it impossible to talk to each other. They slowed when they reached the woods, letting the horses walk side-by-side down the forest path.

"I'm impressed at how well you ride," he said.

"Don't the Metalkin guards learn how to ride? And I've seen Kaelen ride."

"Sure, but they have years of training."

She laughed. "I did have years of training before I came here."

"Right," he said, blushing a little. "I forget. It's not something the Metalkin Princess would usually learn."

"Maybe she should," Mallory said. "Maybe that's part of the problem. I mean, I get it that you have Spirit Guides and you have to follow specific career paths, but what if you learned something about the other provinces too? Everyone should know basic animal care, feeding, brushing, how to get the animal to a healer. Everyone should know how to pick their own food, even if a select few have to grow it. Look at the guilds that employ people from more than one province, they are more prosperous and more politically stable."

Devin admired her passion, but these political arguments were out of his depth. "That's something you should bring up with the new high priest. A new, younger, high priest means there's a real chance for things to change now."

She nodded. "Yes, I think I will do that."

"You'll have a hard time convincing the nobles though, here especially. Here, nobles teach trades and run guilds, they make their money that way, or through investments. They don't work with their hands." It wasn't something he had ever been comfortable voicing to anyone, but Mallory was so different, so honest, he hoped she would understand.

"That's another thing that should change," she went on, not noticing his momentary discomfort. "When the upper class loses touch with the commoners there's real problems. Out in the Wide World we've seen problems like that become bloody."

"We haven't had a war here in over eleven generations." He sounded shocked.

"I wasn't talking about war, I was talking about revolution. When the poor get desperate, they'll overthrow a corrupt and oppressive government system with violence, and that ends with nobles losing their heads."

His face twisted in disgust. "The Wide World sounds like a horrible place."

She nodded in thoughtful agreement. "Politically, it is. But there's so much there that's good and beautiful too. I grew up in India, the buildings there were works of art. And there were animals there that you've never seen or heard of. The animals, the different cultures, the people working for peace and equality and freedom, the art and the music and the books." She sighed.

"You'd go back if you could."

She smiled sadly. "Is that so bad?"

"Do you like anything about the Isle of Light?"

She looked over at him and was surprised to see real concern on his face. She took a deep breath, ready to tell him that she liked this time with him, when a deer bounded onto the path no more than a foot in front of the horses.

Both horses whinnied and bolted, thankfully in the same direction. Unfortunately, that direction was straight into the trees. Mallory held on tight and kept her body low over the horse's neck to avoid as many branches as possible. They were making an awful racket and had probably scared off every animal for a clear mile.

Just when Mallory thought maybe the horse would slow enough for her to regain control it bucked and turned sharply, bolting in a new direction, spooking at something Mallory didn't even see.

Please let Devin be behind me!

Devin had regained control of his horse and was chasing after Mallory, trying to keep her in sight between the trees. They were going far too fast for the terrain. A log in the wrong place, an animal hole, even an uneven bit of ground, at this speed could result in the horse snapping its leg. But all that was a minor concern now.

First, was getting to Mallory and making sure she was safe. Second was getting them both back to the city before dark. They were riding away from Golden Hall, and at a good speed. *This was supposed to be a short ride.*

Mallory's horse startled and turned and he responded to head them off, finally starting to close the gap between them. He came up beside Mallory and leaned, reaching for the halter.

Where the damn badger came from, Devin didn't know, but he heard it's snarl just as he got his hand around the halter.

Both horses stopped short and reared. Devin lost his grip on the other horse and tumbled from the saddle, narrowly missing a large stone. He heard Mallory scream and then the thunder of hooves and the crashing of large animals through the trees. He sat up with a groan, grabbed a stick, and threw it at the badger with a yell. He could see Mallory laying nearby, which was good, because if she'd stayed on her horse he'd have no way of catching her.

He stood and whistled for the horses. If they heard him, they didn't respond. He looked around, getting his bearings. They were in the middle of the bush, probably a mile or two off the road in any direction, if not more. *Damn our luck. Stupid deer. Stupid badger. Stupid horses!!*

Devin whistled again, staring after the horses. He could no longer hear their hooves in the underbrush. He wanted to kick something or scream at the trees. Behind him Mallory whimpered.

The anger drained out of him and he whipped around, returning to her side and dropping to his knees. He lifted her head and shoulders into his lap and brushed a strand of hair from her face.

"Hey, I'm here. It's going to be okay," he said.

Her leg was bent at an odd angle, most definitely broken in at least one place, but more concerning was the blood soaking through her skirt. A broken bone didn't bleed, not unless there were other injuries, or if the break was so bad the bone had ripped through the skin. His gut twisted at the thought. He'd seen horses with breaks like that, had helped to put them down, knew how much pain a break like that would cause.

"I'm sorry," he said. "I need to see your injury."

She nodded weakly. Her usual rosy cheeks were grey.

He tugged her skirt upwards. Her riding boots held her ankle in place so while that was the most likely place for a break there was no way to tell without feeling for the bone or removing the boot. There was a slight but unmistakeable bend in her lower leg and no joint there to allow for it.

If she's lucky it's a fracture and not a completely break. At least the skin isn't broken. Aside from a few minor scratches and scrapes caused but the bushes and undergrowth her skin was unmarked.

"I'm sorry," he said again, still inching the fabric higher. Her knee looked fine aside from the start of a nasty bruise. Taking a deep breath, he pulled the skirt higher.

Her thigh was the problem. She'd hit a branch when the horse threw her and the one-inch across branch had buried itself in the muscle of her leg. The force of her roll had snapped the branch and she now had at least two inches sticking out on one side of her leg, and probably just as much on the other side.

His breath hitched, and he reached for the pack at his waist.

"How bad is it?"

"You're fine," he said.

"Fine doesn't feel like this," she said. "I know I'm hurt."

"You'll be fine," he corrected. "And yeah, it's bad. You need a healer, but the horses ran off and you can't walk. I'm going to apply a tourniquet on your leg to slow the bleeding."

"How far are we from the city limits?"

"Far enough to be a problem. The sun's going down." He eased out from under her, unrolling the scarf he kept in his pack for those hot days when he wanted to tie something wet and cool around his neck. "I'm sorry," he said again. "Excuse the familiarity of my touch."

"It's fine," she said. "I'd rather not bleed to death."

"This is going to hurt," he said.

"Just don't apologize again."

"I'll try." He started working the cloth under her leg, trying to jostle her as little as possible. "It might help if you keep talking."

"Why is everyone on this island afraid of the dark?"

"What do you mean?"

"You said the sun's going down like that's a problem. No one has ever let me travel past dark."

"The Dark Spirits come out at night," Devin said. "Didn't anyone teach you about them? It should have been one of the first things you learned. It's extremely important."

"I heard the stories. Sounds like the boogey man back home."

"What's a boogey man?"

"It's a monster, a dark man who lives in the shadows, usually in dark closets or under the bed. He's the creaky sound of an empty house shifting, the sound of the wind moaning, or anything else that makes you feel afraid."

"You make it sound like he's not real."

"He's not. He's something we use to scare children, or to explain away a scary feeling you get for no reason."

"You think the Dark Spirits are like that?"

"They sound like something out of a cartoon."

"I don't know what that is."

"You don't know what television is either so it's pretty hard to explain." She sighed. "It sounds like something out of a storybook."

"I suppose they do. But they're very real. You saw them yourself, didn't you?"

"What do you mean?"

"On the road, those first days. Don't you remember the attack?"

"Yeah, we were attacked. Kaelen stayed with me in my tent. I could hear men screaming and fighting. I wasn't allowed out of my tent."

"He didn't tell you what was happening?"

"He told me he was in love with me and explained all about soul mates, that was it."

Devin swore under his breath.

"What? Is it worse than you thought?"

"Your leg? No. I'm almost done. *Prince* Kaelen should have explained what was happening that night. The Dark Spirits are the single biggest threat to our island and the soul purpose of you being here …"

"Safety, The Pact, yeah, I got all that from Emilio."

"No, you didn't," Devin said. "Or you'd understand that the Dark Spirits are very real and they're after you more than anyone else. You and the other princesses. They always have been. And that's why you have never been allowed to travel after nightfall."

"They're really real? I thought people just believed they were real. We don't believe in monsters anymore where I'm from. We have science instead of superstition."

"We have magic here," Devin said. "Spirits are real, the good ones and the bad."

"I didn't know. I didn't understand." She took a deep breath and let it out slowly. "So, we're in very real danger out here?"

"Yes," he said. "In more ways than one. Hold on, I have to pull it tight."

She reached out, her hands searching for anything to hold on to. One came up with a handful of leaves, the other found a tree root. She gritted her teeth and squeezed her hand tight as he pulled and still a shout of pain escaped her. She panted, gasping for breath, as the world shifted in and out of focus.

Devin took a deep breath before firmly gripping the ends of the cloth. His heart was pounding. He didn't want to hurt her, but if he didn't do this there was a real chance she could bleed to death and he felt it deep down in his core that it would be a very bad thing for everyone on the island if Mallory Brock died in the woods tonight. He clenched his teeth and pulled. Her scream tore through him like a knife and he bit his lip to keep from crying out in response.

He kept his eyes on his hands, too aware that the sun was descending in the sky and the shadows between the trees were deepening. All he had to do now was tie a knot, but his fingers kept fumbling the job. When it was finally done, he said, "There, that's it. I don't think you'll bleed out tonight."

She didn't answer, didn't make a sound. He glanced over. Her eyes were closed. Most likely she had passed out from the pain.

He rolled his shoulders and tried to relax. She wasn't going to die from her injuries, but they still had to survive the night. Even if he could carry her all the way back to the city, and they were far enough away that he wasn't sure he could do that in a single try without resting at some point, he'd have to do it in the dark. He was a trained hunter and tracker, but the woods in the dark were full of dangers – unseen branches and holes to trip them up, wild animals, and of course, Dark Spirits.

There was nothing they could do except wait and hope that the horses had run back to the city and not in some other direction and that the arrival of two riderless horses would prompt a search party to come for them.

Until someone came, or until the sun returned, all he could do was guard her.

Right, how are you going to keep her safe? They've been trying to keep her safe from you for months. What's going to happen when the sun finishes setting, and your Dark Spirit takes over like it does every night? Who is going to keep her safe from the monster inside of you?

In all of the confusion of the horses running and tending to Mallory's injuries he hadn't even thought of that. In an hour, two at most, Devin would disappear, and Hunter would take over.

The woods were most often considered the holy space of the Evergrowth, what with all the trees and bushes, but Devin knew the spirit of his people lived here too, in the bird and the deer and the rabbit. Kneeling beside the princess, he prayed, not to Airon, not with his light fading from the world until morning, but to the old spirits, the guides of his people, spirits that hadn't bothered to directly answer a prayer in generations.

There was a sound in the bushes, a light rustling. He wanted to believe it was the wind, but the woods had gone quiet and still, too much so. His heart pounded as his gaze scoured the shadows between the tree trunks. No matter what he wanted now, it was not the wind he heard. He eased the knife from his belt, still searching for any sign of movement, fearing it would come too fast from too close and that he wouldn't be able to stop it.

His eyes were drawn to a flash of white, ahead and off to the left, but when he turned to look whatever had made it had disappeared behind the trees again. Another rustle, another shimmer of white, closer this time but moving slowly, purposefully, towards them.

What stepped out of the bush was a white deer, with a mature, elegant face, and the petite horns of a mature female, only this deer stood a mere two and a half feet at the top of its delicate ears. One of those ears flicked back, listening, as the animal paused at the edge of the trees. Finally, it took another step forward, its dark glossy eyes on Devin.

This was no ordinary deer. Devin had grown up in the woods, had sat in the low branches of the trees watching lines of deer pass beneath him, and never once had he seen one this colour or this size. He dropped the knife. It seemed disrespectful to stand, or even kneel, armed before one of the spirits when only moments earlier he'd been praying to them.

They stared at each other a moment longer.

"Why me?" Devin said. "I am cursed, and she is Metalkin."

The deer licked its nose, its tail flickering back and forth. It did not speak, Devin wasn't sure it could speak in the tongue of man, but stepped closer still, walking up to Mallory and lying down beside her.

"Please. If the Dark Spirits come, we have no way of fending them off."

She ignored Devin, her attention fixed on Mallory. She carefully sniffed the length of Mallory's injured leg. She paused to lick the place where the branch had pierced her thigh, and then rested her chin just above the tourniquet.

It was dark now. The sun had gone down, and the moon was neither high enough nor full enough to provide light this deep within the trees.

Devin heard something in the dark, a whisper that touched his ears and his soul, calling to the horrid thing that had taken hold of him, stirring it towards waking.

His whole body shuddered with the effort it took to keep the *thing* caged. It was a battle he could not win. He looked down at Mallory. All he wanted was to keep her safe and now she was at the mercy of the monster inside of him, and this time it would take the opportunity and destroy her, he was sure of it.

A dark pleasure was building inside of him at the thought of causing pain. "No, please no," he whispered.

The deer turned her big, dark, eyes towards him again. She lifted her head, staring intently. Instinctively he reached out towards it, running a timid hand up her nose, as he might do to a nervous horse, then along the side of her face, and down her neck. She settled again, resting her chin on Mallory's leg, and he kept a hand on her shoulder, the short fur stiff and yet strangely soft under his hands.

Peace washed over him.

31st of Thornfall, 24th Year of the 11th Rebirth
Golden Hall, Metalkin Province

Devin woke with a sore back and the start of a headache. He sat up with a groan, trying to stretch his legs while he took in his surroundings. There was a weight there and for a moment he panicked. *What did Hunter do now?* He'd woken up in some strange places these past weeks, but the woods? He looked around, and then down at his legs.

Mallory was still lying there, one hand tucked up by her neck, her eyes closed. She was breathing easily and some of the colour had returned to her cheeks. He breathed a sigh of contentment and smiled at her.

The events of the day before came back to him in a whirlwind jumble and he looked around the woods for any sign of wild animals, Dark Spirits, or the white doe, but saw nothing. Mallory's skirt was covering her leg again and he didn't think it proper to check her wound without permission. As much as he'd enjoyed the ride with her, and the time spent talking with her, as much as his whole body ached to be able to spend more time with her, she was still the Metalkin Princess, and he was just a Carainhithe outcast.

She's already found her prince. And besides, she's Metalkin, and you're Carainhithe. You knew from the start you could never be anything special to her. No matter how special she is to you.

He reached out and shook Mallory's shoulder gently. "Princess, it's morning."

She took a deep breath and then groaned. "Oh, my back," she muttered. "Where am I?"

"We're still in the woods," he said.

"So, that wasn't a bad dream then." She stiffened suddenly. "My leg. How bad is it?"

"Does it hurt at all?"

"No."

"Wiggle your toes."

She sat up and did as he instructed. "Nothing, no pain, not in either leg."

"I do not want you to panic," he said. "But last night you were tossed from your horse."

"I remember that," she said. "My leg hurt like a son of a gun."

"That's because you had a one-inch thick piece of wood clear through your thigh."

Her hands went to one leg and then the other and then her gaze returned to his face, silently questioning.

He took a deep breath and told her about their strange visitor. When he had finished, she started pulling her skirt up. He averted his eyes, but he heard her gasp.

"There's nothing there," she said. "No branch, no hole, no mark." After a moment she added, "It's okay, you can look. I covered my legs again."

Blushing he looked at her. "We have to get you home."

She nodded. "I know. I just …" She took a deep breath. "This was nice, well, except for getting thrown, and now they'll probably lock me up forever. I never wanted to be a princess."

"I'm sorry," Devin said. He pulled himself to his feet, pausing to shake the stiffness out of them, and then offered her a hand up. "When you came through the gate, I could see it on your face. You never believed this was possible, and you've never stopped wanting to go back."

"I don't belong," Mallory said. "I try, and I try, and I don't fit in. I do everything wrong. Everyone is always angry with me for something I've done or said or some decision I've made."

"Not everyone," he said gently. "Look, I come from another province, another people, I knew there was no way I could be anything special to you, but somehow I feel drawn to you. I will serve you, in any way I can, for as long as you'll have me in your service."

She smiled softly. "You are special," she said. "You're one of very few people on this island I can call a friend."

The silence between them stretched long and intimate until Devin looked away and cleared his throat. "I have to get you back to Golden Hall."

"Okay," she said. "You're the tracker, which way do we go?"

It was difficult walking through the forest with no path and no horses, especially in a full skirt, but Devin was always there to give her a hand over or around whatever obstacle they came across. He was leading them in a fairly straight line, as far as Mallory could tell, but she didn't know what direction they were headed in. Enough sunlight filtered through the leaves that she could tell it was day, but the sun was too obscured for her to tell east from west.

Her feet were starting to hurt and more than once she'd nearly twisted her ankle. Her hands were scratched from when she'd tripped and caught herself on a tree trunk, one with thick, rough bark. Her hair kept getting in her face, she was hungry, and she was quickly becoming disenchanted of the whole peaceful magic of the forest.

She was just about to ask how much further they had to walk when she heard a sound, far off yet, drifting between the trees. She stopped and looked up. Devin was standing stock-still, his eyes focused off in the distance. He'd obviously heard it too so she waited silently. He brought both hands to his mouth and called, "Here! Here!"

From off in the distance a voice answered, "Hello! Hello!"

"Here! Here!" Devin called again. He turned to look at Mallory, his face lit up in a grin. "Someone's looking for us," he said. "Come on."

"Shouldn't we stand still and let them find us?" she said

"You need food, and water, and a healer to look at you. Come on."

She sighed, hiked up her skirts again, and followed him. Every few yards he'd stop and call out again, listening for the response from the search party and adjusting their path accordingly. She just trudged along behind him. As much as she did want a hot meal and a hot bath she didn't really want to return to the castle.

She was lost in thought and watching where she put her feet and nearly walked into the back of him. "Hey," she said, stopping short.

"We're close," he said. "We'll wait here." He put his hands to his mouth and called again.

Mallory could hear the reply distinctly now, and someone moving through the bushes. She glanced about and then half-sat half-leaned on a fallen tree with a huff.

She half expected Kaelen to come blundering through the trees like an angry bear, ready to scream at her for her reckless behaviour, but it was the kind and weathered face of Jeremy White-Hart that first appeared from behind a tree. "Thank Airon, we've found you," he said. He looked over his shoulder and called, "I've found them!"

More footsteps and branches snapping and soon Devin and Mallory were practically surrounded. A few of the men were Metalkin guards, but most were Animal People and Evergrowth, and from their clothes, commoners or working nobles. Everyone was talking at once. It reminded Mallory of Airon's Gate.

She huffed a little and stood up. "Can we have these conversations when we get back to Golden Hall?"

"Of course," said one of the guards. "Let's head back."

They had to walk back to the horses, but they'd thought to bring extras, so Mallory and Devin could ride most of the way back to Golden Hall. They went at an easy pace and Mallory found herself fighting the urge to kick her horse into a canter and ride away from them all.

As soon as they were through the gates at the castle the procession was halted and Mallory was helped down from her horse.

"I should help brush her," Mallory said. "It's only right."

"You need food and medical attention," the guard insisted. "Your stewards want to see you, and the prince. You have to come with me now."

"Look, it's not proper riding etiquette," she said. "You take care of your sword, don't you? I have to take care of this horse."

"Princess?"

Mallory spun to face this new voice. "What?"

Devin cringed a little at her tone. "I'll take the horse. I'll make sure she's properly tended. You need food at least. You missed dinner last night."

She stared into his pleading eyes a moment and then nodded. "All right. I'll go eat."

"Thank you."

The guard led her inside, staying at her side the entire way to her rooms, even though she'd known her way around for months now. She let Cecilia brush her hair and she gladly shed her torn and bloody dress for a clean one.

"What happened?" Cecilia whispered, staring at the dress.

"You' wouldn't believe me," Mallory said. "But I'll tell you later. I think people are expecting me."

"I think people are waiting to yell at you."

"I'm not surprised." When she stepped out of her room the guard was waiting for her in the hallway. She frowned. "I can find my own way," she said.

"Prince Kaelen's orders, Ma'am. I'm sorry."

She stifled her exasperated sigh and nodded. "Lead on."

Kaelen was waiting for her in the dining room, along with Emilio and Jaspar. Plates had been set out and servants were setting out the food and tea. She forced a smile. "It smells lovely. I'm absolutely famished."

"What were you thinking?" Kaelen bellowed.

She cringed.

"You're Metalkin. You don't go riding for pleasure. Horses are a means to an end, nothing more. You were foolish! Reckless! You could have been killed!"

"Your concern is touching," Emilio said. "But perhaps we should eat and *talk* about this over breakfast."

Mallory could see Kaelen was still fuming but he nodded and pulled out a seat for Mallory. When they'd all served themselves Mallory said, "I'm sorry for worrying everyone. I didn't mean to be gone overnight. There was an accident, and …"

"Were you hurt?" Emilio said.

She wasn't quite sure how to answer that question, so she said, "I'm fine."

"What were you doing out there in the first place?" Kaelen said. "And without telling anyone! And no guards."

"I had a guard," Mallory said.

"I agree with Kaelen," Emilio said. "Your choice in companion was … surprising. Generally, the princess takes official guards with her, not just the castle tracker."

"He brought me back safely," Mallory said. "None of this was his fault. A deer came out of the bushes and spooked the horses. In the resulting confusion we wound up off the trail and we were both tossed from our saddles. It was too late to walk back to the castle and Devin wisely decided it was safer to stay put than to try to make the journey in the dark."

"He put you at risk," Kaelen said. "He shouldn't have been out with you in the first place. You need Metalkin guards looking after you, not that hunter. You could have been killed!"

"Could have," Mallory said. "But here I am, alive and well. I can't change what happened …"

"It won't happen again," Kaelen shouted, slamming his fork down on the table.

"Stop yelling at me," Mallory shouted back. "I'm not a child. I've ridden horses before, without armed guards. I took two years of fencing too, but I wasn't any good at it. I was studying science and medicine, learning things you can't even imagine. But you treat me like a fool! Or an idiot."

"I'm sure Prince Kaelen simply means …"

Mallory cut Jaspar off. "You're just as bad. I know full well you were handling petitions without informing me because you thought I couldn't handle it." She pushed her plate away. "I'm not hungry anymore. I'm going to take a hot bath."

"I'll have Madam Bella check in on you," Emilio said.

Mallory nodded sharply, agreeing to the suggestion, and stormed out.

"She's impossible!" Kaelen said.

Jaspar nodded in eager agreement.

"The two of you haven't exactly been easy to deal with," Emilio said. "Do you really think yelling at her over breakfast is going to make this better? Did you really think keeping her from court was a wise idea?"

"I'm the political steward," Jaspar said, puffing out his chest. "It's up to me to decide what is best for this province ..."

"No, that's Mallory's job," Emilio said.

"It's my job to help her in anyway she requires."

"She's made it clear you've done more than required."

"You wouldn't understand," Jaspar said. "You're not a Metalkin. I have work to do." He set his napkin on his empty plate and left.

Kaelen and Emilio ate their meal in silence, an awkward weight hanging over them the entire time.

When his plate was empty, Kaelen said. "He's right, you're not Metalkin. You're just here to advice Mallory on historical or religious matters. Leave the politics to Jaspar and I."

32nd of Thornfall, 24th Year of the 11th Rebirth
Golden Hall, Metalkin Province

"Thank you for your continued support," Kaelen said, setting the signed contract on his desk and extending a hand to the Gold Guild representative. He fully planned to burn the contract as soon as the man was gone. *I just need to keep up appearances until I get confirmation from Emelia.*

"You're welcome. The Loyalists can count on the Gold Guild in these endeavours. We've already seen the benefit of what you're doing." He cleared his throat. "We also heard about the princess's mishap yesterday."

"Yes. She's headstrong and she doesn't yet fully understand our ways. You know she didn't grow up here." This was his last appointment of the day and he just wanted it to be over with. *If it's not too late, perhaps I have time to go visit Emelia yet tonight.*

"I understand that, I'm just glad she wasn't hurt. What are you doing about him though?"

"Him?"

"I understand a young man from the Animal People was involved. I also understand this same young man attempted to sabotage your connection to Princess Mallory at Airon's Gate and that this same man was spreading unrest about Dark Spirits."

"Oh, well, yes, I suppose he was. I've had very little contact with him since Airon's Gate."

"What about your wife? How often does she see him? How often does she talk to him? Was this a plot on his part, perhaps to prove how dangerous Dark Spirits are? Or is he part of a larger plot, something the Animal People thought up to weaken us?"

"I was under the impression that she ordered him on this little outing," Kaelen said.

"So, he's been grooming her for a while then, convincing her that he's a friend, and putting dangerous ideas in her head. She could have been killed."

And that would have served the Loyalist agenda just fine. You're just upset because you wouldn't have been ready to take advantage of the situation if it had arisen.

He took a deep breath. "She wasn't killed."

"Praise Airon for small favours. I hope you're planning to take a firm stand against this man. His continued employment at the castle would be a troubling sign. We have the utmost faith in you, Kaelen."

"Thank you for your confidence," Kaelen said, his knees trembling.

When the man had gone Kaelen dropped into his chair and buried his face in his hands. *What am I going to do?* He took a deep breath. *Just keep up appearances a little longer. You can do this. Just take all the anger you've been feeling towards your father and all his cronies and let it all out on that fool. You have to do this.*

He knew Devin Sun-Stag had rooms in the castle, he also knew he was most frequently seen around the stables, especially in the evenings. He pushed away from his desk and made his way out to the yard with long, powerful strides. He must have looked impressive because servants skittered out of his way, avoiding eye-contact with him.

Devin was just coming out of the stables. Kaelen closed his eyes and took a deep breath. *You have to do this. You know how to be angry.* With renewed purpose Kaelen approached the smaller man.

"Master Sun-Stag, a word," Kaelen called, stopping Devin in his tracks.

Devin sighed but bowed his head. "Prince Kaelen, how can I be of service?"

"You can explain your actions," Kaelen said in a voice loud enough to draw the attention of passing servants, guards, and guests who happened to be out in the yard.

"Of course," Devin said. "I followed orders, simple as that. I had no choice. I could not have anticipated either the deer or the badger but I did everything I could to keep Ma… Princess Jewel-Rose safe once the accident did occur."

Kaelen noticed the slip immediately and his cheeks heated up. "You dare to refer to the Metalkin Princess by her first name?"

"My apologies, Prince Kaelen. I only ever addressed her by name when she was in distress. It calmed her. I meant no disrespect."

"You've never once shown the proper respect or deference to either the princess or to me," Kaelen bellowed. "And after this foolish, reckless act, I should have you charged with treason!"

"You look fine," the Madam Bella said. "There isn't even a mark on your leg. I don't know what happened out there, but you're completely healed."

"Thank you," Mallory said.

"Don't thank me, I didn't do anything," the healer said.

"You said the magic words," Mallory said. "Now maybe my stewards and my guide will stop hovering."

"You were with Devin Sun-Stag, correct?"

Mallory nodded. "He saved me from bleeding out."

"Did anything strange happen?"

"Not that I saw. Afterwards, he told me about the doe."

"You didn't see any Dark Spirits? Or any strangers?"

"No. Why?"

"I'm surprised, that's all. You were in the woods at night." She went to the counter and began fussing with the little glass bottles there.

"You were asking about Devin specifically. Is there something I need to know about him?"

"Of course not," the Madam Bella said. She offered the princess a tight smile. "You're safe, that's all that matters."

"Yes, I suppose so."

"I have a meeting with Master Spirit-Light, not about you, but I will mention to him that he can stop fussing."

"I'd appreciate that," Mallory said, still feeling confused about the healer's questions. "Do I need to come back?"

"I don't think so. If anything does hurt, or if something else happens, I am here to serve."

"Well, thank you again," Mallory said. She let herself out. Both of her stewards had insisted she take today easy to recover from her ordeal and Mallory was starting to feel bored and cooped up. *I'll go to the stables and apologize to the stable master. I'm sure people have been scolding him since I went missing.*

It was a lovely day outside; the sun was warm, and the gentle breeze smelled fresh and clean. That was one of the nicest changes, the smell of the air. No smog, no smoke, no exhaust fumes, just the smell of green things, horses, and clean, fresh air. She'd had dinner already, but it wasn't yet dusk and she figured she had a few hours before worried servants or guards came looking for her.

I'm inside the walls. I'm perfectly safe. I'm not even going into the city proper.

She nodded in response to the bows of the passing servants as she made her way around the castle. She came to the main yard and paused. Something had drawn a crowd between the stables and the main doors. Frowning, she picked up the front hem of her skirt and hurried to see what the commotion was.

"And after this foolish, reckless act, I should have you charged with treason!"

There was no mistaking who that bellowing voice belonged to. Mallory didn't bother trying to push through the crowd. With skirts in hand she clumsily climbed the paddock rails and made her way along the inside of the fence, around the side of the crowd, until she could see.

Kaelen was standing too close to Devin, his finger pointed in the smaller man's face, everything about his posture and voice meant to be imposing.

"You endangered the princess!" Kaelen was yelling.

Devin felt something shift in him, something dark and familiar. *Not now. It's too early yet. Please Airon, not now.* "I didn't put her at risk," he said, trying to keep his voice even.

"You endangered her, and you did it knowingly and willingly!" Kaelen said, shoving Devin backwards.

Devin closed his eyes, turning his face away from Kaelen. "I live to serve. I would never do anything …"

Kaelen shoved him again. "Treason, do you hear me? And if I can't have you charged with treason I'll have you removed from the city!"

His control snapped, and Devin burst forward, snarling. "I didn't hurt her! I didn't arrange this! But, Airon help me, if you shove me one more time, I will hurt *you*."

The action was so fast Kaelen stumbled backwards as a gasp went through the crowd of onlookers. "It's treason to threaten the prince," Kaelen said, standing up as straight and tall as he could.

"Treason. Treason. You keep saying that word. I wonder why you're so fond of it? Or perhaps afraid of it?"

Kaelen sucked in a breath with a hiss. "How dare you accuse me of …"

"I accuse you of nothing," Devin said. He could feel his control returning and he knew he had to remove himself from this situation as quickly as possible. He was likely already late for his meeting with Master Spirit-Light. "If you want to press charges, have the princess issue a warrant. I won't resist a guard following her orders. Otherwise, excuse me, I have somewhere I need to be." He stepped past Kaelen and hurried across the yard towards the servants' entrance.

Kaelen blustered for a moment then spun on his heel and stalked back inside. The crowd quickly dispersed, very few of them noticing Mallory hovering near the stables.

Mallory twisted and pulled at her fingers. Her heart was hammering in her chest. *There was something off about that argument, something …*

"Princess Mallory," Master White-Hart said, stepping out into the sunlight. "You're not here to plan another ride, are you?"

"Not right away," Mallory said, laughing. "I'm not sure the guards would let me out the gate no matter how loudly I demanded it."

"I suspect you're right. I'm glad to see you back in one piece."

"I did have a reason for coming down here though. I wanted to thank you for coming after me, and to apologize."

"A princess apologizing to me? Now that's a first. Whatever do you need to apologize for?"

"I'm sure that you took more than your fair share of scoldings from a great many people the last few days, and the blame for what happened to me is solely on my shoulders."

"They can't yell at you, you're the princess, so they yell at me instead."

"They yelled at me too," Mallory said.

"You scared them. They care."

"Some of them," Mallory murmured. "I was happy to hear that the horses made it back safely. I would never have forgiven myself if something had happened to them."

"Thank you, Princess. That means the world to me."

An idea suddenly came to her and she acted on it without hesitation. "I don't suppose I could just brush one of the horses? If I promise not to put a saddle on it?"

"I'll let you brush one horse, but you have to do it in the stables so that I don't get in anymore trouble on your account," he said with a familiar and slightly cheeky grin.

"Thanks," she said, returning the smile.

He set her up with a young mare and a bucket of brushes and left her to the soothing work. The stables reminded her of home and she could almost pretend that it wasn't the Isle of Light waiting for her outside. But she wasn't here to pretend, she was here to think.

There had been something about Devin during that argument that bothered her. The Devin she knew, though she had to admit she didn't know him well, was reserved, polite, almost soft-spoken. Even in the face of a crisis he hadn't yelled at her, or anyone else, and she'd seen him in two emergencies now.

Kaelen could be difficult, god knew she'd wanted to scream at him more often than she gave into the urge. Far more often, and the urge had gotten worse since Taeya's wedding. Even given Kaelen's effect on people, Devin's explosive behaviour, the way he'd threatened an unarmed man with violence, it just wasn't right, it didn't fit what she knew of the man.

Stress can make people do funny things, she thought. A little voice in her mind chimed in, *Why was Madam Bella asking about him? Why was she asking about a stranger? Who …*

"Princess?"

Mallory looked up.

Jeremy White-Hart was hovering nearby. "I need to get her put away for the night. And I should send you back to the castle proper."

"Before someone comes looking for me. Yes, you're right. Thank you for this."

"Excuse me for saying so, Princess, but this is the first time I've ever heard of any Metalkin wanting anything to do with animals."

"I guess it's just because I didn't grow up here," she said.

"Perhaps," he said. "But if I didn't know better I'd say you were the Animal People's Princess."

Mallory laughed. "They already have a princess, and I already have a Metalkin prince."

"Then it must be the influence of the Wide World. Good-night Princess."

"Good night."

Now, *that* was something new to think about. When she'd come through the gate everyone had told her she was the Metalkin Princess and she'd accepted it because they knew best, and they already had four other princesses in the four other provinces. She hadn't paused to consider that they might be wrong because no one else had paused to consider the possibility. There had been no reason to consider it.

But now, now Taeya, the Animal People's princess had married an Evergrowth man and everything was different.

That doesn't change the fact that you married a Metalkin man.

"Hey!"

Mallory's gaze jerked upwards and she saw the man on the path in front of her a split second too late to stop herself from walking into him, knocking herself off balance.

Hunter reached for Mallory, stopping her from falling.

"I'm sorry," she said. "I wasn't watching." Though, to be fair, he was all in black, even his face hidden by the shadow of his hood, and it had started to get dark – he'd been easy to miss. They stood there for a moment, his hands on her arms, her heart and breath racing.

"It's no problem. Princess."

She was getting very warm. She cleared her throat. "I was just on my way inside."

"Really? You're not off on some new adventure?"

"No."

"That's too bad. I should very much like to take you on a grand adventure."

His familiarity should have bothered her, should have offended her, but she felt herself blushing. "It wouldn't be proper," she said.

"I never bother with what's proper or not," he said. The corner of his mouth crept up in a sly smile. "Proper is boring. You feel it too, don't you?"

"I don't know what you're talking about."

"You're not from here. You crave the freedom of your old life in the Wide World and the confines of being proper make you feel like a caged animal. You'd go back if you could."

She'd started to pull away but those last six words made her stop and stare.

He grinned, leaning in closer to her. "Perhaps I will see you again soon, Princess." He released her, stepped around her, and disappeared into the shadows.

She stood staring after him for a long time, her heart still beating too fast. When she felt calmer, steadier, she returned to the castle, almost running into Emilio at the door.

"Princess! Where have you been? Do you know how late it is?"

"I didn't leave the gates, I didn't even go near the walls. I'm fine."

"You don't understand how dangerous it is."

"I was told my own castle was safe from Dark Spirits."

"Of course it is, but that's not the only …"

"You mean, you're worried about Hunter. Because Hunter and Devin are the same person."

"How did you …? When did you …?"

"Today. I'm right though, aren't I?"

"Come with me," Emilio said, putting a hand on Mallory's shoulder, looking over his own. "This is far too public a place to have this discussion."

As Emilio closed the door of his private study Mallory started speaking again. "He was possessed at Airon's Gate. But that was seven, almost eight months ago. Taeya told me all about Henry Canter when I was in Dinas Rhosyn. Shouldn't he be dead by now? Or a raving lunatic?"

"Yes, he should be."

"What happened?"

Emilio sat and pinched the bridge of his nose. "We don't know. We've been monitoring him since he returned from Airon's Gate. Hunter is a newer development. He appeared while you were in Stones Shore for Rheeya's wedding. He surfaced every night for a while, and then only about once a week, then every night again. It seems to come and go in waves like that, but after every bad period the good periods are worse."

"The thing inside of him is getting stronger." There was conviction in her voice.

There was exhaustion in his. "Yes."

Mallory settled into the other chair. "How long have you known that they're the same?"

"I discovered the truth while you were at the Sun Temple for Vonica's wedding."

Before Hunter attacked a guard, she thought. "So, the letter and the gold at court that day …"

"I had Devin write that after charges were brought against Hunter in court. And then I had Devin take a tour of the hunting camps in the area so that Hunter would be out of sight."

"Because if Hunter had been arrested, we would have found Devin in the cell the next morning."

Emilio nodded, "And I couldn't be sure that Hunter would allow himself to be peacefully apprehended. I didn't want someone to die."

"Admirable, but why isn't Devin in custody? Don't you lock up the possessed?" She had to ask, the curiosity was burning at her, even if she was grateful they'd broken the rules.

"As you said, Devin is a unique case. Bernard and I wanted the chance to study him, find out more about these possessions and the Dark Spirits. Devin assured us that, if he ever became violent or unpredictable, that he would hand himself over without a fight."

"But Hunter has been violent, and the very appearance of Hunter was unpredicted, and unpredictable."

"Do you want us to imprison him?"

"No." She blushed and looked away. "Devin is my friend. I don't have many friends here. I want to save him, not condemn him."

"No one has ever been saved from possession before."

"No one has ever lived this long with a Dark Spirit before," she countered. "There must be a way."

"I wouldn't even know where to begin. I like the man too, but there are more pressing things to deal with."

"I know," Mallory said. Cecilia's warning and the things she'd seen with her own eyes were proof of how bad things had gotten. "Eight months. It doesn't feel like long enough to learn how to run a government, but I'm out of time. I'm needed."

"Yes, you are." Things with Devin and Hunter were bewildering, a complete unknown, but this, Emilio knew as certainty. Whatever was happening, they needed Mallory now more than ever.

"It's time for me to start making decisions on my own, without a prince or a steward." She took a deep breath. "And they aren't going to be happy about it."

7th of Daggerfall, 24th Year of the 11th Rebirth
Golden Hall, Metalkin Province

Kaelen didn't feel that the apprentices' courtyard at the Blacksmiths' Guild was an appropriate place to discuss private business matters, but his father was teaching and refused to be interrupted.

"You can walk with me, or you can wait for me to finish," he told his son before stopping to correct a young man's swing. Around them the pounding of hammer on metal filled the air.

"You summoned me here. You should have asked me to come at a better time," Kaelen said.

His father frowned. "Watch your tone with me."

"You asked me here to discuss private affairs. Do you really trust these young ears enough to speak so openly around them? Do you really trust them to keep what they overhear to themselves?"

His father nodded sharply and waved over Kaelen's brother, Shawn. "Watch the youngsters. Make sure no one loses a hand or an eye today."

"Yes, Father."

"Come sit in the shade with me then, Kaelen."

"Thank you," Kaelen said, following his father to a wooden shelter against the courtyard wall.

Shane Iron-Heart poured two glasses of wine, handing one to his son. "Your indiscretions have to stop."

"I don't know what you're …"

"The girl, Kaelen. I know you haven't stopped writing her or speaking with her. What do you intend? You can't marry her. Are you going to have a child with her anyway? Do you realize the scandal and ruin that could bring on all of us?"

Kaelen's heart was hammering. He and Emelia had been discreet but there was always a stable hand or servant who could reveal their secrets, not matter how careful they were. They'd been trying for a month now, but they still didn't know for certain if she was with child. *It's just coincidence, just something to intimidate you. He doesn't know. He can't know.* "Do you realize Holy Week is approaching?" Kaelen said, trying to take the focus off of Emelia long enough that he wouldn't reveal something by accident.

"I know the time of year. Your point?"

"We were wed less than a month after Holy Week. That means it will soon be a year since Mallory arrived here, and then a year that we've been wed."

"And?"

"And, she still insists I remain in my own rooms. She won't even allow me to dine with her in her rooms. If we dine together it is in one of the dining rooms. All the servants are aware of this. I wouldn't be surprised if most of the nobles in the city have heard rumours of it."

"You aren't trying hard enough. You're distracted by this affair. You've been seeing this girl the entire time, and don't try to lie about it."

"Mallory has always kept me at a distance!"

"Keep your voice down."

"You're the one that wanted to meet here."

"You'll put an end to this affair, now, before it becomes public knowledge."

"You don't have the right to command me to do anything."

"I'm your father, the head of your family and house …"

"I'm Kaelen Jewel-Rose now, I don't owe allegiance to my *family* anymore. That's what it means to be the prince."

"You're not the real Metalkin prince and you know it. You only have claim to the title of prince because of me, because of other men like me."

"You can't expose me without exposing yourselves and your whole insane plot."

"Master Iron-Heart, I'm sorry to intrude. The farrier is here. He says you asked him to come and work with the apprentices, something about shaping horse shoes."

"Yes. I'll be right there."

The page bowed and hurried off again.

Shane turned to Kaelen. "This isn't something I can pass off to another. I have to supervise. We'll continue this conversation after the demonstration."

"I'll come with you," Kaelen said.

Shane stepped out of the shade of the shelter, stuck two fingers in his mouth, and whistled sharply. All banging in the courtyard ceased. "Let's go you lazy lot. We're learning about horseshoes."

Some of the higher born apprentices grumbled but that stopped after a sharp look from Shane. The young men followed Shane to the other end of the courtyard where the farrier waited for them with the castle stable master and two horses.

The farrier, Corey Irons, waited until they were all assembled before addressing them. "One of the most common and most important jobs you will do as a black smith is shape horseshoes. It's not as glamourous or exciting as other things you will learn to make but it is essential."

"Aren't all horseshoes the same?" one boy said.

Corey nodded. "At first, yes. Then I take them and fit them to the horse and mark where you need to reshape them for the best fit. A farrier and a smith work hand in hand to ensure each horse is cared for properly. Now, each of you will have the chance to come and take a close look at the difference between a raw horseshoe and a fitted one."

"We can't work with the horses," one of the boys said, taking a step back.

"Don't worry," Corey said, chuckling. "We grabbed some quiet old girls from the stables at the castle for you. They won't give you any trouble. I work closely with stable masters and stable hands doing this job, something each of you will have to get accustomed to. Master Shane will hold this horse while I give each of you the lesson. Jeremy will give the same lesson, so we get through this in good time. He'll need someone to hold the horse."

"My son can do it," Shane said.

Kaelen glanced around but his brother had disappeared. He shrugged and stepped over, accepting the lead from the stable master. Once his hands were free, the older man bowed. "Prince Kaelen, an honour to work with you."

"Prince or not I'm still a son," Kaelen said, hating the words.

"You teach these lads a strong lesson in respect and duty by being here."

Kaelen just nodded stiffly.

"Bring the old girl over here and hold her steady so I can lift her foot."

Kaelen took a step in the direction indicated. The horse refused to follow. Kaelen pulled harder. The horse leaned back, straining the lead.

Jeremy White-Heart chuckled. "Not like her to be stubborn."

"Maybe someone else should do this."

"I've got it," said Shawn, jogging up. "Sorry, needed a moment to relieve myself."

"She's all yours," Kaelen said, shoving the lead into his brother's hands. "I'll wait inside."

"Yes, yes," Shane said, waving a hand.

Kaelen stalked off between the two horses. No one was paying attention, but even if they had, it happened too fast for any of them to stop. He'd nearly passed the horses when the one his father was holding took a half step to the side, bumping Kaelen's shoulder with her hindquarters. It wasn't a hard bump, but it was enough to knock him off balance and change the course of his path. His next step put him behind the stubborn mare.

Her hind leg came up and shot out, her shoed foot slamming into Kaelen's hip. He let out a pained and startled cry, drawing everyone's attention, and dropped to his knees.

The second kick connected with the side of his head.

Mallory was enjoying a rare quiet moment with a glass of wine and an adventurous account of one of the acolytes who had supposedly travelled with the Prophet Abner on his journey to unite the provinces. It wasn't as good as Agatha Christie, but it was better than economics. Court was over, she had no meetings, and Kaelen was off at some meeting of his own. Which was good, because she was still mad at him for yelling at Devin.

She sighed, feeling content. It had been nearly a year since the priests had appeared before her on that busy city street, nearly a year since she'd stepped through the impossible portal into an impossible world, and she was finally beginning to feel like she fit.

She almost didn't notice the door open but she couldn't ignore the servant speaking her name.

"I'm busy," she said, sipping her wine.

"I'm sorry, it's an emergency. There's been an accident at the Blacksmith's Guild and Prince Kaelen has been injured."

She should have felt a rush of panic, but after the fight the other day, all she could muster was a feeling of indignation at being disturbed. She slammed the book shut. "Fine. Let's go."

Mallory had never been to the Blacksmith's Guild which, looking back, was quite odd since it was the guild Kaelen had belonged to before marrying her, the guild his father and brothers belonged to still. She was led straight inside to a back room where the Guild Master awaited her. "Princess Jewel-Rose. Thank you for coming. Please accept my most humble apologies. This shouldn't have happened."

"I was told it was an accident."

"Yes. A horse brought in for a horseshoe lesson kicked him."

"Did you anger the horse?"

"No, Princess," he said, obviously taken aback by the suggestion.

"Then you have nothing to apologize for. Where is he? Can I see him?"

"The guild sent a healer over, she's with him now," the Guild Master said. "She did not want to be disturbed. I'm certain though that you …"

"No, we will not disturb her. Is there somewhere we can wait?"

"Yes." He waved over a younger man. "Take the princess to the day room where Kaelen's family is waiting."

Mallory hadn't seen Shane Iron-Heart since the wedding. Kaelen had mentioned several times that they should visit his family but somehow the occasion had never presented itself. Now, Shane rose and bowed, his body stiff, his eyes vacant. The two other young men in the room, likely Shane's other sons copied the movement, their faces confused, bewildered.

"Were any of you there when this accident happened?" Mallory asked.

Shane nodded.

"Sit, please, all of you," she said. "And someone can tell me what happened."

"It was the horse," Shawn said.

Mallory turned to him. "We haven't met."

"Shawn Iron-Heart. Kaelen's brother. I'm older by a year."

"Yes, you have the look of him. You were there?"

"Yes, Princess. We were showing the apprentices how to work with the farriers shoeing the horses. Kaelen was going to wait inside. It happened so fast. He seemed to stumble and then the one mare kicked him. That's when we all started forward. I was holding the horse. I pulled her forward, but she wouldn't budge, and she was already kicking out a second time."

"I see. Being kicked by a horse once is never a pleasant experience, but twice in one day? Kaelen will be surly until he can walk on that leg again."

Shawn looked down at his hand. "It's worse than that, Princess. The second blow struck his head."

"I see." Even back home, in a world with MRI machines and medically induced comas, a swift kick to the head by a sufficiently powerful horse was fatal at worst, and severely life altering at best. *If* Kaelen woke up he could be a vegetable, stuck in bed for the rest of his life, or suffer brain damage that left him with the wits of a child.

None of them seemed like good options. The dazed faces around her made more sense now. They weren't sure if their son was going to wake up.

"The horses came from the castle stable," said the younger man.

"You are?"

"Will, the younger brother."

"Were you there?"

"No, M'Lady. I was at work. I work with a sword smith in the city."

"You say the horses came from the castle? Given that the stable master there is one of the best in the province, wouldn't that make it one of the best places to get horses for training purposes? Especially when you're training youngsters who aren't supposed to be good with animals?"

"That's why we do it that way," Shane said. "The castle stable master and castle farrier were there to give the lesson. They promised us two quiet horses."

"The one I was holding," Shawn said, "The one that injured Kaelen, she'd already shown a dislike for him. He was holding her a moment, before I got there, and she wouldn't listen to him at all. Wouldn't listen to me either."

"Horses can be stubborn," Mallory said. "They have a mind of their own."

"The Animal People have uncanny control over those beasts," Will said. "They can whisper them calm when they panic, urge them faster than our guards can. What if that Tracker that Kaelen was suspicious of did something to the horse before it came here? What if this was intentional?"

"I don't think …"

Shane cut her off. "Yes, that's it exactly. What was his name?"

"Sun-Stag," Will said.

"I highly doubt …"

"That was it," Shane went on, still ignoring her. "He was critical of Kaelen's claim to the throne from the beginning. If my son dies, I'll … I'll …"

Mallory went to the door and leaned out, waving to the page. "Send up one of my guards immediately."

"Yes, Princess."

When the guard arrived Mallory said, "Send someone to the castle and have Devin Sun-Stag put in protective custody."

"What does that mean?"

"It means I want you to take him to the dungeon but explain to him it's for his own safety and that the Princess doesn't believe he's guilty of anything."

"Yes, Princess. I'll see to it immediately."

"Thank you."

Shane was still raging when she came back into the room.

"It's done," she said.

"What is?" Shawn said as Shane's rant stuttered to a halt mid-insult.

"I've sent a guard to the castle to take Devin Sun-Stag into custody. If Prince Kaelen dies because of this accident, then we will have a trial."

"Thank you, Princess," Shane said, bowing as best he could while sitting.

Don't thank me yet, she thought. *You might not like the outcome of the trial.*

The door opened, and the page bowed. "The healer says you should come. All of you."

"Thank you," Mallory said. She allowed Shane to go first before accepting the arm Shawn offered to her.

They had Kaelen in a classroom, stretched out on a counter. He had a meager pillow beneath his head and a blanket over his body. Mallory could just see the shallow rise and fall of his chest.

His mother ran over and took his hand, weeping openly.

"There's nothing more I can do," the healer said softly. "The leg wouldn't have been a problem. It was a clean break. A few weeks bed rest and a few weeks careful use, and he'd have been right as rain. The second kick …"

Mallory could understand the healer's hesitation to go on. There was a dangerous light in Shane's eyes. Mallory pulled the healer aside. "What about the second kick?" she prompted.

"There's a break, in his skull. The skin was intact, and I could feel swelling there. I made a small incision to relieve the pressure, but I don't think it's enough. We aren't made to bleed there. I can't set the bone. I can't get inside to stop the bleeding. I don't even know where the blood is coming from." She stopped and took a deep breath. "Unless that bleeding stops, and soon, he will die."

"Thank you for your service today. It's hard when you cannot save them, I understand that." Mallory lowered her voice further. "If the family gives you any trouble come to the castle and speak to me directly. Not Master Black-Kettle, you insist on speaking to me."

"Yes, Princess."

With a final glance at Kaelen's body Mallory started for the door.

"You're not staying?" Shawn said.

"He's already dead," she said. "His body just hasn't figured it out yet. I have letters to write and a funeral to plan and you have a son to mourn. When you are ready, come to the castle and we will discuss laying him to rest." She left with their stunned stares on her back.

Masters Black-Kettle and Spirit-Light were waiting for her when she returned to the castle.

"Where is Prince Kaelen?" Jaspar asked.

"At the blacksmith's guild. We will need to arrange for his transport to the temple."

"But, shouldn't he go to his room?" Jaspar said.

Emilio put a hand on Jaspar's shoulder, but his gaze stayed fixed on Mallory's face. "It was that bad?"

"The healer says it's a matter of time. His family will be here later today, maybe tomorrow, to finalize arrangements. Notify Honourable Bernard."

"This has never happened before," Jaspar said. "For a prince to die within a year of being crowned? Never. What about the soul bond? What about …"

"I've only been here a year," Mallory said. "But I seem to be hearing 'that's impossible' and 'that's never happened before' a lot. We will figure it out, somehow."

"What about the man you had arrested?" Jaspar said. "Was he involved?"

"Devin Sun-Stag? Kaelen's family seemed to think so. I was more afraid that a grieving man might do something he'd later come to regret."

"You think him innocent?" Emilio said. There was something about his expression, something too tightly controlled.

Mallory deflected for the time being. "I think a trial is only fair. Master Black-Kettle, I need you to go speak with Honourable Bernard now, and then send out the needed letters to the needed people concerning the funeral. Except for High Priest Silver-Cloud. I will write him personally."

Jaspar bowed. "Yes Princess."

"You sent him away," Emilio said.

"You want to speak about Devin, but you don't want to speak in front of Master Black-Kettle. Is that right?"

Emilio stared at her, mouth agape. "How did you …"

" You looked distressed by this whole thing, and I know you're not fond of Jaspar. You think Devin might have done it."

"Yes. I understand that you and Devin have become friends, of sorts, but he is dangerous."

"Because he and Hunter are the same person."

Emilio nodded. "Devin Sun-Stag would never harm a man, not without good cause and no matter how much he disliked Kaelen, he did not have good cause. Hunter, on the other hand, is quite capable of killing a person with little provocation."

"I'll take that under advisement. Oh, there's a healer, she helped Kaelen after the accident. I'm concerned his family could become belligerent, looking for someone to blame. I've instructed her to come here if there's trouble."

"That's wise. The Iron-Heart family isn't known for their kindness."

"I'm going to write that letter to the high priest. And I think this is an occasion that calls for a Sun Hawk."

"Yes, you are right about that."

"Would you go and speak with Devin, let him know what is going on? If I must sit as judge for this trial it would be a bad idea for me to speak to him until then."

"Of course."

"And see that he has food and drink and some small comforts. At this time, I don't consider him a criminal."

"I'll see what I can do." *Now would be a bad time for anyone to figure out that he and Hunter are one and the same.*

Mallory preferred writing to the other princesses over guild reps or other nobles. The girls had come to accept her casual way of writing and didn't pressure her into using long lists of titles. This letter, however, had to go to the high priest, and given the subject, definitely required every official title she could use.

To the Most Honourable Silver-Cloud, High Priest of Airon,

I received your letter after my accident. Thank you for your concern. I am doing well. There is no mark on my leg at all, which everyone agrees is odd.

Since Betha left for Caranhall, I have been working tirelessly to find the gemstones and the foals but to no avail. I have my suspicions, however, as to why my attempts met with failure and I believe things are about to change on that front.

None of this is why I am writing you. I suppose I am avoiding saying the words. I regret to inform you that there has been a tragic accident in the city and Prince Kaelen Jewel-Rose of House Iron-Heart was killed.

At the time of writing this he is still alive, but the healer says it is a fractured skull with bleeding on the brain. I'm sorry. That's the other-world me speaking. He was kicked in the head by a stubborn mare. The blow cracked his skull. The healer says there is bleeding that she can neither locate the source of nor stop. I have seen this type of injury before coming here. It is a matter of time, hours or days, before he dies. You do not yet have the medical instruments needed to treat this injury, and even with the technology we have in the Wide World this type of injury is often fatal.

We are preparing for his funeral now. If this is something you need to attend due to his political status, please write me so I can delay the service until your arrival, if needed.

I'm sorry this letter could not contain better news.

Princess Mallory Jewel-Rose

She took the scroll to the aviary personally and requested a Sun Hawk from the Hawk Master.

He frowned. "So, there is bad news afoot then."

"Rumour travels fast," Mallory said. "That doesn't surprise me. I suppose I will need to make an official announcement."

"That bad?"

"Probably worse. This needs to go to Most Honourable Silver-Cloud. When the response arrives have it sent directly to me, not to my stewards."

"Of course, Princess."

8th of Daggerfall, 24th Year of the 11th Rebirth
Golden Hall, Metalkin Province

The healer arrived at the castle shortly after breakfast and the poor woman was shaking so badly she couldn't hold her tea cup without spilling. After the third try she set the cup down and folded her hands in her lap.

"Did they threaten you?"

"Me, the horse, the farrier, the stable master, some man I've never heard of or met … As soon as you left yesterday, they started shouting. They said that if I didn't save his life, I would face consequences. I told them I needed something from the Healer's Guild, some ingredient to make medicine, and I left. I thought it was over, but a page from the Blacksmith's Guild arrived at our guild hall this morning asking after me. My Guild Master contacted me and I came here."

Mallory nodded. "You're safe here. You did everything you could, and his death is not your fault. I will have a room made up for you here until this can be settled."

"I'm sorry that this is necessary."

"So am I."

There was a knock at the door and Jaspar strode in. "Princess, the Iron-Heart family is here to see you. Shall I show them in?"

"No."

Jaspar's pompous attitude faltered. "No?"

"I'm in the middle of a meeting. Show them to another sitting room, provide them with refreshments, and tell them I will be there as soon as I can."

Jaspar looked at the healer then back at Mallory. He looked a little pale. "Of course, Princess. I'll use the sitting room off the main hall."

"Thank you." Mallory turned back to the healer. "You will stay here, at least until the trial is complete. I will have one of the girls bring the palace healer up to keep you company."

"That's kind of you."

"Now, I am going to see what the Iron-Heart family wants."

"Princess, be careful. The Iron-Hearts are a powerful family in this city."

"And I am the princess. What are they going to do? Threaten to arrest me?"

"I don't know, but please, be careful."

Mallory nodded. "I will."

She reached the sitting room just as a servant came rushing out, tripping over her own feet and nearly dropping the thankfully empty tray she was carrying. She stumbled, catching herself on Mallory's arm. When she realized who she'd nearly run into she took a step back, her cheeks going red.

"Forgive me, Princess."

"I'm glad you didn't fall," Mallory said. "What's your hurry?"

The girl glanced over her shoulder.

"Go."

The girl nodded and bolted down the hallway.

Mallory went into the sitting room. "I'll not have the staff here abused just because you're in a foul temper," she said.

Shane scowled at her. "Where were you? We are the prince's family! This is a matter of …"

"My business is my own," Mallory said, cutting him off. "Sit, please, all of you. I assume, if you're here, that Kaelen has died?"

"No thanks to that incompetent healer," Will said. "She should be in a cell next to that Sun-Stag character."

"Why would I do that? The healer didn't kill your brother."

"She didn't help!" Will said.

"She *couldn't* help, there's a difference," Mallory said. "In the Wide World they have machines you can't begin to imagine, machines that take pictures of the inside of your body. Even with machines like that, people regularly die, especially when they are struck in the head."

"Where is Devin Sun-Stag?" Shane said.

"In custody," Mallory said. "And none of you have permission to speak with him at this time. If any of you attempt to set foot in the castle dungeons, I'll have them prepare a room there for you and you can stay there until the trial."

"You're threatening us?" Shane said.

"Yes."

He'd likely been expecting her to backpedal or deny it. Her simple answer left him blinking in surprise.

She took advantage of the silence and carried on. "Master Black-Kettle and Honouarble Bernard have begun preparations for the funeral and Most Honouarble Silver-Cloud has been notified. Of course, the entire Iron-Heart family will be given a place of honour at the service. Where is Kaelen's grandfather interred?"

"We have a family crypt," Shawn said. "All of the cremated remains of our ancestors dating back to before the pact are interred there."

"Then Kaelen should join them," Mallory said. "You will require an urn?"

Shawn nodded.

"The crown will, of course, pay for it. Gold, you think? Or silver? Or is iron more fitting?"

"Now wait a minute," Shane said. "The princes of Metalkin are interred here at the temple with their princesses."

"I don't plan on dying anytime soon," Mallory said. "Let him rest with his family until my time of passing comes. Then he will be moved in a grand procession to join me."

"That is most generous," Shawn said.

"That is most suspicious," Shane bellowed. "Why won't you let him be interred at the temple now?"

"I assume you left the body at the guild hall. I will have arrangements made for him to be taken care of. Do you have a preference regarding the urn?"

"Now wait just a minute!" Shane shouted.

"The trial will likely be held after the funeral, unless we have to wait for Most Honourable Silver-Cloud to arrive for the service, in which case we will hold the trial first. And keep in mind that such outbursts will not be permitted at the trial."

"I don't like your tone," Shane said.

"And I don't like yours. However, since your son has just died in a horrible accident, I'm choosing to overlook your poor manners and excuse them as grief. Aside from the local noble families, is there anyone I should be extending an invitation to for this service? And is there anyone who should be excluded?"

"No, no one," Shawn said quickly, before his father could suck in a big enough breath to begin whatever shouted rant he had in mind. "I'm sure Master Black-Kettle will be considerate with the invitations."

"There will also be a period of public mourning, before the service. This will allow the common people to mourn the passing of their prince."

"What about the farrier and the stable master?" Will said. "Are you putting them on trial as well?"

"I will be summoning them to the trial," Mallory said. "I will require their testimony and if I find anything damning against them it will be easy to arrest them. And no, the horse will not be harmed."

"It seems you've already made up your mind in all matters," Shane said. "Why are we even here?"

"So that you know what is happening. And so that I could get information from you."

Shane stood. "Do you require anything else?"

"No. Not at this time."

"Then, if you'll excuse us, I must speak to the rest of my family and see to it that the crypt is prepared."

"Of course. I will see all of you at the service." She waited, smiling, while the three men filed out, Will and Shane with their backs straight and their heads held high, only Shawn flashing her an apologetic smile as he passed.

**11th of Daggerfall, 24th Year of the 11th Rebirth
Golden Hall, Metalkin Province
The Funeral of Prince Kaelen Iron-Heart**

    The message from Baraq Silver-Cloud had arrived early on the eighth and had read, "My presence is not required. My condolences to you and the Iron-Heart family. If you have not already written the other princesses, I suggest you do so but inform them that they are not expected at the funeral." Mallory had expected more but at least she knew to get the funeral over with. She'd spent part of yesterday writing letters to the other princesses.

    They'd opened the temple to the public on the tenth, setting Kaelen's urn on a pedestal in the center of the compass rose floor mosaic. There were three men, either priests or acolytes, standing watch over the urn at all times and guards at every door but there were no problems. The people who filed through over the day were quiet, respectful, and likely more curious than mournful.

    Today the temple was filled with nobles, all in somber dress. All except Mallory herself.

    "Is there a colour for grieving?" she had asked Cecilia that morning. "Are they expecting me to wear black or something?"

    "No, Princess," Cecilia said. "How could the colour of cloth indicate grief?"

"Different cultures have different ideas. I'll wear red, today, the most vibrant red you have."

There was little talking, even before the service began. Kaelen's brothers and father, were seated in the front row with Mallory. She wasn't looking forward to their close proximity, but it was necessary in order to maintain appearances for the time being.

Honourable Bernard talked at length about the wisdom and courage the young prince had shown in his short life, but Mallory wasn't paying attention to the flattery. She was more interested in the crowd, in the misty-eyed women dabbing their faces with handkerchiefs, the stony-faced old men, the bored-looking young men. She wasn't sure what she was looking for but the longer she watched the more she was sure some of the older men were exchanging angry looks with each other. She made mental note of the suspects.

In a moment of silence between prayers a particularly loud sob was heard. Shane scowled at the sound. Curious, Mallory tried to locate the source, expecting a distraught aunt or cousin. The only face that looked like it had been crying at any length was a pretty, dark-haired girl at the opposite side of the temple from Kaelen's family.

Is this Kaelen's secret friend? What was her name? Emily? Amelia? Something like that.

The service ended with a reassurance from Bernard that the soul bond had been completed and thus, Kaelen's death would not affect the strength of The Pact. Kaelen's ashes were carried from the temple by a procession of guards and loaded into a carriage. Mallory and Kaelen's family followed the procession, climbing into a second carriage.

They rode to the Iron-Heart family crypt where Kaelen was laid to rest with his forefathers. *And let him stay there,* Mallory thought as the door was closed. For the first time in nearly a year, she felt free.

14th of Daggerfall, 24th Year of the 11th Rebirth
Golden Hall, Metalkin Province
The Trial of Devin Sun-Stag

She'd made up her mind a week ago about the outcome of this trial which didn't make her the most impartial of judges, but it did fill her with confidence as she dressed and made her way down to the main hall. She'd spent much of the last week trying to anticipate every hurdle she would face in holding the trial, and every argument they would try to present so she would be prepared no matter what.

They'd brought in extra benches because of the number of nobles expected to attend. Even so, some of them had to stand.

A boy rushed in moments before Mallory was to enter the hall, out of breath, a letter clutched in his hand. "Apologies," he stammered, wheezing and trying to catch his breath. "A letter from Most Honourable Silver-Cloud."

"Another one?" Mallory murmured. She took the offered scroll. "My thanks. I will look at this after the trial."

"The Royal Princess, Mallory Brock Jewel-Rose, the Eleventh of her Name, Princess of the Metalkin," Jaspar said as she entered.

She settled quickly and addressed the crowd. "I will have no outbursts today. If you can't keep quiet, leave. If I have need of your opinion or testimony, I will ask for it." She hoped the very visible presence of guards in the room would make her point crystal clear.

"I'm sure by now everyone is aware of how Prince Kaelen died. His brother and father seem to think there was misconduct or conspiracy involved. Normally, a horse-kick to the head doesn't require investigation or trial, but given that the deceased was the Prince, I thought it best to have the clearest possible picture of his passing. Master White-Hart and Master Irons please come forward."

The two men approached the steps and bowed.

"Tell me how you selected the horses, when the selection was made, and what you saw while at the Blacksmith's Guild."

Corey Irons started. "I went to Master White-Hart the evening before the accident. He said he was available to help with the lesson and agreed to have two docile mares ready. He was waiting for me with the horses and we went together to the guild hall."

"I had it in my head which horses to take," Jeremy White-Hart said. "But I didn't pull them out of their stalls until maybe an hour before they were needed. I had a few lads clean their hooves and give them a brushing."

"At any time in this process did you tell Devin Sun-Stag which horses you intended to bring with you?"

"No Princess."

"The man, Hunter, is a known associate of Devin Sun-Stag. Was he aware of the horses you'd selected?"

"No Princess. And neither of them were in the stable when we were preparing the horses that morning."

Mallory turned to the farrier. "Did you inform Devin Sun-Stag, or Hunter, that you had this demonstration coming up? Or where you were taking the horses?"

"No Princess."

"Is it safe to assume that Devin Sun-Stag had no contact with the horses after they were groomed on the day of the accident?"

"Perfectly safe. We groomed them and then left. Those two horses were never out of my sight," Jeremy said. "And we didn't encounter Devin or Hunter on the trip to the Guild Hall either."

"What happened at the guild hall?"

"Prince Kaelen volunteered to hold the horse for me," Jeremy said "While his father held the horse for Master Irons. The girl was being stubborn, which was odd for her. That's when Prince Kaelen's brother took over holding her and the prince declared he was going to wait for his father indoors. He walked between the horses and stumbled. He took a step, to regain his balance and that put him right behind the old girl. She lashed out twice with her hind leg, catching Kaelen once in the leg, and once in the head."

"That all seems clear enough. You're both free to have a seat. I'll have the head of the Blacksmith's Guild come forward."

Mallory had not warned him that she'd be asking for his testimony and was pleased by the look of surprise on his face as he hurried forward.

He bowed deeply. "I was indoors when the accident happened. I don't know what I could tell you that …"

"Aside from the farrier and the stable master, were there any other guests at the guild hall on the day of the accident?"

"No Princess."

"Did anyone report seeing a stranger hanging around? Someone suspicious looking? Someone out of place?"

"No. And it's highly unlikely anyone came in undetected."

"Thank you. That is all."

"That's all you wanted from me?"

"Yes. Thank you. You've been most helpful."

The guild master looked over his shoulder at Kaelen's father, then bowed to Mallory. "An honour to be of service," he said and hurried back to his seat.

"Shane and Will Iron-Heart, you may come forward and state your case before I question the defendant."

Shane marched forward, his chest puffed out, his chin up. His son followed a step behind, copying every outward sign of his father's arrogance.

"Princess, your accident in the forest is already publicly known and I'm pleased you were not seriously injured or lost to a Dark Spirit. My son, Kaelen, informed me that it was Devin Sun-Stag who was acting as your guide that day. My suspicions are rooted in the fact that both you and my son suffered horse-related accidents only weeks apart."

"Did your son also inform you that it was Devin Sun-Stag's quick thinking and ingenuity that saved my life that night?"

Will jumped in. "Kaelen had a loud argument with Devin after your accident and Devin said things that were not appropriate, given that he was speaking to a prince."

"I'm not sure Kaelen's choice of words was entirely appropriate either, but I will note that the two men had an altercation shortly before Kaelen's accident," Mallory said. She kept the fact that she'd witnessed half the altercation to herself.

"Kaelen often spoke of this Devin Sun-Stag and his lack of trustworthiness."

"Odd that he was chosen to guide the party that was sent to find me, and odder still that he was working directly for Master Spirit-Light and Honourable Bernard in the time between if he was so untrustworthy. Kaelen seems to have been the only one with suspicions regarding Devin's character."

"Kaelen suspected that Devin was possessed by a Dark Spirit during the fight at Airon's Gate," Will said.

Mallory burst out laughing. After a moment she let the sound peter out and took a few deep breaths. "I've been here nearly a year. As I understood it, the longest any man has gone between being possessed and becoming a raving lunatic has been two months and even then, he showed serious symptoms within weeks. How ever did a simple guide manage to keep his possession a secret from *everyone* for nearly a year?"

"I – I don't know," Will said. He glanced at his father but was met only with a scowl.

"Why was Kaelen at the guild hall that day?" Mallory asked.

"He was a member of the guild before his marriage to you," Shane said. "He's always been welcome there."

"I realize that. I was wondering the purpose of his visit, not the legitimacy of it."

"He was meeting with me about family matters that had nothing to do with the guild. We chose to meet there because I was working with apprentices that day."

"Thank you. I won't pry into your personal family matters at this time, and not at all unless they become relevant. Is there anything else I need to be aware of? No? Then the two of you may have a seat. Bring Devin Sun-Stag forward."

Mallory was pleased to see that Devin looked no worse for his time spent in a cell and that someone had thought to provide him with clean clothes.

He bowed and when their eyes met Mallory had to force herself not to smile at him.

"Devin Sun-Stag, I have a few questions for you. Where were you on the seventh of Daggerfall?"

"I was out of the city with several other castle staff reviewing a hunting camp."

"When did you leave?"

"Just before dawn. We arrived back maybe an hour before your guards came to escort me to my temporary accommodations."

"Did Prince Kaelen mention his plans to you?"

"Prince Kaelen and I have not spoken to each other since our public disagreement after your accident."

"Did any of the castle staff, or members of the Blacksmith guild inform you where Kaelen was planning to be on the seventh?"

"No. And I had no interest in the information."

"Did you have any contact with the two horses that were taken to the Blacksmith's Guild that day?"

"Not on that day or the day before. I have helped in the stables before and have worked with all of the horses at one time or another."

"Did you know that the stable master and farrier were going to the Blacksmith's Guild that day?"

"No."

"Where were you the evening of the sixth?"

"In a meeting with Honourable Bernard and Master Spirit-Light. I'm sure both men will confirm where I was, and when I was there."

"I'm sure they will." Mallory stood. "Is there anyone else with important or pertinent information that I may have overlooked?"

No one stood but Mallory noted a few people shooting apologetic glances towards Shane Iron-Heart before looking down at their hands.

"Then there is only one verdict I can reach. There is absolutely no proof that Devin Sun-Stag could have been involved in the accident in any way. Horses, even calm, well-handled ones, are unpredictable animals. I'm certain that Kaelen is not the first man in the history of this island to die of horse-inflicted injuries, nor will he be the last. Accidents can and do happen, sometimes to tragic ends. We will mourn Prince Kaelen's passing but nothing criminal has occurred."

Jaspar stepped up beside her. "Is that all?" he asked.

"Yes. I'm finished."

"Court is dismissed," Jaspar said.

"Oh, one last thing," Mallory said as people were already starting to move. "I would like to see Shane and Will Iron-Heart in my sitting room, right away." She turned on her heel and marched out her private door.

It took a few minutes for her guests to find their way to the sitting room and Mallory greeted them with a wide smile.

"What is this about?" Shane said. "I have to get home, after what happened here today I have many things to take care of."

"Have a seat, please, this won't take but a moment. I didn't think you wanted this made public."

"You have no right to pry into our family business," he said.

"At this time, I don't, no. No, I didn't call you here to ask more questions, only to issue a warning."

"What warning?" Shane said, sounding wary.

"No harm is to come to Devin Sun-Stag, Hunter, the healer, or either horse, not by your hands, nor by a hand hired by anyone in your family or at your suggestion. Should any harm come to any of them your family will fall under immediate suspicion and a full investigation will be held. If you think hiring someone will help you escape justice, be warned that most men will say or do anything to save their necks from hanging."

"You insult me with the suggestion that I would …"

"That you would threaten a healer for doing her job? That you would accuse an innocent man?"

"We are grieving. Tempers ran hot …"

"So, let us be clear. There will be serious consequences if your temper doesn't cool quickly. Do you understand?"

"Yes, Princess," Shane said. "If you'll excuse us?"

"Of course. Your family must be anxious for news. Give Shawn my regards. I'm sorry he wasn't able to attend today."

The two men stalked out.

Mallory sat back and breathed a deep sigh of relief. She stretched and ran her hands over her skirts, still smiling. She stopped, hands on her legs, and tried to decipher why the fabric of her dress felt stiffer on one side.

The letter. I put it in my pocket.

She pulled out the flattened scroll and unrolled it, smoothing it against her leg as best she could.

To Mallory Brock Jewel-Rose of the Metalkin,

Holy Week is approaching quickly. This is your first Holy Week on the Isle of Light. For the last twelve years the princesses have celebrated in their own provinces, renewing oaths to Airon and their individual spirit guides in the temples in their capital cities. This has been tradition for several rebirths.

Given that this is your very first Holy Week, and that this is Taeya's first Holy Week in Dinas Rhosyn and Betha's first Holy Week in Caranhall, I thought it best that you all to stay home. Upon further reflection and meditation, I am requesting your presence, and all the princesses', here in the Sun Temple for Holy Week. You are expected to arrive at least one full day before Holy Week begins.

I advise that you inform your temple priest and your stewards of this change as soon as possible.

Most Honouable Baraq Silver-Cloud

PS: Betha claims to have found her prince, a Metalkin man. You and I have one month, give or take, to figure this out. Bring records of whatever you find when you come for Holy Week. We must set this right.

Mallory read the post-script four times. Suddenly a lot things started to make sense to her.

Devin.
Kaelen.
The white hart in the woods.
The horse lashing out at Kaelen.
Her own unrest and inability to settle.
"What if I'm not the Metalkin Princess?"

17th of Daggerfall, 24th Year of the 11th Rebirth
Golden Hall, Metalkin Province

Immediately after the trial, Mallory had requested that Kaelen's study be set aside for her personal use and firmly informed everyone that no one was to enter for any reason, not to disturb her or bring her letters, not to clean, nothing, not unless she expressly requested it. She'd spent most of the afternoon and evening in there following the trial, and most of the next two days as well.

Now, as they were heading for dinner on the third full day, Emilio was beginning to worry. Servants had reported Mallory's requests to him. Some were not surprising, like paper, ink, pens, and food. Others were quite odd: a large board, a hammer, a bag of small finishing nails, balls of string, and seemingly random record books.

She'd barely eaten, barely spoken to anyone, and had left Jaspar to handle day-to-day petitions. After her promise to take more control of government affairs this surprised him even more than the hammer and nails.

It was equal parts curiosity and concern that brought him to the study door this evening and he knocked softly and politely.

Mallory opened the door much quicker than he expected. Her fingers had ink stains on them, her hair was pulled back from her face but more than one strand had escaped, giving her a disheveled look. He half expected her to tell him to go away, instead she reached out, took his hand, and said, "Come and look at this and tell me if I'm seeing what I think I'm seeing."

If Mallory looked less than put together, the study was a complete mess. There was a pile of books on the floor, papers strewn across the desk, and a tray of half-finished food on the side table, but most impressive, and bewildering, was the board Mallory had leaned against the far wall. Using the finishing nails, she'd attached a map of the island and surrounded it with notes, letters, and even a few hastily drawn pictures, all connected with different colours of string.

"You've been busy," he said.

"Sit," she said. "Oh, wait." She started clearing scrolls off the chair for him.

"Have you been eating enough? Have you had any sleep?"

"I had an idea over lunch the other day and it sort of snowballed from there."

"We haven't had snow for …"

"Grew on its own," she said. "A saying. Look at the map," she said.

Her highly kinetic, almost frantic, energy intrigued him. "What am I looking at?"

"Rheeya's dealing with mine stuff, Vonica with the bank, Taeya with whatever still needs to be dealt with … the point is, we were all working on what we thought were separate issues. I don't think they are. I put a nail on the map everywhere something odd or dangerous took place."

Emilio got up to study the map more closely. He touched one of the nails. "Black Mountain Mine."

"Yes. This string goes to the notes on the mine incident, then to Jared Iron-Smith."

"What's this string over here? It goes from the mine into the Sun Temple Province."

"The fire."

"The gems."

"Rheeya said they found gems in the mine, so they had a lot of leverage for when it came time to negotiate with the Iron Guild again."

"You think it's connected?"

"Yes. Come, sit, I've been laying it all out. I'll run over it for you." She cleared a second chair and reached for a stack of papers. "This is what we know so far. A mine collapsed in the mountains, a mine being mismanaged by the Iron Guild. Why? I know Metalkin nobles have an appallingly low opinion of commoners, especially in other provinces, but from a financial stand-point it makes more sense to take care of the mine then allow for its collapse. We know the gems were found before the collapse, but Tomas didn't know about them until afterwards."

"So, who found them, and when, and did Jared know about it?"

"I'm betting he knew. I'm betting he wanted those gems out of there *before* the Stone Clan miners found them. That's why he kept ordering Metalkin workers into the mine, against Tomas' orders."

"To do what with them?"

"Cut out the middle man. I'm betting these Cultural Scholars no one can track down started their work with the gem guilds. They posed as jewellers and worked closely with gem cutters until they thought they could just do the job themselves. Betha's friend Talia got a brand-new necklace from a local jeweller for a ridiculously low price, while the Gem Guild is claiming that costs are rising."

"But the gems won't be as good, the cuts won't be as clean."

"I'm sure a talented jeweller could hide most of that with the settings. And the fire and collapse happened around the same time."

"You had a string from the fire to the Sun Temple capital."

"Yes. The steward at the Sun-Song estate was employed by someone who wanted a bank archivist dead. The fire is what led Vonica to the corruption in the first place."

"And since the fire was tied to the gems …"

"I have learned a little history and the Metalkin have always resented the Sun Temple being in charge of the bank."

"Aside from the bureaucratic power, what good would it do to have control of the banks?"

"The gold. Vonica has found a lot of errors in the Gold Guild books. I just got the letter yesterday."

"That's good timing."

"No, I wrote her and asked for the information. She was going to tell me at Holy Week. Here." She handed him the letter and waited while he read.

"But, this points to dozens if not hundreds of pounds of gold not being shipped to the bank for minting. Where is it?"

"Probably with the foals and the gems," Mallory said. "If I had to make a guess, I'd say the Metalkin working at the bank have been gold-coating other metals when making coins."

"Why?"

"For the same reason they have gems. And foals, and herbs, and seeds, and apple tree seedlings. The same reason they want to know how to fish and grow things and …"

"Self-sufficiency."

Mallory gestured at the map. "I've been at this for three days now and that's the only solution I can come up with."

"Loyalists," Emilio said.

"What?"

"Of course, your historian didn't tell you about it. Jaspar probably instructed them not to bother." Emilio sighed. "When The Pact was first formed, many of the Metalkin hated the idea. They were traders and they wanted to expand into markets beyond our shores. The ones that supported The Pact were called Protectors, the ones against it were called Loyalists, but they called each other all sorts of names. Rosies supported the Roses of Airon, you, while the Loyalists were called Foggies, or black-bloods."

"You didn't think this was important earlier?"

"The scholars at the Sun Temple believed the Loyalists eventually faded away. The Pact was solid, after a few generations people stopped complaining about it, stopped protesting."

"But they didn't."

"The scholars didn't realize that this split was the cause of much of the political intrigue in the Metalkin court over the years. Your Joseph Rose-Gold comes from a Protector family."

"He's not my Joseph," Mallory muttered, but since Baraq had asked her to keep Betha's revelation a secret she moved the conversation away from Joseph. "Let me guess, Kaelen was from a Loyalist family."

Emilio nodded.

"These cultural scholars, they were likely agents of the Loyalists then. And while I don't know where they have everything, I'm betting that if we raided every estate owned by a traditionally Loyalist family, we'd start finding things."

"That would be a lot of houses."

"Yes. And they'd all warn each other. We don't have enough men to hit everywhere at once. But, that's not the biggest of our problems. Somehow Betha and Taeya got sent to the wrong provinces. Was that an error made by a priest, or something else?"

"Something else?"

"That part was confusing me, but now, with what you've said about the Loyalists … bear with me, I haven't had as much time to think this through. The Loyalists didn't want The Pact in the first place and now they seem to be pursuing self-sufficiency. To what end? And why now? What if it had to do with me?"

"How so?"

"What would you do if you wanted to be free of The Pact and only four baby girls were brought to the island? It's the perfect opportunity to be free. No princess, no obligation to the contract."

"They couldn't have known that the missing princess was the Metalkin princess."

"No, you're right. But when it turned out that was true? They've had twenty-some-odd years, ever since the identity of the princesses was announced, to plan this and implement it."

"We need proof."

"I need a list of which families supported which side," Mallory said. She stopped as her stomach growled loudly. "And I need food."

"And maybe a walk outside?"

"Perhaps. If there's time. I need to write to Most Honourable Silver-Cloud for information about the selection ritual or however they decide on which girl goes where."

"Why don't I do that while you go eat?"

She nodded. "All right. Just, don't tell him too much yet. I don't have all the pieces."

"At least one of the five of you has been working on some part of this mystery for half a year now. You're not going to solve it in three days."

"I have to have it solved before Holy Week. Send the letter by Sun Hawk. I need a swift reply."

"Of course, Princess. Now go."

She nodded and went out, leaving Emilio with her notes and her map. He got up again and went to study the board. He'd never have dreamed of a set-up like this but as he followed the criss-crossing strings, he could see how it made sense and allowed a person to see connections not obvious otherwise.

He turned and rooted through the papers until he found a blank one and started on the note for Baraq Silver-Cloud.

Mallory hadn't realized how tired or hungry she was until she sat down at a table that wasn't covered in papers and started eating. She'd been reluctant to stop working, even to send for food, but now she ate with gusto, consuming far more than she expected. When she was done, she found she wasn't overly eager to return to the stuffy study and the piles of papers and books and dangerous ideas.

She decided to take a walk through the parts of the castle she rarely visited. She had time now to wander aimlessly and get a little lost. She lingered over tapestries and paintings but refrained from opening random doors since she didn't know which were private or which were in use.

She turned down one long hallway lined with doors. There was nothing here to distinguish it from any other hallway, and yet she felt she'd been here before. She was about to turn around when the door ahead of her opened and Devin Sun-Stag stepped out.

He froze when he saw her, his hand still on the doorknob. "Princess Mallory, I didn't think I'd see you down in the servants' wing again."

"Ah, I thought I recognized it. I was just exploring, and I was just ready to turn back. I don't want to make people uncomfortable."

"I'll walk with you," he said.

"All right." She felt a delicious flutter in her chest and she averted her gaze, suddenly feeling shy.

They walked in silence for a moment. Devin opened his mouth to speak several times, each time returning to silence instead. Finally he said, "I wanted to thank you, for not charging me with Prince Kaelen's death."

She cringed. "Please, don't call him prince anymore."

"I'm not sure it's proper for me to call him by his first name. Twice-named or not, I'm just an employee here." *And no matter my personal feelings about the man, I'm supposed to be respectful.*

She chanced a glance in his direction. "I suppose that's why you're still calling me 'princess', even after what we went through together."

"After what we went through, I have even more reason to call you Princess. I was too casual with you, I forgot my duty, and you got hurt."

She laughed. "It was an accident. You couldn't have stopped it by using a formal title. Please, I have so few friends here. I'm tired of 'princess' this and 'my lady' that. I just want to be Mallory, plain ordinary Mallory, at least sometimes."

"I'm honoured to be counted as your friend, and if you want me to call you Mallory when we are visiting, then I will."

"Thank you."

"How are you faring, with Kaelen's death and all?"

"Better than I should be, honestly. I think his family would be offended by how little grief or sorrow I feel. I knew you weren't involved. I only held the trial to prove that, to keep you safe."

"It's my job to keep you safe," he said. They were almost back to where Mallory had started from and here, in the middle of the empty hallway, he stopped. "That's part of serving you."

"You already saved me once. I had to return the favour."

"I thank you for that, more than you could know," he said, reaching out and touching her arm.

They were standing close now, and Mallory felt the warmth of his hand seeping through the sleeve of her dress. She was caught up in the little details of his face, the way his hair didn't part quite at the middle, the errant strands that hung over his forehead, softening his face, the arch of his eyebrows, the creases at the corner of his eye caused by his little one-sided smile.

"I have to go." His smile was suddenly gone.

His voice broke whatever spell she was under and she focused on his eyes again. "Because of Hunter."

"You figured it out. I'm sorry." He took a step back, panic straining his features. "I shouldn't even be here."

She reached out, catching his hand before he could turn away. The touch sent her pace racing. "Why are you sorry?"

"He's dangerous."

"Maybe."

"No, you don't understand. The longer this possession goes on, the less control I have. I know it's going to reach the point where I just become Hunter, and then I'll be locked up in a cage like an animal and left to die. I'm losing myself and I ... I promised I would serve you, in anyway you needed, I promised to be your friend, and I'm not going to be able to keep that promise."

"I don't know if you know, but I've encountered Hunter a few times already. I don't think he'd hurt me any more than you would."

"Yes, he would."

"You sound so sure."

"He's inside of me, in my head. I don't remember all of what happens when I'm Hunter, and that scares me, but the parts I do remember scare me just as much. He wants to hurt you, he wants to end you, especially because you never found your soul mate."

"You knew. When did you know?"

"I didn't think the accusation that Kaelen was not your prince would be well received. Neither Kaelen or Master Black-Kettle have ever been fond of me."

"I wish you would have told me," she said, softly.

From around the corner they heard a voice say, "Yes, Master Spirit-Light, I think she was having dinner in the east sitting room."

They weren't in the east sitting room but they were close enough that Emilio was going to walk right past them in a moment. "If he sees me here with you, so close to sunset, he'll be furious," Devin said. "And he's right. I'm sorry." He pulled his hand free and rushed off down the hall.

Mallory wanted to stare after him, more than that she wanted to chase him or call after him, but she squared her shoulders, turned her back, and marched in the other direction. She met Emilio at the corner.

"You've finished dinner?" he said.

She nodded. "You were right, I needed the break."

"Are you going back to the study to work?"

"No. I'm going to my room. I want to let things sit for a few hours. Maybe tomorrow I'll see something I missed, fresh eyes and all that."

"I've just returned from the aviary. You should expect a reply from Most Honourable Silver-Cloud soon."

"Thank you."

Once in bed for the night she stared at the ceiling, her mind still busy. She was onto something, she was sure of it, she just had to ask the right questions, find the connections. They were running out of time. She couldn't afford any distractions, and yet, she found Devin now occupied most of her thoughts. She could picture his face as clearly as if he were standing before her now.

She should have been thinking about politics and economics. Instead a single thought replayed in her mind until she finally drifted to sleep.

Kaelen was not my soulmate, he never was. What if I'm not the Metalkin Princess?

18th of Daggerfall, 24th Year of the 11th Rebirth
Golden Hall, Metalkin Province

Several times over the course of the day Mallory found herself daydreaming instead of reading. Devin's face kept dancing across her field of vision and she'd start thinking about how to cure him instead of how to unravel twenty years of political and economic corruption without starting a war.

She took a break around midday, coming out of the study to eat in the hopes that Devin would come find her again, but she returned to her work disappointed. It was nearly dinner when someone knocked on the study door. She leapt to her feet and rushed to open it.

A servant stood there, a scroll in hand. "This arrived for you from the Sun Temple. I was told to bring it straight away."

"Thank you," Mallory said. She took the scroll back to her seat and unrolled it.

Mallory,

I received your steward's letter. The matter of provincial selection isn't generally taught in detail to the princesses, so I'm not surprised it was completely passed over by your tutors. This is something I hope to change in the next rebirth, if I live to see it.

Airon sends signs to the priests when it is time to go through the gate to find the girls. Just as Airon led the priests to you, so too does he lead the priests to the proper infants. The infants are brought here where a small group of women takes care of them. In this rebirth they were led by Madam Olga. After the girls have started walking and are learning to speak, but years before they are ready to begin their formal education, they are brought, one at a time, to a small chamber for the selection.

The priests have in their possession five artifacts, one from each province. These five items are laid out before the first girl and she is permitted to pick one and only one. It is believed that Airon will guide her hand to the proper item.

In this rebirth, Vonica was the first to select, and she chose the Sun Temple relic. Rheeya was next, and she chose the Stone Clan relic. Those two relics were removed before Betha was brought it. I'm told she took far longer to choose than the other girls but she eventually settled on the Evergrowth relic, leaving Taeya with only two choices. The Metalkin relic was left behind, unclaimed, which is how we knew where you belonged.

It is obvious that something went wrong when Betha made her selection, leaving Taeya with two incorrect relics. The pressing question then is, why did Betha choose incorrectly? And if Betha has now fallen in love with a Metalkin man, why did the Metalkin relic go unclaimed?

I hope this information will help you with whatever you are working on.

Baraq Silver-Cloud, High Priest of Airon

Why didn't Betha claim the Metalkin relic as a child? Something was tugging at her thoughts and she went back over her notes, looking for something to spark a clear idea out of the fog.

It was something Emilio said yesterday. Four girls. How do you take advantage of four girls instead of five? "They couldn't have known that the missing princess was the Metalkin princess." That's it. That's it!!

She scrambled to her feet, sending pages drifting to the floor, and raced back to the door. She stopped the first servant she saw. "Fetch Master Spirit-Light, quickly. And see if you can find Master Sun-Stag as well."

"Yes, Princess."

She went back to the desk and grabbed another sheet of paper, scribbling down her thoughts as fast as she could, barely keeping up with the flood of revelations and ideas.

She responded to Emilio's knock at the door with a quick, "Yes, come in," and kept on writing.

"Your summons sounded urgent," he said.

"It was meant to. Sit. I think I know what happened."

While she kept writing he carefully cleared the second chair, amused at how quickly she'd refilled it with papers and books. Finally, she slammed the pen down on the table and sat back. "A break through?"

"*The* break through. And it's all thanks to you."

"Me? What did I do?"

"You asked the right question, or at least pointed me towards the right question. 'They couldn't have known that the missing princess was the Metalkin princess,' that's what you said yesterday, right?"

"Right. The selection process wasn't done until the girls were nearly ready for school. No one knew which girl was missing."

"They use holy relics," she said. "And they take away each relic as it's selected. Betha was third to choose."

"And Taeya fourth?"

Mallory nodded.

"But I don't …"

"How do you ensure that it's the Metalkin Princess that's missing?" When Emilio just stared at her, obviously confused, she went on. "You change the relic out with a replica. There was no Metalkin relic. When Betha went to choose there was no relic there for her to choose. But the priests demanded she choose something so she grabbed one at random, the Evergrowth relic. When Taeya, the real Evergrowth princess went in to choose, her relic was missing. The fake relic had no sense of the divine in it, but the Animal People relic would have so she chose that one because at least it felt a little right."

Here words made his stomach churn in an ugly way that left him feeling sick and light-headed. "It's not possible. Those relics would be kept under lock and key and only priests, senior priests, would have access." *Please don't let it be possible.*

"A Sun Temple steward killed an archivist because of Metalkin influence."

"You're suggesting a priest was paid to change that relic."

"Can you tell me with one hundred percent certainty that it would be impossible to bribe a priest?"

Emilio just stared at her, his heart beat too obvious against his ribs and in his veins. He wanted to say yes, he wanted to say it was impossible, beyond chance, but the words wouldn't form. He'd held out hope that the corruption hadn't spread to the priests, the honour of his people, the heart of Airon's faithful, and that hope was crumbling around him. Finally, he said, "No. There's always a chance. And with the corruption we've seen everywhere else …"

"It makes sense. It's terrifying but it makes sense."

"So, the Loyalists make certain the Metalkin Princess is the one declared missing, why?"

"They've now had twenty years with no oversight, no princess to guide them or control them. They've been able to spread, to change things, to influence other courts and other guilds. They want to be self-sufficient. If the trip to the Wide World had failed, if the priests hadn't found me, the Loyalists would have seized power and declared themselves free of The Pact and all its requirements. And if it succeeded? Well, they planted Kaelen on that voyage to woo the princess so that the Loyalists would control her."

"You're saying that Kaelen was not your soulmate?"

"That's exactly what I'm saying."

"To what end? What were they trying to do? We all need The Pact to survive. Without it ... what was all that you said about being tied to the world but invisible and intangible?"

"I don't know. I suppose one possibility is that the island would resynchronize with the world and 'crash' into Ireland. Or, the ties could snap completely and the island could drift so far out of touch with the rest of reality that you'd never be able to cross back over."

"They say the Dark Spirits appeared after The Pact. They come from the edges and are drawn to chaos. I think that if the ties snapped, they would be the end of us. They would become more numerous and would overtake us. By Airon, they would have let their greed destroy us all."

Mallory shuddered. "Let's not let that happen," she said.

"How do you propose we stop it? We have no proof any of this happened. The priest they paid might be dead for all we know, it was more than twenty years ago. And if he is alive, he'd never admit it. We'd never get admissions from the Loyalists either."

"Listen, right now the Loyalists think we're looking for foals and apple trees, right? Maybe we can catch them off guard. If we get them together and start asking questions, maybe we can get someone to slip. Maybe we can convince Jared Iron to turn if we promise him a second name again."

"I doubt it, but at this point the only other choice we have is to raid every single property owned by a Loyalist family."

"Let's keep that as a plan B," Mallory said.

"So, if Kaelen wasn't your prince, do you have an idea who your real prince might be?"

"Yes, I'm fairly certain of it. But I don't dare say anything now. Is two days enough time to get someone from every family here?"

"Yes. It might not be the head of the family, but I can get several members of each family to court by the twentieth."

"Do it. And I want Joseph Rose-Gold there as well. And Kaelen's father."

"I'll see it done."

"And don't inform Master Black-Kettle of our plans. He was working with Kaelen and I don't want him warning anyone."

Emilio opened the door to find a servant standing there, preparing to knock. The servant took a step back, bowing until Emilio had left. Mallory smiled at the young woman. "What news?" she said.

"I'm sorry, Princess. I couldn't locate Master Sun-Stag. One of the guards says he's not within the castle or yards today. He left very early this morning."

"Check with the guards and the stable master, see if anyone knows where he went or when he'll return. I need him in court in two days."

"Yes Princess."

Mallory went back to the desk and looked around at the papers for a moment before huffing and stalking out of the room again. She made her way down to the Madam Bella's rooms.

Madam Bella was in her personal rooms enjoying her dinner when the princess called on her. "Don't let me interrupt your meal," Mallory said. "We can talk while you eat."

"Shall I ring for a second plate?"

"No need, I'll eat later."

Bella nodded. "What can I do for you today? How is your leg?"

"My leg is fine. I'm here about Devin Sun-Stag and the elusive Hunter."

"I'm not sure what …"

"I already know the truth, and I'm guessing that you do too. Let's speak honestly with each other, please."

Bella nodded. "Of course, Princess. Forgive me, Master Spirit-Light requested secrecy."

"That was wise of him, but now I need the truth. When were you informed?"

"After Hunter assaulted the guard. Devin was brought to me here and I kept him under observation for a week. During the day Devin was completely normal, if a little tired. During the night the change was complete but unlike any possession I've ever witnessed. Hunter is a different person from Devin, he is blunt, rude, arrogant."

"Yes, I've noticed that."

"You shouldn't have any contact with that man," Bella gasped. "He's dangerous."

"That's what Devin said too. Where is Devin now?"

"I believe Master Spirit-Light sent him on an errand. You could ask him."

"No. Master Spirit-Light thinks the no contact order should extend to Devin as well. Is there no cure then?"

"Princess, in eleven generations we have tried every herb, every medicine, every poison, we could imagine. We have tried every prayer and ritual, every incense, we've tried praying during Holy Week or on High Holy Days, and nothing has ever worked. You must understand, this is not an illness. The Dark Spirits devour men's souls."

What if there's a difference in Devin's soul? "Has a prince or princess ever been possessed before?"

"No, Princess," Bella said, her eyes going wide. "Never. For that to happen ... no, that would mean the end of The Pact. You and the other princesses are vulnerable until you find your soul mate. If a Dark Spirit devoured your soul before it was made whole that would end the cycle of rebirth and end The Pact."

That must be why Devin said Hunter wanted to end me. Why didn't he? Twice now Hunter could have cut my heart out or snapped my neck. Why didn't he? "What would happen if the possession happened after the soul was complete?"

"I ... I don't know. It's simply never happened."

"Thank you. I'm sorry to disturb you like this. If you think of anything else that might be useful, please let me know."

"Of course."

From Madam Bella's Mallory was going to go down to eat but changed course part way and returned to the study to grab a few scrolls to review while she ate. As she came down the hall she saw a figure walking away from the study door. Her steps quickened and she called out, "Devin, wait."

He stopped and turned around. She could see the war of emotions in his eyes, the smile that fought to emerge on his lips, and the fear that dimmed the sparkle in his eyes. "Mallory."

"I was looking for you earlier."

"I was out."

"Come into the study for a moment. Will you dine with me? I was on my way to dinner."

"I shouldn't. Master Spirit-Light ..." His words trailed off as his gaze settled on the string covered map. "What have you been doing?"

"Trying to unravel a very big mystery. A big piece just fell in my lap today. We're having a trial on the twentieth. I want you to be there."

"Who are you trying?"

"I have no idea. Honestly, I'm still looking for proof of a lot of things." She was digging through a pile for the scrolls she wanted.

"What was this big piece?"

"I'm not the Metalkin princess."

His heart leapt at her words and he felt a ringing in his body, as though someone had rung a very large bell very nearby. "You're not?"

"No. But I didn't tell you. You don't know. No one except Emilio knows. There are too many people working against me right now. I have to keep it secret. I didn't even tell Madam Bella today."

"But you're telling me."

"Yes."

"Why?"

"Because maybe it will buy us more time. I have what I need. Are you sure you won't dine with me?"

"No, I can't. Mallory, be careful, please. I'm keeping myself away to keep you safe. I don't want you to go and throw yourself into the path of some other danger."

"I'll try. Don't miss court on the twentieth. Promise me."

"Whatever you ask of me," he said. "I live to serve."

She nodded. "Thank you."

"I need to go. Hunter …"

"I know." She reached out and took his hand for a moment. "Stay strong for me, please. I don't want to lose you to him either."

20th of Daggerfall, 24th Year of the 11th Rebirth
Golden Hall, Metalkin Province

Court was not going well. Even with everything she and Emilio had figured out, she couldn't get a damning word out of anyone and she was coming dangerously close to revealing her hand, something she wanted to avoid at all costs. No one had any connections to the priests in Sun Temple, in fact it was well known that Metalkin nobles held a great dislike for the priests of Airon. Talking to Jared had proven futile too. While he was honoured to have the chance to serve her, he *claimed* his actions at the mine were his and his alone, and not a part of any plot or conspiracy.

Mallory summoned Kaelen's father, Shane Iron-Heart, before her next. "Why was Kaelen sent to Airon's Gate?" she asked.

She saw Shane hesitate. "I can't be certain. The final decision was made by the priests."

"All right. Honourable Bernard, please step forward." As the priest approached, Shane turned to return to his seat. "No, you stay as well, I have more questions for you. Honourable Bernard, how was the selection made?"

"The original party consisted of myself, the other priests, a selection of guards, and Master Sun-Stag, the palace tracker. The guards were selected based on service records and recommendations from both of your stewards and the captain of the guard."

"Original party. What changed?"

"One of the guards had trained a few years in his youth as a smith before being recruited as a guard. He was coming along to ensure we had no problems with the horses. A farrier would have been better, but we hoped that between Master Sun-Stag and the guard we could handle any minor emergencies on the road."

"Let me guess, something happened to that guard."

"Yes, Princess. He fell quite ill just days before we were set to leave. Kaelen came highly recommended, though he was a noble and a smithing instructor. We had little time to interview replacements, so we accepted him."

"I see. Was the guard treated by the palace healer?"

"I believe so," Honourable Bernard said.

"Madam Bella, would you join us?"

The old woman took her time coming forward, even though the Metalkin nobles grumbled with impatience.

"Did you treat the guard in question?"

"I did, M'Lady."

"What was wrong with him? Fever? Flu?"

"Whatever it was, it was not natural. It came on fast and was gone just as quickly. I'd say he ate something that disagreed with him."

"Something like a bad piece of meat? Or something like a mixture added to his food or drink to make him ill at a convenient time?"

"I've rarely seen a reaction so strong to a bad piece of meat or sour milk. I cannot say anything more definitive than that."

"Thank you for your honesty in this matter. I will keep in mind that the possibility the guard was removed on purpose exists but cannot be proven by the healer. Madam Bella, you may return to your seat. If I have need of you again, I will call on you then."

"My old legs thank you," the healer said.

"I have a question," Shane said. "Why all this interest in Kaelen now? It was fate that he was along on that trip. Airon destined it so the two of you could be brought together and your soul bond recognized."

"He wasn't my soulmate." She wasn't sure if it was the words alone, or the dry, matter-of-fact, delivery of them, but the room went silent. "No, I will not answer questions on that matter at this time. Yes, there is proof from several sources."

"Princess," Shane stuttered. "This is unsettling news."

"Yes, it is. *IF* the guard was deliberately injured to create and opening and *IF* Kaelen was sent with the express purpose of asserting his claim as my soulmate then treason has been committed." She regretted the words as soon as she said them. She'd never get another Loyalist to say another word in this court.

"You claim you have proof," someone shouted. "You claim Kaelen committed treason and now you look for conspirators, but what proof do you have?"

She wasn't allowed to tell anyone about Betha and Joseph. Her connection to Devin hadn't been proven by anyone so she couldn't use that in court, and she didn't want these men to know about that yet. *What proof can I offer them?*

"I have proof." Everyone looked towards the speaker, a young raven-haired woman in a fine-cut, high-waisted dress.

"Sit down!" A man yelled. He grabbed her arm.

"Both of you come forward," Mallory said.

The man glared at the younger woman and marched towards the throne, his hand still tight on her arm. Shane was frowning deeply and around the room several men were grumbling complaints.

"What's your name?" Mallory said, even though she was guessing this was the woman Kaelen had been meeting.

"My name ..." the woman started.

The man beside her cut in. "I am Fredrick Iron-Forge, and this is my daughter. I can assure you that she knows nothing of value."

"Please have Master Iron-Forge removed until I need something from him, he's interfering in my investigation," Mallory said.

Fredrick started to protest but a sharp nod from Shane cut him off and he followed the guard quietly.

"Your name please," Mallory said again.

"Emelia Iron-Forge."

"Emelia, what proof can you offer that treason has occurred?"

"I have papers and can recollect conversations for you. My father, Shane Iron-Heart, Will Iron-Heart, Lord South-Mine, and many others, even Kaelen, though I have proof he wanted out, they were all active Loyalists. Kaelen was sent on that journey to woo you, convince you that he was your soulmate, and arrange for his marriage to you."

"To what end?" Mallory pressed.

"To ensure you would support the Loyalist agenda, or, failing that, that you would not interfere."

A great cry went up among the gathered nobles and Mallory wondered just how many Loyalists were quickly switching to the other side to avoid the coming backlash from their peers.

"I grew up in a Loyalist household," Emelia said over the din. "They saw your absence as an opportunity to leave The Pact. They thought they could farm without the Evergrowth or the Animal People, that they could train Metalkin to be healers and hunters and anything else they needed. There are villages around the province where anyone who was not Metalkin was subtly pushed out. You'll find your foals and whatever else you're looking for there."

The entire time she was talking the background noise continued to increase in volume until, by the end, she was screaming to be heard.

Mallory stood, taking a deep breath as she did so. Her next words came out calm, but loud enough to bring every conversation and argument in the room to a halt. "If you want to sleep in your own bed tonight, shut your mouths, now."

After a few heartbeats of silence, Emelia pressed on. "Kaelen didn't want to marry you, he did so under threat from his father and the other Loyalists. His father volunteered him because they didn't like the woman he'd fallen in love with, they didn't approve of the marriage. By the time he died, he'd been working against the Loyalists for weeks, while trying to keep up a front of cooperation. He burned contracts between the crown and the Loyalists, delayed bribes, and ensured that no one would be able to refute the fact that he was not your soulmate. He was waiting on proof of that last before coming to you."

"He was conspiring with you," Mallory said. "I have evidence that he visited you."

Emelia nodded emphatically and her tone became desperate, pleading. "I begged him to come to you sooner. I told him you would pardon him if he gave you the proof you needed to set things right, but he was afraid that he would meet his end at the hands of a Loyalist thug."

"You say you have papers?"

"Kaelen gave me things for safe keeping. Others, I stole from my father's desk."

"I will need them. I will also need to know what proof Kaelen had, other than his own admission, that he was not my soulmate."

Emelia took a deep breath and pulled her shoulders back. "I'm the woman Kaelen loved. He intended to propose to me." She took another deep breath. "And I'm pregnant with his child."

No amount of yelling could bring silence back to the court.

A few quickly issued orders from Mallory had Emelia, her father, Shane Iron-Heart, her stewards, and her captain of the guard, brought to the safety and privacy of a roomy sitting room down the hall. The rest of the crowd was ushered out by the guards. Before joining her guests, she issued one last order to her guards.

"Close the city gates. No one enters of leaves Golden Hall until this matter is closed."

Master Iron-Forge and Shane Iron-Heart sat at one side of the room, with two guards standing just behind them. Mallory and Emelia sat across from them, Captain Shield-Forge standing at attention beside his princess, his face grim and his hand resting on the pommel of his sword. Jaspar and Emilio sat off to one side, making a loose horseshoe, Jaspar looking anxious, Emilio looking amused.

"There, that's better," Mallory said. "Emelia, do you have the papers with you?"

She nodded and from a small satchel at her waist she produced a pile of papers, bound in bundles. "These are what Kaelen left with me. These are letters between my father and other Loyalists. These are account records."

"She's a thief," Fredrick said.

"She's acting in the best interest of the crown and her people," Mallory replied. "Besides, I'm not sure it's a crime to steal from a criminal."

"You have no proof!"

Mallory held up the stack of papers. "Apparently, I have lots of proof."

"I should review and sort those papers for you," Jaspar said, holding out his hands.

"I wouldn't give him anything of value," Emelia said. "Kaelen said Jaspar Black-Kettle was one of them. He's the reason Kaelen wouldn't turn. He knew if he said anything, that Jaspar would report it back to the others."

"This woman speaks nonsense," Jaspar spluttered. "You're going to take the word of this indecent woman, over the word of the man who has aided you and your people for ..."

"You tried to keep me away from court, and you tried to train me to be docile and helpless," Mallory said. "So yes, I have every intent to believe this young woman. I cannot risk anyone disappearing while I investigate. I want Shane Iron-Heart and Fredrick South-Mine arrested and put under lock and key. As I discover their allies' names, they will have plenty of company. Oh, arrest Jaspar Black-Kettle as well." She turned to Emilio. "I'll need your help tomorrow, going through all of this. For now, I would like tea for two sent to my room, and a servant to show Emelia the way there."

"Of course," Emilio said.

All three men were protesting loudly as the guards led them away but seemed to be going peacefully enough and the whole thing may have gone without incident if Devin Sun-Stag had not been waiting in the hallway to speak with Mallory.

Shane spotted Devin, before Devin spotted him, and shot forward, pulling out of the startled guard's grasp. "YOU!!"

Devin took a large step back, but it wasn't enough, and Shane got a fist full of the younger man's shirt. His other hand, clenched tight in a beefy fist, swung up. Before he could bring the blow down upon Devin's head Captain Shield-Forge's hand closed around Shane's wrist.

"I wouldn't do that," Captain Shield-Forge said.

Red-faced, Shane released Devin and followed the guards.

Mallory stepped out and paused. "Master Sun-Stag, how can I help you?"

He almost questioned her formal tone but Master Spirit-Light stepped out behind her and he straightened up. "Princess Jewel-Rose. I see you're busy. Will you have time to see me tomorrow?" He was trying to keep the desperation out of his voice.

She noticed his tone, and the pleading look in his eyes. "I'll make time. If you'll excuse me, I'm on my way to an important meeting."

He bowed. "Of course. I will see you tomorrow." With a slight nod to Master Spirit-Light he retreated.

"I never imagined I'd be sitting in this room, having tea with you of all people," Emelia said while Mallory poured tea.

"I never imagined I'd be a princess on a lost island dealing with this level of political turmoil, but here we are." Mallory sighed slightly. "But here we are. What you've done today, it was brave of you, incredibly brave. How at risk do you think you are?"

"You mean, will I come to harm?" She seemed to consider the idea for the first time. "I don't know."

"We'll get a room for you here. You can stay until we've cleaned up this mess."

"Oh. I couldn't ask for that, not after what we did behind your back, what this child means."

"That child means my freedom. Kaelen never loved me. You were just as wronged by this as I was. And as much as I came to hate Kaelen, I realize now that he was wronged too. What remains now, is to right as many of these wrongs as we can."

22nd of Daggerfall, 24th Year of the 11th Rebirth
Golden Hall, Metalkin Province

Mallory and Emelia had stayed up late, taking dinner together in Mallory's rooms, so that they could talk until the words ran out. The next day had been full of paperwork. Mallory read through every document Emelia had provided and then spent several hours filling out arrest warrants.

By that evening the dungeons were dangerously full, with two, even three, noblemen in each cell. They protested loudly every time a guard or keeper came down, either to add another prisoner or to bring food or water. By the time Mallory toppled into bed, her hand was cramped, and she was exhausted.

Today was likely to be more of the same and the thought of being stuck behind a desk for hours on end, deciding who to arrest and who to investigate further, was not a thought she was looking forward to. Not without some sort of break.

After eating she went out to the stables to get some fresh air before allowing herself to be locked away for the remainder of the day.

"Are you wanting brushes?" Jeremy asked her when she arrived.

"No, I don't have time for that. I'm just going to walk through the stables and maybe try to coax someone over to the paddock fence for a nose rub before I have to go in."

"Help yourself then. I have some new lads to train today."

"Don't let me interrupt. And I promise, I won't steal a horse and take off on you."

He chuckled. "You'd best not."

She wandered down the aisle between the stalls listening to the horses snorting and fussing. Down at the end was the big door out to the paddock. Just before she reached it, Devin came in. At first, he was just a silhouette but as he came further in she recognized him and hurried forward. "Devin."

He turned to face her and the look of sorrow on his face stopped her in her tracks.

"Devin, what's wrong? Oh. Yesterday. I'm so sorry. You wanted to see me. I got so caught up in the new evidence and …"

"And you don't really care that much about me, do you?" he snapped.

Tears sprung to her eyes. "I'm sorry."

"I didn't mean that," he said. "That wasn't me." He took a deep, gasping breath, more like a drowning man would. "I can't control it anymore."

"What are you talking about?"

"The last few mornings, I'm waking up later and later, and even when I'm awake, it takes hours for me to shake the horrible thoughts Hunter leaves behind. I want to hurt things, people. I keep saying horrible things to people. They're all beginning to suspect."

"What are you saying?"

"I have to say good-bye. I promised Master Spirit-Light and Honourable Bernard that if I got to this point, I would go to the Healers, turn myself in, let them lock me up. I have to. For everyone's safety."

She grabbed his arm. "No. I forbid it. I'm the princess. I won't let you. You can't disobey a direct order."

He chuckled. "Yes," he said. "You are my princess. That's why this hurts so much. I failed you."

Her thoughts were tumbling through her mind too fast.

Betha. Joseph. Devin. Kaelen — kicked by a horse. What if you're not the Metalkin Princess? What if there's something different about his soul? Our souls resonate at the frequency of the Wide World and our princes' souls resonate at the frequency of the island. That's why we have to come together, the harmony of the two frequencies creates stability.

Kicked by a horse. A horse. A white doe in the woods — she healed me. The horse protected me. What if you're not the Metalkin Princess? There has to be a way to save him, he's my friend. What if there's something different about his soul, something that protected him? What if you were protecting him? Your soul, the harmony, the soul bond ...

What if you're the Carainhithe Princess?

"Oh hell," she muttered. "It works in the stories." Before he could voice his confusion, she stepped into him, holding tight to his sleeve. "Devin Sun-Stag you are not going to give up and die, I won't let you." And then she kissed him.

Emilio Spirit-Light went to Mallory's rooms to find she'd already left for the morning. She wasn't visiting Emelia, and she wasn't in the dining room or study. Feeling frustrated by her absence and the amount of work they had to do, work that was falling unfairly to him now that Jaspar Black-Kettle was in prison and they hadn't yet found a new steward, he stormed off towards the next likely place she'd be: the stables.

What her fascination with those animals is, I don't know. This has been the strangest rebirth by far. It was little consolation that his name would be in the history books alongside all this commotion. There was no glory in pushing papers, and whatever honour was there was dull indeed.

The stable master was in the paddock speaking with a group of lads, all dressed for work. Emilio waited impatiently by the fence until Master White-Hart finally came over. "She's inside," he said, without even waiting for the question. "Said she was only passing through on her way to whatever duties she has today. Actually, I'm surprised I haven't seen her come out the other door yet."

Emilio nodded and managed a curt, "Thank you," before heading into the stables. He didn't like it here. It was dimly lit and musty.

As his eyes adjusted, he saw two figures down near the paddock doors. They were standing close, their attention on each other. *Mallory, but who is she ... Devin Sun-Stag.*

He took two hurried steps forward, his arm raised, her name on his lips, but before he could call out to her, she'd kissed him.

"NO!"

Mallory heard the protest somewhere behind her, faint, unimportant. She felt Devin's body against hers, felt his hand on the small of her back, felt the heat of his lips, heard her blood pounding in her ears. The kiss was everything a kiss should be and more.

And then the heat started. She felt it radiating from Devin's chest first, but it spread quickly until they pulled away from each other, scared and confused.

"What ...?"

Before she could get a question out, Devin's face contorted in pain and he fell to his knees. The light from the doorway seemed brighter, too bright. She reached for him, but something stopped her. She turned and saw Emilio standing there, his hand on her arm, pulling her back. She tried to pull free.

Devin groaned and she turned. The light was definitely brighter now, there was no mistaking it. There were no shadows at all. On either side of them the horses were whinnying and kicking at the sides of their stalls. Somewhere behind there were more voices, yelling, panicked.

Devin fell silent, his chin against his chest. He was panting. He struggled to bring his face up, and when he did his gaze locked with hers. "Mallory," he whispered, and yet, over all the other noise, she heard that one word more clearly than anything else.

And then threw his head back and screamed. Another voice seemed to join his, a deeper voice, one that echoed in a way that didn't sound human. Both voices climbed in volume, while the horses continued their racket in the stalls around them.

The light flared suddenly, just as the voices reached fever pitch, and then silence. The horses were still, the screaming ended, the light returned to a normal that seemed dark after the brightness of what they'd just witnessed. Even the shouting of the other people, Emilio and Jeremy and the stable lads, had been cut off by the light.

Devin lay on his back, his eyes closed, his arms and legs splayed out about him. Mallory managed to pull free from Emilio and dropped to her knees next to him. He was breathing, but it was shallow.

"Get the healer," she said. "Please." No one moved. "PLEASE!" Several people took off, she didn't see who, but she heard their running steps. She picked up Devin's hand and held it in both of hers.

"That was foolish," Emilio said behind her. "He's cursed."

"He's my prince," she said, softly enough that Emilio was the only one that heard.

"Then we're all doomed," Emilio replied.

It was dark. That was never a good sign. Fearing the worst, Devin tried to open his eyes. If Hunter was in control there was no telling what he'd see, what he'd remember. If not, he'd have to figure out why his whole body hurt like he'd been kicked by a mule.

He opened his eyes. There was light, shadows, people maybe? He closed his eyes and opened them again. The people came into focus. Master Spirit-Light off to one side, Madam Bella, but right over him, staring down at him, was Mallory.

He took a breath, wanting to say her name, but the act of breathing hurt, and he cringed, the only thing escaping his lips was a feeble, "Ow."

"Don't," Mallory said. "Just rest."

"What ...?" He licked his lips.

Before he could try again, she said, "We're not sure. Let the healer do her job, okay?"

He nodded and he could feel the back of his head rubbing on a hard, rough surface. He tried to take in more of his surroundings. It looked like he was still in the stables. He took a few breaths, each a little deeper than the last, until he thought he could get enough air to speak. He licked his lips again and then said, "How long was I out?"

"Not even an hour," Bella said. "Follow my finger with your eyes please, no, don't move your head, that's it." After a few moments of that she placed both hands on his neck. "All right, he can move, but slowly."

"What happened?"

"You got hot," Mallory said.

He put a hand to his chest. "I remember that."

"And then it got bright. You screamed, and I think Hunter screamed too, and then there was a flash of light and you were on the ground."

"Do you think ...?" He looked at Emilio, and then Bella. "I was going to come to you. I was ... it was time."

"We need to observe you, probably until tomorrow morning," Emilio said. "And Princess Mallory has work to do."

Two of the lads helped Devin to his feet as Emilio said, "Take him to the healer's rooms. Princess, you should change your dress."

"I suppose horse manure isn't a suitable look, is it?"

"No."

"Okay." She turned to Devin. "I'll check on you later."

He nodded. "Okay."

23rd of Hooffall, 24th Year of the 11th Rebirth
Golden Hall, Metalkin Province

Mallory paced outside the healer's exam room. She'd skipped breakfast, feeling too nervous to eat, but that meant she was very early this morning. Madam Bella had been understanding but had taken her tea and breakfast anyway before beginning Devin's exam.

"We had someone with him all night," said Emilio from his seat by the fireplace.

"And? What did they report this morning? Did he turn into Hunter again?"

"No. He slept, deeply and peacefully."

Mallory resumed her pacing.

"You have other work you should be doing."

"This is the most important thing on the entire island at this moment," Mallory said.

"Because you feel he's your prince?"

"He is my prince. It makes perfect sense. That's why he lasted so long with the Dark Spirit inside of him. That's why he got worse when I left the province for each of the weddings. After Kaelen died that thing must have gotten desperate."

"You have no proof of any ..."

The door opened and Madam Bella came out, drying her hands on a towel. "He's awake, and as far as I can tell, there's nothing at all wrong with him. There are very few physical symptoms of a possession until the Dark Spirit begins to take hold, but Master Sun-Stag was in the late stages of a possession. I should have been able to find some sign. There was none. He also says he has not slept the night since Princess Stone-Rose's wedding, that he has spent every night as Hunter and has had to catch up on his sleep whenever he could."

"So, he's cured?" Mallory said.

"It's impossible to say," Bella said with a shrug. "It's never been done before."

"I'm cured," Devin said, coming out of the exam room behind Bella. "I don't know how, but it's gone. From the first moment I could feel it there and I don't anymore."

Emilio shook his head. "It's too big of a risk."

Mallory stomped over to Devin's side and grabbed his wrist. "We're going to the temple, now. Airon did the whole light show thing for Rheeya, and Vonica, and Taeya. He's going to do it for us now too, you'll see." She started walking, dragging Devin behind her.

"Shouldn't we talk to Honourable Bernard first," Devin said.

"Look, I was dragged here, into this whole strange mess of an island, with soulmates and spirit guides and Dark Spirits, and you said I had to adjust. I got stuck with a man who was not my prince, and everyone told me I'd get used to him. Now I say I've found my prince, and everyone is doubting me? No. We're getting this sorted out. Now." The whole time she was ranting Mallory was marching down the hall with Devin behind her and Emilio trailing behind him. Everyone they passed gave them an odd look, but Mallory didn't stop or even slow.

She barged into the temple, startling the acolyte who was sweeping the floor. She ignored him as he rushed off, probably to fetch Honourable Bernard. "Which point is Caranhall?" she said, pointing to the compass rose on the floor.

"Northwest," Emilio said.

She switched to pushing Devin ahead of her down the aisle between the benches and onto the compass rose. Five arms of the compass rose were outlined in gold and from that she figured out which one was northwest and that's where she directed Devin. She stood next to him on the point and waited.

"Well?" Devin said. "Now what?"

Mallory tapped her feet a few times. "A prayer?"

"You could kiss me again."

She blushed.

"What's going on in here?" Bernard said, storming in with two other priests on his heels. "There's no service right now."

"Mallory is trying to prove something." Emilio sat on one of the benches, his expression amused.

"I'm demanding that Airon prove it," Mallory said.

"Prove what?" Bernard said.

"That I am the Carainhithe Princess and Devin Sun-Stag is my prince."

As the last word left her lips the entire compass rose began to glow. Bernard fell to his knees. "Airon, preserve us," he said.

"Is that enough proof for you?" Devin said.

"I didn't need proof," Mallory said, turning into his arms. "I just need you."

Smiling, he leaned over and kissed her.

24th of Hooffall, 24th Year of the 11th Rebirth
Golden Hall, Metalkin Province

There was a lot more chaos involved in getting ready for this trip than for past trips and Mallory was impatient to get moving. They took two carriages, one for Mallory and Emelia, the other for Cecilia and a handful of other servants. Emilio had never organized something like this before and consequently was little help to Captain Shield-Forge or Master White-Hart. He was able to help Mallory sort and load all the necessary papers and books though.

"Are you sure I need to come?" Emelia said.

"Yes. Your testimony will be important. And I can guarantee your safety if you're with me."

"But you're the Animal People's princess now," she said. They hadn't made that fact fully public yet but those travelling with them had been informed.

"Yes, and I want to introduce you personally to your new princess," Mallory said. "If I don't explain things she may hate you just because of Kaelen, and that's not fair. Besides, I think, given the chance, the two of you could be friends."

They got a late start and didn't get as far as they'd hoped by the first evening, but they had a few days to spare before Holy Week started so Mallory wasn't worried. *Better to be a day late, then travel at night,* she thought as they settled into the inn that evening. *Besides, they can't very well start without us.*

29th of Hooffall, 24th Year of the 11th Rebirth
Sun Temple Complex, Sun Temple Province

Over the last few days the four princesses had arrived with their entourages. Baraq had stayed out of the way, letting Vonica and her stewards handle getting everyone settled into guest rooms and finding study space for everyone's notes and evidence. Including today, they had just over a week until the start of Holy Week. He hoped it would be enough.

Mallory and her guards and guests were the last to arrive. She nearly burst out of the carriage saying, "Oh, fresh air."

Baraq shook his head and helped her down. "I got your letter," he said. "I've met Joseph Rose-Gold, he came on his own and arrived two days ago."

"You know, I didn't even see him when he came back from Stones Shore. He probably didn't want me to give him another assignment."

"You've brought this Devin Sun-Stag with you, I presume."

"Yes, but good luck speaking with him until he's got his horse looked after."

"No, I'm here," Devin said, coming around the back of the carriage. He bowed. "Most Honourable Silver-Cloud, it is a pleasure to meet you."

"If Mallory's claims are true, then it is a pleasure to meet you as well. I'll just be in the way if I stay out here much longer. I'll see both of you at dinner."

Devin stopped a few times on the way to their rooms to admire the art and architecture and Mallory had to keep nudging him onwards. "You've been here before," he said. "This is all new to me."

"You can see it later," Mallory said. "Keep up."

They were given three rooms, Mallory in the middle with Devin on one side and Emelia on the other. After everyone had bathed and changed they went down to join the others for dinner.

It was a large group: all five princess, three official princes, two proposed princes, Baraq, James, and Emelia. Introducing Devin and Joseph was easy enough, though Taeya was shocked to learn that Betha was the Metalkin Princess and Mallory was the Carainhithe princess.

After a moment of staring she threw up her hands. "Why am I even surprised?"

Introducing Emelia was more complicated. "She's a key witness," Mallory said, choosing to leave it at that for now, at least as far as public statements went.

After the meal was over Mallory pulled Emelia and Betha aside and explained the whole situation to Betha.

Betha took a deep breath and held it, finally letting it out slowly. "This changes things," she said.

"I'm going to petition Baraq," Mallory said. "I think Emelia should be given the name Iron-Heart so that her child will have his or her father's name."

Emelia gasped. "You didn't tell me that!"

"You'll be a widow then, instead of an unwed mother," Mallory said. "And your child will have a lineage and no one will be able to claim the child is illegitimate."

"Thank you," Emelia said. "Thank you so much."

Betha nodded. "It's a good idea. But it's the last official thing you get to do as the Metalkin Princess."

Mallory laughed. "Don't worry. I'm leaving all those Loyalists to you."

"Good. I need a little fun and games," Betha said, smirking.

"What happens if Talia gets mixed up in all of this?" Mallory said.

Betha shrugged. "I'm guessing she didn't know where that stone came from or why it was so cheap. But, I will deal with that when the time comes. What about you? You've barely settled in and now you'll be moving again."

"I think this time it will be a lot easier," Mallory said. "For both of us."

36th of Hooffall, 24th Year of the 11th Rebirth
Sun Temple Complex

They'd spent the last week holding meetings and presentations and trials and ceremonies. In the end Baraq set up a private ceremony for the princesses and their princes and confirmed that Betha was the Metalkin Princess and the Joseph Rose-Gold was her prince, and that Mallory was the Carainhithe Princess and Devin Sun-Stag was her prince. "Betha Jewel-Rose and Mallory Brock Living Rose," Baraq said. "And that is the last of you so there will be no more surprises!"

"I wouldn't count on it," Vonica said. "This has been, by far, the strangest rebirth on record.

An entire day was spent sorting through Mallory's discoveries, putting together a rough timeline of the Loyalists' actions at the mine, the Sun-Song estate, the Merchant Bank, across Evergrowth, and into Metalkin territory. Emelia had talked for two hours, explaining everything she knew and helping Mallory present all of the evidence she'd brought to the Metalkin court two weeks earlier. The list of names implicated in the Loyalist plot was staggering.

"Golden Hall, and the rest of the province, is going to look very different when I'm through with it," Betha said. "Is there a limit to how many men I can behead?"

"I'm not sure yet," Baraq said. "Not all of them, all right?"

Betha pouted a little. "Fine. I'll leave one or two as examples."

"I was thinking you could just behead a half dozen ring leaders and be done with it," Baraq countered.

"I'm inclined to agree with the High Priest," Joseph said.

"Fine. But I'm stripping titles and lands and bank accounts."

"And we won't even try to stop you," Joseph said, kissing her cheek.

"The priesthood is going to look very different as well," Baraq said. "Someone switched those relics, and I hope for their sake, they're already dead."

"Has a priest ever been executed for treason?" Mallory asked in a hushed voice.

"Never," Baraq said. "But I would make an exception for this."

Tomorrow was the first of Holy Week and the first of the two weddings that needed to be held, so today was set aside for personal matters, like visits with seamstresses, sight seeing, and visiting.

Johann took all of the princes on a tour of the complex to look at the carvings and the art and the historic places where the other provinces had left their marks on this place, leaving the girls to their visiting.

As Mallory finished handing the last of the Metalkin dresses to Cecilia to be packed and taken to Betha's rooms, the maid said, "I guess this is it."

"What is it?" Mallory said.

"I'm employed at Golden Hall, I work for the Metalkin Princess. I suppose I'll be going with these trunks and dresses and jewellery into the service of Princess Betha Jewel-Rose."

"I don't think so," Mallory said. "And never see each other again? No. Absolutely not. I don't care what Betha said about last official duties as the Metalkin Princess. I'm firing you."

"What?"

"That's right. You no longer work in Golden Hall. And since you need a new job you might as well come and work for me in Caranhall, if you can put up with all of the Carainhithe everywhere."

Cecilia smiled and curtsied deeply. "It would be an honour, Princess Living Rose, but are you sure you still need me? You have a prince now."

"As if he knows the first thing about doing hair or running a bath." Mallory's smile softened and she took both of Cecilia's hands in hers. "Besides, you are my friend, and no one could replace you."

1st of Holy Week, 25th Year of the 11th Rebirth
Sun Temple Complex, Sun Temple Province
Wedding of Betha Jewel-Rose

This was not what Betha had imagined, and definitely not what she'd been raised to expect. Not once in the history of the Isle of Light had any princess other than the Sun Temple Princess been wed in the Sun Temple itself. Then again, the unprecedented mix up was also a first in the history of the Isle of Light. It was fitting that the conclusion broke tradition.

She'd brought the traditional wedding dress from Caranhall so she'd at least have *something* to wear for the ceremony and was delighted to discover that Mallory had brought the traditional dress from Golden Hall as well. They'd traded as soon as their true identities were made official.

It didn't matter one bit that nearly a year ago Mallory had worn this same dress in Golden Hall to marry a liar and a traitor, Betha was just happy to be wearing something so grand. They spend hours on her hair and let her wear bold, shining jewelry. And when she walked into the temple it was all dimmed by her radiant smile and her joyous laugh when Joseph's jaw dropped, and his eyes went wide.

The ceremony served as her official coronation and re-naming as Princess Betha Jewel-Rose, rightful princess of the Metalkin, eleventh of her name, as well as her wedding, making the prayers dreadfully long. She kept looking over at Joseph and smiling when their eyes met, looking away before either of them could start laughing again.

There was no dinner or ball after the service. Baraq didn't want everyone showing up late and bleary-eyed for Mallory's wedding the next day. "We can't combine the ceremonies, but we can combine the celebrations," he said.

"Oh," Mallory said. "I already had a big ball and everything. I don't' want to take away from Betha's wedding."

"You're not taking anything away from me," Betha said, feeling more at peace, and more generous, than she had in months. "You've given me a home, you've given me my identity. And you've found yours too. That's something we all need to celebrate."

And truthfully, once the ceremony and the quiet dinner with the other princesses was over, she was grateful for the time alone with Joseph.

"I feel like I've hardly seen you since Stones Shore," he said.

She laughed. "We did spend nearly a month apart."

"I know. And you've been so busy since we arrived here." He sighed. "I'm glad it's all over. I was terrified Most Honourable Silver-Cloud would deny our claim and I'd be barred from seeing you again."

"Baraq Silver-Cloud is a good man, but I'd watch out for him."

"Oh?"

"Once all this happily-ever-after, lovey-dovey stuff is done, I'm certain he means to root out ever last trace of corruption and elitism on this island."

"That's not such a bad thing."

"No, but he's ruthless, or I get the feeling he can be. I wouldn't want to cross him. And I just know his crusade is going to mean more work for me."

2nd of Holy Week, 25th Year of the 11th Rebirth
Sun Temple Complex, Sun Temple Province
Wedding of Mallory Brock Living Rose

After nearly a year, Mallory didn't feel so bewildered by the whirlwind of preparations that accompanied her second marriage. Her hair was longer now so it took longer to put it up in a style everyone would approve of, and she didn't even mind too much.

She'd given the glorious wedding dress with the cascade of silk roses to Betha in exchange for the traditional Carainhithe dress. The linen hadn't been lightened, keeping its natural creamy hue, and it came with a hand-embroidered corset that Mallory could not stop running her fingers over. Looking in the mirror she felt more alive this time around, and less like a ghost.

She walked into the temple full of confidence, and she didn't get lost once in the prayers and responses. When she walked out again, after all of the wedding vows, and coronation oaths, she was Mallory Brock Living Rose, Princess of the Carainhithe, and she was arm-in-arm with her soulmate, the love of her live, Prince Devin Sun-Stag.

Author's Note

When Mallory realizes that the name Jewel-Rose doesn't fit her character properly Emilio Spirit-Light has an explanation, but the truth is, the fault is mine.

Partway through writing the first book I stumbled across the gemstone theft subplot. Before that, gemstones were the territory of the Metalkin. After conferring with my husband, we agreed it made more sense for them to be the territory of the Stone Clan. And I forgot to change Mallory's last name.

By the time I realized the mistake, I was 30,000 words into the fifth book! And so, an explanation had to be written because I was sure a reader would catch it at some point and ask.

Upcoming Titles

Turn Coats: Underground Book 6

Why didn't Shawna call? What is Ethan up to? Will Trevor help? Who can be trusted? Ethan, Shawna, and their friends are past the point of safely turning back. They must press forward until they find what they are looking for. Or until someone in power finds them and stops them.

Sunlight: Underground Book 7

The moment of truth is at hand. Or perhaps it is the moment of ruin. Find out what happens to Shawna, Ethan, and everyone else in the Complexes in this conclusion to the Underground Series.

Cheyanne: An Underground Bonus Novel

Ethan & Shawna's story isn't the only one. See what life was like on the other side. Meet Cheyanne, a normal girl, growing up on the surface, until her life is changed by a chance encounter.

More Books by Casia Schreyer

Rose Garden
Rose in the Dark
Rose from the Ash
Rose without Thorns
Rose Alone

Picture Books
Nelly-Bean and the Kid Eating Garbage Can Monster
Nelly-Bean and the Adventures of Nibbles
Janelle et le Monstre de la Poubelle Mangeur d'Enfants

Underground
Complex 48
Separation
Reunion
Training
Rebels

Nothing Everything Nothing
Pieces

ReImagined
The Ultimate World Building Book

By Yvonne Ediger
Recipes and Memories

About the Author & Cover Artist

Casia Schreyer lives in Southeastern Manitoba with her husband and two children. She is the author of over eighteen titles, including the first four books in the Rose Garden series. Writing and being a mother are her full-time jobs.

Sara Gratton lives in Southeastern Manitoba with her husband and three children. She works as a photographer and graphic designer. She is the creative mind behind the Rose Garden covers, her first book cover project. She also took many of the photos Casia uses for her author photos in books and other promotional materials.

Made in the USA
Columbia, SC
03 September 2019